Abbot Kinney

The Conquest of Death

Abbot Kinney

The Conquest of Death

ISBN/EAN: 9783337387525

Printed in Europe, USA, Canada, Australia, Japan

Cover: Foto ©Andreas Hilbeck / pixelio.de

More available books at **www.hansebooks.com**

THE CONQUEST OF DEATH

BY

ABBOT KINNEY

AUTHOR OF "TASKS BY TWILIGHT," ETC.

NEW YORK
1893

CONTENTS.

INTRODUCTION.

N EARLY twenty years ago the fact was brought to my attention that two of the sovereign States of our Union had lost
population between the years 1860 and 1870. These States
were Maine and New Hampshire. The loss in one case was over
six thousand persons, and in the other over sixteen thousand. This
loss occurred in the face of a considerable immigration from Canada,
Ireland, etc. It occurred in two of our most intelligent communities.
The two States named have indeed increased in population during
the last census, but only as to their cities. The rural population has
fallen off four per cent. in Maine, and in Vermont there is in the
whole State an absolute loss of some four hundred inhabitants.
Similar conditions now appear in the West. Thirty-two counties of
Illinois, for instance, show a large absolute decrease of population.

This may not seem alarming without further knowledge of the
conditions existing among us. When, however, we see items like
the following taken from serious publications :

Instruction in Abortion.—The *Medical and Surgical Reporter* says that it
has received a pamphlet which is evidently being widely distributed. This
pamphlet offers for sale a translation of a book by Velpeau, in which instruc-
tions may be found how to produce abortion in a variety of ways, some of
which are "not known to the medical world," and also "valuable hints as to
the best means by which evasion of the law can be accomplished when a
physician is so unfortunate as to be 'suspected' of having been guilty of the
step."—Dec. 27, 1890.

The Prevention of Conception.—The Detroit Medical and Literary Association recently discussed the question as to the justifiability of preventing conception. Almost every speaker contended that the practice was proper and
right, and many said that prevention could be accomplished mechanically
without injury to either the man or the woman. There were apparently but
few members of the society who opposed this view, or at any rate there were
but few who expressed their opposition.—*Med. Record*, Nov. 29, 1890.

When we see in every daily paper advertisements of nostrums to
bring on the menses, or in other words cause abortion, and when we
see in our own acquaintance the few children to a marriage or those
totally sterile, we may well conclude that American breeding is not,
as a rule, done by its intelligent and dominant families. A physician

of fair practice in a popular summer resort informs me that in the treatment of women for the sequelæ of recent abortions, these cases bear the ratio to conceptions going to term of six to seven. Six abortions to seven births is a condition worth looking into. Reflecting further that many abortions are likely never to be mentioned, that prevention of conception is widespread, and that our labor is recruited from immigration, a judicious person cannot but feel that some slight increase of these tendencies will result in an extinction of the old American stock.

In France and Greece the population, independent of immigration, is slowly decreasing. Our last census shows that we have come to a similar condition. This condition may best be seen by the following table :

	Increase of population.	Increase from births.
1870 to 1880	11,598,000	8,891,000
1880 to 1890	12,225,000	6,950,000

There were consequently 2,941,000 less births in the last decade than in the first, and this, too, in a population twenty-five per cent. larger in the last decade. Had the birth-rate been the same in the two decades we should have had an increase of over 10,000,000 by births instead of the 6,950,000 actually noted.

The loss of population in a State like Nevada or in the mining counties of California may doubtless be justly attributable to emigration owing to resource-failure, but such a cause can not be properly credited in the face of a large immigration as in New England.

In a wagon trip through New England in 1877, I found many farms being worked by the Irish, whole districts in manufacturing towns inhabited by French Canadians, with French signs on the streets, stores, and houses. I found the Catholic religion dominant, where a few years before it was not to be found. Children born of the old American stock were rare, while those of foreign parentage were numerous.

I made it a point to call on a physician or druggist in every village I visited, and to ask about the conditions of marriage, childbirth, etc. The result of these inquiries was a unanimous testimony that American men and women of the old stock not only no longer cared for large families, but that they very frequently took means to prevent having them. Both acts to prevent conception and to cause abortion in case of conception were stated as general in every village visited.

The impression confirmed in many cases by statistics was that a large majority of the rural communities in New England had a birth-rate too low to replace the losses in the native stock by death.

The rarity of full-blooded American children, compared to those of foreign parentage in these communities, was striking. I was not surprised later to see such figures as those of Holyoke in Massachusetts. In this old American town of 6,297 minors, but 843 were of American parentage. The birth-rate, in all cases, amongst what we call the native population was decreasing, the marriage rate was about stationary, but the divorce rate and the death-rate were both increasing.

In general conversation, those of the old American stock seemed nearly unanimous in expressing disregard, distaste, or positive opposition to procreation. They made no bones about it. From the preacher to the prostitute, infants were intruders. Progeny was prevented, destroyed, occasionally endured, rarely sought or welcomed. The works of Allen, Clark, etc., gave some years ago the alarming figures as to the vital movement of our native population now familiar to political economists. In Western trips, I found the same conditions fatal to the family growth. In San Francisco, for instance, the last school census shows a shortage in the number of children to be expected in the total population, upon calculation found correct in general practice.

This shortage reached the large total of 14,000 children. The papers on the publication of this fact cried out "Where are our children?" For a moment there was a ripple in the current, a splash of protest, and on the people whirl to destiny.

The testimony is uniform that this shortage of children in San Francisco, as in other places, is nearly all due to the absence of progeny in American families. The families of the foreign-born seem to average up to the standard. When we consider that about one third of the San Francisco population is of foreign birth, we can perceive some other relation of the figures in that census that is still more alarming for the American family. With a continuance of the practices leading to no children or small families, it cannot be long before the original settler stock will be gone. Their intelligence, self-reliance, capacity for a liberal form of self-government, their religion, and perhaps their language will go with them.

It is only proper to state in connection with the child shortage in San Francisco that it has been at-least in part attributed to a former dishonest census. The fact remains, however, that the proportion of children in the well-to-do American families is far below the normal. Now we hear that in the last five years there have been in San Francisco 21,000 deaths and only 8,000 births. It is again proper to state that the record of deaths is substantially correct, while it is certain that the birth record is incomplete and unreliable.

I have not even taken the trouble to verify the figures, so little confidence would I place in any vital statistics from San Francisco.

We may touch casually on the growing lateness of marriage and the increased proportion of those who never marry, and then take up the extraordinary increase of divorce. One curious investigator states that in a period when there were 23,000 divorces in the United States, there were 21,000 throughout the rest of the world. In divorce, America comes first, with all other countries combined a poor second—

Se non è vero, è ben trovato.

But while many of the records are incomplete and unreliable as to close details they are not so as to the general drift of society. What the records stammer out and what we have in official whispers has open confirmation in our social environment. Houses or rooms to let to families—without children,—and families—without children—advertising this advantage when seeking houses or apartments, advertisements of sure cures for suppressed menstruation "from whatever cause," appear every day in city newspapers. Married and single women are equally notified in open newspaper advertisements that conception—the new-lighted life in the uterus—can be painlessly, certainly, and safely done away with. Every such notice is a lie, but that does not matter as to the picture of wants it shows to exist. A physician friend with a large general practice tells me that in his time he has noticed, not a diminished desire for children only amongst American women, but a marked decline in their child-bearing capacity. His experience only goes back eighteen years.

For some twenty years, fact after fact has forced upon me the reluctantly received opinion that the present vital movement in our population can only eventuate in the elimination of the old American stock through non-reproduction. It is impossible to disguise the fact that in many places the population is maintained or increased by immigration, or by the children of recent immigrants. The fidelity of these to the duties of marriage and to procreation is largely due not to the reason but to useful superstition. Intellectual inquiry invites infidelity. Skepticism has no soul, nor has it breeding power. Man must have a belief to be in earnest. The skeptics disappear, the superstitious survive, but progress cannot live without intellectual activity. This is incompatible with the infallibility demanded for the integrity of superstition. So long as there is progress, there must be intellectual independence. Here then is the dilemna—SKEPTICISM and STERILITY, or SUPERSTITION and STAGNATION. Progress to extermination, or perpetuation of life without improvement.

This problem and others kindred to it are those for which I have sought a solution. This work was prepared for my children. Interest in my race and country induces me to make it public, with the exception of one chapter. I have, indeed, little hope of stemming the tide to the extremes of extermination or superstition now running in the public. There is, however, ground to expect that the grand motive of immortality of the body instilled into children may become a material and practical religion securing reproduction, while not subject to the periodic overthrow of systems based on the undemonstrable dogmas of revelation.

My religion of reproduction has no fight to make with those religions derived from revelation. It can live with or without them. Many hypotheses and doctrines are mentioned in this volume ; much advice is given. Some views of men are attacked, some defended. Doubtless, there is plenty of error scattered through the book. All these things are intended to be nothing but the plain truth. Many of them are, perhaps, the correct course for man to-day, while in the future, if persisted in, they might bring ruin. What is truth to-day may be error to-morrow.

These various views are written merely to attract attention and secure interest in the object I have in view.

They are all second and servant to the main motive of the work. This is the necessity of reproduction in man to enter any demonstrable future.

ABBOT KINNEY.

THE CONQUEST OF DEATH.

CHAPTER I.

SEX.

HUMAN beings are divided into two sexes, male and female. The difference between the two sexes is considerable, reaching its maximum in the period of greatest vitality and being least marked in youth and old age. Even before birth it can be recognized by the heart beats. Those of the female fœtus average 144 in the minute, and rarely fall below 135. Those of the male fœtus average 120 in the minute and very rarely go above 130. The heart beats continue more frequent and more variable throughout life in the female than in the male.

At birth and as the growth proceeds, the differences of the sexes remain well defined, and at the age of puberty and fertility increase.

In the new-born babe, milk is sometimes found in the breast. Speaking comparatively, this is frequent in the male child and rare in the female. (Recent researches indicate little if any difference between the sexes in this particular.—Variot.)

The mammary gland or breast develops in the female into a capacity for secreting milk at the age of puberty. After childbirth it performs this function common to the females of all mammals. This milk is the food designed by nature for the infant. Exceptional cases of the secretion of milk by the female without childbirth and after the menopause have been recorded. The secretion of milk by the generally rudimentary mammary gland of the male have been authenticated in a few instances. This may be accounted for on the ground that the male, being the last feature of evolution, must pass through the female type. Another similar indication of this is the minute rudimentary uterus in the male.

The external organs of generation in both sexes show the same development in the fœtus, up to the time of their permanent form in the female. The male organs continue to develop beyond this point. For the detail of this change and the parts in the female which correspond to those in the male, or rather from which these grow, see *American System of Obstetrics*, Hirst, vol. i., pp. 199 and 200.

The male babe is also more difficult to rear than the female, and the proportion of deaths and still-births is greater among them. To neutralize this increased death-rate there are more male children born than female, the proportion varying between 111 (Servia) to 94 (Greece) male to 100 female. (Another census gives Greece 111 boys to 100 girls.) The general average is about 105 males to 100 females in civilized communities. Amongst the well-to-do class in cities and in some country districts, the general excess of male births is found reversed, as in Asiatic Turkey. This is not, as a rule, a favorable sign for a community. Communities with an excess of female births are generally situated unfavorably as to climate, customs, or other conditions to the vigor of the race. A point to consider in this connection is the curious fact that in some of our Western communities, where the males greatly outnumber the females, there is found a tendency to the production of a larger proportion, than normal, of female children. In Arizona they are actually in excess of the male infants. We might think this due to some obscure equalizing process of nature, were the same fact not true of Louisiana, Delaware, and North Carolina. After several very deadly wars, in which the males were much reduced, notably in those almost continuous wars of Frederick the Great, the proportion of male births became and remained for some time much above the normal in the populations affected. An abnormal excess of female births may be a good sign at one place or time, while very unfavorable at another.

Amongst savages and barbarians, as well as the civilized, there are marked differences in the proportion of the sexes born. In polygamy there is an excess of females born, in polyandry an excess of males much above our figures. Hardship seems to produce most males, and ease and idleness most females. Inbreeding tends to males, and crossing to females. These matters and tendencies are true of the higher animals also.

At birth the average weight of a male child is 7 pounds; of a female, 6½ pounds.

The male is taller, heavier, and fiercer than the female. He has a larger proportion of muscle and bone in his weight, while the female has a larger proportion of adipose tissue or fat. Thus a man with a beautiful arm must be muscular and strong in that arm. A civilized woman with a beautiful arm may not be strong. The lines of beauty in the one are made by muscle; in the other, partly by an adipose layer.

The blood of the two sexes varies. The observations of Dr. Mikulicz show that hæmoglobin is present in the blood in largest quantities between the ages of twenty and thirty years. It is at its minimum in children under ten. In females it is less at all periods of life than in males. It is always found reduced in persons with tuberculosis, syphilis, and malignant tumors. The loss of blood of course diminishes it. In females during menstruation the chemical composition of the blood changes, and the carbons are reduced. After the climateric women's blood more nearly resembles men's.

There are some differences in the use of foods. G. Munro Smith of Bristol states that where a man of stated weight and activities eats nineteen ounces of food, a woman of the same weight and activities eats from fourteen to fifteen. In other words, there is an average difference of four or five ounces in the consumption of food between the sexes of the same weight and life. This would indicate a better digestion in the female, or an additional and expensive unformulated use of the extra food in the male.

The male uses the greatest amount of narcotic and stimulant amongst all races. Some rational explanation of the use of these agents is attempted in an article of mine on Diet. The conclusion arrived at is that the general use of narcotics and stimulants is due to an effort to escape from the nerve strain and pressure consequent on change and progress in society.

The thyroid gland, commonly called "Adam's apple," is proportionately larger in the male than in the female. The function of this gland is not known. It seems, however, to have some obscure connection with the intelligence, for its entire extirpation is usually followed by imbecility.

The comparative sitting height of women is greater than that of men ; that is, the body is longer and the legs shorter proportionately than in men.

The arm-stretch more nearly equals the height in women than in men.

The knee-joint in women is characteristic. The articular surfaces of the tibia and femur are narrower and the patella smaller. Consequently a woman's knee, when bent especially, is smoother and rounder than a man's.

Women have a superior expectation of life at all ages over men. Consequently childbirth, whatever its dangers are, is more than neutralized by other conditions favorable to women's lives.

The articulations and shape of the bones are different in the two sexes, being less suited to physical and continued effort in the female. In the woman the clavicle or collar-bone is quite a different shape from the same bone in the man; it is also proportionately longer. From this cause all overhand action is awkward to the female. This seems a provision of nature against this movement, as it is one of the most dangerous for a pregnant woman. A forcible overhand movement is likely to rupture the membranes and cause an abortion. It must be said, however, that the shape of the clavicle varies considerably in men, and seems to bear some relation to the amount of physical exercise performed. Consequently, the difference in the shape of this bone in the two sexes may not be due entirely to inheritance of sexual variation. (See Holden's *Osteology*, p. 131.)

The bones of the male are not only larger than those of the female, but they are different in structure. This difference of structure has the effect of making the bones of the male human being the hardest. The bones in the female skull are thinner than those in that of the male. The shape of the female skull is similar to that of the male child. The variations in the skull are as follows (see table, opposite page):

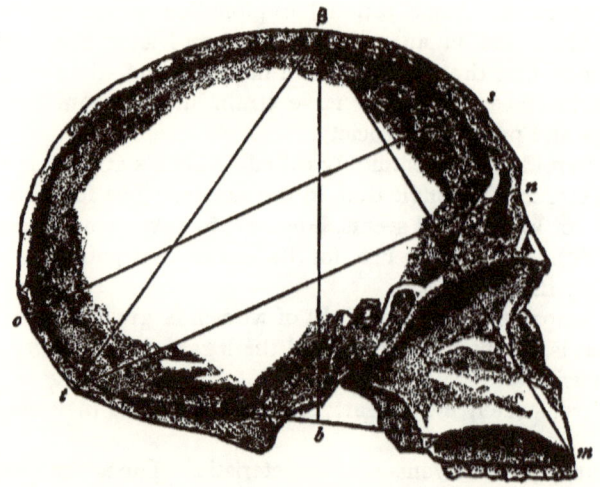

"Variations dependent upon age:

"The proportions of the skull change most considerably in the first year, and continue to change up to the fourth year. After that, modifications are slight in amount and appear more slowly. By the end of the seventh year the skull has nearly reached its full size (see table), more nearly in girls than in boys. The chief measurements during childhood are given in the table. The protuberances and ridges are less marked in children.

"The orbital index, *i. e.*, rates of height to width of orbit, undergoes great changes during growth. In young children it is 100, *i. e.*, the height and

Table of Cranial Measurements in Centimetres, by C. L. DANA, M.D., based on work of Benedikt, Peterson, and Liharzik.

	Adults M.	Adults F.	Physiological variation.	New-born M.	New-born F.	End of 1st year M.	End of 1st year F.	1st to 7th year M.	1st to 7th year F.	10th year M.	10th year F.	7th to 18th years.	18th to 24th years.	End of 12th yr.	
1. Greatest circumference.	52.0	50.0	48.5 to 57.4	34.0	34.0	42.0	42.0	34 to 46		49	47	46.0 to 49.5	49.5 to 52.25		Taken around glabella and maximal occipital point.
2. Binauricular arc	32.0	31.0	28.4 to 35.0	20.0	20.0	25.5	25.0		27					30	Measured from b over through bregma to b, or opposite ext aud. meatus
3. Volume	1,500	1,300	1,201 to 1,751	385 to 450		700 to 1,000				1,300					{ Benedikt and Huschke.
4. Naso-occipital arc	32.0	31.0	28 to 38	22.0	22.0	28.0	28.0								$n\,\beta\,l.$
5. Naso-bregmatic arc	12.5	12.0	10.9 to 14.9	7.7	7.7		10.0				12	12			$n\,\beta.$
6. Bregmat. lamb. arc	12.5	11.9	9.1 to 14.4	9.9	9.0		10.0			12					β to $a.$
7. Lamb occipital arc	7.0	7.1													a to $l.$
8. Antero posterior diameter	17.7	17.2	16.5 to 19.0												s to $e.$
9. Greatest transverse diameter	14.6	14.0	13. to 16.5												
10. Cephalic or length-breadth index	82.2	83.8	76.1 to 87												
12. Facial length	12.37		10.5 to 14.4												From n to lowest point of chin.
13. Empirical greatest height	13.3	12.3	11.5 to 15												The empirical greatest height, $b\,\beta$ is obtained by measuring the sides of the triangle $m\,\beta\,l.$
14. Dolicho-cephaly			70.0 to 74.9												
Meso-cephaly			75.0 to 79.9												
Brachy-cephaly			80.0 to 84.9												
Eury-cephaly			over 100 to 150												

breadth are equal. In adults it is 84.6 (Weisbach), *i. e.*, the breadth is a fifth greater than the height. The naso-bregmatic arc is relatively smaller. Women have relatively narrower orbits (Zuckerkandl), corresponding to smaller frontal lobes.

"The posterior half of the naso-occipital arc is greater relatively in woman. The lambdo-occipital arc, indeed, is actually absolutely longer in woman (Benedikt's figures. See table). The cephalic index is greater in women (Germans), *i. e.*, their skulls are relatively broader. The empirical greatest height is relatively much lower in women; in other words, women (Germans) have lower as well as broader skulls.

"To sum up, the female skull is larger posteriorly, is broader, lower, with higher orbital diameter, often it has no glabella, no super-glabellar depressions, and is less well marked as to its ridges, prominences, and sutures.

"Variations as regards race :"

The length-breadth index and other cranial indices, and the volume, are the only radical differences so far extensively studied. Even these are too indefinite factors to be of any practical value. In general we may say that the Dolichocephalic or long-headed races are the English, Irish, Scandinavians, Negroes, 73; Arabs, 74; Chinese, 76.

"The Brachycephalic, or broad-headed, are the Germans, 81 : Russians ; Turks, 81.

"The Mesocephalic, or medium-shaped heads, are the American Indians, 79; Hollanders ; Parisians, 79."

Dolichocephaly, or long-headedness, is due to a development of bones which varies with age and sex. In the infant it is occipital ; in the child, temporal ; and in the male adult, frontal. In the woman it is always temporal. This is but one of many facts going to show that the development of woman is generally arrested at a certain point below the male, doubtless to liberate the energies for the development and functioning of the reproductive organs.

Another instance of the same kind is the nasal index, which is greater in the female than in the male in all known races. It is greater in the infant than in the adult, and consequently the female, in this respect, resembles the infant.

These details are presented to indicate a brain difference due to sex, but no question of superiority or inferiority of brain quality is pretended to be shown. In fact, the whole question of intellectual manifestation as related to brain mass is in an unsatisfactory condition. Even in prehistoric remains we find skulls showing a larger cubic capacity than those of our own people. One instance of this may be cited in the skulls taken from certain caves in France together with stone implements showing the life of their people to have been similar to that of savages in our day. The average of these Cromagnon skulls is not only larger than our own, but even the skulls classed as female have a larger cubic capacity than modern male skulls. In this connection it is well to call attention to an unpleasant presumption in regard to evolution. It is that the life of a savage hunter and warrior is such that close attention, skilled observation of nature, self-reliance, and a wide knowledge of topography are essential to existence, and that brain qualities may consequently be better developed than they are amongst the great mass of civilized men living by a narrow specialized routine. Ancient British skulls (prehistoric) show a larger cubic capacity than those of the modern English, and their average is higher than all but a few of the most noted skulls measured.

The methods of brain measurement have not been uniform ; no account has been taken of age, condition, or cause of death. All of these things influence brain weight. These sources of error are great. In a private letter to Sir Daniel Wilson, Dr. Wyman states the cubic capacity of Daniel Webster's skull to be 122 cubic inches. This is equivalent to 65 oz. of brain, but the Doctor gives the brain weight as 53.5 oz., which is the accepted figure. One must realize that the brain weight of Daniel Webster in full health and at maturity would be different from that of Daniel Webster old and dead after a waste of tissue due to disease.

The noted brain weights are those of Cuvier, 64.5 oz. ; Abercrombie, 63 oz. ; Byron, 63.5 oz. ; Spurzheim, 55.6 oz. ; Dirichlet, 53.6 oz. ; Webster, 53.5 oz.

But these, taken with measurements by Dr. Peacock of a sailor's, a printer's, and a tailor's brain, which gave from 61 to 62.75 oz., and the measurement by Thurman of the brain of an ignorant butcher (62 oz.), show how unreliable brain mass is as an indication of brain manifestation.

The brain of the ant is minute, but its manifestations of intelligence are remarkable. After an examination into these matters the Peabody Report of '74 gives a good summary of the situation as follows :

"All this goes to show, and cannot be too much insisted upon, that the relative capacity of the skull is to be considered merely as an anatomical and not as a physiological characteristic ; and unless the quality of the brain can be represented at the same time as the quantity, brain measurement cannot be assumed as an indication of the intellectual position of races any more than of individuals."

The thigh bone or femur is relatively shorter in women than in men. At the same time the diameter of the thigh is larger than in men and is the one measurement which in all ages is greater in the female than in the male.

The angle formed by the neck of the femur with the shaft is smaller in women than in men (Humphrey).

The neck of the woman is longer, the shoulders are more sloping, are set farther back, and are less broad than in the male, while the hips of the female are relatively the broader. The skin is smoother in the female.

At Meudon during the Reign of Terror in the French Revolution, there was a tannery of human skins. The skins were taken from the victims of the guillotine. In the course of this extraordinary industry it was found that the skins of men made a good tough wash-leather superior to chamois, but that the skins of the women were unserviceable owing to the softness of their texture. The skin, it must be said, is influenced as to its texture or toughness by uses. Whether a difference in uses between the male and female victims of the guillotine, largely aristocrats, existed to such an extent to account for the skin variations found is a question.

The breathing of the female is done with the chest muscles, while the breathing of the male is performed with the abdominal muscles. This, however, may be partly due to the practice of wearing corsets, which, by their constriction of the abdomen, lower the normal position of the uterus from two to five tenths of an inch, diminish its natural mobility, push the vital organs up on the lungs, and prevent the expansion of the abdomen necessary to the male type of breathing.

Certain examinations of Chinese and Indian women tend to confirm the supposition that the costal breathing of women is thus caused. On the other hand, the experiments on the women of civilized countries by Drs. Hutchinson, .Gibson, and Riegel show that the costal type of breathing commences in our females at about the tenth year, and before they wear corsets at all.

These experiments go to show that whatever the type of breathing of women originally was, in civilized women it has come about the age of puberty to be costal, and they give some reason to think that this is the case irrespective of the corset.

The costal type of breathing is the only safe way for civilized women to breathe during pregnancy. It may be surmised that the difficulties of reproduction, increasing with progress, have forced this type of breathing generally upon the higher-race women. Vierodt in his *Physiology of Childhood* shows that the sex of a child may be determined at the tenth year by the breathing alone. In the male it is deeper and more regular.

According to the recent investigations of Dr. Masge of Zurich (1888), the radiation of heat from the skin was found to be more intense in men than in women, in boys than in girls, in young persons than in old, and in the vigorously healthy than in the feeble, or those convalescing from illness.

The average woman can withstand the cold of surf bathing longer than the average man. At a seaside resort much frequented, the male companions of the female bathers may be observed every day in the season, cold, blue, and shivering, while the women are in full enjoyment of the bath and not at all cold. Whether this female superiority is due to a smaller radiation of heat or to the adipose layer which all normal women have under the skin, or a combination of both, is not known.

The average lung capacity of the male in America is ninety cubic inches greater than that of the female (Sargent). In England, eighty-one cubic inches (Galton). "The female also exhales less carbonic acid relative to the weight than man, showing that the evolution of energy is relatively less, as well as absolutely less, in women" (Sargent).

The step of the woman averages twenty inches; that of the man twenty-five inches. The woman turns her feet out more than the man, an action unfavorable to rapid motion (Dr. Gille de la Tourette).

The growth of the pelvis in the female about the age of puberty throws the articulation of the femur, or the thigh bone, out farther than it is in man, inclining the knees together. This peculiarity again makes rapid movement more difficult than it is with the male, and is opposed to long standing. Both of these acts would be injudicious in a pregnant woman.

Women generally button from right to left and men from left to right. The drawing of circles for the two sexes usually follows the same opposition.

The senses are less acute in women than in men. Women can neither see, hear, taste, nor smell so well as men. In the recent experiments of Nichols and Bailey, the sense of smell was found to cease at the following dilutions:

	MALES.		FEMALES.	
Cloves,	1 part in	88.128	1 part in	50.667
Nitrite of amyl,	1 " "	783.870	1 " "	311.330
Extract of garlic,	1 " "	57.927	1 " "	43.900
Bromine,	1 " "	49.254	1 " "	16.244
Prussic acid,	1 " "	112.000	1 " "	18.000

Prof. Cæsar Lombroso has made experiments which show women to have a keener sense of smell than men, but to have a much less delicate sense of touch or of pain. Here is the *Medical Record's* summary of his article:

THE INSENSIBILITY OF WOMEN.

Professor Cæsar Lombroso contributes to the *Fortnightly Review* an article on the insensibility of women, in which he reaches some rather novel conclusions. Professor Lombroso states that accurate studies as to the relative sensibility of woman as compared with man have never been made. He has himself tested the delicacy of the sense of touch, pain, general sensibility whatever that may mean), smell, and taste in one hundred women and men. He finds that the tactile sense in men, as measured by the æsthenometer, averages about 1.6 mm.; in women of the lower classes it is 2.6, of the higher classes, 2 mm. The sense of pain, tested by the electrical algometer, is in young men 64, in older men, 78 mm. ; in young women, 53, and in older women, 70 mm. In other words, the sensibility to touch and pain is less in women. Smell and taste are rather keener in women. He does not speak of those most important of all the senses, sight and hearing. Lombroso states that he has been informed by surgeons that women show greater insensibility and less shock from the pain of surgical operations. Their lesser degree of sexual sensibility is generally admitted ; their inferior moral sensitiveness is accepted as a fact by Lombroso. It would probably be denied by most women, as well as by many of their chivalrous, if not scientific, admirers. The supposed lesser sensibility of women is thought to be one reason for their greater longevity.

These contradictions are certainly unsatisfactory

On the other hand, it is said that women make excellent astronomical observers. Miss Maury at Harvard is a notable instance of this.

The voices of the sexes distingush them from each other, the voice of the woman being pitched higher than that of the man. That of the male, in early life of the same type as the female, changes at the age of puberty and becomes gruffer and more forcible in its tones.

The hair grows differently in the two sexes. The woman has, as a rule, little hair except on the scalp of the head, about the pubic region, and a little under the arms. With the man the hair grows also on the face and often on the arms, legs, and breast. The beard enables a man to hide his emotions, while Nature makes no provisions for woman in this respect.

I am informed by several professors, having charge of the higher education of our universities, where co-education has been introduced, that there is a difference in the aptitudes of the two sexes. The men are more progressive and the women more diligent. The men excel in mathematics, and the more abstruse studies, while the young women are stronger in the languages and in literary studies. Some of the young lady graduates confirm this view. In Cambridge, England, a number of remarkable instances of female capacity in mathematics have been recorded.

Professor Jastrow has made some interesting experiments in the mental differences of the two sexes. Amongst them one in which he took 25 men and 25 women out of a class in psychology and got them to write as rapidly as possible the first hundred words that occurred to them.

The women used 1123 different words, the men 1376. The women wrote 520 words occurring but once in the list, and the men 746.

In the civil-service examinations about one half of all candidates pass, but of the female candidates four fifths pass. This shows either that the females are more industrious, of a superior class, or of larger capacity.

Professor Jones, of the University of California, a bright and observant man, has been unable to notice any difference in the average of the standing of the sexes in any study. The views of this professor may be summarized as follows:

The strongest minds without exception are amongst the males.

The average standing of the sexes, however, is about the same.

The women seldom select the scientific or mathematical courses.

The women students come of their own will, somewhat against the fashion, with a keen desire to obtain the university education. On the other hand, the men, in many instances, come without interest, sent by parents to conform to custom. Therefore the women are a picked class in the university, and must be for some time yet. There seems to be no more demonstrated tendency in the female university students at Berkeley against marriage and child-bearing than amongst the well-to-do classes generally.

It might be surmised that the knowledge acquired by these young women should improve their view of marriage and maternity enough to counteract the increased strain on their nerves and consequent diminished capacity for reproduction. It must be admitted, however, that a full university course postpones marriage and tends to make it come dangerously late. The girl's chances with such postponement must be diminished, and one would infer that she would be less likely to marry, both on account of her age and on account of the high standard she is likely to set for her husband.

In the *Seventeenth Annual Report of the Massachusetts Bureau of Labor Statistics* an examination is made of the condition of the graduates of female colleges from New England to Kansas. This examination must give cause for considerable reflection to the judicious.

The histories of 705 graduates of female colleges are tabulated in the report. The average age of the 705 is 28.58 years, or several years more than the average age at which women marry.

Of the 705 at this average post-marital age, 509, or 72.2 per cent., were still single ; 196, or 27.8 per cent., were married. The average duration of the married life of these was 6.7 years, or sufficiently long to indicate the fertility of the marriage. Of these 196 married ones, 130 had children and 66 had none. In other words, almost half of the marriages were still absolutely sterile. The 196 had 263 children, of whom 232 were alive, or an average of one living child and thirteen hundreths of a child per marriage.

Of the 705, 417 report suffering from disorders. Of these disorders, 137 were of the nervous system, 26 of the urinary organs, and 112 of the generative organs, or a total of 275 disorders especially inimical to child-bearing.

In looking over the returns and the comments, one is impressed with the idea that the graduates are desirous of leaving a favorable impression of the results of female education. These facts, when properly sifted, are far from doing this. At the same time, it seems fair to say that these figures show that the college life itself has had no generally unfavorable effect upon the health of the graduates.

In estimating the value of the marriage- and birth-rate amongst these highly educated young women, we must bear in mind a fact also set forth in the *Reports of the Massachusetts Bureau of Labor Statistics.* It is that, as a rule, fertility diminishes in Massachusetts with the ability to care for children. Thus the average number of those dependent on the wage-earner is 3.08 persons, while the number of those dependent on the salaried-class individual averages 2.64. The marriage-rate is also smaller in the salaried. The family of the well-to-do class is still smaller than either of the above, and in some districts of native Americans the birth-rate is one insuring prompt extermination.

It may therefore be that the birth-rate of these nearly twenty-nine-year-old collegians is only the generally fatal and exterminating one of those into whose aims, ambitions, and beliefs their education brings them.

I am informed that there is a society of female graduates keeping a record of the post-graduate life of each member of the society, which must be very valuable and become more so every year. I have, however, been unable to obtain this record.

The vital statistics of England, as worked out by Galton, show that it requires an average of six children to a marriage to maintain the population of England stationary. It requires an average of four children to a marriage to perpetuate two lives continuously in reproduction. In other words, counting those who do not marry, those who are sterile, together with the deaths before maturity, it requires six children to a marriage to maintain the population of England. Counting the chances of death, impotence, sterility, or celibacy an average of four children are required for the perpetuation of two lives. When we find that the number of children to a marriage amongst intelligent Americans in many parts of this country is insufficient to perpetuate even those married, and that the unmarried are largely confined to this class, we cannot but fear that the present so-called higher system of education of women is fatal to the best interests, nay even to the life, of the race.

We have now two extremes of women in our society : the highly educated woman, who becomes a writer, painter, teacher, lecturer, actress, etc., on the one hand ; and, on the other, the mistress or prostitute. The first class comprising the best educated (?) and probably the best minds of American women ; the second class comprising, amongst the poorer classes at least, the most beautiful physiques.

Both classes do not, as a rule, breed. Both classes are growing faster than the population. Thus we are losing our best minds and most beautiful bodies in women through sterility.

What will Americans be in another generation, or will there be any of the old stock ?

While infertility is frequent in the highly educated, it is by no means confined to them. Quiet reflection on the facts will bring to us the realization that infertility both natural and artificial is due to causes independent of college curriculums. But such a realization need not blind us to the probable cumulative influence toward sterility of an education of women not in harmony with their functions or duties to the race.

It may be noted that the adaptability of young women to a college course, as shown in their successes at Cambridge, Berkeley, etc., indicates forcibly that the home influences, to which they were more subject than boys, are in no way unfavorable to subsequent success in study.

The fashion of sterility and child limitation, now so widespread, may in the end be cured by a higher education of women. It may in fact be curable in no other way. Certainly, a high and true education in harmony with nature ought not to produce any disinclination to the highest function of humanity—creation. No less eminent authority than Sir William Gull of Great Britain is reported to have said that the benefit derived from a university education, such as girls get at Newnham and Girton, makes them and their children stronger and healthier ; also that the percentage of childless marriages is less with the educated women, and the percentage of children that survive infancy is larger.

This opinion of an eminent man may or may not be correct, but it is encouraging. My own observation is that the best mothers, and those realizing and glorying in the grandeur of procreation, are women of large capacity and wide information.

Recent examination of class histories of both males and females force me to the unwilling conclusion that the higher education, as exemplified in university graduates, is sterilizing in both sexes. One of the male classes had a history covering fifty years, and showed a procreative power too small to maintain the orginal number of the class and the wives of such as married. Whether this showing would be different from that of an equal number of lives in the superior ranks without university training is not within my power to say, but in any case it is a very unfavorable showing for our educational system. The female classes show the greatest sterilization.

It has been generally remarked that women, when allowed the opportunity, are more devoted to religious forms than men, and adhere to such forms long after men have lost interest in them, as is the case in society, when the development of institutions becomes unsuited to the religious forms. Women, also, run from conservatism to the extreme of radicalism more frequently than men. The scenes of the French Revolution and the later French Commune, the accounts of the saints in the overthrow of old religions, or in the support of orthodox ideas, our own experience with slavery, temperance, etc., almost invariably show the women, when associated in a movement, either at one extreme or the other.

In the woman, as a rule, we find that the emotions dominate the reason, and it is safe to say generally that the civilized female, when mature, has motives, emotions, and reason more like those of the child or of primitive man than has the male.

It is claimed, and with strong color of reason, that these characteristics of the sex are the product of the conditions in which they have lived from time immemorial. We may admit this without abandoning a conservative position in face of the extraordinary changes proposed in sex relationships, and for that matter already largely prevalent.

The condition of the polyandrous Thibetan woman is superior. She dominates, as a rule, her husbands. The Thibetan civilization, however, is a failure.

So it is with other present communities with the female dominant. In the past we find a number of records of women taking activities different from what the old fogies think wise, but we find no case where the type of civilization thus ordered was perpetuated.

The pulse is more rapid and irregular in woman than in man. The average weight of the adult American man is 141 1–2 lbs. ; of the adult American woman 124 1–2 lbs. These figures are not from complete examinations but from partial examinations of a number of men and women in similar conditions of life, and may be considered to approximate the truth.

Sargent's figures for America are different and make the male exceed the female by 21.5 lbs., while Galton's English figures give the difference as 22 lbs. The relative difference in height of the sexes

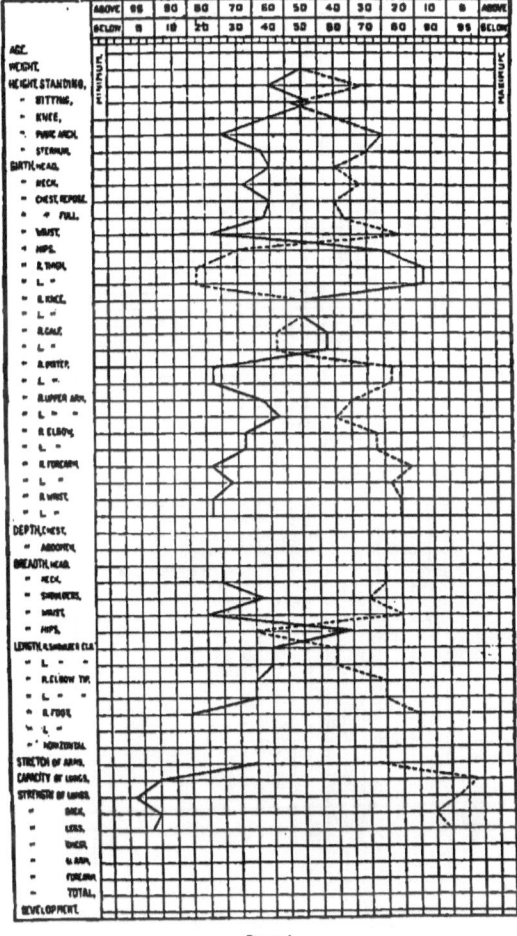

Chart I.

in America is, 5.1 inches and in England 4.6 inches. The accompanying charts, with comments taken from D. A. Sargent, M. D., will prove of interest.

"In order that we may form some idea of the physical condition of women, I shall first compare the physical condition of girls with that of boys of the same age and condition in life. For this comparison I have taken for tabulation the measurements of twelve hundred girls and boys from the student class of the community, the age of each class ranging from thirteen to sixteen inclusive, the mean age being fifteen. When plotted on a chart by themselves all the mean measurements of the girls come upon the 50 per cent. line, for their chart, and all the mean measurements of the boys upon the same line for the

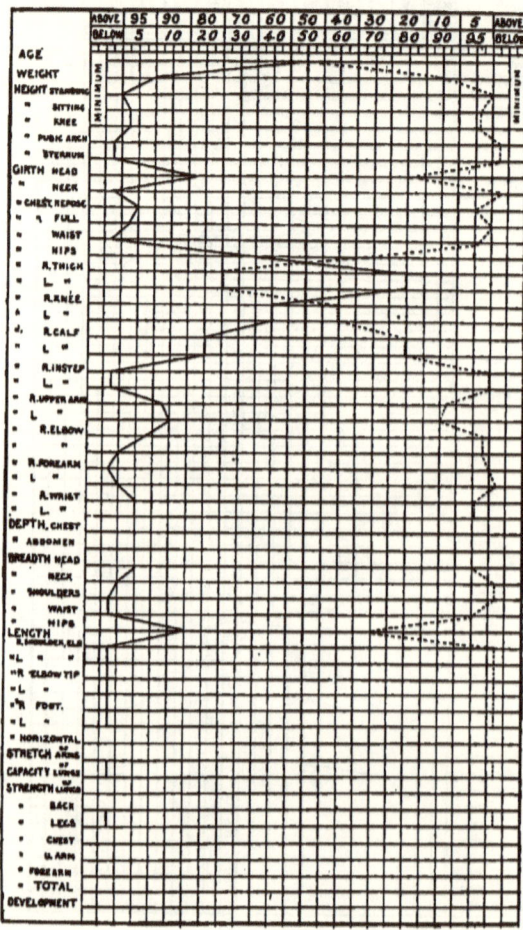

boys' chart. When the mean measurements of the girls, however, are plotted on the boys' chart, they fall at the points indicated by the irregular full line (Chart 1), and the mean measurements of the boys fall on the girls' chart at the points indicated by the broken line on the same chart.

"In following the two lines on the chart, some interesting facts are brought to light. We find that at the age of fifteen the mean weight of the girls and boys is the same. At the age of thirteen the girl is heavier and taller than the boy of the same age. It will be observed, however, that at the age of fifteen the boys exceed the girls in height about three quarters of an inch. The height of the knee is only a trifle lower than that of the boys, while the sitting height of the girls is actually greater than the mean sitting height of the boys. How then shall we account for the superior tôtal height of the boys? In looking on the chart for the height of the pubic arch in girls we find it on the 25 per cent. line of the boys' chart. This means that 75 per cent. of the boys surpass this measurement, while only 60 per cent. of them surpass the mean total height of the girls. The difference in height, then, is due to the shortness of the bones below the pelvis. I have already shown that the height of knee is nearly equal to that of the boys, so we must look to the comparative shortness of the thigh bone in girls to account for the difference in stature. Although the body length in girls is greater than that in boys, the difference as shown by the sitting height is largely due to the greater length of neck and head in girls, as shown by the superiority in boys in the height of the sternum.

"In girths the differences are more marked, the mean girth of head in the girls being only about ¼ of an inch below that of the boys, while the neck is about ⅝ of an inch smaller. There is but little difference in the natural chest of the two sexes at this age. The boys, however, show a superior expansive power when the chest is inflated. In the girth of waist the measurement of the girls is 1¼ inch smaller than that of the boys, while the girth of the hips is 1¾ inch larger. The greatest difference, however, is in the girth of the thighs. Here the actual measurements exceed that of the boys by two inches, while the relative difference is much greater. It will be observed that the mean girth of the knee is the same in both sexes, but that the girth of the calf is ⅝ of an inch greater in the girl. In the bone measurements, as indicated by the instep, elbow, and wrist, the superiority of the boys becomes more manifest. There is but a slight difference in the girths of the upper arm, but the right arm of the boys is ¼ of an inch larger than the left. This makes the left arm of the girl appear larger than the right, though both are of the same size.

"At the time these measurements were taken, the depth of the chest and abdomen had not been added to the list, and have consequently been omitted in the plotting. The difference in the mean measurements of the breadth of the head and neck is less than ¼ of an inch for each part. The shoulders of the boys are about ⅝ of an inch wider than the shoulders of the girls, while the hips of the girls are ⅝ of an inch broader than those of the boys. The actual difference in the breadth of the waist in the two sexes is quite marked. Even at this age the girls' waist is ¾ of an inch narrower than the boys'.

"The relative difference between breadth of waist and breadth of hips of the girls is greater, when compared with the same measurements of the boys, than the relative difference between the breadth of waist and breadth of shoulders in the two sexes.

"The length of upper arm of the girls is about ¼ of an inch less than that of the boys, while the forearm and hand is ⅝ of an inch shorter. In length of foot the boys have the start of the girls at this age by over ¼ inch, and in stretch of arms by fully two inches. The girls compare less favorably with the boys in the point of strength. In capacity of lungs the girls are seventy cubic inches behind the boys, and in the strength of expiratory muscles the weakest boys in the 5 per cent. class are stronger than the average girl. In strength

2

TABLE I.—*Showing comparisons in certain measurements of American and English men and women.*

Subject of measurement.	Unit of measurement.	Sex.	Nationality.	Number measured.	Age.	ABOVE 95 / BELOW 5	90 / 10	80 / 20	70 / 30	60 / 40	50 / 50	40 / 60	30 / 70	20 / 80	10 / 90	5 / 95
Weight*	Pounds	Male	American	2,235	16–26	111.3	116.3	122.8	127.2	131.2	135.1	139.1	143.3	149.2	156 9	165.3
			English	520	23–26	111	115	121	125	129	133	137	140	146	155	162
						+3	+1.3	+1.8	+2.2	+2.2	+2.1	+2.1	+3.3	+3.2	+1.9	+3.3
		Female	American	1,901	16–26	92.6	97	102	108	111	114.6	119	122	129	137	145
			English	276	23–26	92	95	100	104	108	112	119	122	126	132	139
						+.6	+2	+2	+4	+3	+2.6	0	0	+3	+5	+6
Height, standing	Inches	Male	American	2,235	16–26	64	64.6	65.7	66.5	67.1	67.7	68.3	69.1	69.1	70.9	71.7
			English	811	23–51	63.2	64.6	65.7	66.5	67.3	67.9	68.5	69.2	70	71.3	72.4
						+.8	0	0	0	−.2	−.2	−.2	−.1	−.9	−.4	−.7
		Female	American	1,835	16–26	59.1	59.8	60.6	61.4	62	62.6	63.2	63.8	64.6	65.6	66.3
			English	770	23–51	58.9	59.9	61.3	62.1	62.7	63.3	63.9	64.6	65.3	66.4	67.3
						+.2	−.1	−.7	−.7	−.7	−.7	−.7	−.8	−.7	−.8	−1
Height, sitting	Inches	Male	American	2,225	16–26	33.3	33.9	34.5	34.8	35	35.4	35.8	36	36.4	37	37.4
			English	1,013	23–51	33.6	34.2	34.9	35.3	35.4	36	36.3	36.7	37.1	37.7	38.2
						−.3	−.3	−.4	−.5	−.4	−.6	−.5	−.7	−.7	−.7	−.8
		Female	American	1,833	16–26	30.7	31.5	31.9	32.3	32.7	33.1	33.3	33 7	34.1	34.6	35
			English	775	23–51	31.8	32.3	32.9	33.3	33.6	33.9	34.2	34.6	34.9	35.6	36
						−1.1	−.8	1	−1	−.9	−.8	−.9	−.9	−.8	−1	−1
Stretch of arms	Inches	Male	American	2,216	16–26	65 4	66.1	67.3	68.5	68.9	69 7	70.5	71.3	72	73.2	74.4
			English	519	23–51	65	66.1	67.2	68.2	69	69.9	70.6	71.5	72.3	73.6	74.8
						+.4	0	+.1	+.3	−.1	−.2	−.1	−.2	−.3	−.4	−.4
		Female	American	1,854	16–26	58.7	59.5	60.8	61.6	62.4	63	63.8	64.6	65.4	66.5	67.7
			English	276	23–51	58.6	59.5	60.7	61.7	62.4	63	63.7	64.5	65.4	66.7	68
						+.1	.0	+.1	−.1	0	0	+.1	+.1	0	−.2	−.3
Capacity of lungs	Cubic inches	Male	American	1,113	16–26	170	180	200	210	220	230	250	260	270	290	310
			English	212	23–26	161	177	187	199	211	219	226	236	248	277	290
						+9	+3	+13	+11	+9	+11	+24	+24	+22	+13	+20
		Female	American	1,045	16–26	80	95	110	125	135	140	150	160	170	185	200
			English	277	23–26	92	102	115	124	131	138	144	151	164	177	186
						−12	−7	−5	+1	+4	+2	+6	+9	+6	+8	+14
Strength of forearms	Pounds	Male	American	2,112	16–26	44.7	50.7	59.5	61.7	68.3	72.8	77.2	83.8	86	97	103.6
			English	519	23–26	67	71	76	79	82	85	88	91	95	100	104
						−22.3	−20.3	−16.5	−17.3	−13.7	−12.2	−10.8	−7.2	−9	−3	−.4
		Female	American	1,923	16–26	26.5	29.8	35.3	38.6	41.9	44.1	47.4	50.7	55.1	60.6	65
			English	276	23–26	36	39	43	47	49	52	55	58	62	67	72
						−9 5	−9.2	−7.7	−8.4	−7.1	−7.9	−7.6	−7.8	−6.9	−6.4	−7

* A deduction of 10 pounds for clothing was made from the original weights of the English men and women.

of back, legs, chest, and arms the showing is a little better for the girls, though considerably below what it should be.

" It will be seen that the mean strength test of the girls falls below the 10 per cent. line of the boys' table, while the mean strength of the boys exceeds the 90 per cent. line on the girls' table. This indicates that 50 per cent. of the girls fail to reach a point in strength that is surpassed by 90 per cent. of the boys."

The investigator was not prejudiced in favor of the male, as the following sentences will show :

"In taking the sum of certain important measurements such as the head, chest, waist, legs, and arms, we find that the mean total of the girth dimensions of these parts in the girls is equal to that of the boys. We are accustomed to regard the sum of these measurements as indicative of the potential strength of the individual."

"Why, then, is not the girl of this age equal to her brother in strength, activity, and endurance?"

As age increases the measurements change and the man forges ahead. At full maturity he exceeds the female in every measurement except the diameter of the thigh. Proportionately, however, the woman exceeds the man in breadth of hip.

At about twelve years of age the two sexes average nearly the same weight. This is owing to the fact that at about the age of puberty a rapid increase of weight takes place in each sex ; the girl, reaching puberty first, for a short time about equals the male in weight.

In America at thirteen the girl is taller and heavier than the boy, at fifteen the boy is taller by three quarters of an inch, while the girl is still the heavier ; after this the boy's physical larger size becomes rapidly more marked.

The female matures physically and mentally sooner than the male.

We see, for instance, boys' parts in plays almost invariably taken by girls. It is to be presumed that this fact is due to the comparative incompetency of the boys at any of the early ages for such work.

At an age varying between the sexes, and also varying with climate, with city or country residence, with race and with occupation, comes the age of puberty.

It is at this time that the powers of reproduction develop in each sex. The female reaches this period from one to three years sooner than the male, and loses the reproductive power much earlier.

At the age of puberty the constitution is in a semi-confusion consequent upon the change of balance of powers to be maintained. New ideas, new blushes, new yearnings come to both sexes. It is a time when great care is required for the mental, physical, and moral welfare of the individual. The girl at this period develops, rounds out, and becomes more peculiarly feminine than before. The boy changes still more in the other direction. The beard commences to grow, the voice changes its timbre, and becomes rougher, and the body takes a new development of height and weight.

The system in the East of making eunuchs of the boys prevents these sexual changes. In eunuchs the character is as mutilated and incomplete as the body. The spayed female also, if young, never progresses in female characteristics. If mutilated when older, there is sometimes a tendency in voice, beard growth, etc., to the male type.

Sex is an evolution presumably necessary for the highest forms of life. Life in its most primitive conditions has no sex,—reproduction is by division. Then we find an added germ type evolved—still without sex, the main reproduction continuing by division; then comes the next step, a budding process by which, as in corals, the renewed life buds out of the old ; then a condition of sex, but both sexes in the same individual, as is still the case with most plants ; and lastly the sex separation of the individuals, with, however, many of the primitive types temporarily asexual in reproduction by parthenogenesis. Each step finds a place for a higher life. Sex is not to be obliterated nor assimilated, but further differentiated if the same path of progress is to be followed. Whether the male or female is superior, is a question of naught. Which should do the outside fight for life and subsistence, is important.

The fact noted by Darwin of the tendency in the hen when too old to breed to vary toward the male type in hackles, comb, and disposition, is a suggestion that there is a type for each kind of life, from which the necessities of reproduction and the perpetuation of such life demand variations by both sexes ; that such variations are only necessary during the reproductive period, and consequently they may be expected to be little notable before puberty and tend to disappear after the climacteric. The assimilation of the chemical character of women's blood after the climateric to the blood of men is an indication in the same line. The progressive atrophy of the mammary gland after the menopause is another.

The *Evolution of Sex*, by Geddes and Thompson, is a valuable condensed compilation of the information now accumulated in books on this subject. As a summary of this information, we may say that the male and female characteristics pervade all life. As life is of simple organization so are these characteristics least notable, while as life is of complex organization so is sex most marked. In unicellular life already a beginning may be perceived. Cells often meet or merge together, after which reproduction takes place by division. In the merging we may note that it is between a large, nutritive, and sluggish cell and a small, hungry, active cell. This foreshadows sex. No matter under what variations we find life, we find these types in reproduction. At last differentiated in sex, we find the female sex always anabolic and the male sex always katabolic.

The female type is anabolic—nutritive, conservative, sluggish. The male type is katabolic—destructive, originative, active. In the ultimate sex-elements the same generalization holds good. Compared to the sperm, the ovum is always large, nutritive, and quiescent.

The higher the type of life in a general way, the greater and more radical are the sex differences. The necessities of life perpetuation furnish the only explanation of this condition. If it is necessity that makes, perpetuates, and increases sex differences, we are doing something dangerous when we endeavor to neutralize such differences by social rules and laws.

When the male is inferior to the female in longevity, vitality, etc., as amongst some insects, the condition has accompanied an arrest of progress, or at least such inferiority of the male is nowhere an accompaniment of the highest types. Darwin observes in speaking of animals :· '' Characters common to the male are occasionally developed in the female when she grows old or becomes diseased, as, for instance, when the common hen assumes the flowing tail feathers, hackles, combs, spurs, voice, and even pugnacity of the cock.''

It is a very prevalent custom amongst breeders of animals and birds to unsex a certain proportion of the increase of their herds or flocks. The facility of doing this with the male and comparative difficulty with the female has practically confined the operation to the males. The result is usually an increase in size, an improvement in tenderness of flesh, and a loss of courage and endurance.

Amongst horses there have been scarcely any great gelding racers. Parole is the only one that I can recall. Geldings lack the courage and ambition for a great race. Stallions in long races will often dominate or apparently overawe both geldings and mares. The great race won by the stallion Swillington, in which, when he found the other horse beating him, he seized the jockey's leg with his teeth and pulled him out of the saddle, illustrates the determination and ambition of the male horse. The Arab idea, and the idea of the early Californians, that only a stallion amongst horses was fit to ride, may have good foundation for it. Stallions are the best mounts for soldiers on account of their courage, and, in fact, are the only reliable horses in a battle, taking them as a class.

The effect on the brain of unsexing the male is shown in some recent examinations of horses. The proportion of weight of the cerebellum to the cerebrum is :

In mares 1:5.57
" geldings 1:5.97
" stallions 1:7.07

The virgin female has a membrane called the hymen. This, as a rule, guarantees virginity. There are, however, a few recorded cases even of impregnation and delivery without the rupture of this membrane, and others where a congenital absence of the hymen has occurred.[1]

There is no means of ascertaining the chastity of a man. Nature demands purity on the part of a woman to secure the paternity of the children and the purity of the breed, which is to be protected by the male of mankind, as it is to a less extent by the males of lower animals. From this reason it may be understood why nature has fixed a test for woman's purity. It must be confessed that this explanation is without much force and unsatisfactory.

Sexual intercourse with a virgin involves, as a rule, the rupture of the hymen and is accompanied with some blood discharge. The linen thus stained was kept by the parents of the bride amongst the ancient Hebrews. Moses makes these tokens a conclusive evidence of the previous chastity of a bride, whose reputation might be attacked by her husband. We must, therefore, suppose that the token of virginity, or first intercourse, was practically universal amongst the Hebrews. Such tokens are considered important among many races, such as Arabs, Slavs, etc. There is no available means of knowing whether such tokens are now as general as in antiquity, but there seems no good reason to suppose that they are less so amongst healthy women of our race than they formerly were amongst the Hebrews or our own ancestors, who also demanded these evidences of chastity. Undoubtedly, disease of the reproductive organs or vaginal examinations, digital or instrumental, may destroy the hymen, but in such case the woman is, though carnally chaste, physically contra-indicated for matrimony.

The function of the hymen in the woman may be to exclude foreign and irritating substances from the generative parts before the age of discretion. In little girls it is about ⅛ of an inch from the surface, while in grown virgins it is from ¼ to ½ an inch below the

---

[1] Playfair's *System of Midwifery*, p. 44.
Leishman's *System of Midwifery*, p. 7.

surface. This explanation is also unsatisfactory, because the generative organs are more subject to injury by foreign substances after
than before childbirth.

The foreskin in the male probably plays a protecting part. It
has, however, no known conditions that would indicate a non-user of
sexual functions.

The vulva is the external female generative organ and the
vagina the internal canal by which the fertilizing spermatozoa
may be so introduced into the generative organs that they can
penetrate into the uterus or Fallopian tubes. For a full description
of the human generative organs, Hirsch's work, already referred to,
is good. Acton goes somewhat farther into sexual matters in his
work, *On the Reproductive Organs.* He has, however, a proper
fear of a thoroughly complete account of all the reproductive functions, and, besides, has many personal prejudices which he allows to
control his advice. He has, for instance, the ridiculous idea that the
female has little or no enjoyment in the reproductive act. There is
no full and scientific description of the whole reproductive function
in man with which I am acquainted, and I am afraid to violate the
prejudices of society by any attempt to supply this deficiency. In
fact, this fragmentary sketch is already too full to be palatable to the
general reader. I have a work in which there is what purports to
be a copy of the old rules of the Jesuits for the examination of married women at the confessional. This comes nearer a complete exposition and instruction in sexual function than anything else I have
ever seen. I must admit that, while I believe in complete instruction on reproductive matters, the most complete work on the matter
I know of produced a very unfavorable impression on me. There
are a number of works such as *Philosophy of Marriage, Tokology*,
Naphey's books, etc., etc., that go very extensively into reproductive
matters, description of the organs, together with more or less good
suggestions and advice on the uses of the function, and still none of
them have dared to tell the whole story. In strictly obscene works
one may find an account of this function, true, indeed, but again
limited, and this time without dignity and thoroughly disgusting.
It is delicate and dangerous ground.

In the healthy female about once a month there occurs a period
called the menstrual period. At this time an egg bursts from the ovary
and passes into the uterus, and if not fertilized, it dies and is eliminated. From the wound thus formed and from the uterus blood
flows for from one to seven days, or even longer. Exceptions have
been noted where no menstrual flow preceded conception, consequently the egg must have descended without it. But the rule is so

general that the absence of the menses in a virgin is accepted as a sign of disease or defective organization.

A number of savage tribes celebrate the first appearance of the menses in the girl by a feast. Her friends call and congratulate her on becoming a woman. This custom when boys reach the age of puberty is also found amongst many peoples. The time or age of the boy is, however, conventional and fixed. In both cases the age varies with climate and race.

The secretion of the uterus usually precedes the descent of the egg. If this secretion persist and be excessive, the egg may be washed away, even after union with the spermatozoa of the male. Thus excessive nerve activity or strain, which often deranges this function in women, may induce sterility.

In explanation of this function, some say that it is the escape of energies stored in the female for procreation and that it is the waste of disappointed Nature; others say that it makes the opportunity for the egg fertilized to fix itself in the prepared uterus; and we may say that we do not know.

The menstrual period is generally considered by women as a nuisance. In truth, it is a glory, and no greater misfortune can befall a woman than the loss of this sign of her reproductive power before the normal time, at between forty and fifty years of age. Such a loss means sterility, ill-health, loss of self-esteem, and unhappiness.

The human being is different from all other animals in reproduction. In man during the productive age, procreative power is continuous. In woman it is monthly and only intermitted by conception, lactation, disease, great hardship, or exposure to cold. In Greenland women, for instance, menstruation is generally suppressed during the winter months. This is generally true of women living in severe climates. With wild animals in natural condition and birds the reproductive powers are limited to a short season varying with the necessities of reproduction in the animal. In most animals this period occurs but once a year. We very suggestively term it the period of rut or "heat."

In great labors of mind or body in either sex the powers and inclination for reproduction are diminished. The egg which has thus descended into the uterus or into the Fallopian tube near it may be fertilized by man.

The crisis through which the constitution goes at this time requires reduced effort and work and increased precaution against exposure to climate or disease.

The lessened vitality of females at the time of puberty and adolescence is a striking fact, according to Sir James Crichton Brown.

Throughout life, in every quinquennium, the mortality of males from small-pox exceeds that of females, and that in a very marked degree, except in one quinquennium, from the tenth to the four-teenth year, when the female exceeds the male mortality, being again but very slightly behind it in the succeeding quinquennium, from the fifteenth to the nineteenth year. At all ages the male death-rate from enteric fever exceeds that of females, but the female mortality is very considerably higher from the third to the twentieth year of life. In infancy, and also in old age, the male mortality from diarrhœa and dysentery exceeds the female mortality, but in the child-bearing period, from fifteen to forty-five years of age, the mortality is distinctly higher among females. And even more striking in this connection are the statistics of phthisis than those of zymotic diseases. Phthisis is more fatal to males than females under five years of age ; but then a change takes place, and from five to ten it is much more fatal to females than to males ; while from ten to fifteen it is more than twice as fatal to females as to males. From fifteen to twenty, phthisis is still much more fatal to females than to males ; from twenty to twenty-five, the mortality from it is exactly equal in the two sexes, and from twenty-five to thirty, and at all subsequent ages, the mortality from it is much greater among males than among females. Dr. Brown is inclined to attribute this to over-pressure in education ; but surely there are many other factors more important in lowering the vitality of young women.

Dr. Dimitri Ott, of St. Petersburg, at the International Medical Congress at Berlin, in 1890, showed by extensive examinations of women and girls of various ages that, in addition to the nervous phe-nomena observed in women at the menstrual period, there is a series of variations of normal functions appearing periodically in typical form. The curves of temperature, muscular strength, blood pres-sure, respiration, and nervous irritability all attained their maximum shortly before menstruation.

A description of the generative organs of the male or of the acts leading to generation must be sought in a book like Flint's *Physi-ology*, Acton *On the Reproductive Organs*, or some similar work.

Acton's work is valuable, but he falls into errors and makes posi-tive statements on questions the evidence on which he must have taken by hearing. He says, for instance, that a normal woman has only exceptionally sexual desire. This is probably a complete reversal of the truth.

One reading his book should be careful to sift somewhat the proof of Acton's statements.

Man possesses in the testes an organ for forming the spermatozoa, not, as I know, periodically, but at any time, and by the erectile power of the penis of injecting these living and mysterious spores into the generative organs of the female. In the generative act the male takes the superior and aggressive position, the female the inferior and expectant.

The male has the power of fertilizing an indefinite number of females within the period of gestation of one child—*i. e.*, nine months. In this period a woman can conceive and bear children but once, and may bear one, two, or, at most, three healthy children, while man, without the artificial restraint of monogamous marriage, might have a large number of healthy children by different mothers.

The normal secretions in the lower female generative organs, that is, all below the os uteri, are acid, while those of the male are alkaline. This difference is thought to induce electrical phenomena favorable to generation.

A curious similarity of opposition in chemical reaction exists in the intellectually creative part of our bodies. The gray matter of the brain has an acid reaction, while that of the white is neutral or alkaline.

When through disease or inflammation the discharges of the female generative organs become abnormal, generation does not generally take place, and may never take place. We are not now sufficiently informed on these points to speak with precision, but can only give the general results.[1]

This is equally true of the male organs. Gonorrhœa is the venereal disease that most often causes absolute sterility in both sexes. The mucous inflammation with which this trouble commences often extends to the Fallopian tubes and closes them, imprisoning the eggs, or, completely involving the uterus, prevents conception. In the male the inflammation may close the ducts through which the spermatozoa should pass, or may destroy the power of the testes to properly perfect them.

The male principle in this most wonderfully creative act has a capacity of independent and continued motion ; that of the female, the egg, has none. This is the normal relation of the sexes throughout. The man has the initiative, the woman the passive.

In the male during adult life spermatozoa are found, as a rule, indicating no periodicity of their formation. They have been found by Duplay and M. A. Dieu in men of advanced age. The figures

---

[1] Thomas' *Diseases of Women*, pp. 262, 626, 627.

as given by Dieu are of twenty-five sexagenarians ; spermatozoids were found in 68.5 per cent. Of seventy-six septuagenarians the per cent. was 59.5 ; of fifty-one octogenarians the per cent. having spermatozoids was 48 ; four having passed the age of ninety gave negative results. It is probable that the spermatozoa persist in many cases when the generative power is lost.[1]

Ovulation, or the capacity to conceive, usually ceases in mothers between 43 and 50 ; in virgins or women without children, between 38 and 45. Very notable exceptions sometimes occur. A Scotch woman is reported recently as having borne children at the following ages : 47, 49, 51, 53, 56, 60, and 62. The following case is authenticated by affidavits : Mr. and Mrs. W. D. Green, of Pike County, Arkansas, have had 23 children, of whom 18 are still living. They have 72 living grandchildren and 12 living great-grandchildren. Mr. Green when married lacked 25 days of being 23 years of age, and at the time of the birth of his last child he was 67 years 7 months and 15 days old. Mrs. Green at the date of the birth of her first child was 18 years 4 months and 6 days old, and at the time of her last child's birth lacked 11 days of being 62 years old. The children were all born singly.[2] There are a number of reliable cases on record where women have continued to bear children between 50 and 54 years of age.

If the woman does not become a mother by the age of twenty-five there is a continuous tendency to degeneracy and atrophy of the reproductive organs, therefore a virgin, everything else being equal, cannot be as healthy as a mother after that age. Every additional year makes the change more notable. These changes are especially unfavorable to marriage duties. Conception is less likely to occur after intercourse ; the child conceived is delivered with more difficulty and danger, and it is less likely to live. Experience warrants the general presumption that a woman, a virgin at thirty-eight, can, in only exceptional instances, become the mother of a living.child, or of one that may be reared. A few exceptions to this general truth have been brought to my attention. The most striking is that of a woman whose first child was delivered in her forty-second year. This woman had one other child. One of them lived, which, however, is not now ascertainable, but probably the second.

Another case of a claimed first conception in the forty-ninth year of the woman has been published. The woman lived and the child was delivered by forceps at term.

---

[1] See Flint's *Text-Book of Human Physiology*, p. 886.
[2] *Medical Record*, June 8, 1889.

Dr. Lawson Tait says that the human female is an exception amongst animals, in that she has a menopause. He states positively that ovulation continues indefinitely amongst the females of other animals. Cats have kittens at fourteen and fifteen years of age, which would correspond to eighty and ninety in the human being. Mares the same.

Women married at the proper age, on the other hand, usually continue to bear children well into the forties. Extraordinary cases of prolonged virility are also noted in men. I have personally noted a case of gonorrhœa infection in a man of eighty-six, and there are a few fairly reliable records of men having had children after their one hundreth year, that of Thomas Parr being perhaps at once the best authenticated and the most remarkable. Much question has been recently thrown on the Parr history.

The Old Testament gives us some notable cases of fertility in advanced ages. From this book we learn that Sarah had her first child at eighty, and that the males retained their virility to wonderful ages. Whether the periods of time mentioned in the Bible correspond with those now received may, however, well be doubted.

The female has in the menstrual period a sort of safety-valve for her instinct of reproduction. The man has none except in the performance of his part of the act of generation with the woman, or by a destructive abuse of these his highest powers. Nocturnal emissions, it is true, can occur naturally without any injury whatever. They are, however, usually the result of abuse or excessive sexual indulgence. Complete continence to the male is comparatively easy ; incomplete continence, however, is most difficult.

When the male principle unites with the female, the egg, it fertilizes it, stamps it, and fuses with it. From the point of contact life begins and radiates. The life is given by the male. It is he who lights the flame. The egg then becomes attached to the uterus. The chorion and placenta develop, thus bringing the child in direct connection with the mother, by whom it is nourished. The blood passes by endosmose and exosmose from one to the other. The child and mother are one. The child is a part of the father ; thus the father is also in the woman, blood to blood, and nerve to nerve. Thus we can understand how it is that a wife comes to resemble a husband after bearing him children, or bears children to a second husband in the likeness of the first. His blood, nerves, and constitution in the child are in and connected with the blood, nerves, and constitution of the woman pregnant by him. He is in her but she is not in him. So, the influence telling, she comes to resemble him, not he her, and the child of the second husband resembles the first through the stamp on the woman by the first. I do not wish to be understood to claim that the spermatozoa of the father contain blood or nerves. The spermatozoa, however, do possess a power in generation similar in effect to that of the individual brain in intellectual creation.

The brain receives blood from the vital organs, and is largely influenced in its activities by the character of that blood, which nourishes and vitalizes it. At the same time the quality and character of an intellectual creation depend upon and are limited by the brain matter through which the blood passes. It is in the brain itself that the individual stamp is given to our thoughts.

In generation, the spermatozoa and the ovum fuse and become one. The life of the father and mother is there renewed, and the life thus lighted has the power of moulding and forming all the nourishment, giving it growth to the image of the united pair, as fixed in the fertilized egg. The growth of the fœtus, and the development in it of bone, blood, nerve, and brain, is the growth of the father united to the mother. The character and identity of the individual man is fixed and maintained by a stamping or individualizing power of his or her vitality. The cells, molecules, or atoms forming our bodies are ever changing. From year to year, from day to day, from second to second, these atoms die and are swept away to be replaced by others. The process only ceases when Death coldly commands a halt. The force that thus is ever alert to mould each new aliment introduced into the man after birth to the human type, is equally powerful to mould the mother's nourishing blood to the individuality of the unborn child.

For about nine months the child grows, going through various stages. Commencing with an egg from which all life starts, it has a progress which is a living history of animal evolution. First the semen when liberated from the tubercles of the testes divides up as does the most primitive life. Nuclei have to divide, nucleoli to multiply, and each division of the nucleoli to become, through a gradual adolescence, adult spermatozoa.[1] From this early increase of life by division we find now the two sexes necessary for reproduction. The female perfects the simple egg as it is in the next step of evolution, then comes fertilization, by union with the male, and wonderful, indeed, we find in this fertilized egg growth and development, conditions succeeding each other, which make it similar to the fish, to the reptile, to the lower mammals, to the highest mammals below man, and after birth a still further progression and each change cor-

[1] See Acton *On Reproductive Organs*, p. 91.

responding in order to the chronology of life established by the geological record.

During the period of gestation safety to the woman and the life of the child demand a quiet, orderly existence without extreme exertion or excitement. For six weeks after the birth of the child, the civilized woman should have absolute quiet and repose. For some months longer great care is required.

While it is true that many women do well without so long a period of rest and quiet as has been named, it is equally true that a large amount of disease and misery among women results from a neglect or inability to observe the rule for rest and recovery laid down. The risk of uterine trouble, displacement, etc., after labor is beyond a doubt greatly increased by premature exercise or work. Abortion or premature expulsion of the child caused by weakness, by accident, or by intention requires still more care and is frequently followed by long and distressing illness.

A medical writer has spoken of abortion as the picking of unripe fruit and compares its effects on the woman to those of such picking on the tree. The green fruit is firm in its fastening to the tree ; to get it off one must pull and twist, with the frequent result of bruised fruit, torn twigs, and broken limbs, and after all it is of no account. The ripe fruit, on the other hand, comes off almost with a touch, perfect in texture and flavor. So with the woman ; before term nothing is ready and the separation of mother and child is under a protest of nature. Hemorrhage, injuries, and even permanent invalidism are a frequent consequence. In all the stages before the sixth month the child is lost, after that and before term it is generally lost or reared with the greatest difficulty. While at term a fatty degeneration has gone on in the parts, resistance is at a minimum, and everything is ready for a return to the conditions before conception.

Under a protest of nature against a violation of her intentions the delicate generative organs are liable to injury. Thus the child is lost, the mother injured, nature's efforts for the future of the individual are frustrated, and we have as in the orchard only a nubbin and a broken tree. Abortion consequently cannot do away with the necessity of care after conception, but rather increases it.

The woman has a considerable development of the mammary gland or breast. After childbirth this gland in the healthy woman secretes milk for her child. The child first nourished by the mother's blood is next nourished by her milk—always by her love. If this function be suppressed, the recovery of the woman from childbirth is delayed and endangered. The generative organs are slow in reestablishing their old conditions if the child be not suckled. Many female diseases start from this cause. The life of the child is also endangered, the mortality in hand-fed and even wet-nursed children being from ten to ninety per cent. greater than in those suckled by their mothers. The mother loses also a great joy. The suckling of her child will prove one of her greatest pleasures.[1]

The man has no mammary glands developed. This statement is a general truth as to the male, but abnormal developments of these glands in the male are on record, and even milk has been secreted by the man ; but such departures from the rule are ever found in nature. Men have been known with breasts of milk and women with thick growing beards.

These exceptions do not vitiate the rule as to the development of the sexes.[2]

During the period of suckling, exposure, overwork, all excitement or careless diet on the part of the mother will injure the babe and may kill it. Such injudicious acts may also bring on abscess of the breasts or other painful troubles in woman.[3]

This function should be properly performed about nine months. Childbirth and its immediate duties occupy about seventeen months, and after this is complete still no one is so well fitted to care for the helpless child as the mother for the first five or six years of life.

These necessary maternal duties prevent the woman from fully taking part in the outside contest during the period of her greatest vitality. If she do not perform those duties she exterminates her individuality and life. So nature rids herself of useless incumbrance. It is, indeed, difficult to see how the interests of the race can be advanced by a return to the system of savages and barbarians, in making the woman carry the burden of bread-gaining as well as that of breeding. Many civilized people living in continual poverty follow the savage system, somewhat mitigated however. These people for the most part are peasants now, and have been peasants in the past for an indefinite period of time. The tendency of civilization and of advance, at least till recently, has been toward a liberation of woman from the drive of drudgery. Under this advance she has grown more beautiful in body, morals, and mind. Unfortunately, humanity has been continually confronted with a point at which the nerves are not balanced by the body, and the reproductive powers of the races disappear.

[1] See Jos. E. Winter's articles, *Medical Record.*
[2] See on mammary glands, Leishman's *System of Midwifery*, p. 154.
[3] Even so simple a matter as bathing on a full breast instead of after the child has nursed may cause serious consequences.

While it is true that an extreme point has sometimes been reached in which idleness productive only of inanity has been the lot of women, and in which neither body, morals, nor mind could develop or even hold their own, it is not true that the liberation of energy in women for reproduction, consequent upon their activities being largely confined to the home, has proved unfavorable as a whole to the interests of humanity. This higher nervous organization in advanced societies doubtless demands more care in generation or force for reproduction in their women than is required in less mentally developed women.

The woman's rights agitation, and the change in the status, education, and activities of women are all the results of a condition. This condition has produced also the increasingly high standard of life. Amongst the consequences are increasing difficulty of attainment of the standard, progressive delay or avoidance of marriage, and in marriage the avoidance of children.

These things hold women back from child-bearing. This, again, takes away the main object of men in protecting them or caring for them, as it also takes away much, if not all the necessity of their being protected and provided for. All this to the extent that women do not have children. The results we see before us. The high standard of life is now difficult for man to attain to alone, without providing for a wife or family. The women are therefore in increasing numbers pushed out into the fight of life. Considerable numbers, having nothing to hold them back, go voluntarily into the world's contests—nay, often force themselves there.

These are usually the most intelligent and capable. The reason for this seeking of interests in the drudgery of life is probably threefold :

1st. Not having the glory of reproduction to occupy them, their intelligent minds demand an interest.

2d. The frequent weakening in so-called highly educated women of both the reproductive instinct and the reproductive power.

3d. The difficulty of satisfying a woman of superior intelligence and high education in the matter of a husband. We perceive this from the fact noted by Galton that the daughters of eminent men marry less frequently than the sons, and consequently create fewer children.

The present movement in women's status will doubtless do good in eliminating the extreme and disadvantageous idleness still found in many women's lives, and the substitution for these errors of a wholesome and safe series of activities in which body and mind may be developed and the morals strengthened. It is difficult, however, to reconcile the interest of the race with the idea of opening to women all forms of life activity. Take politics for instance. Public officers have terms ranging from one year to six, with the possibility of re-election. In fact, a successful political life demands a considerable period of office-holding in one or another position of trust. Many of the highest judges hold for life. Take the term of a United States senator, six years, or take any of the terms of office usually held before this dignity is reached. Is it possible to conceive that a woman in political place could attend to her official public duties as well when bearing children as when sterile? Must she, then, for the highest political achievement remain single, or, if married, refuse conjugal intercourse, or use preventive measures, which physicians unite in saying injure and undermine the health? If a woman be single when she enters public life she may marry while in it, if no law provide to the contrary. If she marry, conception and childbirth must be expected. We have already seen that a woman with child could not safely take the risks which an unfertilized woman or a man could. Neither can she that suckles her young. The result of putting women in politics would be first a recognition on their part of the handicap of child-bearing, and second, a refusal of at least the majority of those going into it to submit to the handicap. On the supposition that the most intelligent women would take hold of politics, their probable failure, as a rule, to perpetuate their superiorities to the next generation in children, we must admit would be to the disadvantage of the race.

The brain of the high-class white women probably runs over the average of her sex and race (44 oz.), but even if it does not, it is proportionately superior to that of the negro male, which is 44 oz., with; however, on his part superior bulk of flesh, which makes his brain relatively inferior to the female white brain of the same weight. It is, of course, unreasonable with these facts before us to assert that the male negro is mentally better fitted to vote than the female of the white race. It is also quite ridiculous to assert that a Madame de Staël, George Sand, George Eliot, Mrs. Somerville, Mrs. Julia Ward Howe, or a thousand others we could name are unfit to vote, or less so than the ward striker or "politician for plunder," we all are so familiar with.

The policy, however, of throwing these women into careers discouraging to matrimony or at least to child-bearing may well be doubted. No activity could serve their country or humanity so well as the perpetuation of their superiorities, not in ideals alone but in LIFE. Were I a tyrant with absolute power, I should be inclined to make it a legal obligation on every superior woman to breed. I believe that at present this is their moral obligation.

3

In the nervous and brain organization of the two sexes, differences are observable. As might be expected, knowledge of the internal and invisible sex differences is much less complete than knowledge of the external and visible differences. The whole sympathetic nervous system is more developed in the female ; hence the greater frequency of hysteria and kindred troubles in women. As it is proportionately more developed in woman, so it is also more delicate and more subject to be upset by shocks or rough usage.

The average weight of the brain in the white man in America is a little over 49 oz., in woman a little over 44 oz.[1] The relationship is as 100 to 90. In the lower races the difference between the brains of the sexes is less than in the civilized. This is the case also in all sexual variations. Even in the apes these sexual differences are greater in the gorilla, orang, and chimpanzee, the highest members of the order, than in the lower apes.

The following summary, from the *Medical Record*, of Sir James Crichton-Browne's oration at the annual meeting of the Medical Society of London is of interest :

The orator maintained that the growing tendency around us to ignore intellectual distinctions between the sexes is unphysiological, and he adduced numerous interesting facts in support of this view. The radical explanation of sex, he said, was to be sought in what Michael Foster had called "the protoplasmic movement," that is to say, in the integrative and disintegrative changes of living matter. Anabolic and katabolic processes were manifold, varied in their relative ascendency in different individuals, and were influenced by environment, so that in tracing their operation through the animal kingdom, qualifications and explanations were from time to time needful, but subject to these it was everywhere obvious that the female was the outcome and expression of predominant anabolism, and the male of predominant katabolism. A study of the organic and functional, primary and secondary sexual characters, of the normal development of the tissues, and of their pathological modifications, made this evident, and a study of the emotional and intellectual characteristics of men and women led to the same conclusion. Differences in intellect implied cerebral differences, and first among cerebral differences between the sexes he would refer to mass and weight. Tables were produced showing that, allowing for differences of stature, there was still an excess of brain weight of more than an ounce in favor of the male. It could also be shown from the tables that organic diseases, and the atrophic changes they induced, lowered the normal difference between the male and female brain. That the smaller size of the female brain was a fundamental sexual distinction was made clear by the fact that the same difference in brain weight between men and women had been found in savage races. Not only was the male brain heavier than the female, but it had a wider range of variation in weight. There were also grounds for believing that there was a difference in the balance

[1] Flint's *Text-Book of Human Physiology*, p. 689.

of parts in the male and female brains respectively. Broca had declared that the occipital lobes were more voluminous in the female, and Sir James Crichton-Browne said that his own observations confirmed this conclusion and showed that, while the frontal lobes were equally developed in both sexes, the parietal lobes, which corresponded roughly with the motor area of Ferrier, were larger in the male than in the female, and the occipital lobes, certainly sensory in their functions, were larger in the female than in the male. The third brain difference between the sexes was one of convolutional arrangement ; mere ocular inspection would bring home to any one who diligently used it the superior symmetry of the female brain, due to its comparative poverty in secondary gyri. He had also found the specific gravity of the gray matter generally lower in the female than in the male brain. Another momentous difference was in vascular supply. In an investigation carried on jointly with Dr. Sydney Martin, he had found that the diameter of the internal carotid and vertebral arteries, taken together, was slightly greater in the male than in the female. When the smaller size of the female brain was taken into account, it appeared that the female brain received a larger supply of blood in proportion to its mass than the male brain did, but it must be remembered that the blood was somewhat poorer in quality than that going to the male brain. The distribution of blood to the brain in the two sexes differed considerably. The internal carotid arteries, with their great branches, the anterior and middle cerebral arteries, supplying the supra-orbital convolutions and island of Reil, the gyrus fornicatus, the Rolandic area, the angular gyrus, and the first temporo-sphenoidal lobules, were much larger in the male than in the female brain, but the vertebral arteries, which supplied the occipital and temporo-sphenoidal lobules, were larger in the female, and the basilar artery, which was practically a continuation of the vertebrals, was also larger in the female brain. The posterior communicating arteries were incapable of adjusting the balance between the direct currents of the carotid and vertebral arteries, and the result of the difference mentioned was that the anterior region of the brain was comparatively more copiously irrigated with blood in men, and the posterior in women. The region of the brain which in men was most richly flushed with blood was that which was concerned, we had reason to believe, in volition, cognition, and ideo-muscular processes ; while the region which in women was most vascular was that which was mainly concerned in sensory functions, and we thus saw that there was a relation between the size of the cerebral arteries and what observation had taught us as to the intellectual and emotional differences of the sexes. Differences in brain structure and function had a special pathological significance at the period when sexual divergence was taking place most rapidly, and when education was being pushed forward with most vigor. The orator then proceeded to speak of the methods of education. He said he did not hesitate to affirm that overpressure was rampant in high schools for girls in this country, though there were those who believed that it was a medical myth. He protested against home evening lessons, and also against girls proceeding to school without having first had an adequate morning meal. He quoted in conclusion, as an argument against the equal education of the sexes, the remark that " what was decided among the prehistoric protozoa cannot be annulled by Act of Parliament," and he said that the essential difference between male and female could not be obliterated at a sweep of the pen by any Senatus Academicus.

In the whole matter of cranial capacity, in absolute brain weight or in its relative size to the rest of the body, we have but a partial and general guide that in our present knowledge is at least unreliable in all minor details or differences. The elephant has a greater brain weight than man, and a number of birds and animals have brains relatively larger to their bodies than man. The brain of the infant is larger in comparison to the body than that of the man. The proportion of the brain of the savage to that of civilized man in a rough, general way is about 5 to 6, but the difference in intellectual force is more nearly, as Galton has said, 1 to 1,000.

The female brain, considered relatively as to the whole body weight, is very nearly in the same ratio as that of the male.

All these things show a lack of complete connection either as to absolute brain size or comparative brain size in intellectual force.

In taking up cranial capacity, for instance, we would find the Chinese below the Esquimaux, and the neolithic man of some districts above the modern Parisian. We can hardly believe this to be correct. In America we find the negro cranial capacity, measured while the race was still under the influence of slavery, to have been 83 cu. cen., or less than that of the native African ; other measurements make the difference greater in favor of the African. We generally consider the American negro the more mentally developed. Still slavery, by taking away individual self-reliance and initiative, and by thus leaving part of the brain faculties unused, may have actually diminished them.

RACES.	MEAN.	MAX.	MIN.	DIFF.
English	96	105	91	14
Germans } Anglo-Americans }	90	{ 114 97	{ 70 82	14 15
Arabs	89	98	84	14
Greco-Egyptians of the Catacombs . .	88		74	23
Irish	87	97	78	19
Malays	86		68	29
Persians				
Armenians } Circassians } Iroquois } Lenapes }	84	94	75	19
Cherokees . . . . Shoshones		104	70	34
African Negroes } Polynesians }	83	{ 99 94	65 82	34 2
Chinese } Creole Negroes of North America } . .	82	{ 91 89	70 73	21 16
Hindoos } Ancient Egyptians of Catacombs } Fellahs } . .	80	{ 91 96 96	77 68 66	14 28 30
Mexicans	79	92	67	25
Peruvians } Australians } Hottentots }	75	101 83 83	58 68 63	47 15 20

Broca's measurements of a vast series of Parisians' skulls would lend color to this view, for the cranial capacity increases with the intellectual manifestations of the various epochs examined. A curious thing in these cranial measurements is the way in which the maxima and minima of races cross into each other. This shows the importance of careful selection in marriage, not only as to race, but as to individuals. Morton's table (see opposite page) showing the various race cranial capacities is considered the best made. Its surprises are worth examination.

We must be satisfied to say at present that while brain size is a general guide to brain capacity, it is after all the brain quality which is most influential in intellectual manifestations.

The brain texture is claimed to be different in the sexes. The specific gravity of the brain in man is heavier than in woman. The convolutions are more extensive and the gray matter relatively in larger proportion in the man.

The fissure of Rolando separates the upper or reasoning part of the brain from the lower or emotional part. If we take the entire length of the brain to be 100, there will be found in woman 31.3 parts in front of the upper end of this fissure, while in man there will be 43.9 parts. Thus the emotional is more developed in woman's brain, the reason more in man's.

Woman is the more delicate, refined, sympathetic, and loving. She it is whose intuitions seem to come from Heaven, so tender and so true are they. It is to her, this delicate and loving being, that the child-bearing and child-nursing function is given. The woman lives for others, for her children. Her body, her nerves, her brain, are perfect for this glory of motherhood.

Nature has said it—woman in reproduction carries the race beyond the clutch of Death. Man with heavy bones, powerful muscles, no recurring wound like the egg bursting from the ovary ; no uterus to bear the babe, no breast to suckle the young ; large-brained, coarse, and strong,—it is he who is to make the fight in the hard world, to protect and support the mother and babes, both helpless for so long. The decree of nature is plain. " He who runs may read." There is no inferiority of the sexes. Both have grand duties to perform that, if well done, are full of joy and pleasure. The man cannot enter the field of woman. Woman enters the field of man only as an inferior, no longer a woman, nor yet a man.

Perfection is that each should be in his or her place. It is there that each can work best. The glorious function of woman handicaps her unalterably for anything else. Nature's decree to her is to bear children, for this she is made. Can you violate a law of nature without paying the penalty ? Jump from a housetop—will the law of gravity forgive you ? Take poison—will its deadly action spare you ? Cut open your heart—will it go on beating ? So the woman who violates the laws of nature laid down for her will be neither healthy nor happy.

So also the man who violates these laws, who does not take wise measures to reproduce and improve, will be neither healthy nor happy. It may be said here that the defects of society and the degeneracy of marriage are more due to the ignorance, idleness, and crime of man than they are to the shortcomings of woman. The errors of the women are in large measure due to the initiative of the men.

The accumulated experience of mankind crystallized in the customs of society follow in a general way the law of nature in regard to the relation and position of the sexes and are not to be lightly cast aside. The married man has better prospect of life than the bachelor. The wife-mother has equally a better prospect of life to about the same extent over her single sister. Thus we see that avoidance of maternity on the ground of its danger to life, a doctrine making nature a fool, is the result of ignorance.

Some occupy themselves with the justice of the position of woman in nature. It is an idle waste of breath. We might with as much reason occupy ourselves with the justice of the size of the mouse as compared with the immensity of the elephant, the rapidity of the horse compared to the slowness of the snail, the limitation of the cow's diet to grass and seed compared to the omnivorous capacity of the bear. With equal utility we might discuss the justice of the destiny of the graceful porpoise playing for hours with its mates about a ship—intelligent, social, and interesting, condemned to live in the sea, while the ugly, poisonous snake glides about amongst the beautiful glades of the ever charming land. After deciding the destiny of the porpoise to be unjust, we might, if fools enough, decree that it should be placed on land and proceed forthwith to drag the poor animal-fish out of the water only to see it linger in agony, flapping awkwardly and fruitlessly about until an early death came to relieve it. So we might go on talking of the justice of the delicate flower being the prey of the caterpillar, the caterpillar of the bird, the bird the game of the wild cat, and the wild cat the game of man. All this would be in the air, and the arguments about it so many balloons of gas that have only to be pricked to collapse in a formless mass while the stink of them rises to Heaven.

Most of the discussions of sex by the women's rights people are of this character. They overlook or defy nature and they would pull the woman out of her element willing or unwilling with the fact under their noses that the mass of women out of their sphere, through ignorance or a hard fate, are, by their weakness in an unnatural position, forced to inferiority. They are women, not men. When they fight man there may be one here and there found to hold their own, but the mass are driven to the ragged edge or into the gutter.

These remarks apply especially to the results of this movement in discouraging marriage and in promoting prevention of conception or inducing abortion, so that the woman can fill some supposed high destiny. By these means in many places the American population has lost its power of reproduction and is not even able to hold its own. No reflection is intended on a woman's learning how to support herself, or in her doing worldly work, or in her following any outside career so that it does not interfere with the grander destiny of maternity.

There is no organized movement to induce men to avoid procreation, but the drift of society has for some time been in this direction. The bachelor's life has now fewer drawbacks than it has ever had. Society tolerates sexual promiscuity on the part of the male in this country as it has not done before. The standard of life is high and difficult to maintain a family in, while club life enables a single man to meet the demands of the times with comparative ease. The men consequently shirk marriage, and when married shirk the responsibilities its high and grand creative work imposes. In historical civilizations, dissipation and degradation have always commenced with the men and have thence communicated to the women. When the women sink into that slough of despond—sexual lewdness and avoidance of maternity—the intelligent or ruling class disappears and so the civilization ends for want of perpetuation of the minds and morals that made it.

Small families is one of the first signs of this condition, and then come no families at all amongst the upper classes.

The time may arrive when the best interests of humanity and progress will be served by small families. It is true that in nature the rule is, as complexity increases so does fertility decrease. As yet, however, there are no indications that a small family is advantageous to man in the struggle for immortality and advance by the child. In a small family, one or two children, the chances of extermination by death of these before procreation has blessed them, or of sterility or impotence, etc., are greater than in a large family, but besides this there is not only this relative advantage to the large family, but the individuals are also superior to those of the small families. Only sons and daughters are rarely celebrated. As a rule, they are physically and morally below the average of their class, they are more often childless, and at this time they are a sign of weakness in the breed and should be avoided in marriage selection.

Woman's present emancipation as compared with her condition in the past is a result of a drift of society that has overcome great opposition. To curtail woman's freedom as it exists in well regulated families now is a reactionary policy not to be thought of. A man, however, in Solomon's time, or even Solomon himself, might have considered the female freedom of to-day quite incompatible with the security of the family and the perpetuation of the best minds of the race. So doubtless it would have been if suddenly given without preparation to the women of the harem.

We to-day are doubtless equally unable to properly judge what means can be best availed of to at once improve woman, and improve the race in children born from her loins. Consequently no rules are laid down as to the advisability of any of the measures proposed to improve women.

Voting and political duty is now the immediate goal of their champions. This has been tried in numerous places from the wild tribes of the Amoor to the American Territories of Wyoming, Utah, and Washington. It does not seem to have improved society or the condition of women. Polygamy in Utah, for instance, had nothing to fear from female suffrage while it lasted. General female suffrage seems likely to prevail before very long. Its effects can then be studied. In all these details as to woman's sphere, the benefit of the doubt should be given to cautiously conducted change, demanding only one conservative stronghold, the security of reproduction. The women who have gone out into the fight of life, emancipated, have in many cases fallen by the way. Thus while in the higher classes of women a freedom from supervision is allowed, which has been found consistent with perfect chastity or fidelity in marriage, on the other hand it must be admitted that under this system there exists a vast army of prostitutes, not found under the old and primitive patriarchal regime. But again, every one with experience seems to agree that harem women have less capacity to protect their chastity themselves than our own women, and appear ready often at the first occasion to let it go. We can thus perceive that the necessity, so plain, that the man must have a security in the paternity of his children to insure progress by the protection of the mother and young during their increasing period of helplessness going with their increasing improvement, has not suffered by the gradually enlarged freedom of the woman. On the contrary, an increased self-reliance has improved the female, or most of those, at least, who breed.

It is not so many centuries ago that the Anglo-Saxon virgin could no more go out alone, where she would meet men, than the Continental lady virgin can now. In morality the English or American girl will not suffer in comparison with any others or with those of the past, and the married women at least with the same religious training are or were more reliable in England and America than in the more conservative countries of Europe. The word *were* is used, because it must be admitted that the moral tone of both England and America in regard to the chastity of men and women is lower than it was from thirty to fifty years ago. It is still true that we have no condition in our race similar to that in some of the Austrian provinces, where nearly half the births are illegitimate, but on the other hand the prevention of conception or induction of abortion in America gives us no room to boast. Of the two, the illegitimate child or no child, the first, of course, would be the choice of every one believing in the immortality the child gives.

The tone of morality and regard for female chastity has gone through many ups and downs, but through it all there appears a history of improvement. In the past an army generally committed rape on conquered women. In the earliest times they either massacred the whole conquered population or used them for slaves, the women being destined for the sexual indulgence of the victors. Now no one would think of expecting such acts from a conquering army. So a woman of the Turks floating about unguarded can not be deemed by them virtuous, while we find our highest-class women more reliable as to chastity than any experienced person has ever found the women of the harem with all their guards.

Progress may continue in this line, in fact it must, and the time will doubtless come when a father can have implicit faith in the chastity and fidelity of the mother of his children under any circumstances. Progress may go so far, that a man and woman unmarried may go to sleep in the same bed without any more suspicion of improper conduct than now exists when they walk together. Human nature, however, must change before this can be a received opinion, and we should consequently avoid too much temptation.

A woman who is single, childless, and making the fight of the world, is certainly not doing that which gives the largest amount of health, happiness, bodily pleasure, or of material results.

A general review either of the past or of the present shows that thus far in the evolution of society a position of women with ambition or duties inconsistent with maternity has not been and is not favorable. We find women soldiers, not only individually as Joan of Arc, but collectively as in the Amazons of the past and in the present

female guards of the King of Dahomey, vowed to chastity. Under
such systems the women do not gain power, nor is the strength of the
society made superior.

We find women, as has been said, exercising the privileges of
citizens, as voting in barbarous communities as amongst the tribes
on the Amoor River, also in more civilized places as amongst the
Mormon settlements of Utah, in the school elections in Massachusetts,
etc. We find women engaged in general industry to the same extent
as man in many primitive societies, and generally amongst savages
the women do the work while the men look on. With many such
tribes the women seem now to be constitutionally industrious, while
the men are constitutionally lazy.[1] In the higher types of slavery,
such as that formerly prevalent in the United States, the slave women
were obliged to work to the extent of their powers.

In all these cases the productive power of the society has not
been increased nor has progress been as rapid as in societies where
the superior woman bore children more generally than has ever been
recorded in societies where they take part in public, military, civil,
or industrial affairs. These create ambitions inconsistent with
maternity.

In our own day we can make a comparison between England and
France. In the first until very recently women have had comparatively little opportunity in engaging in the outside fight. This is
especially true of the highest classes of women. In France, on the
contrary, the women have for a considerable time played an important part in both politics and industry. Their political influence as
court favorites and as centres of literature or politics is a matter of
history. Their industrial influence may be observed generally. A
Frenchman and wife unite their capital for business and the wife
does her full share of the management. Such is not so generally
the case in England.

We find upon examination that the per capita production of the
whole population is greatest in England; per capita commerce
ditto, per capita consumption ditto, per capita service of money
ditto, children to family ditto, general birth-rate ditto, stability of
government ditto; achievements of great men, as discovery of circulation of blood by Harvey, power of steam by Watts, law of gravitation by Newton, desent of man by Darwin, social evolution by
Spencer, political economy by Adam Smith, etc., etc., ditto.

France has had an ambitious colonial policy for 200 years with a
strong naval power to back it up, still there is but one real colony of

[1] See Spencer's *Sociology.*

Frenchmen, that of Lower Canada, and in that the social conditions and position of women are entirely different from those in France; while England taking up the colonial policy later has occupied large portions of the world with people from its own loins and with its own language and development. The native population of France is slowly retrogressive, being maintained by immigration like the native population of New England. In forty-two departments in France the deaths exceed the births, while the population of England is overflowing. In the one case there is scarcely internal and native reproductive power for the continuance of the French people, while in the other there is a surplus for the peaceful conquest of the world.

In our own country we may perceive already the effects of an untimely or too great change in the ambitions and duties of women. In those sections such as New England, where the movement is greatest, greater probably than anywhere in the world, there also is the reproductive power of the native population weakest, weaker, for instance, than amongst the native whites in the South under a more unfavorable climate for this race. So also in those classes (unfortunately the superior ones) where what are called woman's rights are most believed in and lived up to, we find equally that the females are unable or unwilling to breed to an equal extent with the females of immigrants, such as those mockingly called the Pope's Irish, the Canucks, or French Canadians, etc. Should the present disposition or capacities of our own native females remain the same in this respect as it now is, the laugh will soon be on the other side—in fact, is fast getting there now.

In New England, as well as in nearly every northern State, it is the mentally weakest, most ignorant, and least developed who are, speaking generally, doing the breeding and fixing the character of the next and of the succeeding generations. This is certainly not to the interest of the nation, of the race, or of humanity.

The Catholic religion is thought to play a prominent part in the continued breeding of its communicants, and as far as official precept goes it evidently does so ; but as the Catholic population of France is rotten to the core with prevention, abortion, and infanticide, it cannot be the only cause. Whatever the cause of sterility is, nowhere do we see women's rights so ardently preached as in certain sections of America, and nowhere in the whole world do we see the birthrate so low as amongst the native Americans in the most infected sections. It is also in America and amongst our own race that we see the greatest crimes against nature and reproduction in *both* sexes anywhere known. Nowhere else is abortion, infant murder, masturbation, and the prevention of conception so general. Where these crimes are most frequent there also is the woman's rights' movement strongest. These errors are not so much due to women's rights perhaps as are women's rights due to a diseased condition, the common parent of both these tendencies to sterility.

The past history of mankind shows us women in prominent positions or equal to man in the outside fight in primitive and in some advanced societies. These conditions thus far have not proved favorable to progress. The reason doubtless is that the superior women at a certain point of intelligence refuse to breed, and the best of the society is in that way exterminated.

A higher and better position for woman, in which she has more dignity and receives more consideration than in any primitive time, is a universal accompaniment of progress beyond the pastoral-patriarchal type. Before that stage woman's position in progress was, from a relatively equal position to man, to one of greater subordination to him, out of which change came permanent marriage and security of paternity.

We may say, in a general way, that a. woman who is not or cannot be a mother has neither the perfection of hope, health, or happiness. While, on the other hand, the mother, the woman in her sphere as nature has decreed, is in the mass happy, healthy, and superior,—I may say, grand with the aureole of maternity sanctifying her, for the mother is a "holy of holies" and a fountain of life.

The comparison to be made in every-day life one might think would be enough without very deep inquiry into the science of the matter as to what woman's happiest sphere is. On the one hand, the work-girl, by no law of man, but by the law of nature, is weak in the outside fight. She is forced to the lowest wages of her vocation. Always on the verge alone on her way to work and on her return to a lonely room, to what temptation is she not exposed? If she will cede her virtue she can be in affluence, if pretty, in a moment. The money may support some poor relative, she thinks. The first step taken, and the doors of a hell in this world have opened for her.

Promiscuous intercourse soon brings inflammation, maternity becomes impossible, she is no longer a woman, only a slop-pail of infamy. What degradation there is in a prostitute, what despair, no one who has not seen them in their early decay can tell! For them death strikes off a chain. How will you blame the poor child? She is so delicate, sympathetic, full of emotion, ready yearning to love, with the monthly periods when continuous work is wellnigh impossible. She is in competition and contest with rough, hard man. She is a child of hope and trust, unprotected, homeless, un-

husbanded.   Can you expect her to starve both body and heart for
the good opinion of a society that will not know her?

Here, on the one side, you have the woman, as we see, thrown
into the relentless contest of life.   How many fall a prey to shame,
that living death ; alas, an evening walk in the streets of any city,
thick in fallen women as autumn is in fallen leaves, will but too
sadly tell.

Let us take the other condition of women in our midst : married,
a mother, queen of her home; her lisping children at her knee.
The husband, fighting the bitter battles outside, comes back with joy
to his home.   His little triumphs in the world are nothing to the
triumph she has borne him and achieved in immortalizing him and
herself in their children.   Nothing that he has, nothing that he has
done, does he consider of value compared to one of them.

Such a woman, as Michelet says, is a religion.   So tender, so
true, so loving, so loved.   Sweet cares of the wife to love, soothe,
and encourage her husband, and see his energy renewed at her dear
touch.   Sweet cares of the mother to nurse her child, to watch its
powers unfold, with the devotion, tenderness, and insight alone possessed by woman.   She travels on the path of life hand in hand with
her children, happy and glorious.   Oh, holy mother, they who
would raise their finger to prevent your joyous destiny are full of
folly, full of crime !

I do not wish to be understood as advising a prohibition of woman's
entry into any sphere of life.   On the contrary, I believe fully in the
utilization by women of all their powers, physical and mental, both
for their own improvement and for that of the race.   But I hold that
all such secondary activities should always be subordinated to the
one great function of woman—child-bearing.   Nor do I overlook the
fact that procreation is the one great function of man also, to which
everything should be secondary.

Some men and some women have an idea that there are duties in
life and acts, such as teaching or creating works of art, literature,
etc., which are grander and of more value to the race than the creating of human beings in their own image.   This idea I believe to
be erroneous.   I have sufficiently set forth the individual aspects of
this matter in other chapters ; a few words, therefore, on the interests
of the race will be sufficient here.

In the lowest geological state in which evidences of man are
found there is unity in this, that all implements credited to man are
of the most primitive types.   In succeeding strata, while these primitive types often persist, higher and higher types take possession, and
we have thus in the earth's crust a history which demonstrates man

to have progressed from a race or races uniformly lower than any known to-day, to our present highest civilization. In this era, however, all have not come to the highest plane. Large bodies of human beings, even in the most developed countries, are far below the highest men and women in brain power. Brain power is the line on which humanity has improved. This power depends largely on brain size, convolutions, etc. Taking the first two we find that in the primitive tribes of our day both brain weight and convolutions are deficient as compared to these conditions in the highest men.

Amongst Andaman Islanders and Australians the convolutions of the brain are comparatively simple, while the total weight of the male brain has been noted as low as 38 oz., and will probably average about 42 oz. In the male negro in America it is 44 oz. In the male American the average brain weight is a little over 49 oz. The most primitive savage has no mental grasp compared to ours ; he cannot count over five ; his language has but few words, and his numerals give out after three or five, and are replaced by the word "many." The negro, a few steps higher, shows his deficiency in being unable to cope with the white man. He has not yet become a composer or an inventor of importance.

Now the history of this development of the highest types of brain power gives every indication of having occupied a long period of time, probably tens of thousands of years, perhaps hundreds of thousands of years. The point that I make is that no mere book, statue, picture, invention, work of charity or philanthropy, possible to be done by an individual man or woman, can compensate the race for the loss through non-reproduction of the brain developed through ages of time to the capacity of such a work. In other words, it is more important to the race to hold by reproduction the brain of an Aristotle, Shakespeare, or Spencer, than to have the works they have done, and to toil through ages more to develop their powers again in developed brains.

To the highest type of brain all human things are possible. As the brain is inferior in structure, so its manifestations must be inferior. It is probable that the lower types of brain, even amongst the developed races, would require thousands of years to reach the highest brain power in the same races. These considerations should accentuate the importance of careful selection in breeding amongst men and clearly show the value to the race of perpetuating superior brain development in children.

A brainy woman can do no work to compensate the world for the extinction of her brain in sterility. It is at sterility that the line must be drawn.

There are still other differences in the constitution of the two sexes. As the woman has the highest capacity of devotion in the use of the reproductive power, as she has the tenderest and most spiritualized capacity for the highest love, so, unfortunately, she also has the capacity of prostituting these powers, and of sinking into an abyss of infamy deeper than is possible for man or any animal.

With man the use of the reproductive powers depends not only on consent and the will, but also on desire or instinct. He must be attracted, he must have passion. This is not the case with woman. Consent is enough. As a corollary of this we find another difference. A man cannot be forced to the sexual act ; a woman may be. Thus if a man, we will suppose, was in the power of some Asiatic despot, and was given the choice of immediate death or of having a child by a woman loathsome with some horrid disease, her face sloughing away with cancer and revolting to smell, look upon, or be near, he might wish to save his life, he might be willing to prostitute his powers by taking the alternative proposed, and still he could not,—it would be impossible. With a woman it would be different : offered a similar alternative—death or to have a child by some misery of a man,—she by the mere will could consent to the act, receive the man, take his impress, carry him for nine months, his blood in her through the child, and then bear into the world his diseased image to martyrize her maternal love, and she still stamped in her very nature for life with the man.

The man must be the head and protector of the breed and family. For though he can sink low in the use of the reproductive powers, it is impossible for him to become a prostitute, or to sink to the depths possible to the female.

A man in youthful levity, with untrustworthy companions, may be led off, take too much stimulant or narcotic, and pass the night insensible and no one knows where. The next morning he rises full of headache and repentance. If there is good stuff in him he determines to do such acts no more, and that is the end of it. His reproductive powers are safe. A young girl with the same liberty may be similarly misled, but how terrible may be the result ! Her maidenhood ravished, her purity gone, her maternity capacity seized by the fertilizing germ of some drunken pimp, perhaps outraged again and again !

Again, a boy or man passing in a lonely place may be set upon by a band of robbers, wounded, knocked down, his money taken; he rises, his cuts are bound up; in a little while it is as though nothing had happened. The girl or woman thus lonely and attacked may lose more than money, more than consciousness, more than life. She may, and as a rule when so exposed does, lose honor and purity. She may carry from the place the germ of some repulsive life.

If a doctor were required at the dead of night, and had to be sent for through a country infested by roughs, whom would you send, your son or your daughter, your boy or your girl? The question answers itself. The girl, being exposed to so much greater risks so deadly to fall under, and she being, besides, so much the better nurse, the boy would be sent by the judicious parent, while the girl, with her sympathy and her tenderness, watched with the sick. So it should be in all life matters. From these causes we can clearly perceive that what is proper for a man or boy may be highly improper in a woman or girl,—not merely by reason of the prejudices of society, but by reason of the imminent peril some situations have for the sex. A woman or girl ought not to go about alone in rough or doubtful places. Protection and succor should never be far away from the female.

To recapitulate, we find man the stronger of the sexes. The woman is the more delicate and sympathetic. She has smaller bones, less muscle, has less power mentally and physically for organization and the contest of life, while, on the other hand, she has a larger vitality and development of the sympathetic nervous system. If she remain a virgin, she has, during the period of her human force, fourteen to forty (Anglo-Saxons), the menses at least once a month. The menses cease upon an average several years sooner in the virgin than in the mother of a family. This indicates that the vitality of the mother, instead of being diminished by childbirth, has been increased.

If she enters man's occupations, this function often increases in violence and frequency, or becomes altogether suppressed, with accompanying general nervous derangement. Thus, for some days in every month, she is at a disadvantage in any contest. It must be clear that even when she refuses or cannot enter the career of a mother, she still remains at a disadvantage for any other. If she perform the duties of a mother, that is enough of greatness. She is by this function handicapped for outside occupations, for childbearing must take place in the period of greatest vitality, when the battle of life is hottest.

Women must have children or farewell to the race. Children or extermination, such is our alternative. Women cannot have children and also fight men in the contest of life; the handicap is too enormous. The logical conclusion is beyond escape. Women for the home, men for the fight. Women should not be deceived by the foolish into thinking this destiny inferior. A correct measure in this regard is influence. Woman as mother in the home not only influences her own time, but the future through the child; for the child is almost always what its mother makes it—that is, as far as any influence outside of its own special individuality after birth can make it.

In infancy the impressions are most permanent. Those impressions come from the mother, or should do so. Thus she holds the generation that follows her, and has really the superior position, if there is such an one. The contest of life, where the man belongs, is nothing but a quantity of drudgery and detail subsidiary entirely to the main point of perpetuating the race through the child. As woman has most to do with this, the main and essential question of life, she again may be said to have the superior position.

Let no woman be led willingly to the slaughter. For her to fight with man is a losing fight, ridiculous and useless. She should take the hand the strong man offers when she is true to her duties, and go with him. He for the battle, she for the serene home. Let her be earnest, loving, and virtuous, and she will not lack a man to do his part. Exceptions do occur where the woman is all she should be, but the man is wanting. Such a situation is indeed unfortunate. The great number of unhappy unions of men and women is due to the ignorance of the man and woman of the grandeur of their functions, and of the peculiar difference of sphere of man and woman.

A discreet, virtuous, and loving woman, who has knowledge, will, as a rule, have a happy home, and a happy home contains for woman more possibility of joy and of greatness than any other place. The home is created by woman, defended and supported by man.

What the future may have in store for us no one knows. We must from the limitations of our faculties be guided by what little we know of the past and present. From this point of view there is nothing to indicate that society can even exist with women unable or unwilling to bear children. There is nothing in the history of nature to give any color to the belief that the reproduction of the race is going to be less complex and force-requiring than it is. There is nothing to show that women can be emancipated from child-bearing.

An examination of nature would lead to quite a contrary view. Development has been from the simple to the complex and from generalized functions of matter to specialized ones. The first and simplest life reproduces by division and is sexless. All the functions of this earliest life seem interchangeable. In some low forms of life, by no means the most primitive, the living being may be turned inside out, when the stomach performs the duties of the skin and the skin performs the work of the stomach.

From such simple forms we see life becoming more developed only as it becomes more complex and specialized. One of the first specializations of function both in plants and animals was sex. At first reproduction went on without sex, so life went on without specialized organs. Thus a living being of the most primitive type might be cut in two and each part live on as though nothing unusual had occurred. Developed human beings cannot thus part from their specialized organs. The loss of the liver, the kidneys, of the lungs, of the heart, is in either case at once fatal. Equally the loss of the function of child-bearing by women would sweep humanity from the earth in a hundred years.

Development seems to necessitate the passage of advanced individuals or classes through all previous stages of progress before becoming useful in their new sphere. Thus the young of man starts with the spore, goes through the egg period, resembles a fish, then a dog, then a monkey, then the lowest intellectual man, and so on up to the highest standard he is born to, passing meantime through innumerable and inseparable stages of change.

From this cause the young of man having the most ground to pass over as compared to the young of any other creature, is by far the longest time helpless and dependent.

Early specialization in reproduction shows us the eggs dropped out and fertilized externally as in the fishes. Next we see eggs fertilized in the female, but the egg laid and left to care for itself; the young reptile coming from the egg to the warm sand being fully able to care for itself. In birds the egg is laid and watched and sat upon and the young looked after for a time. In the marsupials the period of gestation is longer, but the young are so immature that they are carried by the female in a natural pouch for a certain period, thus going through a sort of internal and external gestation.

The higher we go the longer is the period of gestation and helplessness combined. Some animals, as the elephant and the cow, have longer periods of gestation than woman, but the young of no animal is so long, or anything like so long, in passing from the time from the fertilization of the egg to the time when they are self-maintaining.

The young of man being so long helpless requires additional time and care from the mother. Woman's form, mind, sympathies, and, in fact, her whole nature, have developed in harmony with this necessity.

As a recapitulation we may say that sexual reproduction in all the simpler forms of life was short in duration for but a comparatively small compass of previous evolution had to be repeated in the young. The egg generally matured outside of the mother and independently of her, and the young when coming from the egg were at once ready to care for themselves without parental protection.

As evolution and improvement progressed, the young passed through longer and longer periods of helpless infancy either in or out of the mother, or both, and needed more and more protection and care. As the necessities of the case changed, so the relation of the sexes changed. At first reproduction demanded the female for the egg and the male only for fertilization ; consequently in plants, insects, and the less developed forms of life, we find the male sex generally inferior to the female.

But as the young made more and more demands upon the mother, and eventually the young came to be born helpless as in man, demanding care and help for the long period required by them to pass through former stages of development, the necessities for a protector arose, and we find the male sex in all the superior animals the strongest and most capable outside fighters From the necessities of the highest improvement arose marriage and the family in man.

This sketch of the outline of the necessary development of motherly qualities coincident with the development of life gives every reason to suppose that a farther advance and development of man will leave the chain of experience unbroken, and that accompanying it will be a development of further motherly qualities and capacities to carry the young through a still longer period of helplessness. The female sex is a necessity of development. As time and development have progressed, the sex has become more and more individuated.

Even in man we see the male and female differ less in all respects amongst the primitive races than amongst the highest, so also we see the children of savages mature far more quickly and cease their mental growth much sooner than those of civilized man.

In this connection it may not be amiss to call attention to the fact that it is amongst savage and primitive races that woman's right to work is not denied, but that, on the contrary, she is continually forced to the unexciting drudgery of industrial work in societies of the militant type. As the savage child is able to take care of itself much sooner than the civilized one, this was not so much a hardship to primitive women as it would be to the highly civilized.

Progress in mankind first demanded the enslavement of women for the foundation of the family. The family once secured and society established firmly on it as a foundation, we find farther progress accompanied by a relief for the female from excessive drudgery or the outside industrial fight, leaving her more opportunity for the grand duties of reproduction, of child-bearing, and of forming the next generation.

Amongst the mammals the female must fight, and for the most part secure her own subsistence as well as that of her young. It is only amongst the higher types that the male protects the female and the young. With savage man the woman no longer has to fight, but all the drudgery is hers. It is amongst the most civilized men and during the most progressive periods that we find the woman given most time for reproduction. Considering this fact, it may well be deemed doubtful whether the present tendency of society by late marriage, avoidance of childbirth, etc., to throw women on their own resources and to make of them outside industrial and political competitors, is not a reversion to an inferior type rather than an advance,

A number of facts in the history of mankind and in the present social organization of primitive industrial societies give a strong probability to this view. While it is true that those primitive militant organizations from which the marriage, polygamous first and monogamous afterward, the security of paternity, the family, and the government of the present dominant races sprang, have shown disregard toward the rights of women, it is not true of all primitive societies. On the contrary, primitive industrial societies all place women in a much better position from the woman's rights' point of view than the militant societies. In those industrial organizations where sexual intercourse is more or less promiscuous, in those where the unions are temporary, and in those where they are polyandrous, the first idea of inheritance must be on the maternal side, for there is little if any security of paternity.

The importance of women in society, owing to this fact, must be increased. They are not captured, because these societies are peaceful, and the lack of chastity makes it useless to buy them. They are not, then, looked on as property, and not treated as such. Women in primitive industrial societies, and in some militant ones, as the Iroquois, derived, doubtless, from them, have a considerable choice in selecting their husbands, are often chiefs or rulers, and on separation or divorce have a share of the property, usually one half, and take the children. Their right to inheritance of property is recognized. With this high position of women for barbarians, we find a weak social organization. Nowhere have such societies been able to survive the competition of those societies where the patriarchal form has prevailed, in which women have had a comparatively much inferior standing, often to the extent, in the earliest militant type, of being treated with great cruelty. These primitive industrial societies, as far as they exist to-day, are confined to localities either incapable of supporting a high civilization, or so isolated as to protect them from the destruction of their fellow-men. Thus we find the Lapps and Esquimaux within the arctic circle, the Thibetans on the high arid table-lands of the Himalayas, the Andamanese and Dyaks on tropical islands, the Nairs on the hills of India, the Pueblos on the deserts of Arizona, etc., all of this type. We must, then, be brought to the conclusion that in primitive man the freedom and high position of woman was not, and is not, conducive to chastity, to the security of paternity, which gives the man a definite object to protect and provide for a mother and *his* children by her, and consequently to the creation of the family, from which our civilized forms of government spring. Without security of paternity the progressive increase of the helpless period in the young essential to the improving man has no means of being provided for. Therefore, these primitive industrial types have been swept away or into corners by the more progressive patriarchal organizations. We are now ordering our civilization more and more on the industrial type. Our women now inherit property, may take the initiative in divorce, and are commencing to vote, as in the primitive failures of society (natives of Amoor River). Woman's chastity, as with them, is less considered than it was in the militant type, and few people think of stoning adulterers, or of killing the seducer of a wife or daughter, Where it is done, for the most part, is amongst the militant ex-slave-holders of the South. The position of prostitutes, while still deservedly damned, is much more tenable, in this country at least, than it was twenty-five years ago.

The family has less cohesion and respect than formerly. The state has taken many of its functions, such as infant education. As Spencer says : "It may well be surmised that in some directions the change in woman's situation has gone too far, but this need not and ought not to put any limit on her progress in true directions." What these true directions are is not now known, but the true measure for woman's position now and hereafter must always be the interest of the generation, and generations to come.

The cruelty and oppression of woman by man in the social organizations that have everywhere preceded man's civilization, took the form of forcing the women to do all the work of which they were capable. The men fought, the women worked. The limit of abuse and drudgery was the line beyond which the women could not bear enough children to sustain the tribe. With all this heavy outdoor labor child-bearing and child care could not be fully developed, and it is this reason which has given societies giving their women better treatment and work more suited to their reproductive duties the advantage.

A strong indication that sex cannot be aborted in its reproductive function without injury, is the effect upon the body and character of men or women by the destruction of their respective reproductive organs. The mutilated man at once loses physical force and endurance. His voice changes, approaching the feminine type, and his moral tone and force of character are impaired, if not destroyed. The gait, attitude, and tastes all take on a feminine quality, and eunuchs as a rule lose with their manhood the timbre of voice and courage of their sex.

Women who have their ovaries removed generally depart from the female type and assimilate to that of man. Often the beard commences to grow, the mammary glands become atrophied, the voice becomes gruffer and more masculine—the gait, attitudes, and tastes become more and more those of men ; yet the force and structure are lacking. A sterilized woman can never be a man, though destroyed as a woman. A sterilized man destroyed as a man is not by far made participant in the glories of woman. Both from something become nothing.

These reflections should cause us to bear in mind the limitations of sex both on the male side for some things and on the female side for others, and to consider them in life plans and actions. It cannot be good economy to undertake a man's work with a woman, nor a woman's work with a man. In many things nature has issued her fiat and it is impossible for the one sex to do the duty of the other.

The little boy seeks enjoyment in the contest, playing horse with the tin soldier, with a drum, in hunting or adventure. The books he first takes to are histories, accounts of travels, adventure, piracy, or war. The girl is from the first naturally pleased with playing home and housekeeper with her doll, its dresses, and its house. It is an exception ever with the freest choice that a girl takes to the rough games of the boy. When she reads, it is the novel with love leading to marriage. The boy seldom takes to the amusement of the girl.

Thus the instinct in the individual of the two sexes, at its earliest manifestations, is without difficulty seen to be different. The outward appearances of the body characterizing so distinctly the two sexes is but an index of the internal workings of the flesh functions and of the nerves. To an observer these internal qualities are as different in the sexes as is their outward appearance.

The difference in appearance, in temperament, in tastes, and in action between the two sexes is so considerable that it is beyond escape from even the inattentive. The natural lives of the two sexes in their relation to each other are perhaps best shown when circumstances break down the usual conventional relations that surround us. In case of sudden àccident, trouble, or danger the woman looks to the man for help and protection. When the danger is so great as to place the instinct of self-preservation above everything else, the fight for life is won by the strongest in muscle, vitality, and judgment, as the case may be. It is on such dreadful occasions as panics, fires in public places, and wrecks at sea that we observe the men either grandly and voluntarily sacrificing their lives to the women and children, or in a frenzy of life instinct trampling them down in theatre doorways, crowding them out of the boats of sinking vessels, or abandoning them to the fearful fate of fire or flood. Sad events these are, sometimes showing grand qualities of character and heroism, sometimes uncovering a relentless demon of selfish cruelty. In either case, the power of man and the weakness of woman in the outside fight are brought into strong relief.

The tendencies of our time are toward a greater assimilation of the activities of the sexes than has hitherto prevailed. This assimilation in our civilization commenced in the feudal ages, and has several culminating points, one coincident with the collapse of the Italian municipal republics, one at the fall of the French feudal aristocracy, and one now. In the civilizations of the past we find, as in our own time, the rising period to correspond with a strong family life and a marked differentiation of the activities of the sexes. The early Egyptian, the early Greek, the early Roman, like the Knight in growing feudalism, was the head of a family in which the wife was a homebody. It is in Egypt dying, in Greece upon the verge of the abyss, in Rome rotted to its core, in Florence failing, in the French aristocracy going to the block, that we find women and men most assimilated in their life activities. An incapacity or unwillingness to procreate séems to have been a general accompaniment of all these periods, resulting in the extermination, through non-reproduction of the dominant classes, of those who had made and who supported the civilization or system involved.

The Queen of Sheba demonstrates the capacity of woman, and may have been the evidence of a national condition of woman active in the same fields with man in Sheba ; at any rate, it is the last we hear of Sheba. The glory of Palmyra goes out with Zenobia. Aspasia burns bright at the death of Greece. Cleopatra marks the extinction of the Ptolemies and the absorption of Egypt into Rome ; and later, as the sun of Egypt's civilization sets forever in clouds of super-stition, clouds bloody-hued with the glare of fiery fanaticism, we see Hypatia rise on Egypt's horizon, pure and bright as an evening star, as a souvenir of a glory departed and dead.   Boadicea leads the last hosts of Britain's dying life, and Lucrezia Borgia shines in an expir-ing system.

The rule seems quite general that, as far as the past is concerned, the shining of women in the activities before their time monopolized by men, is a forerunner of destruction.   The exceptions to this gener-alization, which are quite numerous, on examination indicate that celebrated women in fields occupied by men, when not noted at the period of downfall, or shortly preceding it, are never and in no sense an evidence of a general change in women's activities to an assimila-tion with the outside activities of men.   In the more general case of noted women at the downfall of races, governments, and systems, they have quite as invariably been the salient exposition of the general altered relation of the sexes.   Queen Elizabeth was a noted and childless woman acting in the field usually occupied by man, but she represented no general change on the part of the women of the time from the home life to the ambitions of the contest of outside life. The legal condition of women on the other hand had completely changed in Rome at the time of Nero from what it had been in the days of Scipio. The examination of past human records shows strong and splendid women indeed in the rising periods of races, but their general activities were in the home or family, and not in the field.

Strangely enough it is in the extremes of race life that we see this assimilation of the sex activities.   It is the barbarous Nair, the Veddah, the Negrito, the Andamaner on one side, and the extremes of luxurious civilization on the other, where we find the sex activities most similar.

In some polities the females are given great power.   Dahomey, for instance, makes them soldiers, and we there find the celebrated Amazons.   These Amazons are all vowed to chastity and virginity. Certainly there is little in the condition of Dahomey to encourage us to follow its example.

We may indeed be convinced that women are capable of being good soldiers, but we see nothing in military virgins looking to the highest progress of the state.

Evolution has ever been from the simple to the complex, from the general to the special.   The simplest life is without sex.   Sex, then, is a specialization accompanying all life's higher progress.   It is least specialized in its functions in the lowest life, and most in the highest.

An exception in low forms where there is a high specialization runs through insect life. Insect life seems to be a no-thoroughfare of evolution ; at any rate, it is only in this line that we find specialization with general domination of the female. It is amongst an allied form of life that we find the female of a certain species of spider, when annoyed or satisfied with the attentions of its diminutive male companion, turn and devour him. Many similar relationships of the sexes may be observed amongst insects. It is, however, in this form that we find the Queen Bee specialized for breeding alone, but amongst bees the male is still the inferior form.

It is in those forms of life called parasitic that we find at once a general retrogression, a decay and loss of higher organs to fit a lower method of life, and a general domination of the female.

It is in the scale parasites infesting trees that we find and observe the female doing the most damage. The male is smaller and short-lived. The tapeworm is the female of the tenia, and so on through the whole class.

The specializations of sex in mammals, and especially and increasingly in the highest forms of mammals, provide variations in the female suiting her to care for the helpless period in her young, increasing as progress increases, and variations in the male suiting him to provide for her and his children, helpless for periods in proportion to their progress. It is in mankind of all mammals, and in civilized men of all mankind, that we first find an evolution of the female in the higher types, making her the most beautiful and attractive of the two sexes. It is amongst civilized men also that we find the greatest physical differences between the sexes ; not only the greatest difference of voice-timbre, of skin quality, of figure, but also of bones, nerves, and muscles.

We can doubtless by breeding and training change this, and assimilate the activities or capacities of both sexes.

Where would such a course lead us ? It is clearly reactionary. It is apparently not in the line of the plain requirements of progress.

The conditions necessary to evolution or progress, the lines hitherto followed, and the general aspect of the sexual relations are such that we should lend ourselves slowly and with an ever vigilant eye to the preservation of reproductive power, to the exaggerated and hasty radicalism on sex matters growing out of the drift of a society now meeting wealth, luxury, and scepticism—the destroyers of former societies.

The past gives no promise of a solution of society's salvation through sexual similarity. Quite to the contrary the line has been : family strength, sex diversity; progress ; wealth ; luxury ; scepticism ; family weakness, sex similarity ; death.

Here is a stew for humanity. When it is put on the fire it sends smells of high hope to the nostril, but in the mouth it is rotten and rancid. The last ingredients of this pretty kettle of fish must be changed or we too must meet the fate of societies laid to rest before us.

In considering life from the point of view that the grand aim and object is self-improvement continued in children to perfection, we demand reproduction as the one unchangeable necessity. The necessity is such by reason of individual death, and is the only means to overcome this. Children vary in sex, so that one may have mainly boys who in their turn may have mainly girls. In each case the life goes on. The mother is perpetuated in her boys as well as in her girls, and so also the father; a female trait in the mother will appear in the daughter of her son, and so a male trait may pass to a grandson through the daughter from her father.

Immortality of the body through children is a grand object. Through it we can perpetuate improvements in individual action. If we accept the religion of reproduction we certainly should rise above the prejudice of sex and discuss sex relationships from the grand outlook of immortality and eternity. The little squabbles of sex standing must not dominate and blind us. In the effort to immortality by children one sex passes into and through the other continuously: the man by reproduction having daughters becomes a woman, and so the woman having sons becomes a man. We have no interest in setting one sex over the other for a transitory and immediately personal triumph. We have no interest in establishing any false system fatal to race reproduction. If such change be made in the interest of men, the father may at once suffer personally in his daughters. If it be in the interest of women, the mother suffers personally in her sons. In both, immortality of the vital flame is endangered by error.

For immortality through reproduction we must have reproduction, but this being secure we are willing to discuss secondary questions. We see that amongst low life the female often dominates and still reproduction takes place, reproduction with female similarity of activity or actual superiority. But we can see in such conditions no high types. Nor do such conditions seem to meet the requirements of the highest development. Progress upon the same lines as those already followed by life-evolution means an increased preparatory period, an increased duration of helpless youth, and an increased length of time to pass through former and lower stages of existence in the embryo and young.

Sexual similarity in form or function gives no expectation of meeting such requirements.

The honeymoon is a period in the lives of the married immediately after the ceremony of union in which all the old conventionalities and reserves that had properly kept the lovers apart before marriage are cast to the four winds of heaven. The pair prefer solitude, it may be that of the country or of the crowd, but they abandon and avoid friends and family and forget prejudice, education, and everything in the first transport of the union of their loves. It is this return to nature that makes, as a rule, the honeymoon happy, though bad education, bad surroundings, or absolute ignorance of the true relations of marriage may, as they so often do, make the subsequent married life, when these influences establish their power, a failure. It is both interesting and instructive to watch with tender sympathy young couples in the honeymoon. At this time when nature has broken down the barriers of convention, we see the sexes bearing more nearly their true relations to each other than in ordinary life. It is a joy to the young husband to protect and watch over his wife, it is a joy to the young wife to be protected and to look for support from the husband.

In the honeymoon when the woman is superior to the man, happiness results from the vanity and blindness of the man in not knowing the truth and in the self-deception of the woman whose wise instinct still insists on looking up to the man even when there is nothing to look up to. In the honeymoon the observant looker-on may always note the sweet desire of the woman to find in the husband a power to which she can look for protection.

The loving bride always thinks her husband physically and mentally superior and stronger than herself. She wishes him to be so, and the wish is father to the thought. The continuance and increase of the honeymoon happiness into the future home depend on the man's being the strongest in these qualities of the outside fight. It is indeed rare to see a happy woman who is superior in such qualities to her husband. I have never seen such a case, although I have seen to my joy many happy homes. No one ever saw a happy man who was the inferior in these qualities to his wife. The woman, as has been said, has her superiorities, upon the existence of which the happiness of marriage equally depends.

The sweet determination of the bride to be dependent, to be loving and devoted, and to find in her husband the qualities peculiar to the male is an instructive contrast to the protective tenderness of the new husband, to his exaggerated sense of responsibility, to his watchful care against all danger, and to his impetuous rush into every breach through which harm may come to his wife.

It is thus in the honeymoon that we see an abandon that returns the sexes nearer to their natural relations than we ordinarily observe. The conditions necessary for marital happiness are then accentuated. The woman should have the truth of virtue, devotion to one idol who is to re-create her in the child, industry to maintain the order of home, and the tenderness of love to develop further when she is a mother. The man must have the strength to ward off danger, and to support the woman helpless in childbirth, and nearly so in child-care, and the passions of love to drive him to the re-creation of himself and of his wife in the child. The child is the true union of man and woman, the bond indivisible by law, indivisible while life or a descendant of that life exists. We may summarize by saying that a happy home requires the husband to be a man, and the wife to be a woman, each complete in the characteristics of their respective sexes.

Sex is a differentiation in living things that by a specialization of the reproductive function has made improvements in life possible that without it would have never occurred. The greater the specialization is, speaking generally, the higher is the condition of life.

The main object of woman's existence is child-bearing. It is for this that her organs and organization fit her. To her everything else is secondary and inferior, so much overture, interlude, and finale, but the plot and action of her life is child-bearing. So also is it with man. All is secondary to the child. Without child, a man or woman is nothing. Their existence in outside life has no reason without this crowning glory of the child.

The barren woman is a zero. The mother is a patriot, replenishing her country; a creator, immortalizing herself and her husband. She is grand.

CHAPTER II.

MARRIAGE.

MARRIAGE is a regulation of man, now established in some form everywhere. By marriage the family is founded ; by the family the higher social organizations become possible.

Pairing amongst animals is the outcome of the necessity of reproduction. It suggests the line of evolution our own marriage has followed. The strength of the pairing instinct is in proportion to the necessity for the protection of the young. Where the perpetuation of life is insured by large numbers of young, as in most fishes, pairing is weak or non-existent. The fertilization of the egg in nearly all fishes takes place outside of the body, and there is no sexual congress. In reptiles the egg generally is hatched by the sun, and the young are able to care for themselves when leaving the shell. In the higher forms of life, whose young, passing through former stages of evolution, are in this period more or less helpless, more care is required. This care at first given entirely by the female, is, as life becomes more complex, and as its preparatory period becomes longer, shared in by the male. In the highest types the male protects, and often provides for, both mother and young. These necessities of life continuation in man have become formalized amongst all of humanity by custom and code into marriage. Marriage then is a legal provision for reproduction. It is a codified expression of the highest animal instincts for the continuation and improvement of life.

In this convention man strengthens nature, as we see her manifestations in the sexual relations of other animals. The possession given by monogamy to the husband of the wife, and to the wife of the husband, especially the former, prevents the necessity of contests to maintain the purity of the breed, and the certainty of the paternity of the child, necessary to the highest interests of humanity.

The marriage laws of civilized countries bear the same relation to reproduction that the laws of property do to securing to the laborer the results of his or her efforts. Society protects in each case the individual, and the necessity for fighting is minimized. Thus in marriage a large amount of energy devoted amongst animals and uncivilized man to capturing, or holding, or temporarily monopolizing females, is liberated for other uses.

The main thing in marriage, as in all animal pairing, is the procreation, protection, and support of the young.

All the great founders of institutions have been especially particular about marriage. Moses, Lycurgus, Solon, Numa, Mahomet, and the leaders of Eastern civilization have laid great stress upon this essential regulation of society.

In world time it is a recent arrangement. Those things secondarily dependent on it are of still more modern growth.

These noted formulators of law, it is true, only codified existing customs with probably merely moderate modifications in the line of progress. Institutions have developed as man's command over nature has developed. It is after all the creation and acquisition of property that have done most to change primitive marriage forms, to change descent and inheritance from the female to the male, and to supply the dominating reason for the evolution and maintenance of monogamian marriage. It is convenient to mark epochs in man's history with the names of men most prominent in them, but it is inaccurate to attribute to any of these the social system that they may have formulated or represented. Such systems must have been due to long growth, and must have mainly depended on the economic condition of the people where they prevailed.

Surnames are a new idea, depending for their commencement and existence on marriage and the security of paternity. We see the first tendency toward them in allusions to persons as the son or daughter of certain individuals. We see them in ancient history, in the Bible, etc. In our own time many surnames still remain, which, in the primitive dialects of our ancestors, meant son or grandson of some individual. The prefixes Mac and Fitz mean son of, and the prefix O means grandson. Thus MacGregor means son of Gregor, and O'Hara means grandson of Hara. These were continued as surnames and notice of descent, and indicated in their time of origin a shortly previous period in which the paternity of children had become secure.

We may study in the same way the gradual adoption of the husband's surname by the woman, indicating both the recognition of the fusion of the pair in the children and the recognition of the paternity of the children as secured by the marriage monopoly of the woman by the man. The words new and recent are here used in the belief that the human race has existed as such for periods of tens of thousands of years.

Marriage has been and is the greatest promoter of progress that man has ever devised. The highest form of marriage, monogamy, has been the keystone to rapid progress in the human race. As chastity and fidelity has been the base of women's lives, so has been the advance of mankind, slow or rapid. The reason is plain, for with the fidelity of the wife comes certainty of paternity of her progeny.

Thus the strongest motive for thought and work on the part of the man is furnished. With the certainty to the husband that he is growing up again, in a sense immortal, in his young children, with the knowledge that he himself, without a doubt, has planted the seed of life in the children he calls his, comes the motive for work for more than that part of himself which must soon die and disappear, for more than to-day. With the full belief that his life is going on in his own progeny, he will be rewarded for work for that part of himself, the child, which will live, continuing the father's life, really marching the father to immortality, and for the to-morrow which he, the father, can only enjoy in the renewed life he has in his child.

In the history of the human race, the certainty of fatherhood in society has always been a concomitant of greatness, individual and national. License, corrupt morals, and general unchastity leading to uncertainty of paternity reflect ever on those women who remain true, and lessen the value placed by society on virtue and certainty of paternity. Periods when life was so conducted have been slow in progress. When such periods followed periods of fidelity, they have been retrogressive and the human race has gone backward.

The early history of the great races shows an evolution in their governments from a patriarchal form founded on the government of a father over his own descendants and entire household, in which the certainty of paternity was secure.

This is a point of advantage without which no race has achieved even temporary success. We may therefore say that the security of paternity of children is a fundamental necessity for the highest civilization.

The customs and usages of many countries of our day show survivals of the patriarchal views from the early times. Two things in these survivals are worthy of notice : one, the fiction that was so long held in some places, and even very late in Rome, that all the citizens of the country were descendants from a common ancestor ; and the other, the value attached to female virtue, which often went to great lengths. In many cases the tokens or signs of a wife's virginity were taken the day after marriage and kept by the woman's family or exhibited, as is the case to this day in some Slavonic tribes. Moses speaks of this custom of keeping these tokens in Deuteronomy when laying down rules for establishing the character of a wife unjustly attacked by her husband.

It may be asserted with good foundation that mankind escaped from barbàrous conditions through the institution of the family. The first point gives strength to the inference that civilized government in its political base has arisen through and by the family out of a previous social type resting on the gentes, phratry, and tribe, and based on kin, but not on the family as we have it. The second point shows that the chastity of women giving security of paternity was an essential feature of social evolution.

Another consideration in this connection is that in all the historical civilizations that have fallen, the fall was preceded by a period of immorality, a diminished respect for chastity and children, and a decay of the marriage institutions. Thus before the fall of Rome, marriage and child-bearing had both lost their former high repute. In Greece it was the same. Amongst modern nations I am aware of no case where a fall or setback was not preceded by a period of domestic corruption.

A retrogression in power and condition must always be expected when there is a retrogression toward the primitive type in sexual intercourse. The marriage relation has been attacked in every possible way, but without permanent success. Perhaps no more insidious arraignment of it exists than that of the corrupt and cowardly Bacon. In one of his essays, he says, amongst other things : " Certainly the best works and of greatest merit for the public have proceeded from the unmarried or childless men.''

That some unmarried or childless men have done great works is true. It is also true that eunuchs and women have performed great works. Some such have also been accomplished by those of unsound mind, like Joan of Arc. But the progress of the world and of humanity has been the work of fathers and not of celibates nor of the sterile.

From Rameses, the greatest king of Egypt, who had 169 children, to our own Washington and Jefferson we see that the power and desire for precreation is the usual accompaniment of genius. Washington was unfortunately without legitimate heirs, but he appears to have had a number of illegitimate children.

On the contrary, men of creative ability in ideas have, as a rule, been dangerously overflowing with creative ability as animals. Geniuses have usually been ardent lovers and when they have failed to perpetuate themselves, the fault has lain in their sexual excesses or irregularities more than in their coldness or incapacity. The wife, too, must occasionally take the blame, for we know from the careful figures of Dr. Parvin that approximately one woman in eight is sterile.

Dr. Parvin's figures apply to social conditions different from those prevailing in America. The last Massachusetts census shows the general average for the State in sterility amongst American married women to be one in five. In some districts, and those the most exclusively American in every influence, one married woman in four is childless. This extraordinary sterility is accompanied by a lessening regard for chastity, an increase in prostitution and divorce, and demonstrates a reversion to the Syndyasmian or temporary pairing form of marriage, from which patriarchal and monogamous marriage developed. In this country and now, the wife evidently is an unusually important cause of man's failure to reproduce. Dr. R. T. Morris claims that there is also going on a progressive atrophy of the reproductive organs in the American white female. This he undertakes to demonstrate by examinations by medical men of ten Aryan-American women, and comparing these with ten American negresses. His figures show 80 per cent. of greater or less abnormality in the reproductive organs in the white American women, and indicate a tendency toward sexual atrophy. The negresses were all found normal.

No idea could be more false or inconsistent with general history than that great achievement demands celibacy. Were such a fact, the world's deeds would have been done by priests or fakirs. So also the proudest pinnacle of human glory would have been that barren period of the Dark Ages dominated by anchorites, monks, and crazy, childless nondescripts. So also those times of family decay and decreasing birth-rate seen in Greece, Rome, etc., would have been as great in achievement as they were despicable in deeds and sterile in children.

As the true idea of the greatness and grandeur of creation in marriage is comprehended, more and more will the foremost men and women of the world be found looking to love for fortune, and to the child as their noblest work. Some have opposed marriage on the ground of its unremunerative expense; or, if not opposing matrimony on this ground, have condemned child-bearing. Starting even on as low a basis as this, its opponents' opinions cannot stand examination. Do we not breed other animals with profit? What animal is capable of more production than man? Taking slave times as a criterion, we find that the child is not a bad investment:

5

a good-looking black girl was worth, not long since in America, about $900 at fifteen years of age ; a handsome young mulatto, several thousand ; a young man with a trade, $1200 to $1800 ; and had a profession been possible, doubtless the price, as in horses, would have run far into the thousands. Amongst the ancients, when slaves were usually made from all classes of the conquered populations, very extravagant prices were often paid for individual slaves. We may well imagine that the price of an Æsop, or of a Greek female slave similar to the beautiful woman commemorated in the celebrated statue of Milo, would have been high.

I have from curiosity asked great numbers of parents in the medium walks of life what they would take for a child, and have, with scarcely an exception, found them unwilling to even consider a money price which would deprive them of the company, care, and, if you like, the trouble of their baby.

We can thus perceive that there is a real material value in the child as a profitable crop, if we but knew how to utilize it, and also a value in a spiritual way which a parent able to support life is unwilling to translate into money.

It will not do, however, to gloss over the changed social and economic conditions in which we live as compared with those of our fathers. They took pride in a large family ; we dread or avoid many children. In their time a farm was largely self-sustaining ; the necessaries, even to the carpets, were generally made at home. Education was in actual life and on the farm. Every child was a helper, and by so much increased the power and production and independence of the family. A large family under a judicious head meant success and wealth. To-day we have become specialists. The family, as a unit, is not self-sustaining in the old sense. The standard of material condition is higher and more difficult of attainment. Education absorbs increasingly long periods of the child's life. This results in two things. First, the child's education is altogether a burden—that is, excluding any fee for tuition, the child must be boarded and clothed according to the social standard for many years while producing nothing, while formerly the education of the child was accomplished through its participation in the productive work of the family ; schooling was at a minimum. Secondly, the child, separated so much from family influences, hopes, and interests as our modern system demands, loses the family feeling of the old style. Thus a child in our early history was, as a rule, a source of reliance and support to the family, and remained more or less in connection with it. This condition has been and is being weakened to-day. We must in honesty admit that the general view of a large family to-day is that it is an excessive responsibility, costly and burdensome, a source of care and weakness and not a source of solace and strength.

While I have personally found no one willing to sell a child, I know of a large number of cases of adoption, some of which were of children with living parents. In fact every now and then one sees an advertisement of a child for adoption. There must be those, then, who value their children very little even after begetting them.

It is very probable that the present reaction and reversion of women to the outside industrial type of the savage or barbarian comes from the destruction of home manufacture and industry in the family on one side, and on the other from the increased standard of life, weakening of the family tie, and decreasing appreciation of matrimony and procreation.

What dangers we discover in the weakening reproductive power of Americans, threatening their proximate extermination, has far-reaching industrial, social, and religious causes. No law like the French one offering a bonus for a seventh child can have much effect. We must seek the remedy deeper.

Humanity is actuated by motives which must be good if the race is to progress. The strongest motive for thought, invention, action, and work, and especially for great work, which can either not be enjoyed by the worker in his life or only partially enjoyed, is the security that such effort can be enjoyed by one's other self—that is to say, in one's children. For this motive to operate in full force there must be a certainty as to the paternity of children.

From plain, natural causes there always is a certainty of motherhood. Thus we see the reason for the fact that amongst many savage tribes of to-day and of the past, the name, inheritance, and lineage were often derived from the mother and not from the father. The reason is plain that, the marriage institution being undeveloped or of a combined polygamous and polyandrous nature—that is, a group of men being husbands to a group of women,—certainty of paternity did not exist, and therefore inheritance depended only on the certainty of maternity. That this was an inferior condition of society is shown by the fact that the tribes and nations adopting rules that secured the paternity of the child to a husband have surpassed and left all other tribes behind.

In the gentile organization, which prevailed everywhere amongst man as he emerged from the savage to the barbarous stage, and which has been a stage in the evolution of every civilized people, past or present, the inheritance was, like the marriage, to the group or gentes and not to the child. Originally always to the mother's gentes, it only changed to the father's gentes as conditions of progress and acquisition of property by the man made him dissatisfied in not seeing his labors enure to the benefit of his progeny. Pairing doubtless had taken the place of group marriage to a considerable extent when this change was accomplished. The first formulated step in the evolution of marriage from the group or Punaluan to the monogamian form, was the change of inheritance and kinship from the female to the male.

The recent advance of humanity has been confined to peoples having the institution of marriage as we KNOW it. The progeny and condition of a people may be measured by their attitude toward marriage.

When the certainty of who the father is, is a rule of social organization, the resulting motive for work will by sympathy affect even those who have no children, and *vice versa*. Where society makes no case of female fidelity and male parentage is consequently uncertain, even a reasonable security of paternity on the part of some will have less force through the sympathetic influence of the general view and general absence of the motive.

Men have their individual and their aggregate motives. The effect of the opinion of the masses upon the individual is best illustrated by studying panics and the frequent and almost inexplicable enthusiasm or violence for evil or for good seen in crowds. Man is undoubtedly influenced by the social standard of his time although he himself may have a different standard. If he be thus at variance with his surroundings, he will be less influenced, but still influenced.

Man is and must be, from the limitations set forth in the chapter on sex, the outside contester and property accumulator, the fighter in industry, as in war, of the human race. It is he also who may be pressed on in effort by the knowledge always possessed by the woman as to her progeny, that he lives again in his own children ; that his likeness, his life, his spark of immortality is his child, and that he can thus enjoy through this new life in his child the efforts which would otherwise be of little or no benefit to him.

The certainty that a particular life is from you, and the result of your own godlike powers of creation, is a motive of incalculable power for good. It is the man also who may be deprived of this greatest of all reasons for development of human power through loose social rules, more or less promiscuous intercourse, and the resulting uncertainty of paternity of children, or total sterility.

From these reasons it will be plain that it is of the very greatest importance to the welfare of human beings, and above all to their further development, that man should have this grand incentive to use all his powers and faculties, and to improve them in himself re-newed—that is to say, in his child.

The value of the marriage tie, and of the observance inviolate of the wife's chastity, is thus shown to be on a high plane. It involves the godlike quality of creation possessed by man and woman united, the purity of the breed, and the perpetuation of the joined vital flame in the child, which gives humanity a tangible promise of immortality. Its benefits are a peaceful and natural life to the woman; giving her dignity as wife, grandeur as mother and part-creator of the child, and a maturity and old age happy in the love and devotion born only of the blood tie. To the man it gives comfort, the happiness of home, the indescribable delight of conjugal love, to which that of a mistress is as that of Hyperion to a Satyr; and, above all, it gives him the child in which to live again, and for which every faculty may be drawn on, thus making the father doubly great through his improve-ment in his self-renewal.

In the Middle Ages a life of suffering and misery was considered the shortest road to heaven. Under such a doctrine virginity and celibacy were deemed a sure means of reaching paradise. The sup-pression of our greatest natural instinct, reproduction, and the dis-couragement of marriage, in which relation mankind has the highest capacity of happiness and joy, with the consequent ill-health of body and of mind which such abnormal life always brings in a highly organized society, was the *beau ideal* of an uneasy, unhappy, and miserable existence and was in complete harmony with the general view.

The avoidance and disgrace of marriage in those times had two effects : first, an arrest of progress and a stagnation which gave the name to the time " Dark Ages " ; and, second, a license and prosti-tution which pervaded all classes from the Church and royal families to the peasant. Even nuns, monks, and popes, the very preachers of celibacy, were notoriously licentious. Thus nature could not be conquered.

The first result was the sinking out of sight of the grand act of paternity and its perpetuation of the parents in the child ; the second, the impossibility so many were under of a legitimate and honorable exercise of nature's great command.

The effect upon each succeeding generation must have been cumulatively bad. For those persons of a kind, religious, and stu-dious disposition took to the monasteries where celibacy prevented breeding, while those of enterprising or investigating disposition were so persecuted or destroyed as to discourage procreation in them. Galton calls attention to the effects of this system in eliminating from the world the best and the perpetuation of the least worthy. Spain is a striking instance of what such a policy can do.

Toward the end of these ages syphilis, that awful scourge of man visiting the sins of the fathers upon the children to the third and fourth generation, appeared. The rapidity of its spread all over Europe showed the extent to which general depravity and license had gone.

A curious statistical fact is the excessive proportion of insanity, delirium tremens, and suicides amongst the single as compared to the married. So also, according to Becquerel, at seventy there are 26.9 married to 11.7 unmarried men living. There is everywhere more crime among the single than among the married ; the proportion varies, but it is always considerable.

The study of suicides is exceedingly interesting. It is not only that single individuals suicide more frequently than the married (about three to one), but amongst the married childless men suicide twice as frequently as those with children, and childless women three times as often as those with progeny. With widowers and widows the same conditions to a more marked degree prevail.

It is probable that there is a common cause out of which suicides and prostitution both come. As society grows in complexity and its standards become more difficult of attainment, so must we expect to see with sad eyes the weak and unfit in moral or physical power fall by the way.

Again as societies have gone off on side tracks and been lost in some error or exaggeration ; when they have thus developed on lines which bring them to a point where it is impossible for the mass of their humanity to conform to the system and prosper, as in Greece and Rome, we must have collapse with an increasing misery of the individual till the system is reformed or destroyed.

Considerable numbers of persons and families have been unable to keep up with the progress of their societies. There is reason to think that such stranded beings not only fail to keep up with their fellows, but tend to revert to primitive types of social organization and even to conditions of no organization.

Suicides bear a direct relation to the manner of sexual intercourse in a community. When such intercourse is in marriage mainly, then are suicides fewest ; where the most prostitution and sexual abuse exist, there are suicides the most numerous. What is a nun's life on one side of marriage and a prostitute's life on the other, to that of a wife and mother ? What is the life of a celibate or hermit on one side of marriage and a debauchee's life on the other, to that of the husband and father ? Old age in the father and mother,

in a well-regulated family, is a glorious time of repose. The parents'
youth is multiplied and everlasting. In their children they live again.

To the childless human being, old age is a desolation worse to
many than is death. It has no dignity and no alleviation. A death's-
head is on every pleasure of the vanished youth of such unhappy
ones. Age to them is a curse. Death when it comes is complete.
They leave no life.

A virtuous wife, who is a mother, will command not the love of
her husband in her youth and beauty alone, but his devotion in her
old age. A childless wife is but a mistress ; like a mistress she holds
her husband only by the tie of passion, or that of agreeable companionship, which often exists between persons of the same sex whose
characters are sympathetic. As such a wife grows old and loses her
charms, her hold on her husband rests only on the customs of society, and, if she be fortunate, on the habit of companionship. There
can never be the grand, natural, innate feeling for her in her husband
which the united perpetuation of their being in progeny can give.

Children form a chain that binds the married together as nothing
else can. For this chain to have its full strength it is necessary that
not only should the paternity be certain, but that the accumulative
opinion of society should strengthen the belief. Therefore the
children of a mistress, though there be certainty of paternity, have
not the same binding power as those of a wife. Wedded life alone
can give a woman an assured old age. Material welfare is not here
referred to, but the sympathy that smooths the roughest paths of
fortune is what is meant.

Society must consider virtue in marriage absolutely essential, or
the general opinion sanctioning looseness will weaken even correct
feelings in the individual. Such periods of decay have continuously
recurred since monogamous marriage was instituted, and human
progress has been at such times arrested until a new virtue came in.

To avoid the effect of these periods is one of the main objects of
these chapters. It can only be done by fixing the value of chastity
in woman firmly in the minds and lives of a considerable family
circle of sufficient strength to counteract amongst its members the
general depravity to which society will from time to time become
a prey

The importance of the certainty of paternity and of the family
has caused the ancient legislators and others more modern, even
down to our own New England ancestors, to take strong measures
to preserve chastity. These rules varied from the stoning to death
of the adulterous woman to the placing on the breasts of such, the
Scarlet Letter.

And, on the other hand, the punishment for rape was equally strong, as we note from this summary of Dr. McKee's:

THE PUNISHMENT FOR RAPE.

The unlawful taking of the hymen has in all times been visited by the most severe punishment. The penalty was death among the Jews, if the maid was engaged. If a man lay with a betrothed damsel in the city, they were both stoned; if in the country, the man only. It was reasoned that in the city the maid could cry out and have help; in the country she could not. Among the Athenians, Romans, ancient French, and the English, and in many of the United States, in their early days, the offence was punishable with death. In New York, by the law of 1787, rape of a child under ten years of age was punishable with death. In 1810 it was changed to imprisonment for life. In Illinois and Massachusetts the punishment was death. In Texas it is still a capital crime; and only as long ago as April, 1888, a man was hanged, not lynched, at Gainesville, Tex., for rape. In the Isle of Man, in "ye olden time," there existed a very wise custom. The criminal was brought into a public place, and his victim was given a sword, a whip, and a ring, and his punishment left entirely in her hands. She could kill, whip, or marry him. Among the old Welsh, he who robbed a maiden of her hymen, there being two witnesses to the same, was required to present his sovereign a piece of silver as high as the sovereign's mouth and as large as his little finger.—St. Louis *Courier of Medicine.*

But these rules were too severe, more in fact than human nature could bear, and besides no one had arrived at the true idea of matrimony and the necessity of virtue. Therefore reaction has always followed such strict rules, the true basis of conduct which they were made to support not being completely understood.

The public dancing girls of polygamous countries, the Hetairæ or brilliant prostitutes of the Greeks, and the farce into which marriage was at last turned in Rome, where a marriage is recorded, the bride in which had already had twenty-three husbands and the groom twenty-one wives, the former wives and husbands having been divorced, indicate what forms reactions against unappreciated stringencies take. In modern times we see the same protest against unexplained or unreasonable strictness. No more notable one has existed probably than the gallantries and profligacy of the Restoration in England after the Puritan rule. To-day there is nowhere a stronger reaction against marriage and children than in New England, where the rules for chastity were of the very strongest. Such reversions are the protests of decaying societies against the rules on sexual intercourse which had formed important elements in their growth.

While various safeguards are necessary in the rules governing the conduct of women, to secure certainty of paternity two things must not be forgotten : first, that the grandeur of virtue and child-birth must be understood ; and second, that the progress of the race depends on the development of the woman as well as on the development of the man. Therefore these rules should not take unnecessary forms, totally destroying the self-reliance and character of the woman. Such a course will leave considerable portions of the woman's higher qualities unused, and consequently not only unprogressive but retrogressive. These qualities will become atrophied and the children bred and reared by such mothers will inevitably show the mother's weakness. From this cause the harem system of the Turk, although giving certainty of paternity, is non-progressive beyond a certain point, through the counter effect of undue suppression of all development in the women.

It is probable, too, that the peculiar sympathy and completion of humanity in well executed monogamy is not found in polygamy. In polygamy the children of each mother under her special influence are liable to grow up with a feeling of hostility to the children of the father by other mothers.

This is a fact in polygamous households and the rivalries of the mothers are usually intensified in the children. So the stories of bloodshed and fratricide in the ruling families of polygamous peoples are common. One son rules after exterminating his brothers. Fratricide under monogamy is rare, thus showing that the family tie under this system is stronger, and that the affections which add so much to our life joys have a play nowhere else found.

The commonly received ideas as to the suppression of women in polygamous countries are, however, very much exaggerated. In the higher forms of polygamy, the women inherit property, have the right of divorce upon liberal grounds, rule their houses, and play an often important part in government. The memoirs of the Arabian princess, Salme, afterwards Emily Reüte, gives a good idea of the Oriental life of women. Polygamy shows its own weakness by ever tending to monogamy. Almost always in polygamous households there is a favorite who monopolizes the husband, and frequently obtains the lion's share of the husband's property for his children by her to the exclusion of his children by other wives.

The great majority of men in polygamous communities are, however, monogamous. The difficulty of obtaining women, the cost of maintaining, and, as we learn from well-to-do persons with one wife where they are allowed more, the desire to avoid the troubles and contests of the harem, all tend to this result. A positive agreement, in such places as Utah and Arabia, was frequently exacted from the man before marriage, by the bride, that he would have no

other wives.   Another curious thing in this connection is the fact
that the rate of childbirth is less in the most fertile polygamous countries than in the most fertile monogamous ones.   So also in the early
luxury and sexual license of the Roman Empire, when the emperors
desired to have sons and heritors for their greatness and had sexual
intercourse with large numbers of women who might aid them and
desired to aid them in their wishes, few of them succeeded.   Some
had children before their achievement of power and license, but afterwards had none, or such weaklings as to be incapable of sustaining
their position.   This sterilizing of man by excessive sexual indulgence
is a strong argument for the chastity and fidelity of the man under
the grand motive of worldly immortality only attainable in the child.

Promiscuous intercourse on the part of men or women tends to
sterility, as Bertillon says :

"Il ne pousse pas d'herbe dans les chemins où tout le monde
passe."

Sir Henry Maine calls attention to the unfavorable pathological
condition leading to sterility produced by promiscuous intercourse.
Dr. Carpenter refers to the same thing as observed by American
planters and their remedying it by forming the negroes into families.

Where each man in a community has a wife, it is easy to understand that such a balance of the sexes would be likely to produce
more offspring, than a monopolizing of an undue share of women by
some men to the deprivation of others, but it is not so clear that a
surplus of women obtained by capture, purchase, or even the result
of the excessive death-rate of males by battle exposure, bred to by
the males under the polygamous system, would not produce more
progeny than the same number of men with one wife each.   Strange
as it may seem, I am of the opinion that the one-wife system, under
favorable circumstances, is the most productive.   There are no statistics on this point with which I am acquainted, but we obtain
some idea of the size of polygamous families by ancient records, such
as the Bible, the Egyptian genealogies, etc.

Occasionally we come across a record of over one hundred children, as in King Rameses, who is said to have had 169 children ; as
in Augustus the Strong, of Saxony and Poland, who is reported to
have had a large number of illegitimate children ; as in Gordian, a
Roman patrician of the decaying empire, who had, by his 22 concubines, from 60 to 80 ; as in Sejid Said, Imam of Mesket and Sultan of
Zanzibar, who is said to have had about one hundred children by his
2 wives and 75 concubines and left 36 living children at his death ;
as in the Bishop of the 14th ward in Salt Lake, who had 50 children, of whom 20 died in youth ; and as in Brigham Young and

other Mormons. A group of five of the most prolific Mormon men, for instance, had 150 children by 70 wives. The mortality in these children was about 40 per cent.—a terrible rate. But these instances are rare and they are not quite free from doubt. The records we have, it must be remembered, usually only count the sons. Jacob had twelve sons by his two wives and their two handmaids. He may, however, have had some of these children by the large number of concubines he took when he had become established; we hear nothing of his daughters.

David and Solomon had a great number of concubines, but their children were comparatively few. The other biblical accounts of polygamy show families frequently equalled in size by monogamous marriages, when free play is allowed to the productive power of the wife.

In the accounts of the ruling families of polygamous nations, such as the Turks, Arabs, and many Eastern peoples, we usually find the descendants not especially numerous. When the son of a dead prince massacres his brothers, to quiet the title to the crown, he usually has from one to five or six only to kill off. The sons of Sejid Said had few or no children. His successor, Madjid, at Zanzibar, had but one daughter, although a number of women were in his harem.

Mahomet, with a number of women in his harem (nine wives), seems to have had but one daughter, " Fatima."

The Mormon records frequently show a similar condition. Joseph Smith, for instance, left but three children, although he had twelve recognized wives. His living children were all born before he commenced his excesses.

Dr. Samuel W. Gross in his great work states it to be his opinion that one sixth of the cases of sterility are due to defects in the husband. We here have an indication of the importance of this question.

My experience in Eastern nations is that the children in polygamous households are not on the average as numerous as in our own Western pioneer monogamous families, and that their marriages are oftener sterile. The most plausible explanation of this, if it be true that polygamy is not so productive as monogamy, is that the husband becomes intemperate in his sexual indulgence, and that consequently the spermatozoön has no time to become perfectly formed. Thus the frequent intercourse with unimpregnated women is unproductive.

Herbert Spencer incidentally takes an opposite view, which causes me to be more doubtful on this point than I otherwise would be. In polygamy there is jealousy in the wives, hatreds among the children, and absence of opportunity for the women to develop their best qualities. All these things work against the complete influence for good that man and woman derive from a perception of the grandeur of their creative power, as shown in themselves renewed, immortal in the child.

Where polygamy is as fertile as it may be, it must become difficult, if not impossible, to properly rear the children. The extraordinary child mortality in the family of the wealthy Sejid Said illustrates this point.

Monogamy, a single wife and a single husband, ought to produce from ten to fifteen children, which is a good family, not too difficult to handle. In fact, such a family generally results better as to the success of the children than smaller or larger families, because unnatural coddling is seldom practised in a large monogamous family, and still the support of the children in infancy is not so costly as to invite neglect. Fifteen or twenty children is about all a man can really take good care of—that is, give a fair opportunity to develop the best there is in them.

From these reasons, polygamy, when fertility exists, is defective as well as too expensive for a crowded population, and, on account of the unequal distribution of the women, altogether unsuited for a sparse one.

The subject of matrimony is of such vital consideration in the welfare of human beings, the stages of its evolution are so interesting and instructive, the esteem in which it is held varies so much from time to time and in different places, the virtue, chastity, and child-bearing duty of the wife are so frequently uninforced, to the ruin of society and the arrest of progress, that it will be well to go a little further into the subject.

If we accept the theory of development, there is no escape from the conclusion that, at one time, man or his progenitors lived sexually in the same promiscuous or unregulated way that the gregarious animals now do. It must not be overlooked, however, that even the animals and birds have a sort of marriage, and to some extent protect the paternity of their young. The bull chases away from his cows other bulls ; the wild stallion, other stallions from his mares. Many animals and birds have a period of courting, and when they mate go off by themselves on a sort of wedding tour, by which the paternity of the offspring is secured, at least for the time being. Even aside from the theory of evolution, the few facts we have of man's history show that he has progressed slowly from a primitive condition in which he used rude implements of flint and stone, to our present civilization.

While it is true that we know little or nothing as to the social regulations of prehistoric man, still we have traditions, old customs, mythologies, superstitions, systems of consanguinity and affinity, and fragments here and there, which, taken with the actual lives of primitive races still living in a savage and barbarous way, throw some light on what the social laws of our own prehistoric progenitors are likely to have been.

It is but fair to suppose that the lives of a race using stone implements, and generally in a comparatively undeveloped condition now, are like those of other savage peoples, whether past or present, whose stone implements show them to be or to have been in a similar condition. When we can trace a custom, such as that of throwing objects, especially shoes, at a departing bridal couple, common in Anglo-Saxon countries, back step by step to greater and greater simulated opposition, to the carrying off of the bride, until we find amongst many peoples regularly arranged sham fights at every marriage, it is but reasonable to infer that these customs are what remain to us of a period when marriage took place by the actual capture of women, still practised amongst some savages as a part of their resource for marriageable women.

McLellan, in his studies in ancient history, traces a number of customs back to actual living practices now in vogue amongst savage peoples. It is, however, possible that some of these customs, instead of coming from wife capture, are survivals of gens regulations against marrying in the gens.

We must not infer that because marriage was by capture in some tribes, it was so in all tribes, or even entirely so in any. This is far from the facts. We must use the same caution in considering all marriage customs.

The marriage relation, we know, has practically no more existence to-day amongst a few of the most primitive tribes, than it has among animals. These people are unprogressive and live a miserable life. In the promiscuous or temporarily limited sexual intercourse of the Andaman Islanders no family life is possible. As both religion and government have grown out of the family, we can perceive how impossible improvement is under these conditions. In such societies, chastity in the women can have no reputation.

Amongst the Andamaners, for a woman to refuse a man a sexual favor is said be be a serious insult.

All primitive social conditions put but small value upon female chastity. With some tribes, as the Chibchas, a woman, who turned out to be a maid when married, was treated with contempt by her husband, because she had not been able to excite the passions of other men.   Other tribes allow their girls to earn a position for future marriage by prostitution, a primitive condition still prevailing among us, as we see by the marriages of prostitutes, especially in France and Germany, after they have acquired some property.   The Assanyeh Arab's marriages seem to have limited the woman in her sexual intercourse only during a few days in the week or month ; at other times the husband, we learn, felt rather complimented than otherwise by his wife's sexual intrigues.

In most primitive tribes, a wife or daughter is readily loaned to a stranger, and in some it is considered bad manners not to make the offer.   A survival of this feeling is seen in the story of Cato, who loaned his wife to his friend Hortensius, and occasionally in records of our courts of justice to this day.   The formal and customary compliments to women in Japan show a survival from a time when sexual promiscuity must have been greater than now.   Other, to us abnormal, conditions in the sexual relation existed very generally in ancient times, and do still amongst savages.

The royal families of Egypt, Peru, and other places are frequently recorded as marrying brothers to sisters.   Amongst the rulers of the ancient Peruvians this seems to have been obligatory.   With lower tribes we find the males cohabiting with their mothers, daughters, and sisters, as among the Chippeweyanas.

The royal marriage rules of Egypt and Peru were probably survivals in the royal family of the consanguineous marriage after the general community had arrived at the Punaluan type.

Such promiscuous intercourse, especially in close kin, is unfavorable to reproduction.   There is a natural feeling which we may presume to be a useful evolutionary inheritance, that disinclines us instinctively to sexual intercourse with those we have been brought up with as children in the same home.   Out of this has probably grown some of the exogamous customs of marriage, and the general regulations of mankind against such marriages.

In war, primitive men seem to have considered the female as part of the plunder.   After the defeat or slaughter of the males, the females were taken as wives, concubines, or slaves ; the reservation of the males captured in war for slaves came much later.   Primitive men probably, at times, went to war to capture their wives.

Man's improvement by regulation on the primitive promiscuity, which prevented the foundation of the family, developed on the lines and in the order set forth by Morgan in his *Ancient Society*.

Dr. Lewis H. Morgan has made the first complete and rational explanation with which I am acquainted of the social order, customs, and systems of consanguinity and affinity that are known to have prevailed or do prevail amongst primitive mankind. His work gives us a satisfying unity of comprehension of what were isolated and incomprehensible facts recorded in savage and barbarous societies.

He demonstrates by names for kin that the earliest record of man is the consanguineous system of kinship which he calls Malayan.

This system, with its descriptive nomenclature, could only have originated where marriage, or more properly perhaps sexual intercourse, was limited to brothers and sisters direct and collateral in a group.

For instance, all the children in such groups are brothers and sisters, all the husbands and all the wives are equally fathers and mothers to all the children, and so on throughout the system. The Malayan system of consanguinity indicates clearly that sexual intercourse was theoretically and, as a rule, practically free in the group of brothers and sisters, including what we now call cousins, but which they did not and could not recognize as such.

Dr. Morgan's five types of marriage, as formulated by him in *Ancient Society*, are as follows:

THE ANCIENT FAMILY.

I. *The Consanguine Family.* It was founded upon the intermarriage of brothers and sisters, own and collateral, in a group.

II. *The Punaluan Family.* It was founded upon the intermarriage of several sisters, own and collateral, with each other's husbands, in a group; the joint husbands not being necessarily kinsmen of each other. Also, on the intermarriage of several brothers, own and collateral, with each other's wives, in a group; these wives not being necessarily of kin to each other, although often the case in both instances. In each case the group of men were conjointly married to the group of women.

III. *The Syndyasmian or Pairing Family.* It was founded upon marriage between single pairs, but without an exclusive cohabitation. The marriage continued during the pleasure of the parties.

IV. *The Patriarchal Family.* It was founded upon the marriage of one man with several wives; followed, in general, by the seclusion of the wives.

V. *The Monogamian Family.* It was founded upon marriage between single pairs, with an exclusive cohabitation.

There were developed, however, but three systems of consanguinity:

1. The Malayan, which continued into the Punaluan marriage, being still fairly descriptive of the conditions it created.

2. The Turanian, which grew out of the ordering of society on the gentes, which excluded own brothers and sisters from marriage. Under this system mankind were united in tribes or confederacies of tribes, generally limited to a common dialect and derived from a recognized common ancestry. Each tribe was divided into gentes, and these were often again united, in two gentes or more, into phratries. No one could marry into his or her own gentes, not at least until property induced the desire in the gentes to preserve the wealth of heiresses to the gentes, at which time the gentile organization was drawing to its term. The closest consanguine marriages were thereby barred, because brothers and sisters belonged to the same gentes.

The practically universal prevalence, in all races that are or have progressed beyond a certain very low stage, of this gentile organization demonstrated in *Ancient Society* is a remarkable achievement in human history.

I should advise every one interested in marriage and its evolution to read this valuable work.

3. The third system of consanguinity is the Aryan, which is that which we now have in common with the Semitic race. The Aryan system has its most complete and convenient exposition in the Roman terminations. A table of the Roman system is annexed. Its value is apparent. By it one can take any ascending or descending genealogy to the sixth generation on simple unit terms and to the twelfth generation by a duplication of the terms. The poverty of our own language stands in sorry contrast to this old Roman simple fulness of definition. The table is taken from Morgan.

1.	tritavus.................	great-grandfather's great-grandfather.
2.	atavus....................	" . " grandfather.
3.	abavus......................	great-great-grandfather.
4.	abavia.....................	" " grandmother.
5.	proavus....................	great-grandfather.
6.	proavia.......	" grandmother.
7.	avus..................	grandfather.
8.	avia............	grandmother.
9.	pater.....................	father.
10.	mater.....................	mother.
11.	filius.....................	son.
12.	filia......................	daughter.
13.	nepos.................	grandson.
14.	neptis..	granddaughter.
15.	pronepos..................	great-grandson.
16.	proneptis.................	" granddaughter.
17.	abnepos...................	" great-grandson.

18.	abneptis....................	great-great-granddaughter.
19.	atnepos.....................	" grandson's grandson.
20.	atneptis....................	" " granddaughter.
21.	trinepos....................	" " great-grandson.
22.	trineptis...................	" " " granddaughter.
23.	fratres.....	brothers.
24.	sorores.....................	sisters.
25.	frater......................	brother.
26.	fratris filius................	son of brother.
27.	" filii uxor............	wife of son of brother.
28.	" filia.................	daughter of brother.
29.	" filiæ vir........	husband of daughter of brother.
30.	" nepos..............	grandson of brother.
31.	" neptis..............	granddaughter of brother.
32.	" pronepos............	great-grandson " "
33.	" proneptis...........	" granddaughter of brother.
34.	soror.....................	sister.
35.	sororis filius..............	son of sister.
36.	" filii uxor............	wife of son of sister.
37.	" filia............	daughter of sister.
38.	" filiæ vir............	husband of daughter of sister.
39.	" nepos	sister's grandson.
40.	" neptis.............	" granddaughter.
41.	" pronepos...........	" great-grandson.
42.	" proneptis..........	" " granddaughter.
43.	patruus....................	paternal uncle.
44.	patrui uxor................	wife of paternal uncle.
45.	" filius................	son of paternal uncle.
46.	" filii uxor............	wife of son of paternal uncle.
47.	" filia	daughter of paternal uncle.
48.	" filiæ vir............	husband of daughter of paternal uncle.
49.	" nepos..............	grandson of paternal uncle.
50.	" neptis..	granddaughter of paternal uncle.
51.	" pronepos..	great-grandson " " "
52.	" proneptis...........	" granddaughter of paternal uncle.
53.	amita...............	paternal aunt.
54.	amitæ vir....	husband of paternal aunt.
55.	" filius....	son of paternal aunt.
56.	" filii uxor.	wife of son of paternal aunt.
57.	" filia....	daughter of paternal aunt.
58.	" filiæ vir..	husband of daughter of paternal aunt.
59.	" nepos...........	grandson of paternal aunt.
60.	" neptis..	granddaughter of paternal aunt.
61.	" pronepos..	great-grandson " " "
62.	" proneptis...........	" granddaughter of paternal aunt.
63.	avunculus..................	maternal uncle.
64.	avunculi uxor..............	wife of maternal uncle.
65.	" filius..............	son " " "
66.	" ·filii uxor.	wife of son of maternal uncle.

6

67.	avunculi filia................	daughter of maternal uncle.
68.	" filiæ vir...........	husband of daughter of maternal uncle.
69.	" nepos.............	grandson of maternal uncle.
70.	" neptis.............	granddaughter of maternal uncle.
71.	" pronepos..........	great-grandson " " "
72.	" proneptis...	" granddaughter of maternal uncle.
73.	matertera..................	maternal aunt.
74.	materteræ vir......	husband of maternal aunt.
75.	" filius.............	son " " "
76.	" filii uxor.........	wife of son of " "
77.	" filia.............	daughter " " "
78.	" filiæ vir..........	husband of daughter of maternal aunt.
79.	" nepos........	grandson of " "
80.	" neptis............	granddaughter of " "
81.	" pronepos.........	great-grandson of " "
82.	" proneptis........	" granddaughter of " "
83.	patruus magnus............	great-paternal uncle.
84.	patrui magni filius..........	son of great-paternal uncle.
85.	" " nepos..	grandson of great-paternal uncle.
86.	" " pronepos.....	great-grandson of great-paternal uncle.
87.	amita magna...............	great-paternal aunt.
88.	amitæ magnæ filia.........	daughter of great-paternal aunt.
89.	" " neptis.......	granddaughter of great-paternal aunt.
90.	" " proneptis....	great-granddaughter of great-paternal aunt.
91.	avunculus magnus..........	great-maternal uncle.
92.	avunculi magni filius.......	son of great-maternal uncle.
93.	" " nepos......	grandson of great-maternal uncle.
94.	" " pronepos...	great-grandson of great-maternal uncle.
95.	matertera magna.	great-maternal aunt.
96.	materteræ magnæ filia... ..	daughter of great-maternal aunt.
97.	" " neptis....	granddaughter of great-maternal aunt.
98.	" " proneptis.	great-granddaughter of great-maternal aunt.
99.	patruus major..............	paternal great-great-uncle.
100.	patrui majoris filius........	son of paternal great-great-uncle.
101.	" " nepos.......	grandson of paternal great-great-uncle.
102.	" " pronepos.....	gt.-grandson of paternal great-great-uncle.
103.	amita major...............	paternal great-great-aunt.
104.	amitæ majoris filia.....	daughter of paternal great-great-aunt.
105.	" " neptis..... ...	granddaughter of paternal great-great-aunt.
106.	" " proneptis....	gt.-granddaughter of paternal gt.-gt.-aunt.
107.	avunculus major...........	maternal great-great-uncle.
108.	avunculi majoris filius......	son of maternal great-great-uncle.
109.	" " nepos.....	grandson of maternal great-great-uncle.
110.	" " pronepos..	gt.-grandson of maternal great-great-uncle.
111.	matertera major.	maternal great-great-aunt.
112.	materteræ majoris filia......	daughter of maternal great-great-aunt.
113.	" " neptis.. .	granddaughter of maternal great-great-aunt.
114.	" " proneptis.	gt.-granddaughter of maternal gt.-gt.-aunt.
115.	patruus maximus...........	paternal great-great-great-uncle.

116.	patrui maximi filius........	son of paternal great-great-great-uncle.
117.	" " nepos.......	grandson of paternal gt.-gt.-gt.-uncle.
118.	" " pronepos....	gt.-grandson of paternal gt.-gt.-gt.-uncle.
119.	amita maxima	paternal great-great-great-aunt.
120.	amitæ maximæ filia	daughter of paternal great-great-great-aunt.
121.	" " neptis......	granddaughter of paternal gt.-gt.-gt.-aunt.
122.	" " proneptis...	gt.-granddau'ter of " " " " "
123.	avunculus maximus........	maternal great-great-great-uncle.
124.	avunculi maximi filius......	son of maternal great-great-great-uncle.
125.	" " nepos.....	g'dson of " " " " "
126.	" " pronepos..	gt.-grandson of maternal gt.-gt.-gt.-uncle.
127.	matertera maxima..........	maternal great-great-great-aunt.
128.	materteræ maximæ filia	daughter of maternal great-great-great-aunt
129.	" " neptis......	granddaughter of maternal gt.-gt.-gt.-aunt.
130.	" " proneptis ...	gt.-g'ddaughter of " " " " "
131.	vir, maritus.................	husband.
132.	socer......................	father-in-law.
133.	socrus....................	mother-in-law.
134.	socer magnus..............	great-father-in-law.
135.	socrus magna..............	" mother-in-law.
136.	uxor, marita...............	wife.
137.	socer......................	father-in-law.
138.	socrus....................	mother-in-law.
139.	socer magnus..............	great-father-in-law.
140.	socrus magna..............	" mother-in-law.
141.	vitricus...................	step-father.
142.	noverca...................	" -mother.
143.	privignus.................	" -son.
144.	privigna..................	" -daughter.
145.	gener.....................	son-in-law.
146.	nurus.....................	daughter-in-law.
147.	lever.....................	brother-in-law.
148.	maritus sororis.............	" " "
149.	uxoris frater...............	brother of wife.
150.	" soror...............	sister " "
151.	glos......................	sister-in-law.
152.	fratria...................	" " "
153.	vidua....................	widow.
154.	viduus...................	widower.
155.	agnati...................	agnates.
156.	cognati	cognates.
157.	affines...................	marriage relations.

Polyandry seems to have been, as it still is, the prevailing type of regulated sexual association amongst a few primitive peoples of peaceful policy. It is confined to sterile and poor tracts of country. It is of two kinds. The first, that in which a woman has a number of different husbands not necessarily related to each other ; this can be termed the Nair type of polyandry, as it has been well observed in the Nair tribe.   In this type a man may probably be one in several combinations of husbands, and therefore may have more than one wife, as well as the wife have more than one husband.   This type is but a small improvement on no regulation.   In fact it is below that of many animals and birds.   The second form of polyandry is that in which the husbands must be related, as in the hill tribes of Ceylon.   The highest grade of this form is where the husbands must be brothers.   This is the practice in parts of Thibet, and gives at least the security of paternity to one of several of the closest blood tie.   Its superiority over other polyandrous types would lead us to expect that at least some communities living under that rule would show a more advanced social organization than could be found in any unregulated community, or in one regulated upon other polyandrous forms.   This is the case.

But security of paternity is neither regarded nor sought for in any of these types.   The virginity of the woman can be of no moment, and her chastity after marriage cannot be of much import-ance, even according to their own liberal rules.   Under such a condition, a woman's self-respect cannot be very great.   Dignity in reproduction and high breeding are at a low point, and relationship must be through the mother mainly.   Family relationship cannot be as strong as under either polygamy or monogamy.

Polyandry is practised by a number of rude people still, and by at least one fairly organized community, that of Thibet.

In polyandrous communities there are more males than females, a startling variation from our excess of women in civilized communities. The first suggestion to account for this condition was female infanti-cide.   Examination showed this position to be untenable.   We now learn that the births in these communities show a great excess of males.   Dunlop found in one Himalaya district 400 boys to 120 girls. Amongst the Todas of the Neilgherry Hills there were found 455 males to 249 females.   Marshall's general examination of the Todas shows the percentage of the sexes to be 100 males to 75 females.   No female infanticide could be learned of.   Amongst civilized people there is a slight excess of male births.   Between the ages of fifteen and twenty the sexes are in about equal numbers. After that, the females predominate.   In polygamous countries, however, there is generally a large excess of female births.   This is the case in most of Asia Minor, Morocco, amongst the Mormons, etc.   In some of these places there are as many as three to one in favor of the females.

Nourishment and condition seem to have something to do with this proportion. The more hardship and distress, the greater the excess of males.

> Country districts show a male excess.
> City districts show a female excess.
> Rich people show a female excess.
> Poor people show a male excess.

Ploss' Saxon figures show a greater excess of male births in the highlands than in the lowlands. The conditions amongst polyandrous peoples are unfavorable, and the pressure of population is continuously against an inadequate subsistence. This may be an explanation of the great excess of males in the births amongst them.

Evolution of Sex is a very valuable book by Geddes and Thompson. The results of investigation and experiment to the present time are by them shown to indicate a connection between food and conditions and the determination of sex in reproduction. As food is plenty and conditions favorable, so is the proportion of females greatest. The contrary produces most males. Parthenogenetic life is especially affected by nutrition and condition. Under the most favorable circumstances asexual reproduction is greatly prolonged or continuous. It is only with unfavorable change that the male appears and sexual reproduction takes place. The normal sex proportion amongst tadpoles is 57 females in the hundred ; by care and feeding, this has been changed to 92 females in the hundred. Gentry and Treat have shown the same thing to be true of bees, caterpillars, and aphidæ, Von Siebold as to wasps, and Rolph as to the *Artemia salina*. Giron's experiments with sheep indicate similar results amongst mammals. He took 150 ewes on good feed and bred them to two young rams. The progeny showed 60 females to the hundred. One hundred and fifty other ewes he put on poor food and bred to two old rams. The progeny in this case showed 40 females in the hundred. It seems a happy provision that, under favoring conditions, the female— conservative, non-progressive, or anabolic—type of life should prevail, while, with unfavorable ones, the male—variable, originating, or katabolic—type should predominate in the interest of change and progress.

Crossing has a tendency to produce females. Amongst mulattoes there is an excess of 12 to 15 per cent. of females. The cross-breeds on the Pacific coast, Mexico, and Nicaragua show the same. Horses and cattle of different colors generally bear females. Jewish marriages with other races, from the following small example, may be taken to show the same.

Of 118 such marriages, 28 were sterile. To the others were born 145 female and 122 male children. The ratio would be 118.82 females to 100 males.

On the other hand, regular Jewish marriages between Jews show a ratio of 114.50 males to 100 females (Jacobs). Marriages of kinsfolk tend to produce males. In-breeding of animals does the same. The Talmud mentions the fact of crosses running to females. Illegitimate unions tend to female children also (Westermarck's *History of Human Marriage*).

McLellan is the main authority for polyandry. In view of the ignorance of McLellan (*Primitive Marriage*) as to the gentes rules of marriage which his descriptions suggest, it may well be doubted whether this polyandry of his is not after all Punaluan marriage, or at most a peculiar and very local aberration from it. There is no known system of consanguinity to indicate a past or present polyandry, as differentiated from a combined polyandry and polygamy of the group-marriage systems.

These systems of consanguinity are now the evidence to be most relied on as to marriage types. They are set forth in full in Dr. Morgan's works, but are conveniently abridged in his *Ancient Society*.

Polygamy is a frequent form of marriage amongst savages and barbarians. It is more suited to the military type of society than polyandry, and perhaps even more than monogamy. It may have grown out of military contests. Captured women would be looked on as property, as we know that they are amongst savage men. Their use being largely for sexual gratification, their captors would naturally guard their chastity. Out of this feeling could grow the desire to protect the chastity of the women born in the tribe, as well as that of those brought into it, and also from this idea of property probably came that of the purchase and sale of women. However, I wish it understood that I believe the feeling or instinct for sexual limitation, which we have formalized into varying marriage rules, comes to us from pre-human ancestors.

Polygamy strengthens the family by making the paternity of the children secure, and consequently lends itself to a better and more powerful organization of society than any group system. Under it, the strongest and most capable men will do the breeding. It is a form which has had its value and has enabled mankind to progress and to perform great things. Its weakness is that a number of wives are not likely to be, and in practice are not, satisfied with the divided attentions of one man. To secure their chastity, therefore, the women must be mewed up and guarded. So in those polygamous countries, where the type is at its highest, we find the women imprisoned in harems and guarded by that invention of polygamy, the eunuch. Thus the women, having little opportunity to use their faculties, do not improve, and what the child gains from the activities of its father it loses from the inactivity of its mother. The qualities and capacities of the father may be developed and improved by use in polygamy, and the men with strong character will monopolize the women to the exclusion of the weaker individuals. But the women having no chance of improvement, what is gained on one side is lost on the other, and the family cohesion necessary for at least a certain period of human progress is not possible, owing to the divided maternal ancestry and the consequent rivalries.

In the patriarchal governments in which marriage was often polygamous (probably originally pastoral ones), the progress was accompanied by a subordination of both wives and children. This in the end defeated itself, for too great subordination in both cases necessarily prevented the use of the faculties or the development of individuality and character. Society has long vibrated between the extremes of no family control and too much family control. We cannot seem to stop at the *juste milieu* or else that point varies.

Monogamy is also found amongst savages of a very primitive type like the wood-Veddahs, whose mode of life in tropical forests forces the man to live alone, or with his wife only, for a considerable portion of the year. This Veddah marriage is probably Syndyasmian, a pairing to last at pleasure. It must also be noted that, as a practice, polygamy is never universal in a tribe. Either poverty and inability to support more than one wife, or the scarcity and consequent value of women, or both, necessarily limit polygamy to a few. The general observation is that from Utah to Central Africa the majority of married persons in polygamous countries lead a monogamous life.

While it is true that primitive man is found with monogamy, it seems in these cases more a matter of the conditions of life than a recognition of the family or of the importance of procreation. As a lion or tiger will pair off with one female of its species, so do these men with a female of the tribe. This condition is not conducive to high progress. The division of labor and the help of one another, necessary to the highest civilization, are only possible with a certain gregariousness.

In the gregarious life amongst the animals, we see only promiscuity or a sort of polygamy in which sexual intercourse is limited by a fighting male. The monogamy we now have in the world, it would seem, must have sprung from an evolution out of Syndyasmian marriage or from polygamy. In polygamy we have the first sense of ownership of the woman, and therefore the first legal desire to monopolize her body. From this comes the security of paternity. These feelings permeating the tribe and the improved social possibilities advancing their position and developing their capacities, we have a higher standard of living, to the perfection of which fewer can arrive. Consequently few men have more than one wife, and the formation of an opinion favored by the condition of the majority against polygamy is probable. Early Jewish marriages were often polygamous. We may reasonably presume that the evolution from polygamy to monogamy in the Jews has had many counterparts, especially in those societies coming out of a patriarchal system.

Spencer's *Principles of Sociology*, Morgan's *Ancient Society*, and McLellan's *Traces of Early History* are good books in which to study the origin of the family. McLellan, however, falls into many errors. The general view which these works give of the growth of the morals of man in the sexual relation is striking.

From promiscuity to our present condition of monogamy, with only the weaker members falling away into prostitution, is a great and wonderful advance. When, however, conditions become unfavorable, we have periods of decay, and a reversion to these primitive practices of license. Each fall, however, seems less low than the last, and each rise, greater.

The progress in the opinion of men in the license of war is marked. At first the women were captured and held permanently for wives, concubines, or slaves. Gradually we see this practice relaxing, but the armed conquerors, while relinquishing the permanent enjoyment of the charms of defenceless women, still exacting a temporary penalty. So all the wars of the Huns, Goths, Vandals, Saracens, etc., were marked by the rape of matrons and the violation of virgins in the enemies' country whenever opportunity occurred, though they did not carry the women off as had been the case before. The story of the capture of the Sabine women by the Romans and their retention for wives is an instance of the earlier practices in this regard.

The Saracens when conquering Asia Minor were offered by their officers, from the cities to be conquered, the most beautiful women for their use. The Arab soldiers in the trenches and on their deserts, with primitive ideas of sexual intercourse, were exalted by their dreams and ideals which the results of rape could never realize. To-day, in our wars, rape of a general character, such for instance as is said to have been committed on the Romans by the soldiers of Charles V., not so very long ago, is neither practised by the conquerors nor dreaded by the vanquished. This is, indeed, an advance.

While monogamy has advantages which carry man beyond any other system, the liberty of women it allows, and must allow for its best results, or rather best results for the future race, causes many to fall into prostitution. This again weeds out the inferior natures, for prostitutes, speaking generally, breed but little.

In monogamy, for the security of paternity given by the limitation of sexual intercourse, the man gives protection to the woman and child in sickness and in health, and in age as in youth. For woman, the marriage contract is a boon immediate and personal. For the man, it is a boon immediate and personal. Which sex gains the more, it is hard to say ; but which loses the more, where the society or the individual do not live sexually in marriage, is clear. It is the woman.

The strength and position of any nation now may be gauged by an accurate statement of its marriage system in practice thirty to fifty years before the period at which the estimate is to be made. The future condition may be foreseen by its actual practice in this regard.

As soon as a people demanded chastity of the mothers and certainty of the paternity of the children to one man, they passed other nations not taking this course, as though these had been stationary. In this connection, it may be well to call attention to the indication that from the earliest geological epoch, as well as from the earliest traces of man, we have every reason to think that progress has been always increasing its speed. From the almost inconceivable slowness of the first period of organized life, it has come to a pace that in our own time is quite appreciable even in 1,000 years.

The evolution of man has certain well known lines from which the only escape is the final death of extinction. Man is born, develops, reaches maturity, decays, and dies. The atoms and particles of which he is composed go through the same history. They are born, develop, mature, decay, die, and are eliminated from our systems to be replaced by other atoms. The body while apparently the same, or undergoing change but slowly, is in reality entirely changed in its composition within very short periods ; and a young man may within a year not contain a single atom of flesh matter that was a part of himself the year before.

What is true of the individual, is true of society. Its atoms are men. Society changes slowly, almost imperceptibly, like the man ; but men, the atoms, are continually developing, maturing, dying, and being replaced by others, while the society of which they are the living parts maintains its general characteristics.

The short life of man, the unit of society, makes it absolutely essential that he should reproduce himself, or else society must die and mankind become extinct. The atoms in man have different functions : some carry on the work of digestion, as in the stomach or liver ; others, locomotion, as in the legs ; others, elimination, as in the skin and kidneys ; and others, the intelligence that governs the whole, as in the brain. Each set must exist and be replaced by its kind. An ancient Roman saw and used this analogy to society. Human society, however, is not as yet thus fixed in its reproduction. The idea has nevertheless been formulated in governments, most notably among the Hindoos, and is a general tendency of social organizations.

Thus far, however, the brain atoms of human society have been unable to maintain their reproductive power. These brain atoms of society have been continually replaced by other new atoms from lower strata, simply through the loss or neglect of the reproductive power in the higher men. The brain of Egyptian, Assyrian, Greek, and Roman society has died and become extinct. So progress has been retarded.

Thus it is seen that the line of advance of man exacts reproduction. The penalty of non-fulfilment of this law to the individual or to the race is death, permanent death and extinction.

The history of evolution, as written in the rocks, is strewn with wrecks. Mollusks, fishes, and saurians show, each in their special periods, wonderful developments in size and power. Amongst the mammals the mammoth, mastodon, and American elephant showed a greater size and physical power than anything we now have ; so also we see that gigantic horses, deer, beavers, tapirs, and oxen with horns nine feet from tip to tip once roamed on the earth. The fire of true progress, however, was carried by what must have been deemed an inferior animal, the ancestor of man, and the greatest developments in other lines are now dead and extinct.

So also with man, from him of Neanderthal or Mentone down, race after race, civilization after civilization, some remarkedly developed or organized in one line and some in another have arisen, been found wanting, and, like the great saurians and mammals, are now dead and out of sight.

These considerations should cause us to continually study and reflect to see how we may escape a fate so general and move on in the tide of progress.

Marriage has now two extremes, both of which are bad and one is fatal. One is the harem of polygamy. Under this system, sexual pleasure has complete dominion and the reproductive powers are secondary. The girls are sometimes circumcised by the cutting of the clitoris at the age of seven ; after this they become eligible as wives. Usually by ten or twelve they are such, and very rarely over sixteen when married. The consequence of this is that the organs of generation are frequently injured by premature use, and the sterility so common amongst the women of polygamous communities is doubtless largely due to this cause. It is also probably often due to premature and excessive sexual indulgence, and to the almost exclusive cultivation of sexual passion in the thoughts and acts of the harem.

The children born of children cannot be fully developed. The girls themselves, being immured and guarded beyond the possibility of fully using any of their instincts of self-protection, necessarily lack character and self-reliance. The children must inherit these unused functions and be weak in them. From most points of view, the harem system is defective. This system, however, provides for the sterility of a wife, by its permission to marry many without casting off the sterile one.

On the other extreme is what we may call the present native New England condition of marriage. Here we have an intense pressure on the nervous system of young girls, to develop the memory and intellect without a corresponding regard for the body. As a consequence, the women are often physically imperfect and delicate, with a diminished natural taste for the duties and delights of a wife, and a lessened capacity for the grand creative functions of the mother. Besides this absolute lessening of the instincts leading to reproduction and absolute lessening of the physical power to be a mother, the whole tendency of the New England method of bringing up young women is to cultivate ambitions inconsistent with maternity. The sexual instincts are effaced and the godlike power of creation in motherhood is always neglected or belittled and often actually condemned.

This educational system, like its extreme opposite, induces innate sterility, and equally like the Mohammedan leads to practices causing artificial sterility. Under both these systems women become barren from physical causes.

The polygamous system is bad, the New England system is fatal. The first encourages beyond nature the instincts leading to fertility and consequently weakens reproduction. The second discourages both the instinct and its result.

The low birth-rate in New England, the weakness of reproduction amongst the native Americans, and the replacement of the original American stock by immigrants have been attributed to climatic reasons. The Province of Quebec, with a climate more severe than that of New England, was settled by the French at about the same time that New England commenced its life. This French stock, reproductively weak at home, has become strong here and is even flowing over into New England. Seven elevenths of the births in New England are now of Catholic parents. Consequently, with two such diverse results in similar climates, we must eliminate climate as the cause. The difference in reproductive power between the English and French at home was institutions, manners, and customs. The same causes have turned the tables here. The French Canadians are sound on reproduction; the native New Englanders are not. Therefore, the French are replacing them. Unless reform comes, no New Englanders of the original stock will be left in New England within a few generations.

Man must reproduce or become extinct. Monogamy is the best form of securing healthy, well-cared-for, and well-developed progeny. Any system of society or marriage which does not insist on the necessity of reproduction is an aberration furnishing a passport to death and extermination. The instinct of reproduction in civilized man is more and more controlled by the reason and therefore by government. As men develop and as they reach a certain point in wealth and intelligence they continually stumble into this aberration of sterility. As a consequence, the upper classes continually disappear, extinguished by their own acts and sink into the black death of deaths from which no renewed self, no child, no flesh of their own flesh carries on their likeness and their life to the future perfect race.

The sexual reproductive instincts of the lower animals are intensified and spiritualized in all harmoniously developed men. This instinct, in its best form, we call love.

As man has the highest spiritualized instinct of reproduction in love, and has even a still higher capacity of appreciation of the reproductive act by the power of the reason to comprehend its godlike possibilities and its material promise of immortality, so also he has the faculty of a complete abuse and prostitution in lust of this wonderful power, unknown to any lower animal.

Thus man's reproductive acts are lifted by nature, through love, far above those of the animals, and may be still further elevated by the reason, through the recognition of the immortalizing feature of these acts. But man has also the capacity of debasing the instincts leading to reproduction far below those of the animals, and of leading these instincts into fruitless paths of passion.

Love is unknown where marriage is unknown. It is weak where marriage is weak. In times when marriage lacks consideration love is despised. Therefore love may be deemed the outcome of marriage. In primitive life conjugal love arises, when it arises at all, after the birth of children.

The main point of excellence and superiority of marriage is that it furnishes to the man through the certainty of paternity, and by means of his child, his renewed and immortalized self, a motive for thought, invention, and work applying to things he can only enjoy through his child, his new self, which nothing else has given or can give.

From these considerations it is clear that marriage without children is like the rose without its flower, like the fruit tree without its fruit, like the wheat field without its grain. Without progeny it is an idle and unreasonable rule.

The folk-lore of Germany describes marriage without children as the world without the sun. Amongst a number of tribes marriage did not take place until the birth of a child,—a practice we may find traces of in numerous betrothal customs, some historical and others existing. By these customs a betrothal, as far as sexual intercourse was concerned, was equivalent to our marriage.

Sexual intercourse, unhallowed by the creation of the child, is lust. The marriage tie under such circumstances partakes of the character of the laws prevailing in some countries for the licensing of courtesans, except that it licenses and limits both sexes for prostitution.

To the woman without children there might be some compensation for the limitation required by marriage in the security of care in ugliness and old age, but for the male there is nothing in being tied to one prostitute or companion for lust after she has lost her physical attractions.

Our civilization has come to the point come to by others dead and gone in the ages of the past, where the higher types avoid having children or refuse to be bothered with them at all. Prevention of conception or abortion is notoriously the rule in intelligent communities, and marriage may be for companionship, for money, for lust, for anything, but it is not for the child. Still real marriage is for the child, and its whole reason for being rests on procreation. If this be a correct conception of the condition to which conjugal life has come in our community, we can understand one reason why men are more and more marrying late or refusing to marry at all.

Without the desire for children they prefer prostitutes to wives, for the former are changeable at pleasure, and are consequently more studious to please than the wife, and need not be lived with when *passée.* There are good reasons to think that the men have had something to do with this idea of not having children. However it commenced, it is the women who suffer most from it. The men lose a great deal—the cream of life, in fact,—but the women lose everything.

A wife without children is a mere sewer to pass off the unfruitful and degraded passions and lust of one man. It is perfectly certain that a wife without children can never have the regard, respect, and love of the husband that the wife-mother has who in children blends her husband and herself in a new being, who will lift the spark of both lives from their dying embers, and carry it flaming to a possible material immortality.

The experience of those who have sinned can alone give voice to its pain and inferiority over righteousness. Ripe, complete love only comes with the ripe and complete fruit of love—that is, the child.

The kiss and the embrace of the wife-mother and of the husband-father has possibilities of holy and intense pleasure which that of mere lustful companionship never gives, and never can give. The entire relation of husband and wife, man and woman, after fruit in children, may be and ought to be intensified and sanctified in its joy and happiness. Their unity receives its seal in the glory of creation. For parents there is no old age, no death. Their lives and youth are renewed, and blossom in themselves new-born, the offspring of their loins. The parents live again, are young again, and·may be immortal in the child.

Marriage without children is an empty, unreasonable piece of nonsense, a mere aberration, a preliminary of extermination. The child is the bond of marriage. In it the husband and wife are united. The death of the bond is the only divorce.

Love has so ill-defined a meaning with most persons and is applied to so many of our feelings that it is necessary to set down clearly what is meant when the word love is used. The poverty of our language obliges us to use this word for describing sentiments of exceedingly different kind.

Dr. Louis de Séré says : " Of all human passions love is the one that moves and unites souls most powerfully, the one that awakens the noblest and most generous feelings, and above all exercises the strongest sway over the senses to the extent of leading impassioned natures to the greatest excesses." Its manifestations are clearly recognizable in insects, fishes, and in animals. Ornament, color, song, self-sacrifice, and courtship are all found in the life below us. Montegazza in his *Physiology of Love* says that the whole of nature is a hymn of love. The chirping of insects, the croaking of frogs, the songs of birds, the cries of animals, the love dance of the firefly, the colors and odors of flowers, are all intimately connected with reproduction. Humanity has no monopoly in this matter. Our sex love is only different in degree.

As it is here spoken of, love means that budding out and spiritualization of the reproductive instincts coming to humanity after the age of puberty. It may exist without any knowledge of the reproductive functions, and without any recognition of what this springs from or what it ought to produce—that is, children.

While a special Indian Commissioner in the Southwest, I was much struck by the total absence of caresses between the sexes amongst the Indians. An Australian traveller mentions the same fact and says specifically that he never saw a savage man place his arm around the waist of a woman. Monteiro in his *Tribes of Africa* speaks of the absence of love and caresses ; Lichtenstein, Du Chaillu, and others have observed this peculiarity. Spencer's researches confirm this absence of love amongst savages.

The fact that these observations apply largely, if not entirely, to communities where marriage is of the Punaluan or group order gives a reasonable explanation of why love—the spiritualization of reproduction—should be in abeyance or absent.

Love in its complete sense is of modern origin. Its first manifestations were doubtless individualized and recognized sexual desire. This we now see refined into romantic love before marriage in which sexual gratification may play no recognized part. This is the ideal desire for reproduction, and is not real love. The highest form of love is conjugal. This is the real thing, a thing and not an ideal.

Romantic love is full of illusions and extremes, ecstasies of joy or sorrow, hope or despair, running into a sickness like madness. It is necessarily temporary and, if its end be not achieved, recurrent. Conjugal love is smooth and deep, strong and constant ; it cannot exist without respect. The first is the flashing lighthouse that shows us a port ; and the second, the harbor itself in which we command more than the riches of the world by our commerce of love.

In modern love the gratification of the imagination surpasses the gratification of the body, and the sensual is surpassed by the spiritual. Love probably has some development even amongst the primitive societies where these are upon the individual basis, and for that matter amongst birds and animals also.

Numerous observations of male regard for the female in various tribes are of record, and the higher position of woman and her relief from the severity of outside labor would indicate that such must be the case. The stories and songs of the Arabs show also that at least at their stage of development love is known.

Jealousy is an instinct common to many animals and birds, as well as man. It is useful in preserving the purity of the breed and the productiveness of the female injured or destroyed by promiscuity. It is a feeling out of which some of our ideas as to limitation of sexual intercourse and marriage may have arisen. But that it is an outgrowth of the highest form of love is not to be lightly admitted. It would carry us down to the dogs in our ideals.

Jealousy amongst men is generally found strongest in societies where the moral tone as to women is low, as in Southern Italy, Spain, etc.

The jealousy of women in polygamous households is a fair indication as to the extent of the development of their tender feelings. Without some sort of love there cannot be jealousy. So amongst the primitive militant types from which our development comes the absence of the caress is accompanied by the absence of jealousy, and, by inference, of love also. At the same time, we must recognize the evident fact that the modern strength and power of love is still unknown and unfelt by a large part of the population in even our most civilized countries. Its highest manifestation, as a rule, is an accompaniment of brain development.

Love commonly appears in girls and boys considerably before they are sufficiently mature to either bear good children or support the physical effort necessary for this great result. This premature effect may be avoided or postponed by healthy outdoor occupation and exercise. These first flowers of love, like the first flowers of the rose, are never perfect, and this splendid instinct should not be trusted until it is in its prime, say at 25 years in the man, and at 18 in the woman. At these ages the instinct seldom errs.

Love is never complete and perfect, no matter how much the passions common to the lower animals may mislead one, until the fruit—that is, the child—comes. It is then, if ever, that men and women really love each other in a true and complete way. All the other dreams, etherealizations, self-effacement, or gusts of passion are but the preliminaries, the preparation, cultivation, and seeding of the ground.

Love, like the fruit of the grain, is only in existence when the harvest is ready to gather. In some sensitive human beings love's preliminaries are often abnormally developed, and cause sickness, melancholy, and even death. Such sensitive ones must be carefully tended, not noticing much their ailments, or speaking of its cause, but giving them, by action, occupation, or change of scene, a means of diverting the energy from a great but perverted instinct, and allowing the animal balance to become established. Love is much more apt to develop fully and, unfortunately, to become perverted or uncontrollable in the virtuous than in the licentious. As soon, therefore, as the bodily powers are fully developed, marriage should be encouraged, if for no other reason to give love a healthy and moral means of expansion and growth. If this is not done trouble is almost sure to ensue, either to the constitution and body, or to the morals and the mind.

Love is, after all, in the mature, the best guide to marriage. But this is not true in childhood or in old age. Love is the guide the highest development of nature gives us.

Natural marriages, that is, those where the inclinations at the age of full maturity have alone had play, are almost always between persons of different mental and nerve tendencies. It is a commonly received opinion that such marriages are the happiest.

In civilized countries, and in fact in all countries, things other than the natural inclinations play a prominent part in selections of life partners. The chapters on the selection of a husband or a wife discuss this subject. A very important thing to consider in advising early marriage is its bearing on the health of body, mind, and morals.

The vital statistics of every country that has taken the marriage relation into consideration show an increased prospect of life for the married—that is, the death-rate is higher amongst the single than amongst the married. When we consider the amount of disease and misery that each extra death represents, we can perceive the importance of this matter. For each person that dies there are a considerable number of sick. As there are more deaths proportionately amongst the single than amongst the married, there must be vastly more sickness amongst the single also.

Of moral disease we have no account, and probably need none, to know which of the two conditions is healthier. A well considered marriage demands and leads to morality. The immorality of the race is largely monopolized by the single. It must be remembered here that a man or woman without children is really single, though nominally married. Married men, whose wives from one cause or another do not sufficiently fill the position of spouse, are large supporters of vice.

The health of the mind is equally with that of the body and the morals affected by marriage. Insanity is more prevalent amongst the single than amongst the married, and crime and suicide also.

In Switzerland two fifths of the divorces are of sterile couples, while sterile marriages are but one fifth of all marriages. We can thus note the marked effect of sterility in weakening the marriage tie.

The figures compiled by the London *Journal of Institute Actuaries* in 1881 gives the death-rate per thousand amongst married and single women, from the age of 15 upwards, as follows:

Married. . . 89,703.
Single . . . 90,174.

More recent statistics in England are as follows: Of each 1,000 men who marry, 861 are bachelors and 139 widowers, while of each 1,000 women only 98 have been married before, and 902 are spinsters. Twelve marriages out of every 100 are second marriages. The average age at which men marry is about 27, while the average at which women marry is about 25 years. Out of every 1,000 persons, 602 are unmarried, 345 are married, and 53 widowed. Over one half of all the women between 15 and 45 are unmarried. Married women live two years longer than single ones. If the mother dies first the father survives $9\frac{1}{2}$ years, but if the father dies first the survival of the mother is $11\frac{1}{2}$ years as an average. Two thousand four hundred and forty-one births occur in England daily. February is the month in which the greatest number of births occur; June, the month in which occur the fewest. The average number of births for each marriage is 4.33. In every 1,000 births 11 are twins.

Statistics from the census of 1890 show that in a class of Jews sufficiently superior to fill out and return the official blanks sent them, the death-rate of married women is higher up to the age of 35 than that of the single women, but the married women having passed that age the death-rate changes in a marked manner, and the rate is higher amongst the single than amongst the married. The death-rate is always higher amongst these Jewish men when single than when married. The figures for this class of Jews show further that marriages take place later in life than amongst the general population. The excess of married women's mortality over the single is between the ages of 25 and 35, and not before or after. It is consequently a fair presumption that the unfavorable figures for married women covering but one decade are at least partly due to late marriages and the well-known increased risk of first births after the age of 23 or 24.

The life-insurance companies are operated on a business and not upon a sentimental basis. The extra fee of five dollars for every thousand insured which the largest of these companies now impose on single and childless women over married mothers is an indication in the same line.

If it be true that there are 23,000 divorces in the United States to 21,000 in all the other portions of the world, we must admit an unhealthy condition of the marriage relation in our country. If figures for America, therefore, are in any way less strikingly favorable to the married for health and longevity than in other countries, we may presume that the bad and abnormal condition of marriage with us has diminished its good effects. We may claim with some reason that children, being the foundation-stone of marriage, and the only object for its legal limitations in sexual matters, can not be avoided or aborted without so injuring the foundation as to reflect itself on both the health and happiness of the married. Thus we see vitality decrease showing less health, and divorce increase showing less happiness. With all its present shortcomings, however, the married state still shows us the healthiest and happiest of our population. In fact, after the age of thirty-five there is little, if any, health or happiness outside of the marriage relation.

Maudsley, quoting from a number of investigations on insanity, shows that the percentage of insanity is higher amongst single women than amongst the married. If the childless wives, or those with but one or two children, were taken from the married, the figures would doubtless be more striking.

The preventive measures against conception adopted by many married persons are deemed by the best doctors to be injurious to both parties. Incomplete intercourse seems to be the cause of much ill-health in married men who adopt this method of limiting progeny, especially of nervous disarrangements, such as nervous dyspepsia and various forms of paralysis. Amongst wives similar results are produced, and the abortions and miscarriages which they bring on when they find themselves pregnant increase very materially the death-rate. It is said that 9,000 women die annually in America from abortions.

A physician in good practice in a summer resort informs me that in his practice the treatment of women for the sequelæ of miscarriage bears the ratio to conceptions going to term of six to seven. Six abortions to seven births is certainly a bad condition, especially when we contemplate the large number of miscarriages that are likely never to come to a physician's official notice. The summer resort may have offered a temptation to license inviting abortion for escape from social penalties, or have been specially sought for recovery after abortion elsewhere.

Were these abuses of matrimony excluded from the figures, the balance of life in favor of a properly carried out marriage would probably be startling. One thing may be said here in answer to the idea of limiting at once poverty and population by limiting children, and that is that the voluntary limitation of children has always hitherto, in all civilizations and societies, been by the intelligent and well-to-do, with a result of the extermination of the best class and the death of the society. It has not been by the poor and needy.

The condition of marriage in the United States is not good. Many marriages are broken up on frivolous pretexts, and many others are maintained in name but not in reality. The divorces in this country have about doubled in proportion to the population in the last thirty years. In the past twenty years we have granted 328,716 divorces. In this State (California) there is now one divorce to 7.41 marriage licenses. In the city of San Francisco there is one divorce in 5.78 marriages (Dike).

This condition of affairs shows a low and poor idea of the grandeur of marriage, and a large incapacity to realize its pre-eminent happiness. It seems, therefore, appropriate here to give the causes that make a divorce necessary.

1st. Sterility.—Without children no marriage should be maintained.

2d. Insanity.—This demands seclusion, prevents the payment of the conjugal duty, and renders improbable the creation of proper children.

3d. Conviction for Felony.—For same causes.

4th. Habitual Drunkenness.—For same causes.

5th. Adultery of Wife.—By this the security of paternity of the children—the main object of marriage—is destroyed.

The demand for divorces on other grounds arises from the gross and culpable ignorance of the people who thus destroy their own happiness. Of the two most urgent causes of divorce, adultery of the wife and sterility, one, sterility, is never pleaded, and in fact is, in general, not a legal cause of divorce. Here is indeed a condition. Incompatibility of temper a good cause, and sterility, which prevents the realization of the object of matrimony, no cause. Could anything be more inconsequent?

Insanity, as a rule, has to be proven before marriage to make it a legal cause of divorce. And we see further that the adultery of the wife is less and less in proportion to the other causes pleaded for divorces as time carries us on.

Adultery on the part of the husband is a just cause of complaint for the wife. Like polygamy it does not, however, destroy the security of paternity of the children, which is the basis of all marriage. It is in this respect essentially different from the adultery of the wife. We can therefore understand why adultery of the husband has not been a cause of divorce in numerous vigorous societies in which the family was the recognized unit of power, such as that of early Rome. Adultery of the husband in the early history of Rome appears to have been a marked exception. In every strong social organization the family is strong. As it is strong, the ideal and aim of domestic life must be high and pure ; as it is high and pure, so must the life and aims of the husband be high and pure. Adultery or sexual intercourse merely for animal gratification is not consonant with this, and cannot exist with it. The reason that we to-day have so much to complain of in this matter is the weakening of the family, and the gradual substitution of the individual for the family as the unit of society. Nothing is more fatal to the ideal of marriage, than the prevalent prevention of conception and destruction of fœtal life amongst the married. Children once removed as the aim and object of marriage, this convention loses its backbone. Dignity, force, and reason are lost to it, and marriage changes from the staff and support of society to a reed that under any pressure bends into fantastic shapes. When the high aim and the true object of marriage is lost, when the married do not wish children or do not appreciate the children they have, and lose or never have a realization of their renewed life and material immortality in their children, the tie is weak, and marriage responsibilities and limitations become burdensome.

In this condition divorce will be increasingly sought. Without any grand unity of aim, without any ideal, without any true object, we must expect to find small things dominate. Thus incompatibility of temper becomes a legal reason for divorce, and the law, in one frivolous pretext or another, officially recognizes a precedent weakening of family life. The remedy is not in restricting divorce, but in changing and improving the appreciation of marriage—a difficult thing indeed. How far society should go in permitting divorce for petty causes, is an open question. I am inclined to the opinion that when the married have a low view of the institution and wish to cut the knot, they might as well be allowed to do so and thus legalize what is already an accomplished fact. On the other hand, society has heretofore depended on the integrity and strength of the family for its integrity and strength, and it is a question how far it can afford to legalize destructive and deadly conditions, even if they are accomplished facts.

Sexual indulgence may exist between persons of the same sex—between men and men, and between women and women, but marriage has never been permitted between persons of the same sex. Marriage is not for sexual gratification except as an incident.

The century plant blooms but once. Its seeds are perfected in its death. Many insects die in the moment of reproduction. Humanity has nothing so serious to face. On the contrary, children make the one interest in old age, and are always a source of pleasure to persons of normal feeling. Children make life worth living and make it longer. Instead of dying in our moment of reproduction, we step into new interests, new joys, and new hopes. We live anew and multiply our highest hopes, interests, and joys.

As a recapitulation, we say :

1st. That child-bearing is an absolute necessity for the continued existence of a man, a family, or a race.

2d. That marriage—monogamous, one wife, one husband—has been found in the experience of mankind the best to secure and support children.

3d. That the object and only object of marriage is children.

4th. That this relation gives security of paternity and insures the aid, support, and defence of the woman helpless in childbirth, and of the child helpless in infancy, by the man thus knowing himself the father.

5th. That monogamy secures the strongest foundation for the family. The family being the foundation of the state, this form of marriage is an essential to the best interests of society.

6th. That marriage without children is nothing. Marriage being complete only with children, without children necessarily there can be no true marriage.

The conclusion is beyond escape, that it is a religious duty for all good members of society to marry so as to perpetuate the life of themselves and of their family.

True marriage makes complete love possible. The loved one is like the warmth-giving sun—all other lights are by it extinguished. The single person or childless one lives in the night. The heavens for such may indeed be full of stars, but there is for them no life-giving, all-absorbing, creative sun. As a poet has it—

> " The night has a thousand eyes,
>   The day but one ;
>   Yet the light of the whole world dies
>   With the setting sun.

> " The mind has a thousand eyes,
>   The heart but one ;
>   Yet the light of the whole life dies
>   When love is done."

The wedding-ring is a fitting emblem for marriage. The circle is the Egyptian hieroglyph for eternity. The plain wedding-ring is the circle that completes, in so many countries, the marriage contract. It is marriage, the true marriage with children in whom the life of the united ones continues, that presents to us the best hope for eternity.

Marry, then, my children. Make it a religion to have progeny. Be thus natural, be thus happy, be thus great, be thus immortal.

Man in his Love doth blossom and bloom ;
    What beauties he has can then be seen.
The height of the heart appears in the groom ;
    The opening soul of the bride is queen.

The loves of the flowers and the loves of man
    Conquer cold Death in their seeds of life ;
Love is the hand, with immortal span,
    Alone can help us through Death's strife.

No flower with fertile seed can die,
    No man with living child is dead ;
A body cold and dead may lie,
    The old must wither and fade and shed.

Dark and dread is the night of Death,
    The dead lie lost in its dreadful gloom,
A pestilence floats in its midnight breath,
    And Terror's throne is the endless tomb.

Whatever of spirit drifts away,
    Whatever of hope the truth may hide,
The body must go to ash or decay ;
    We know Death's shadow is at our side.

But out of the old a new life grows,
    Love lifts life to bloom anew ;
We cannot die if our child's life shows,
    Immortal life in the child holds true.

What of the flower that blooms so free ?
    In its day of love it spreads its charm,
Odor and color combine on the lea
    To marry the flowers beyond Death's harm.

Out of their charms, out of their love,
    Comes the seed that makes them live,
And so renewed from the life above
    The flower immortal life doth give.

Out of our loves, out of our loins,
  Springs a life never to die ;
We pay for the new in God's own coins
  Our children carry our lives on high.

Silent and cold the conqueror comes,
      Dark
       Terrible
       Death.

Glory I breathe in my child anew,
      Conquering
       Immortal
       Life.

CHAPTER III.

HUSBAND CHOICE.

AMONGST certain birds and animals the female seems to have some choice as to its mate and in many cases to play an important part in this respect. We see at the mating time the cock, of the pheasant, of the peacock, of the turkey, like the males of many other birds, display their feathers and finery to the quieter females presumably to attract their favorable attention.

We may account for the gay appearance of the male and the more sober garb of the female in tame birds, on the ground that the choice in mating seems to rest with the female.

Æsthetic taste is widespread amongst birds and animals ; coloring, crests, ornamentation, delicate odors, and harmonious sounds have proved so attractive at the mating time that in spite of the dangers which must attend the display of these advantages, in drawing the attention of predatory animals, they have been perpetuated and developed by sexual selection.

Reptiles, fishes, and insects also frequently have sexual ornamentation of one sort or another, and their ornamentation must be attended by the same dangers as in animals. In plants beautiful colors and sweet odors are also for reproduction, but in them there seems no special danger in brilliancy or fragrance. This choice, however, may be often annulled by a fighting mate. Thus has female selection favored the evolution of ornament in the male.

Darwin takes this view, but Wallace, the independent discoverer of evolution in the animal world, does not admit that such is the case. His views may be summarized by saying that vigor and beauty go together, and that it is at once the vigor which makes the successful breeder and the beautiful male. The quiet colors of the female bird may be attributed to the necessity of protection by obscurity while they are hatching out their eggs.

In the early conditions of the races from which our present civilization has come, woman has had but very little choice in the selection of her husband—much less than these birds. Perhaps the most remote times of our ancestors, of which, however, we know almost nothing, may have been an exception to this statement. Certain conditions amongst primitive tribes would lend at least some color to this possibility. However, during the times upon which we have information, the woman has played only a passive part in mating.

Amongst certain tribes in Corea and amongst the Puttooalies, it is said that the women are the uglier of the two sexes. It is even ungallantly denied in our own country that the female is the better-looking of the two, although it is a proverbial privilege of the male to be ugly. However this may be, the artificial ornamentation of women would indicate that if they are not now better-looking than men this is the tendency. Consequently they may anticipate a greater influence in marriage selection than they now enjoy ; that is, if we take the ground that the female birds already referred to really flock around the males to be chosen by them.

If this be the correct explanation, then we may anticipate an increased power of choice in the beautiful female, for around her will flock the men competing to be chosen.

Amongst savages, barbarians, and during the greater portion of civilized man's existence, except under polyandry and in a few degraded tribes, a woman has been husbanded by capture, by compact of parents, by purchase, or by the purchase of the husband by dot or bounty as in modern France and other European countries, and not generally by any choice of her own.

At certain epochs and among certain classes, women have had more or less choice in this matter. Amongst the poor, natural selection has had more opportunity to operate than among the rich, which may be one reason for the general incapacity of the rich to breed up. On the other hand, the universal care of the ruling classes, in healthy, civilized epochs, as to the disposition and marriage of their women, and the equal care of their mothers by surviving families in retrogressive times, may be taken as a sign of strength and advance on the part of the superior class.

Amongst many tribes of the industrial type, such as the Pueblos of Arizona, the women have considerable to say in the choice of their husbands. The traditions at least of a few militant societies show a freedom of women in this choice also. It is doubtless a survival from a previous industrial organization, or the story of the sexual relations under that type. *The Arabian Nights* give a number of instances where the women selected their own lovers or husbands. Amongst the Pueblos the daughter is said to mention her fancy for some man to her parents, who then inform the parents of the favored youth, and these arrange the match.

During certain feasts in ancient times, as well as amongst still existing tribes, the women had and still have a freedom of choice, at least of lovers. The curious laxity in this matter during particular celebrations in antiquity is well known to students. It may not be so well known that several tribes of our own Indians had the same custom, and in certain celebrations the girls of the tribes danced and chose young braves with whom they retired, but apparently with no eventual marriage.

In America the woman now has more chance to choose and more voice in making the marriage contract than anywhere else in the civilized world. It may be observed that our civilization is also more nearly industrial than any other. The initiation of courtship is the man's, here as elsewhere, but a capable woman may, without any breach of modesty or manners, do much to attract to her the proper class of men for matrimony.

A woman perceiving a good man may properly do things in a modest manner to attract him. In this matter, however, a young woman must use great judgment. At times an initiative or at least a plain encouragement will be well repaid, while at other times such a course might cool if it did not disgust a suitor.

As a rule, a woman need not fear to make her preference plain, not, however, omitting a judicious spice of coquetry. Widows, no longer fresh and virgin, and from many points of view less desirable than maids, still have a considerable success with men and secure husbands oftener than their real merits warrant. We may attribute this success to the plain preferences they show and to the open encouragements they give.

It is well here to suggest to parents that it is not good policy to show anxiety or even intention to secure a husband for a daughter. It is, however, their highest duty to give their daughter the best possible opportunity to become well mated in matrimony. Parents should on no account neglect this matter of the first importance, and should see to it that both sons and daughters are made acquainted with eligible persons for life partners.

Woman has an intuitive perception as to the character of men, gained probably from manners, intonations, expressions, and minor acts. It is a basis of diagnosis which she is unable to formulate, but her results and judgments are often accurate. She is in the position of the Philadelphia rhymer of the last generation, who wrote of the notorious Dr. Fell.

> " I do not like you, Dr. Fell,
> The reason why I cannot tell,
> But this I know, and know full well,
> I do not like you, Dr. Fell."

This faculty of judgment is of great value to the woman. The man has less of this intuitive perception of character, but his deficiencies are to some extent made up by the experience he gains in the world. A young woman should therefore never forget that while she is judging the man, he is also judging her. The man's method of life is reflected in his manners. His character, in spite of the most studious suppression, will show in his indefinable expressions. So will a woman's.

It is perhaps well for a woman to know that immorality to the extent that it is indulged in, even of thought, will show in perceptible though unformulatable ways. The power of judging character can be developed by practice, and many persons even make a trade of it in various quack and charlatan ways.

A woman should by no means neglect close observation and judgment of persons. She should also remember that the keen man of the world mentally catalogues women with considerable accuracy, sometimes on sight, or at any rate after a short acquaintance.

There are amongst women :

Those who are regularly irregular.

Those who are irregularly irregular.

Those who have sinned once or a few times but have reformed.

Those who would sin if opportunity offered.

Those who do not wish to sin, but who would be too weak to resist under circumstances favorable to the seducer.

Those who could only be seduced under exceptional conditions.

Those who cannot be seduced, but may be violated.

Those who can only be violated when unconscious or when bound.

These classes of character merge into each other. The man does not perhaps consciously place each woman he meets in a class, but if he is interested in her he adapts his manners and acts to the class to which he has unconsciously assigned her.

Immoral and dissipated men are rarely mistaken in their opinions of women. They know the women who can be improperly approached with certainty, those approachable with probability of success, and those who cannot be approached at all. There are some women like common prostitutes, who are so stamped by their sin that they cannot escape from it, and are at once recognized by the most casual glance. There are, on the other hand, women whom one would as soon suspect of being professional poisoners and assassins as being guilty of immorality. Their purity and honor are reflected from their souls into their faces, and they can do things with impunity that would throw suspicion on even good women but of less vigorous virtue.

The importance of this is to show the woman that, in attracting a man for a husband, her best chances are in her best behavior, and that error or immorality, though the act be never discovered, will inevitably show in those undefined signs the experienced so promptly recognize. A desire or disposition to looseness is perfectly perceptible in a person.

The extremes of virtue and vice show so clearly to even the inexperienced, that a moment's thought will show the girl that it is also possible for the attentive observer to recognize the intermediate stages as well, and to order her conduct accordingly. So guarding her own conduct, she may observe with advantage the character of the men who approach her.

While flirtation cannot be recommended to a young maid ready for marriage, and less probably in the future than now, there is a cunning coyness that leads men on. Its success may be due to the general but unsound estimate that the value of a thing is in proportion to the difficulty of its attainment. As humanity is now constituted, we must not set up too rational a standard, or neglect such successful means to an end as the usages of man make most available. Every man of merit has at least a secret pleasure in being considered a hero or a genius. By finding his line of thought and his aims, and by judicious drawing out and commendation, a man's interest is invariably awakened, and he is attracted by the feeling that he is appreciated. Thus may a maid attach to herself the strongest of men. Othello won Desdemona by his heroism and strength, and Desdemona won Othello by her open admiration and attention.

The same course followed after marriage will do much to make the man forget defeat and failure, and persist to success. A wife can do much to prevent the wheat of worth from being choked out by weeds of worthlessness springing strongest from neglect in the richest soil.

There seem to be in this country two tendencies in marriage: one toward the dot system in Europe; and one toward a still greater influence of women, even perhaps permitting to them an initiative in marriage.

It must be remembered that a woman's freedom of choice has come to amount to but little in most cases at this time. If she desires to marry she will be risking much not to take the first good man who presents himself, otherwise she may be left entirely unhusbanded. A woman, of course, of superior attractions, whether of face, fortune, or fascinating manner, can afford to take considerable chances, but it is not safe for even these to let a really eligible man go. As society is now constituted, a young woman after eighteen years of age should not be foolish in holding off from a fair offer in marriage.

The measure to set for the man is what father will he make for the future children of the union. In this is everything. No good father can be a bad husband, and no bad father can be a good husband.. A man to be a good father must have sufficient vitality and physique to give promise of life to his children, sufficient force of character to endow them with this quality of success, and sufficient capacity to support the family and to transmit such capacity to the progeny. A man with these qualities in apparent plenty, but who is positively distasteful to the woman, should not be chosen. There will doubtless be some obscure physical or mental apposition unfavorable to progeny indicated in such case by natural instinct.

Instinct generally guides us more in matters of the physique or of the emotions than in intellectual or character traits. It is a frank friend who should not be forsworn, at least until the reason has gained a far greater control of life than now.

At the same time the young woman should not be governed by romantic folly, and expect from the instinct of reproduction what it cannot give. The idea that a man must be loved before he is married, is good in a sense, but its goodness depends on the definition of love.

Love is a passion that can only be fully possessed after the fruits of union. In its extreme but true sense it has no existence, except as a flower of the reproductive instinct. As flowers differ so does love. It may be like the heavy-odored bloom of the magnolia and the daphne, or like the delicate perfume of the mignonette and violet, or the fragrance of the jessamine, or like the cold splendor of the soulless chrysanthemum, or it may be like an evil-smelling flower.

In fact the passion of love may be scented from the rose to the stinkweed, but few maids, however much they think so, have ever had its flower to their noses. Affection may be accompanied by love, or may not. Love, however, cannot exist without affection. In this it differs from lust. Love is the accompaniment of the highest civilization. Amongst primitive people it is practically unknown. Elsewhere there is some further discussion of this passion.

Love is indeed a high development, but its use is not in its abuse. Many young women, brought up in ignorance of life and with extravagant notions of the feelings that they ought to experience toward a man whom they are to marry, lose chances of good husbands for whom they have every essential feeling required in the contract. More men marry for love than women. The nature of our social arrangements would make this a fact to be as expected as it is necessary.

The unnecessariness of the present supposedly necessary romantic standard set up by some is demonstrated by the very considerable number of matches made on that line that fail in forming a happy home; whereas the French *mariage de convenance* averages decently in results, and is often better than our so-called love matches. These two extremes are bad. The maid should feel an affection and affinity for the man she is to marry; but she should not expect herself, or be expected, to feel the passion of love in its full power before she has had experience of what it means.

It is perfectly true that the instinct of reproduction which draws the sexes together during their period of possible fertility, and sometimes abnormally before or after this time, frequently takes a form in which the sexual function has no recognized part. It is most common to see this preliminary passion either in those ignorant of its practical manifestation or, strangely enough, in those passed the capacity of securing the object for which we inherit it—that is, the child. The love follies of the inexperienced youth are only equalled in the impotence or sterility of age.

This unknowing manifestation of the absorbing desire in the healthy for reproduction, a desire normally recognized by the individual in being driven toward one of the opposite sex capable of carrying out the grand creative act, has in such case its object entirely unformulated in the reason. It is in such ignorance that this overmastering instinct in a sound life may mislead us instead of aid us.

While the pleasures of pre-matrimonial affections and attractions, commonly called love, should not be denied a place in the preliminaries of an engagement for a life union, it is unwise and unjust not to notify the inexperienced maid of the true limits of such feeling, and of the control she must maintain over such manifestations for her own safety. A maid, therefore, should resist the supremacy of the passion. Caresses between the sexes lead to the more full awakening of the physical passion of reproduction, personal liberties often follow, and these may result in the overthrow of the honor of the maid as fixed not only by the standard of society but by nature itself.

No man can feel the same regard or respect for a woman, in advanced societies, who allows unlawful liberties, much less for one

who cedes her virginity except under the solemn compact of marriage to secure herself and her children a support and protection.
Even if a man continue and marry after he has been permitted undue
liberties, he will not have the same confidence in his mate that he
would have had if she had resisted his improper importunities.

In engagements and before marriage, all manifestations of love
should be formal and limited, and a woman should never subject
herself to the dangers and temptations of personal liberties, least of
all from one in whom her interest has been matrimonially awakened.

It is a lover loved who is most dangerous in improper caresses to
a maid. If a man, it may be said, lack respect in action toward the
woman he intends to make his wife, his idea of marriage must be
inferior.

A young woman should certainly recognize that pre-matrimonial
love must be under control and never be allowed full rein. She cannot, for instance, allow herself to fall in love with a man who makes
no advances toward her, nor with a man ineligible from physical,
mental, or race inferiority.

To show how much education and surroundings have to do with
one's power over the sentiment of love, so foolishly supposed by some
to be beyond control, we have only to look at our Southern States
and at Brazil. In the first, education has fixed a proper prejudice
against the marriage of a white with a negro ; in Brazil no such
strong prejudice exists. In the States we see consequently no mixed
marriages, while in Brazil they are more the rule than the exception.
The white races in these two countries are indeed different, but that
it is the educational control which rules their matrimonial choice
must be evident from the fact that the Anglo-Saxon man has often
satisfied his passions upon the negress, and has, when in foreign
lands and liberated from his environment and educational prejudices,
married and had children by the woman of nearly every known
inferior race. The Anglo-Saxon, has, however, been more conservative in this respect than the Latin, and his colonies, being generally
better bred in not being mixed with inferior native races, are more
vigorous and progressive than those of his rivals.

So also the every-day evidence of the effect of education in keeping the classes of society apart in matters of love is an indication of
the control our reproductive feelings may and ought to be subjected
to. Of course, sometimes we are faultily educated in this respect,
and may have a class prejudice that experience has shown to be useless in securing an improvement in mankind. Such a prejudice is
that of the females of the noble families in Europe against marrying
one not of their class. The males of the aristocracy have recognized

that their lines of breeding have not made them mentally, morally, or physically superior to many outside their pale, and consequently, whenever circumstances seem favorable, they marry those not of the aristocracy.

This is also true of nearly all ranks of society. The men do not regard so strictly the often incorrect prejudice that those in other classes are their inferiors, while the women do observe these prejudices. The men, for adventitious reasons, such as those where fortune can be had, will, in many cases, it is true, prostitute their reproductive powers, and marry women who must produce inferior progeny. This, I believe, is largely because they are ignorant of the true grandeur of reproduction and of children, and of the importance of securing a good partner to carry out this main object of life.

So ignorance among young women, allowing their grand and laudable instinct for love and its fruits an unwarrantable license, leads them to the pinnacles of folly. Thus a young woman may consider that there is but one man in the world for her whom she can truly love. Here is truth and error. It is indeed a fact, that a woman can give her virgin body to but one man ; it is indeed probable that the father of her first child so seals and impresses her that his likeness may again appear even in subsequent children by another ; but it is error that before union and conception any one man is essential to a woman's happiness. This pre-matrimonial love breaks out in the life of nearly every man and woman of our present standing, and receives its direction according to the education, surroundings, and location of his or her life.

A New York girl will therefore, by the law of average, marry a New Yorker of her own class. The same girl brought up in San Francisco will be equally likely to marry a Californian, or if her associations of society be with a different class from that to which she was born, she will be likely to marry a man of that class.

At the age of puberty, Cupid drives the new-born powers to use in love. It is often prejudice and association that influence love toward, and introduce it to, those eligible for partners in perpetuating life.

The importance, therefore, may be seen of having the education sound and the association of the best, both for man and maid. As the great rewards of life are largely found in cities, so the strongest men tend toward the cities to obtain them. A young woman should therefore spend a certain time in a city or in a place where city people will be met, when of marriageable age.

Another pinnacle of folly is when the girl, mistaking animal feelings or awakened though unformulated desire for sexual union as

8

true and laudable, or at least as irresistible love, cedes to seduction and is ruined, or, upon an inferior basis of looks alone, gives herself in marriage to an inferior man.

Men have more experience of the world than women, but the very means of this experience introduces them to women of lower classes, and they often wed them, not always with bad effects. Women with less opportunity have less knowledge, and the mesalliances, judging by divorce statistics, are more often on the side of the woman. Carroll D. Wright's figures are for the United States, between the years of 1867 and 1886, as follows :

Divorces granted at request of husband   112,639
     "   "   "   " wife   .   216,077

The growth of love with the improvement of man offers us a prospect that in the future, with further improvement, marriage will depend more and more on love—that is, upon the affinity, affection, and respect mutual between the man and woman. When to this are added the true idea of reproduction and the glorious hopes born of our renewed life in the child, we may expect a wonderful improvement in marriage and a love and joy in this relation as yet but dimly perceived amongst the happiest.

A woman should expect to marry between eighteen and twenty-five. After the latter age her chances rapidly diminish, and, if married, her trouble with the first child will be much greater than before. Her husband should be from five to fifteen years her senior. While these ages and ratios are the best, a woman should stretch a point or two to secure a good husband. With a population that is rapidly becoming redundant by immigration, and with an increasing standard of life and consequently decreasing and later marriages, a woman is not in a position to take many chances, nor should she be too precipitate nor too liberal in this vital matter.

A drunkard or hard drinker, or the victim of any dangerous habit, such as that of opium, should not be chosen, mainly on account of the effect on the children. A reform of action, unless prompt, cannot reform the constitution, and the degenerating effect of the intemperance, in whatever line, must be reflected in the children born from such a parent. Relapse in action must also be deemed as extremely likely. Intemperance in narcotics or stimulants should always be deemed the result of some previous weakening intemperance in work or idleness, or of a constitutional inability to meet the struggles of life on an equality with the average of society.

In any case it is certain that abuses of whatever kind leave indelible injury on the individual thus erring. We now know, for instance, that alcohol, when abused, leaves permanent lesions in the liver and the brain and that the power of these organs is diminished. Constitutional disease, such as consumption or syphilis, is equally dangerous and often fatal to the progeny. Such unfortunates should therefore be barred from the choice. The best means of judging of a man's fitness to bring forth children who can maintain the contest of life with success, is the measure of success attained by the man himself. Other things being equal, a woman should always give the preference to the man who has made his mark in the world.

Fortune in a man is no bar to matrimony, but rather a superior indication. This point, however, must not be misunderstood. Money as a motive in matrimony is meretricious. Its sole value is the indication of the ability and energy of the possessor.

Upon the deserts of Nubia the lioness has been observed to lie and watch a battle between two lions, and, when the contest has been decided, to go quietly away with the victor. So a woman may look out upon her suitors and select him who has achieved victory in whatever line society has set up as most essential for its collective welfare, or in any line she may deem of advantage to her expected children.

It is easy by observation to ascertain what qualities and conditions are best in man for his present condition. But it is difficult, indeed, to appreciate what qualities and conditions are necessary for improvement and for the future.

In the history of man we see both the physical form and the faculties very different in the extremes of barbarism and of civilization. The keen, observant eye of the Bedouin is not possessed by our city citizens even when not near-sighted.

The heavy jaw and full, large, sound teeth of the negro are not possessed by the average American. The latter suffers even in the smallness of his jaw, which crowds his teeth so much that a considerable number decay or are pulled out to make room for the others.

The prize-fighter is not the top of our society, nor likely to be. Keen sight and strong jaws might well have appeared to ancient legislators as points essential to be preserved, or even developed, for the safety of the race. We now, looking back, see that they are not.

The tendency of nature is ever to get rid of the useless. So a man who exercises little soon finds his muscles diminished in size or power, if they have been well developed before. So, also, many of his organs may diminish in activity and the redundant parts tend to atrophy. Some organs may diminish and others not, and disorders ensue on the attempt of nature to set up a new balance. While this is going on many individuals must perish. The difficulty of trusting to the reason alone, in its present benighted state, for our choice in breeding, must be apparent. The ugliness and, perhaps in part, the infertility of the French are strong arguments against the purely conventional marriage.

A man at thirty generally shows pretty well the stuff he is made of, and his capacity can be fairly gauged. It is better for men to marry younger than at this age, but better for the girl to be able to choose a man whose character and capacity are formed and knowable. This it is difficult to do before thirty.

An important reason for choosing a man five or more years her senior is the fact that woman passes out of the reproductive period considerably earlier than man. After the climacteric a woman rapidly loses her sexual feeling and attraction. If a man be in full possession of desire and power, and his wife be without either, we must perceive the dangers that overshadow the union. In America marriages have been largely of persons of nearly similar age. We can consequently explain how it is that in the present decline of the consideration of marriage we find the men most recreant above middle age.

It is an unpleasant thing to speak of, but then, why play ostrich? why shut our eyes to patent facts?

Prostitutes are supported by boys and married men over forty. It is to be presumed that the wives of these men have lost their power to attract. Another fact in the same line is that, excepting certain classes, as railroad employees, soldiers, sailors, etc., whose lives are peculiarly open to temptation, venereal disease is largely confined to the very young men and to married men over forty.

It is indeed painful for a pure woman to face these facts of life, but it is better to do so, and then to be armed by knowledge against placing temptation in the husband's way. This may be done by neglect of her person, by refusal of the conjugal duty, and by marrying a man of unsuitable age. I cannot recommend a young woman to refuse a good offer of marriage from a man of her own age—but then she ought to know that by and by there must come a severe strain on the husband's fidelity.

Very young men, certainly before they are twenty-one, should not be chosen. Such a young man cannot use the privileges of a husband with safety to himself. Premature use of the sexual function has a tendency to prevent the full physical and mental development of such as commit this error.

The progeny born of immature parents is generally considered as inferior, and as life matures the woman must find herself old while the husband is still young. The inferiority of the progeny is of course limited to those first born unless the husband's powers be permanently injured.

Writers on these subjects seem to be of one opinion on the inferiority of children born to the immature. They consider that it is so, but I have seen no conclusive facts adduced to show when man or woman should be considered immature. The first flowers and fruits of plants are usually abnormal; while sometimes superior to the average in size, they are always inferior in texture, flavor, etc., to later fruit produced under equally favorable conditions. Another indication in the same line is the fact that short-lived trees bear sooner than long-lived ones of the same family. An exceedingly unfavorable location may also force a tree to early bearing; so will sickness, parasitic or predatory attack, so will the pruning of man, and so will budding or grafting.

Everything injurious or likely to be weakening or fatal to a plant usually produces premature fruiting. Premature fruiting is therefore a sign of weakness. Some of this is caused designedly by man to secure better fruit. Thus he buds the seedling orange tree to obtain the Navel. A superior selling fruit is produced at some expense to the life of the tree.

A man or woman might not regret shortening his or her life to secure better children, but in this case of the Navel, while the fruit is developed to the taste of man, it has, on the other hand, quite lost its power of sustaining the contest of life. A Navel orange is seedless and therefore depends for its existence upon the attention of man.

It is probable that every variety of fruit perpetuated by budding or grafting would either disappear or revert back to the original at the extinction of the lives of the trees in being. Thus an apparent superiority of product at the expense of the parent is shown to be in a true measure fallacious.

Too young a woman should avoid breeding and avoid too young a mate. This suggests the idea that interest developing at immature age might be met by engagement to marry and postponement till maturer years.

The general rule should be against this or any engagement until the contracting parties are ready to marry. Eight weeks is the limit to allow for an engagement. The time required for reasonable inquiry as to the character of the groom is all that is desirable and all that should be allowed. The reasons for this rule are discussed elsewhere. The consideration of a candidate for matrimony through the glass of the future family to be expected must show more clearly than by any other means the essential good points as well as the essential bad points of the man as a husband.

A young girl brought up to look at matrimony as a means to

immortality in the progeny, and with a knowledge that her husband must be an equal force in her possible immortal life in the child, cannot, it seems to me, be led into open and apparent aberration of choice. She cannot be so easily deceived. For looking for the essentials of a good father for her future self, the usual means of deception—handsome looks, social standing as of a dissolute noble, fashionable dress, or profuse generosity—fade before the grander qualities of fatherhood—vitality of physique, capacity of mind, and force of character. A young maid should attach the greatest importance to the choice of a husband. There is but one thing more important, which is the bearing of the child and the renewal of her life.

In my female as in my male descendants, I will forgive everything but sterility and extinction. Thus as a partner of the opposite sex is necessary for the continuation of life, a partner must be taken, good if possible, but as nothing can be worse than extinction of the vital spark by which all hope and chance is lost, a partner even though imperfect or below what ought to be desired must be accepted.

CHAPTER IV.

WIFE CHOICE.

THE first requisite of a woman to be selected for a wife is that she possess the physical capacity to bear children.

It is, of course, of great importance that the children born should be an improvement on the parents. This subject is worthy of careful study. Amongst the works interesting on this point are those of Darwin, especially that on the changes in animals and plants under domestication, and the works of Francis Galton on heredity, Hutchinson's *Pedigree of Disease*, the works of Maudsley, etc. Galton shows very clearly that capacity, zeal, and vigor, the three qualities which he deems essential for greatness, are enormously more liable to appear in the child of an eminent person than in one of the common average. If both parents be superior, the progeny is certain to be above the average.

The male brains of the lowest tribes we now know about, and who use the same primitive implements which geology teaches were once the only implements used by early man, vary from thirty-nine to forty-four ounces. In convolutions and structure these brains are inferior to those of our race.

Whole races of men are much behind the highly civilized peoples in development, especially in that part of the physical development called nerve or brain quality and force. The brain of the Andaman Islander or Bushman of Africa is simpler in convolution and less in weight than that of, say the Anglo-Saxon. The average brain weight of males in the lowest races is in some cases, as has been said, under forty ounces, and the brain presents in its anatomy an appearance similar to that of one of our idiots. The brains of negroes in this country average about forty-four ounces, while the Anglo-Saxon brain averages nearly fifty ounces.

If an Anglo-Saxon breed to a negress, the lower race traits will appear more or less modified in his children's forms, hair, constitutions, and complexions. It is probable that the brain will partake of the lower qualities also. Such a man handicaps himself in his children and diminishes their brain power to an extent that at the very best will take ages to re-acquire, if happily they do not perish before this is achieved in the struggle with stronger competitors. The same point holds good in reference to inferior white races or families of your own race. It is important, therefore, to breed up rather than down. The children of eminent men should be sought in marriage.

The superiority of the brain of a white American over a negro American is six ounces. The superiority over the brains of other inferior races probably often exceeds ten ounces. Here is a difference in brain capacity which it would take long to overcome under the most favorable circumstances. All men once used no better implements than the lowest savages now do, and all men doubtless in those early times had no better brains than these savages now have. It must have required thousands of years to bring the mind of civilized man to its present superiority, to say nothing of the probable duration of the time of the evolution of mankind itself.

It is consequently more important to humanity to preserve this improved brain and to continue to improve it than to do anything else. The works of man soon become of themselves useless and antiquated and are of little permanent value. The best brain development can always produce the best of work, and work suited to the time. It is more important, therefore, to transmit a superior brain endowment than to do any work of the brain, and better to sacrifice the work rather than the reproduction of the brain. It is equally clear that, in breeding and reproducing, care should be taken not to adulterate and lower the brain capacity of the children to be expected.

The importance, therefore, of selecting wisely in marriage and of securing the very best partner possible for the great work of self-perpetuation is manifest. The attention of the more developed men can hardly be too often called to these radical brain differences.

What careful breeding can do, we see in many animals. In this country, in 1840, the average weight of the fleece of a sheep was 1.85 lbs., in 1887 it had risen to 6 lbs. In other countries careful attention has still further increased the yield of wool. In England the Southdowns have been bred for both fleece and meat. The striking superiority of these sheep, especially in the latter case, is to be noted.

When we consider that the cranial capacity of the European is forty cubic inches greater than that of the native Australian, and that this is four times greater than the difference between the cranial capacity of the Australian and the gorilla, the importance of careful selection in breeding may be understood. As the brains of our babies resemble in their convolutions and comparative simplicity, first those of the quadrumana and then those of the savage, we may surmise that we have risen from this low estate and may reasonably expect that evolution and improvement are still at work to carry some of us through our children to heights impossible for us now to conceive.

While these differences are striking enough, there is good cause to believe that in the leading clans of humanity the difference is still greater. The average of American brains of the white race is said to be short of 50 ounces. But this average is taken from a comparatively low stratum and the ruling class doubtless averages much more. Such brains when occasionally weighed, as was that of Daniel Webster, show an extraordinary excess of power running up even to over 60 ounces. Without the brain with strength to support the strain now necessarily forced on it, we can hope for nothing. In California, one third of the population is of foreign birth ; this third furnishes two thirds of our insane. It is thus indicated that the minds of this foreign one third are not on the average as capable of sustaining the strain of our general progress as are the minds of the native Americans, who have made it. As the negro and the white do not combine to make a strong race nor in all probability one that will perpetuate itself, so we may expect that other differences of less extent between the whites themselves will also be incapable of furnishing a resistant and progressive breed. (There seem at this time no conclusive indications that the negro will not be able in certain climatic belts in America to hold his own or even to supplant the white. Of this, however, it is too soon to speak with certainty.)

In attempting to breed up, the greatest care must be taken not to miss the true line of progress. We cannot now say what the sum of qualities is that is best for our future improvement. We can see the elephant surpass us in physical power and longevity, and the horse in swiftness, the bird possessed of the capacity of flight through the air, the fish with capacity to live in the water, and the lizard to live for long periods without any water. All these have powers we entirely lack. The tiger surpasses us in ferocity and natural weapons, as does the wasp. So also amongst men, we see the average male Zulu surpass our average in physical proportion and strength, and many savages are our superiors in the power of sight and of reading the open book of nature.

Thrown on our natural resources in deserts like those of the Sahara, of Australia, or of the Colorado, we should be at a disadvantage compared to the natives of these districts, and would probably perish where they grow fat. So in brain development, we, as a people, are perhaps below the populations of the old Greek cities, or of the Italian republics, and we may thus see that intellect, while evidently in the main line of superiority and progress, demands for its perpetuation both a physical power to reproduce and the moral qualities leading to its exercise.   Otherwise the superior brain power, like that of the Greeks, must disappear as theirs did.   Another thing to recollect is, that qualities and conditions favorable in a high degree to the present activities of man may be the very ones that will absorb his energy and prevent him from following the true but unseen line of progress in the future.   Thus we may explain the rise of different branches of our race and their fall and extinction. Their development was not even and true.   By premature excess in what will be eventually essential, or in fatal lack of necessary qualities for progress, or in the development of deadly errors, civilization after civilization has fallen.

Marriage without children is nominal not real.   In fact, a sterile marriage is no marriage so far as the fundamental object of marriage is concerned.   The physical capacity to perform the duties of wife is, therefore, an absolute essential in a woman for your life partner. Any condition of chronic disease, or any malformation that would throw doubt upon this capacity in a woman, should at once strike her from the list of your possible choice.   Uterine diseases in woman should be a bar by reason of the tendency, in woman so diseased, to sterility.   The woman with broad pelvis and rounded breast will generally prove a mother when made a wife.   The attractive and well developed girl must be at least handsome as a whole, for the standard of beauty in women is really based on their physical fitness to become mothers.   A woman not capable of being a mother, cannot be a beautiful woman.   The perfection of charms, as in the Venus of Milo, is, also, from a physiological point of view, the perfection of physical capacity to perform the duties of a mother.   A woman anatomically correct, but with a face unusually ugly, should in most cases be avoided.   The reason of this is, that these traits may be transmitted to your daughters, making their marriage difficult and thus interfering with their future happiness.

Women, on the other hand, with extraordinary beauty of face, skin, etc., unfortunately, as a rule, attach undue importance to such qualities.   They notice the effect of their striking beauty in the passing crowd, in society, and amongst acquaintances, but ignore altogether the fact that those they live with forget about their skin-deep beauty.   It requires but a short intimacy in family life to sink the beauty of the face, and substitute, for all purposes of attraction or happiness, the beauty of heart and mind.   Thus beautiful women in society, who have flirted and tasted the delights of adoration in the acquaintance and in the crowd without effort, are apt indeed to consider themselves ill-treated or neglected when the family life a wife must lead gives facial beauty so poor a place.

In every-day intercourse, one's likes and dislikes are based on action, not on looks. Society belles forget, if they ever knew, this fact, and expect devotion and attention from the husband, proportioned to that received from flattering beaux, all based on looks and rattle talk. The husband forgets the looks, finds nothing else, and, disappointed, becomes dull and indifferent. The passing swell attracted by the beauty is all devotion. The wife contrasts the two, knows not the cause, feels injured, then come bickerings and unhappiness, if not divorce.

Next to the physical quality is the moral quality. A wife should possess an unalterable devotion to virtue so as to give the husband complete security in the paternity of his children. Without the reproductive power, sexual virtue has no cause to exist.

The human being is greatly governed by circumstances. Those who are good might, under different conditions, be bad. Those who are bad might, under a more favorable fate, be good. What is sunshine may become shadow, what is shadow may become sunshine. All depends on the situation of the sun or of the clouds.

Therefore, in selecting a wife, her training and surroundings should be considered, for these will without doubt have played an important part in the formation of her character. The woman for a wife should be a virgin. This bars widows. Widows have been in the arms and embrace of another. No thorough man can altogether forgive this. He can never have the same regard or devotion for a woman deflowered by another, as for a woman all his own. He may not think of this in the intoxication of passion before marriage, but it will inevitably occur to him afterwards. The thought is an unpleasant one, and the truer the man the more he will feel it. The woman who has been wived can never have the same modesty, or the same true devotion, to a second husband that she might have had to a first, or that a complete marriage relation demands. The fineness of woman's nature is spoiled by promiscuous intercourse even to the extent of two men. She is like an apple ; an apple mouthed and tasted by one may still be mouthed and eaten to the core with undiminished pleasure by him who first did bite, but to all others there is a rebelling thought, often inexplicable and ill-defined, that prompts them not to touch. An apple partly eaten, with the tooth-marks of another mouth, left in a public place, would be touched only by those in the pangs of hunger. The better the person, the less likely to eat.

The simile fails in this that in such an apple some parts may remain untouched; not so a deflowered woman, every part and portion to her inmost life has been chewed and slobbered with.

Those who have not thought on woman's and on man's nature, and upon the grandeur and unity of marriage, failing to appreciate these points, may marry widows, but they cannot escape the consequences. Such a marriage must be incomplete. There are other reasons why widows should not be married. A woman barren, or in any way defective as to her reproductive organs, should not be chosen for a wife; therefore, a widow who has borne no children to her first or to any former husband should be avoided, as likely to remain barren. On the other hand, a woman who has conceived by a divorced or a dead husband, or by any one, has received his stamp or seal indelibly by that fact. It is a matter of common observation that old mothers resemble and suggest the likeness of their husbands, and that the likeness to the father tends to be most marked in the last children born. The cause of this is apparent when we study fœtal life. The egg bursts at the menstrual periods from the ovary of the female; if the spermatozoa of the man find it, it will be vitalized and more or less stamped by the man. So the child is a part of the woman and a part of the man, and always contains a strong element of both. A child may entirely resemble its father and still have a child like the mother, or the likeness may come out after several generations, and *vice versa*. Thus the child in utero is the man as well as the woman. When the egg is fecundated and becomes attached to the uterus the man-father is actually in the woman attached to her. The connection is complete. By the chorion and the placenta the blood of the mother enters the child, nourishes it, and passes back to the mother. The circulation is one. Thus is the blood of the man for nine months passing in and out of the woman. She is stamped by the man's vitality in the process, and after a while she may resemble him.

But what is most important in this connection is that children by a second husband may resemble more or less the first. What a painful reminder of former caresses by another, such a child must be. The first husband is revenged, and brands the progeny of the second. See *Lessons in Gynecology* by Dr. Wm. Goodell, page 376. I have noted a number of instances of these resemblances myself. Recently I became acquainted with a family in which the mother had borne two children by a first husband and four by the second. The first three children by the second marriage resembled the first father, and were especially like the daughter by the first husband. The case was the more clear from the fact that the first husband was of Latin extraction, had brown eyes, a peculiarly fine complexion, and crinkly hair, while the mother and second husband were Anglo-Saxons, of light complexion and blue or gray eyes and not curly hair. The first three children of the second husband had brown eyes, crinkly hair, and the complexion of the first husband. The second husband and wife remembered no ancestors of this type, but their family knowledge did not extend far enough to eliminate this source of error.

I am bound to admit that this stamping by the first sire is not proven. Most of the breeders of animals whom I have consulted have failed to notice such stamping, and at least one conscientious student, A. Weismann, in *The Germ-Plasma*, denies it.

One of the rules of Moses made it the duty of a man to marry the widow of a deceased brother and raise seed to him. The sect of the Sadducees held such a marriage by a brother to be an important religious duty.

In thinking on this rule and reflecting on the frequently repeated admonitions to go forth and replenish the earth, on the fact that the old Hebrew blessings were so often for the fertility and continuance in children of the life of the individual and that the curses were for sterility and extermination, it has seemed to me that the great importance attached by the Jewish prophets to child-bearing took this now forgotten form to secure real children to a dead man from a wife already stamped to him. It must be confessed that a careful study of institutions gives fair presumption for a different origin of this rule.

It is doubtless a rule that a first fertilization stamps more or less the mother, but it must also be said that the first husband, though present, may not be visible in the children of the second. The stamp may come out in the grandchildren when not visible in the child, but of this I have no recorded observations. See Darwin, *Animals and Plants under Domestication*, vol. i., chap. xi ; Prosper Lucase, *Traité de l' Hérédité Naturelle*, vol. ii., chap. xi., page 64 ; Dalton's *Human Physiology*, chap. xi., page 659, 7th edition ; also Flint's *Physiology*, chapter on Reproduction.

The treatise of Fournier on *Syphilis and Marriage* touches on a point which confirms the view that the mother is influenced by the foetus. Syphilis manifests its first presence by contagion in the chancre and bubo. The only two exceptions to this are hereditary syphilis and the syphilis of conception. The syphilis of conception, according to Fournier, is that syphilis found only in women pregnant or who may have been recently pregnant, whose husbands had no infective sores, and who themselves had neither chancre nor bubo in the course of the disease, but whose husbands had had these symptoms of syphilis. The children born to women thus affected always have syphilis. It is well known that a mother contracting syphilis may infect the child in utero, but it is not so well known that the child in utero inheriting syphilis from the father may infect the mother. Fournier is very positive that this form of infection occurs, and states that the number of cases observed is so great that all source of error is eliminated in the history of the contagion. The father is free from infectious sores, but has syphilis in his blood. He impregnates the wife and the child inherits the constitutional taint which is present in utero. The mother without any of the symptoms of contagion, universal in the history of syphilis, manifests the secondary symptoms as a constitutional taint. It is the constitution of the child in utero which has stamped her constitution. Without any contagion from the father she receives his dread disease from the child constitutionally. The child when born, if alive, manifests its syphilis in the same way by a general order and not by any chancre or bubo.

A number of cases are now on record in which a healthy woman having borne a syphilitic child to a syphilitic father, and without herself contracting the disease, afterward bore a syphilitic child to a healthy man. Two of these cases were very carefully checked to exclude error and are fairly reliable. From the South come a number of cases reported by medical men, of white or mulatto children borne by negro women to negro husbands, the women having borne children previously to a white man.

Thus one can perceive how influential is the child before birth on the mother, and consequently how important a part a man plays in stamping for good or for evil his wife. The same fact in regard to resemblances is known amongst breeders of the domestic animals, and they will not breed a mare to a scrub sire for fear that his stamp will again appear in the progeny of better animals. The case of the Arabian mare first covered by a quagga, whose subsequent colts, though by well bred stallions, still showed the markings of the quagga, is a classic instance. It is said by some breeders that a mare put for the first time to a jack will show mule characteristics in all future colts though sired by horses. The importance of good breeding in horses, which we can appreciate when we recall the fact that the great horse King Herod won £201,505 sterling in prizes and begot 497 winners, and that Eclipse begot 334 winners, has made breeders careful, not of their stallions that can receive no impress, but of the mares, whose breeding powers may be and probably often are ruined by impregnation from inferior sires, and the consequent stamping and sealing to his life they thus received.

The plant louse is impregnated for forty generations (Bonnet); the caterpillar for three or four (Bernouilli); the bee for a year (Riaumur); the hen for her whole brood. We may therefore understand the importance of a first fertilization.

Edward Home, in writing about horse-breeding, relates the story of an Arabian mare first impregnated by an ass, whose colts ever after, though by the finest stallions, resembled the ass. Magne speaks of the understanding of this matter by the breeders in Poitou, and the precautions taken to guard against improper impregnation. The bitch is the same ; the first dog impresses her more than twenty that may follow ; he marks their offspring with a resemblance to himself (Stark, Burdach). The domestic sow surprised by the wild boar retains his fierceness and bears to his peaceable successors bristling pigs (Meckel, Michelet).

This law which plainly devotes the female to her first love, and protests against those which follow, appears to be universal amongst the superior animals. Similar conditions are also noticed in the vegetable world. I have noticed the curious fact that buds used in budding fruit trees varied in their fruit, even when originally coming from the same tree. This may be accounted for by supposing that the fertilization of the blossom impressed, to a certain extent, the wood growth near it. So different parts of the tree being differently fertilized in the blossom, might be permanently affected in character. Thus the male element would not only stamp the character of the fruit, but also, though to a less extent, the fruit twig or branch, leaving an impress that would show on fruit differently fertilized, and on buds or cuttings made from the branch.

In the orchidaceæ the pollen is perfected and disappears before the ovules can be directly fertilized by it. We must in this case presume that the mother plant is fertilized and produces the ovule afterward. This is suggestive of the fertilization of certain insects for succeeding generations by one covering. John Brown, M.D., has made some interesting observations on the cross-fertilization of peas. In his cases not only was the seed affected, but the pod also, showing the reflex on the female element.

You will thus perceive that the first impregnation is a brand upon the woman and upon her future children, no matter by whom sired.

As the certainty of paternity is the main basis of marriage, so the marrying of women, mothers by other men, is in opposition to its fundamental principle, in that they will really bear children to the first husband, though the life flame of the child is kindled by the second.

Another point in this connection which deserves study is the comparative frequency of the procreation of the great by men from second or plural wives, and the rarity of such procreation of the great by women from second or plural husbands (as in prostitution or polyandry). Joseph Jefferson and Cromwell are the only exceptions thus far noted. If, on examination, it turns out that there is a marked weakness on the part of women to transmit superiorities from second husbands, there will be an additional force to the recommendation not to marry widows.

I do not advise widows or divorced women to remain single. If they can find a man ready to take them, they themselves have no dominating reason against accepting a second marriage. For a man, however, the question, as has been explained, is entirely of a different aspect. Nearly every great religious legislator has formulated rules discouraging to the marrying of widows. These barbarous rules included the burning of women after their husbands' death, as in the *suttee* of India ; the killing and burying of women to accompany their husbands, as in Fiji ; and their seclusion from general life more or less complete.

Such women as have lost their maidenhood out of matrimony are still more impossible, for the thought is inevitable that the virtue they have failed to protect once they may fail to protect again. In fact, it does not exist to protect.

The widow's former husband has at least the merit of being dead. The divorced woman's ex-husband may be alive to recall himself and his privileges to his successor. A wife who cannot keep, or will not be kept by, her husband, may well be mistrusted as a life partner. She is considered as dealt with, and condemned as a woman to take to wife in the words spoken of widows. But lest there be misapprehension, the rule is laid down, "Thou shalt not marry a divorced woman."

The Jews owe much of their success in maintaining their race to the laws of Moses. One of these in relation to the marriage of priests in the 21st chapter of Leviticus, verses 13 and 14, is as follows.

13. "And he shall take a wife in her virginity."
14. "A widow or a divorced woman, or profane or an harlot, these shall he not take ; but take a virgin of his own people to wife."

It may be safely presumed that the promise of a Messiah to be borne by some Jewish woman has done much to encourage childbirth and consequently family life in this race.

Many orthodox Hebrew wives for ages have had the secret and exalted hope that some one of them might be glorified in bearing a Saviour for her race. As long as this belief held complete sway in a Jewish woman's mind, no worldly digression from the great work of reproduction could attract her. Perhaps it is on this account that Jewish wives have become proverbial for fidelity and for their attention to home duties, for these are incidents and characteristics of fertility in women.

In recent times with the weakening of persecution and the advance of science, the Hebrew race has not the ancient fulness of belief in the communion of God and Moses, and the Jews now often slight and disregard the wise rules of the founder of their historic life. This change is making rapid way.

A few years past a Hebrew prostitute was a curiosity, in America at least ; now such misguided and irretrievably ruined Jewesses are to be found in every large city.

The Jewish young men are said upon good authority to be often more wanton and lustful than their other fellow sinners of different race. These signs show a weakening of the old rules that have preserved the Hebrew race intact for so many ages.

The unbridled sensuality of the males of a race or nation has always preceded the prostitution of their females. Such license of the males, at first practised on captives or inferiors, has in the end drawn their own wives and daughters into the vortex of dishonor, and has surely diminished the desire for child-bearing amongst women. So less children are born and the grandeur of the reproductive instinct is debased to the level of low lust.

Man cannot long worship in the temples of Cyprus without finding in his own family women the tastes of the Cyprian.

WITH CORRUPTION, WITHOUT CHILDREN—Such is the result to be anticipated within a short period, if the morals of man be loose. The first signs of a decay amongst the Jews are plainly in view. -Their women no longer expect a Messiah.

The rules of many of the foremost of the ancient peoples are now known to have been exceedingly strict in regard to both marriage and family life. A Roman of the senatorial rank could not marry any inferior woman. Their definition of an inferior woman was doubtless defective, and included all women of other races no matter how exalted. Thus Antony could not marry Cleopatra, Queen of Egypt, and was obliged to live with her as his mistress and not as his wife. Cæsar was in the same situation, and his son by her was illegitimate. The story of Titus and Berenice is another illustration of the rule. This Berenice was a granddaughter of Herod the Great of Judea. She was three times married : first very young to Marcus, son of Alexander the Alabarch ; second, to her uncle Herod, King of Chalcis, who left her a widow at twenty ; and the third time, to

9

Polemon, King of Cilicia, whom she deserted. After the capture of Jerusalem, Titus fell in love with her and would have married her had it not been for the Roman rule, which was strongly enforced by the prejudices of the people. Racine has written a tragedy founded on this story.

Every wife should have a good moral character, the principal element of which should be virtue. After physique and morals comes intellectual capacity.

A man marrying should try to improve his blood and life. The children being himself renewed, he should look for their mother not only where physique is sound but where the mind is strong also. He should not choose one who, through imperfect information or abortion of maternal instinct, seeks a career inconsistent with child-bearing, for such tendencies are exterminating and fatal, but he should look for a healthy, well-developed brain.

These three are the main points in selecting a wife—Physique, Virtue, Intellect. The secondary considerations are the social and property standing of the woman and her age. A woman in good social position, when the tone of society is healthy, must have observed the many unwritten laws that govern it. These laws are in the line of good breeding and virtue, and while somewhat considered in all classes, they are only fully known amongst the best and can therefore only be completely observed in that stratum.

A young woman in full standing in society ought to have good breeding, at least in outward semblance. Every endeavor should be made to have the good breeding real as well as seeming. This gives a stamp to the household and to the children, and will tend to good manners. Good breeding acquired in infancy will be of great advantage to the mature life of the progeny thus influenced. The foundation of good breeding is the heart. Never forget this. Cultivate good feeling and action in harmony with it and you have good manners.

A young woman in good social position is there presumably through the forceful actions of her ancestors, and is therefore likely to inherit such qualities, and consequently to transmit them to your children. On the other hand, it must be remembered that the removal of the necessity of productive work which success brings, causes a cessation of such work in almost all cases. The qualities that brought success, no longer used, retrograde and eventually disappear.

Thus men rise, transmit their powers to their children (themselves renewed). These, lacking the motive and necessity, neglect to use the inherited powers, which consequently fail, and in a generation or two sink often below the general average.

The fish in the Mammoth Cave have no use for eyes. The non-use of the eyes has produced a loss of function, and we find now in these fish only rudimentary eyes which see nothing. Rudimentary organs abound everywhere in animal life, not excepting humanity. Such organs have come to this condition through non-use.

The appendix vermiformis, a part of man's intestine, is now not only useless, but occasionally causes trouble and even death. Its function in the marsupials, where it is large and developed, is to digest crude vegetable food. Man no longer eats such food, and consequently has no use for this part of the intestines. Non-use has destroyed it.

A man who breaks his arm has to wear it in a sling after it is set, until the bone knits again. In the meantime no use of it is possible. In every such case a progressive atrophy of the muscles will be noticed, and the power of the arm will be much less when the arm is taken from the sling than when it was put in; frequently the old power is never regained.

So special capacity is born in families, dwindles through non-use, and disappears. Life runs in a circle in which no man or family has been able to gain permanent ascendancy. Some, ay, whole tribes are trampled out of existence and exterminated, but the advance of man is by average of the whole and leavening of all. Each rise is higher, each fall less deep; so while no family knows thus far a permanent conquest of all other families, society at large advances, destroying only the sterile who destroy themselves, and leaving stranded and stationary some few far off stragglers too weak to make the fight of life and progress. Two principles are here in conflict: inheritance of property, which gives the impulse to those great works enjoyable in our own life, projected to the future in our children. This gives motive for great work.

The other principle is this: capacity of body and of brain depends on use. Use in the long run depends on compulsion. Work is the child of necessity. But to work for yourself living in the child, grandchild, and descendant demands inheritance. Inheritance of property involves a diminution of the necessity for productive labor in the inheritor. The labor must be expected to decrease as the necessity for it is removed. With diminished work is diminished use of faculty. As the faculties are unused they cease to grow, then decay.

Thus the family that rises by capacity to wealth and power, with inheritance rises no more, for it works less; working principally from habit, necessity being absent, losing soon the habit, work ceases. The capacity, at first rusty, is now rotten, and the family sinks back to obscurity, if it happily does not disappear, exterminated by the children of idleness, vice, and disease.

The grandest motive for the greatest work is the effect of such work in shaping the human life toward improvement, an improvement that will tend to be repeated in the worker's children. If his children can be moulded to improvement by great thoughts and grand acts, a man has an unquenchable motive for the best use of all his faculties. A woman equally.

Weismann, indeed, denies such influence. His experiment on five generations of white mice, 901 individuals, when he cut the tails off without any sign of tail disappearance showing in the young, is striking. The Jews, too, are an illustration, for they have circumcised for ages without any congenital loss of the foreskin. It appears from this that some mutilations are not inheritable. On the other hand, numerous investigations of nerve mutilation show such to be certainly transmitted. Brown-Sequard has published some recent experiments in this line. Nerve diseases, as insanity, epilepsy, ataxia, chorea, show a strong tendency to hereditary transmission. Pfitgun finds the two end joints of the little toe are becoming fused, 41.5 per cent. in women, and 31 per cent. in men. The musculus sternalis, a new muscle or useful reversion to a very old one, is of advantage in the recently acquired costal breathing of women, and is most often found in that sex. Dr. A. Lane has demonstrated not only modifications of structure in shoemakers and tailors, but also the creation of new structures of use in their special occupation. There is a tendency to inherit these peculiar adaptations, for several cases of children of shoemakers of two generations show the new type before going to work. A thousand such details would prove nothing. But the weight of testimony and a reasonable interpretation of the changes we note in animals make it probable that these changes have arisen largely through use of function, and the consequent progressive adaptation of the form of life to the function necessary for its maintenance and transmission.

Perhaps nothing we now know could lend more strength to this view than the German figures showing 65 per cent. of all cases of near-sightedness to be hereditary. Myopia is primarily due to a changed function and strain on the eye. It would not seem possible that the eye could be the only organ affected in descendants by a change of function.

Carrying out these rules and thus keeping sound on the question of reproduction and so escaping extermination, it may be for you to reconcile these two principles. When you solve the problem, the earth is yours.

Zeal, that quality which drives to effort, whether it be recompensed or not, whether it be necessary or not, is almost always found in the great. Zeal may then be our road out of this dilemma. It is indeed a quality we should seek in breeding. Therefore, while capacity, force, vitality, and intellect should first be sought in the children of the successful, the other considerations mentioned will make it often best to seek a wife amongst those rising and consequently developing their faculties, rather than amongst those risen and leaving their capacities in disuse to be eaten to the heart by rust, and therefore going backward or into extermination.

There is, however, another cause for the return to the general standard of the children of those above it that has been demonstrated by Galton in his *Natural Inheritance.* This is the law of Regression. He shows that in every society there is a certain average as to various characteristics, which we may presume to be the best suited to the conditions in which the society lives. Any variation from this standard has a constant and calculatable tendency to revert to the standard. His demonstrations are in inherited heights and inherited color of the eyes. In height he transmutes the female to the male, on the basis of the female height bearing the ratio to that of the male of 100 to 108, which a great mass of measurements shows to be substantially correct. He then strikes an average between the height of the father and of the mother transmuted, which he calls the mid-parent height. If the height of the mid-parent be above or below the standard of the society examined, there is a constant tendency in the children to regression to that standard. The average of these will be one third less removed from the standard of the society than was that of the parents. Thus the parents transmit two thirds of their united and average variation.

The coloring of the eyes follows the same rule, and so also does that of artistic temperament. We may presume that the law holds good in all human qualities, and thus is partly explained the facts of observation, that the children of eminent parents are not so talented or so much above the average as were the parents, and consequently there is another levelling law at work besides the atrophy and disappearance of organs or qualities that are not used.

Galton further shows that some inherited qualities from father and mother are blended in the child ; one such is height : while on the other hand, some are not likely to be blended but tend to be inherited in their entirety from one or the other parent ; one such is the color of the eyes. The child of a blue-eyed mother and of a black-eyed father is likely to have either blue eyes or black eyes, thus inheriting the color altogether from the father or altogether from the mother or perhaps from some ancestor.

The height of the child, however, may be the exact average of the two parents. Other qualities or characteristics doubtless follow the same opposition. Other curious matters are brought out in Galton's investigations which show another and different law to be at work in the opposite direction.

A peculiarity in a man involves the expectation of finding one third of that peculiarity in his mid-parent. The amount of influence in inheritance of the mid-parent pure and simple on the progeny is figured to be close to one half, of each separate parent therefore one quarter, of the mid-grandparent one quarter, and of each grand-parent one sixteenth ; that is to say, the average of a family of six or more will follow this rule, and upon the average every person owes one half his qualities and characteristics directly to his parents, and the other half to remote influences of ancestors working through the parents.

Galton also explains by his examinations that a peculiar or eminent person is more likely to arise from the great mass of average people than from the few above the average, although each one of the few above the average has a vastly greater chance of producing an eminent person than any one of the common average. He uses the following language to prevent any one from placing too little importance on inheritance.

"The other subject to be alluded to is the fundamental distinction that may exist between two couples whose personal faculties are naturally alike. If one of the couples consist of two gifted members of a poor stock and the other of two ordinary members of a gifted stock, the difference between them will betray itself in their offspring. The children of the former will tend to regress, those of the latter will not. The value of a good stock to the well-being of future generations is therefore obvious."

When the first primitive life appeared in the world, it may be presumed that the conditions were suitable only to the most primitive forms; all deviations toward higher forms must then have been exterminating and the law of regression must have had full sway. As the conditions improved, the law of adaptation to surroundings doubtless added its force to the law of variation and so the two over-came the law of regression. Thus each new condition encouraged and developed a life suited to it.

The various fields of life once occupied, any variation from the standard of those occupying one field to that of those in another must be fatal, for any adaptation would in its various transitory stages be met by a body of beings whose standard was already perfectly suited to the conditions of life in question. This handicap would be too great to be overcome.

We can thus understand the unchanging character of present orders and species of life, and must expect it to continue except as to the ending of lower forms of life in occasional extermination through unsuitable surroundings supervening, and in the highest form, man, in progress adapting him to advances made possible through natural changes of condition either direct or caused by man himself. In such progress man has no superior type to compass his defeat.

In evolution, therefore, it is to be presumed that change in life characteristics can only come where changed conditions offer the chance. Changes causing extermination have already come, ending forever many forms of life. These or other changes have, however, continued to occur, which have made openings for new improvements of life at the top, and have even caused reversions of high forms to suit low opportunities. These changes are now going on. Some are natural and slow beyond appreciation, such as the cooling of the earth, and some are caused by man and make new conditions to which he must adapt himself.

Steam and electricity have made life more rapid and more trying. Thus a being with greater nerve power than the average of past civilized man is best suited to our present conditions. We see this plainly in the proportionately more rapid increase of insane, idiots, suicides, inebriates, etc., than the increase of the population would warrant. Consequently, the conditions of life must be more severe on the nerves than they were. The conditions of life are changing. This is a matter which requires constant attention on the part of the family founder, and it makes an acquaintance at least with the excitements and trials of city life an essential to the development of nerve power to keep one in the current of progress. (See Chapter V., " The Child.")

We can perceive also from these considerations the necessity of the cultivation of the feelings of humanity. We must have a society suited to our growth. A selfish individualism alone is not enough. A sound family is not enough.

Progress demands a favorable environment, which the individual cannot create. Conditions compatible with a higher evolution must be the outcome of a social organization and must be supported by it. Narrow selfishness, then, may as well be discarded at once and for ever. It is a no-thoroughfare. A general and intelligent humanity in action is a necessity for progress. It is a hopeful symptom to note the gradual growth and spread through the ages of a humanitarian sympathy.

We must not be extreme in this, certainly not to the extent of the danger of self-extermination in sterility. In such aberration, the individual would lose himself and the true objects of humanitarianism.

Eminence in goodness or ability, as in the Ancian family of Rome, eminence in badness or incapacity, as in the Juke family of New York, are often long-continued in families, and, by proper breeding, the good could be as certainly maintained and improved as are the qualities of animals.

Great attention has been devoted by man to the development of certain qualities he desired in animals, so we see peculiar breeds of hogs, horses, cattle, dogs, pigeons, poultry, and even of insects. He has submitted vegetable life to his desires also. A thoroughbred in any line is as certain of being superior in its specialty over an ordinary-bred animal, as in the speed and endurance of the race-horse, as the day is to follow the night. Man himself, however, still breeds with reasonable recognition of the true qualities of improvement and success in his race. We can get a thoroughbred man as certainly as we have obtained a thoroughbred horse. The difficulty under which we must labor in such an effort is the probable necessity of changing from time to time the qualities for which we breed, to secure progress and permanent superiority. In glancing back through history, we find the standards best suited to success and superiority to have often changed. At one time we find an industrial type the most necessary and the most promising ; at another, the military and the fighting, with the industrial degraded and enslaved. So wealth and glory, physique and intellect, have alternately, with minor matters, been suited to bring and keep man at the top.

Mind and intellect may safely be supposed to be the eventual road to the promised land of a self-sustaining race. As has been already said, all we want of the physique is to carry the mind with the now necessary powers of reproduction.

It may be remarked here that great differences in life-forms are incapable of reproducing life. Where the differences are less, we may obtain progeny, but a progeny incapable of self-perpetuation, as in the mule. Others, again, are doubtless still nearer in type, who breed, and whose progeny breed, but whose thus mixed life must eventually run out.

It is said that marriages between Jews and Americans are more often infertile than those between Jews and Jews or Americans and Americans. Here is a condition that if true demands careful attention in marriage.

Cross fertilization in fruits often produces surprising perfection of quality, together also with a lack or total absence of fertility.

In the same species, however, varieties combined in breeding give a greater plasticity and capacity for change than we see in members of the same variety. Darwin speaks of cross fertilization as being productive of the most vigorous plants. Fritz Muller shows that, in at least some flowers, the different parts, male and female, in the same blossom do not fertilize each other. The male element must be carried to another flower. This would indicate that in such plants qualities preventing close or continued in-breeding have been most favorable to life.

The most beautiful of California flowers (*Romneya Coulteri*), a poppy, is said to have few fertile seeds when planted alone, but to have a large seed vitality when planted in masses. This is a characteristic of many California wild flowers, which, when found in vigor, grow naturally in beds and masses, and so form striking features in such spring landscapes as are not conquered to the plow.

Consequently, when we are in face of changing conditions as we are to-day, and probably always will be, we may with advantage make excursions out of an established breed of men to secure change and adaptation to advances. At the same time we must be careful not to go too far lest we run up against the dead wall of sterility. It may occasionally be necessary to sacrifice some points of breeding to secure reproductive power. This power is often weak in the well bred of animals, and probably will be equally so in well-bred men.

An incident of success in our present life is usually wealth. A wealthy woman seldom makes a good wife, and still more rarely is she happy as a wife or does she make a happy husband or family.

Women of wealthy families, who have maintained good qualities through several generations are not so much to be feared on account of their wealth as those of families who have come suddenly into riches. One class of rich women, heiresses and co-heiresses, should be altogether excluded. The tendency in such women to sterility is strong. Perhaps the best place to find this tendency tabulated, and to thus learn what it amounts to, is in Galton's *Hereditary Genius*, page 138. He there shows the tendency of able men elevated to the English peerage to marry heiresses to support their new dignity. He goes on to demonstrate that the extinction of peerages so often noted is principally due to the marrying of heiresses. These women are often entirely sterile, or have children without procreative vigor, or leave children without vitality. Galton's researches are very conclusive against heiresses as perpetuators of life.

By heiress Galton means an only daughter with wealth; by co-heiress, one of two children.

A wealthy woman should generally be avoided. If a woman is found in a wealthy family fitted for a wife in other things, she should either be taken on condition that she bring none of her wealth into your family, or that the wealth be made over to the husband absolutely on the wedding day. The first method is best, both in leaving the husband's motives unimpeached and also in leaving the motives for effort in him unweakened.

Few wealthy women have healthy bodies, morals, or minds. Idleness is their destruction; therefore wealth is of all things the most fatal to families in happiness and the most effective extermi-nating agent unless some other strong motive, as the desire of noble or royal families to perpetuate themselves, overcomes these tendencies by early training and constant effort.

It will doubtless occur to many that to turn all her property over to the husband is a great sacrifice and risk for the woman to take. But these should remember that the greatest risk of life is marriage. In taking this step a woman stakes her happiness, honor, and im-mortality. These are her all. Such a trivial incident of life as wealth cannot be considered in comparison to them. If, therefore, upon an examination women controlling wealth after marriage are not found to be happy and do not make their ventures successful, this fact may reasonably be deemed to have been an element in their failure. When we make a great gamble, when the stake is high— say life,—we should never hesitate to put at risk also any small or secondary thing that might bring us to a successful issue. An apparently cautious policy in such a crisis may be the height of folly. Thus by failing to risk a toe when life is at stake we may lose life itself and the toe also. A woman when she marries should hesitate at no minor risk to make the greater gamble a success.

Nature has given man the taller stature, the stronger muscles, and the vital forces best suited to the outside conflict. The woman has her superiorities as clearly defined. These are in the line of child-bearing and child-rearing.

Nature gives man the headship. When marriage was devised by mankind, man took the head of the family. This is the natural condition of the family. Any other position for man is inferior and unnatural. A family thus faultily constituted is in conflict with nature. To contest against nature is a labor of Sisyphus.

The natural position of the wife or mother is not inferior, but is grand and splendid. As the man cannot perform her highest work, so to place him in her position is to degrade him, taking him from what he can do, and can do best, to place him where he cannot perform the duties at all.

To place the woman at the head of the family, and consequently to oblige her to stand the brunt of the struggle of life, is to place her at a disadvantage, in which the family must share. She enters a fight in which, if she be a true woman—that is, a mother,—she is heavily handicapped. She is degraded as well as the man, and diverted from those activities which she can perform best, and turned to those she can only perform at a disadvantage.

Wealth may change the natural condition ; that is, the physical and nerve power of the man may be more than counteracted by the power of wealth in the hands of the woman to purchase those qualities from others. Thus the man may, by this means, be pitted single-handed against thousands of other men, hired directly or indirectly by the woman. The man then, by artificial means, becomes the weaker of the two life partners. Nature is overthrown, and misery is the result.

It is seldom that a wealthy wife is able altogether to resist the temptation to use the power wealth gives, and to more or less upset thereby the natural relation of the sexes in her marriage.

To save your own powers, which are increased by headship and responsibility, and your own self-esteem, the counsel is repeated to take a woman to wife from a wealthy family only on one of the conditions named.

A husband should always be older than his wife. Five years' difference is little enough, and fifteen not too much. Plato advises a difference in age, between the contracting parties in marriage, of twenty years, and Lycurgus laid down the ages of marriage for the different sexes at thirty-seven for the man and seventeen for the woman. These differences are extreme, and demand too long a continence on the part of the male.

The reason why the man should be oldest, is that women lose their sexual attractions sooner than men, and depend for a happy marriage very much on them. Women at about the age of forty-five lose their capacity to have children, while men do not lose this capacity for an indefinite period after this age.

Thus a man marrying a woman of his own age, and, still more, marrying one older than himself, finds after a time the wife diminished in sexual attraction and altogether incapable of bearing children, while he still has the full activity and command of these his most vital functions. This is a dangerous condition for a marriage to get into. It should be counteracted by marrying a woman sufficiently younger than yourself to give a reasonable expectation that both will grow old in these functions together.

Too early marriage is not advisable in either sex. While the age of puberty in the male and in the female indicates the call of nature to reproduce, still we know that the first efforts of reproduction in the flowers and seeds of plants are often imperfect. This is probably true of animals, including man. Besides, the premature use of the generative functions and organs weakens the constitution and character, diminishes the prospect of life, and gives a progeny tending to retrogression rather than to improvement, and sometimes induces sterility.

From 18 to 20 is the best age for a bride, but 16 is not an impossible age. It is not advisable to take a woman as wife who is over 25. Some English statistics show that one marriage in fourteen of women between 15 and 19 is sterile, that nearly all marriages between 20 and 24 are fertile, and that after 24 the proportion of sterile marriages increases with the age of the bride. What these statistics are worth I do not know, nor how the proportion of one sterile marriage in fourteen before 20 is made up. It would seem probable that the first two or three years of this period, say 15, 16, and 17, would make the bulk of the sterility.

In this country the figures would not apply, as over most of our territory the age of puberty comes earlier than in England. Consequently the most fertile age would be from eighteen to twenty-two, if the distance from the age of puberty is a governing cause in woman's fertility and the English figures are authentic. Owing to the increased chance of sterility after twenty-four or twenty-five, that age in women is a pretty good limit to the wife chooser. One marriage in eight is unproductive of living children in England, one in four in Suffolk County, Mass., and probably the proportion of sterility is increasing. The importance of this question will therefore be seen.

In exceptional cases, such as a man marrying a second time when pretty well advanced in life himself, the rule may be relaxed. Under such conditions it might be better to take a good virgin old enough to understand herself, for youth and old age do not always make a happy combination in matrimony.

A woman married after thirty has increased difficulty in bearing children. This is owing to the lack of use of the reproductive parts, which by their disuse become stiff and less yielding and less normal in their action. For this reason first births after thirty have a larger proportion than usual of breech, side, and other presentations of the child more or less hard to deal with, and the perineum and cervix are oftener torn in such women. The proportion of the sexes of first-born is reversed from mothers between thirty and forty, and girls predominate.

The recent studies of Eckhardt (*Zeitschrift für Gebürtshulfe und Gynækologie*, xiv., 1, p. 44) confirming those of Kleinwachter show that the mortality of the children of primiparæ increases with the age of the mother. The mortality is nearly three times as great amongst old primiparæ as amongst the young. The difference becomes noticeable at twenty years of age and increases with accelerating rapidity in each period of four years afterwards. Forceps deliveries occur three times, and perforation five times, as often in old primiparæ as in young.

It may seem to some that all these conditions will be difficult to find in woman, and that marriage will consequently become uncertain on account of the impracticability of carrying out the rules in this chapter.

If such an idea takes possession of you, dismiss it at once. First, I would rather you should marry ill than not marry at all ; and second, the world is full of good girls who are healthy in body, morals, and mind.

The cause of the unhappiness of so many marriages is faulty education and breeding in both men and women. Women correctly educated are to be preferred as wives ; but a woman with the essentials wed to a man of some force, who has been educated in the realities of life, may be expected to turn out well. Women are impressionable, and therefore errors, especially errors of omission in their bringing up, can be overcome. They must be taken young, however, if any change is expected.

In old countries, the principal considerations in the choice of a wife are of a financial or social nature. In a new country, the choice of a wife depends more on personal appearance, character, etc. The latter are by far the safer guides. To make them perfect it is only essential that in youth the man should have become thoroughly impressed with the qualities which constitute a good woman, and familiarized with the object of marriage—that is, the getting of progeny and the consequent perpetuation of his life by means of them and their descendants.

Instinct guides a man to a type of woman best fitted to perpetuate the lives of both and leads him to lack interest in women of types unsuited to his own. In extreme youth this instinct is often immature. By means of romances and imperfect understanding, as well as by the incomplete development of the reproductive instinct, young people often make gross errors of choice, and sometimes come to consider that only one particular individual in the world can become their mates and be truly loved. These ideas, when carried to an extreme, result in much harm, sometimes in sickness, occasionally in suicide and murder when the desire is disappointed.

It is therefore well to bear in mind that this instinct we call love is really more for a type than for an individual, and that its concentration on one person is a matter of convenience which may be transferred to another. Not so the ripe love to a fertile spouse. Here the lives are fused indivisibly in the children. A true man once bound to a woman by this tie must always be bound to her in feeling.

The instinct of love is the outcome of the necessity of reproduction. The young man should respect the instinct, not to become its slave, but to look to it for light and guidance in the mystery of marriage. It has been often said that "love is blind." A saying nearer the truth would be that love can see the spiritual and vital harmonies best for immortality in the child. That a faulty education may destroy the strength and truth of love is only too apparent. The time has come for us to take off whatever bandages convention, ignorance, or error has placed over Love's eyes. Reason should be the salt with which to flavor love.

The only child-god of the ancients was " Cupid," the god of love. Here is a beautiful harmony of truth, the child the god of love. Nothing could be more true. ' Love is the spiritualized instinct of reproduction. In healthy bodies and minds it is confined, to be loosed only to persons of the opposite sex, whose age and vitality give promise of good progeny. Without the child there is no god of love. The child is the origin of love. Love is a sexual awakening that by instinct drives us to perpetuate ourselves. Without the child it is like the heavens without the sun. Without the child, love, born in us to bear again the child, must change. It may cool off to friendly liking, to a sentiment such as persons of the same sex feel for each other, or it may degenerate into fruitless lust where the wife is but a prostitute to one man.

We must admit that the romantic love leading to marriage changes in character afterward with or without the child. Without progeny, its change is for the worse, while with the child it may grow in strength and steadfastness.

In France and in most of the countries on the continent of Europe, a dot or dowry is required from the bride. Coincident with this rule is the custom of unduly immuring the young girls, and thus preventing a proper development of character. By this system the man sees little of the woman before marriage, and his matrimonial views are largely controlled by the size of the dot. Nature is put in a dark closet. I cannot believe that this system is one that will lead to a progressive and improved race. A further feature of this method is a liberty of the woman, after marriage, inconsistent with her previous training, and for which she is not prepared. Theoretically, this system appears indefensible. The dot makes money, and not physique or intellect, the guide in matrimony. And the education of the girl and the style of courtship make it difficult for the man to know anything about the character and type of the woman. Virtue alone is assured, and this in such a way as to make its subsequent maintenance by the woman doubtful. If the size of a dot was an unfailing guide, or any guide to a girl's suitability as a wife and future mother, something could be said for the system, but wealth is, at the best, for this purpose an unreliable guide for reasons already set forth.

A large dot may make a family wealthy, but wealth is not what we live for. As compared to the perpetuation and improvement of life in our children, it is as the refuse in a swill barrel to a Thanksgiving feast spread thick with richest viands.

While the French system does not seem good, there are suggestions in it that may lead to good. Marriages under this system are made according to reason. Instinct has little or no part in the matter. If the reason were but true and reliable, if the objects sought to be obtained were but the true interests of the individual and of the race, who can doubt but that the results of such a system would be better than our haphazard, happy-go-lucky total absence of method. Some things, however, must cause us to pause upon such a decision. If the instinct of love be too grossly violated, nature will be revenged. The intimacies of marriage leave one room enough to pay penalties for error. It is said by some that even sterility may result from a violation of the instincts leading up to reproduction.

Where you are favorably impressed with a young woman as a future wife, it will be well to make a business of seeing a number of the same type. If she be a German, go to a German quarter; if she be English, look up English people, and so on. The reason of this is that an individual representing a type favorable to you for reproduction, but new to you, may at once awaken a strong feeling of what is called love. You are attracted and commit yourself, when perhaps you might easily have found another member of the same type very superior to the one who has led you to perceive what type you should take.

It should also be taught to young men about to marry, that they ought to make a business of seeing under varying conditions those who attract them. Most of us have a mask we wear in public, and one not always easy to see behind. A young lady charming in social gatherings should therefore be sought unexpectedly and in situations where she may be presumed to be off her guard.

With some, love before marriage—that is, the feeling of attraction and desire for an individual—becomes passion, and is not to be regulated by the reason. With proper training beforehand, such cases ought to be rare. When cases of this kind threatening improper marriages occur, travel, separation, and new scenes afford the best antidote. Always in cases involving these instincts, management of a very judicious kind is required. Direct antagonism is seldom advantageous.

When you become engaged, marry. Make investigations and complete probations beforehand, but when you have made up your mind and obtained the woman's consent, complete the transaction at once. I think that a marriage quick from the engagement is the most likely to be happy. For a man of any warmth of feeling, to be engaged is to be in a sort of mild purgatory. If this state be prolonged, it cannot but react upon the health. The awakened reproductive instinct continually repressed may have very serious consequences upon the constitution.

Young women are less subject, but still subject, to the same suffering and injury. Dr. Goodell in his *Lessons in Gynecology*, page 365, attributes this as a frequent cause of uterine disease, and therefore advises against long engagements to marry, where the caresses sanctioned by custom in this country are permitted. He is also outspoken in condemning the kissing, hugging, and forfeit games common amongst our middle classes, for the same reason. I am able to confirm his statements by one or two instances that have come under my observation. Certainly mothers and girls themselves should be careful in these matters.

Use judgment and deliberation in choosing. The choice made— marry. I recommend you to choose by your twenty-fifth year.

Intemperance or insanity in a family should be a bar in marriage, for either of these in the parents will certainly transmit serious weakness to the children, while the appearance of such conditions in a brother or sister of the proposed bride will indicate a constitutional taint likely to break out in her children in some injurious form, if not insanity or intemperance, then consumption or other destructive disease.

You should not marry a consumptive, or one with syphilis or any constitutional disease. Close consanguinity in marriage, from the evidence at my command, is injurious when there is a taint in the family constitution, such as gout, consumption, etc. Otherwise, it seems to have no bad effects, except where long persisted in from generation to generation.

Advantageous variations of the individual amongst domesticated animals have been maintained and increased by careful breeding. One necessity for success in this is now recognized. It is in-breeding, with an occasional cross to add vigor in secondary characteristics, which, by the in-breeding for a special object, are becoming too weak.

In the thoroughbred horse, in the Jersey cow, in the Percheron stallion, and in the Durham bull we see the advantage and necessity of in-breeding to perpetuate superior qualities and its lack of destructive effects.

Still many curious things come out of excess of in-breeding : one is a great increase in the proportion of male to female progeny, and a tendency to sterility.

Doubtless attention to the digestion, vitality, bones, eyes, etc., of these animals would have made them as superior in these points as they are in those for which they are bred.

Amongst animal breeders even brothers and sisters are bred together. Weakness in reproduction is a frequent condition in high-bred animals. How far it may be due to in-breeding is now hard to say. Amongst men also, brothers and sisters as well as cousins and other close relatives have often been permitted to marry. The royal family of the Ptolemies in Egypt, of whom Cleopatra was the last, had a number of marriages between brothers and sisters and other close blood connections. The Ptolemies ruled in Egypt for a long period and probably will rank with the average royal families in all respects. Their frequent close in-breeding was not productive, and the royal line was in only two instances dependent on such marriages for its continuity. Other wives than those of the same family were the means of maintaining the dynasty.

The old myth of Isis and Osiris, a brother and sister married to each other, would indicate that this sort of marriage was not uncommon amongst the still more ancient Egyptians.

There are many reasons, however, to justify the universal rule of civilized nations against the marriage of brothers and sisters, and the almost universal prejudice, often re-enforced by rule, against the marriage of cousins.

This useful absence of sexual love amongst near kindred is now attributed to an instinct, evolved by its utility, against reproduction with those with whom we have been in close association from childhood. In man's regulation it takes the most extraordinary forms as seen in exogamy or the marrying outside of the tribe. In some

10

places (China) persons of the same clan name cannot marry, although not in any way related, while they can marry persons of different clan names to whom they are related.

It is needless to discuss the numerous degrees of consanguinity prohibited or discouraged by the rules of men. It is enough to say that the marriage of parents and children or children of the same family with each other should be barred. Beyond this there seems no good reason for going.

Constitutional taint transmits itself generally by producing its like, but oftentimes there is a sort of transmutation. Thus a consumptive may have consumptive children, but idiocy, insanity, spinal disease, deformity, intemperance, or constitutional immorality, all steadily tending to sterility, may be the outcome of such a marriage. When you find any weakness in yourself, do not on account of these remarks despair. The taint, if not too strongly established, may be eradicated.

I have known of such instances. Careful life under the best conditions and judicious breeding for several generations are necessary to achieve this result.

There is a large risk to be undertaken when marrying one who is diseased. Therefore, while the world has plenty of healthy women by whom you can strengthen your breed, do not marry weaklings, whose defects your children will at least require generations to eradicate. They may, you should remember, never succeed in doing this, the eventful result being to sink your life in theirs under an impossible load.

It is well, as has been said, to avoid *only* children in marriage. Such a child is very precious to its parents. The attention of these is concentrated upon it. The value the parents set on the life of an only child is so great that they generally keep the precious one from every possible risk. This course prevents a due and natural development of self-reliance and character; therefore *only* children are rarely distinguished in after life.

The large value set on them generally results in coddling and pampering, which treatment reacts unfavorably on the child's nature. Only too often do we see the only child ruined, or as it is commonly called spoiled, by the affection of the parents. These misguided ones implant in it vanity, self-sufficiency, bad manners, and withal a plentiful lack of character.

The parental feeling of tenderness, which removes every possible obstacle from the path of the child, removes also the only means the child has for development of force and character.

Speaking generally, the best promise at once of fertility and of a well-formed character is found in girls members of large families. If the parents have had large families, the girls may be expected to inherit their reproductive powers. With many brothers and sisters the edge of unreasonable selfishness and other bad character traits is likely to be taken off. The statistics of T. W. Hollands show that morality is more common in large families than in small ones. Sir W. Gull says that the members of large families furnish the strongest members of the Indian Civil Service (Finck). Franklin advises a wife-seeker to take her out of a bunch of sisters.

Dr. Chervin, a distinguished statistician, states that in the departments of Eure, Oise, Orne, and Lower Seine, where the families have less children, the number of recruits discharged from the military service for physical disability is the greatest. Dr. Luis de Séré says that in French families with a small number of children these are less healthy and vigorous than the progeny of large families. He attributes small families to preventive measures taken by the married. Regarding one of these known as "withdrawal," in which the sexual act is not completed, he cites physicians' opinions to the effect that it is the cause of much ill-health, especially of those forms of progressive paralysis which of late have been spreading so widely. De Séré also expresses the opinion very strongly that all such measures exert a deplorable effect on the cerebro-spinal system in man, and also that such children as are born under these conditions tend to weakness and inferiority. The woman also is injured through excitement without complete satisfaction. The results appear most in her uterus. *Only* children are therefore not desirable. The way things are going it will be next to impossible to marry into an American family if a large number of children is necessary for a choice.

We cannot be strict in this rule, but still avoid an only child. While Americans continue to have two to a marriage the difficulty of securing a proper virgin for a wife, when found, may be reduced by the knowledge of what a woman admires.

The female in marriage needs protection. It is therefore easy to understand that she likes courage and daring in a man as well as energy and force.

A person of one sex is under difficulties when undertaking to portray the inner feelings of those of the opposite sex. There is an element of error in all such portrayals against which we should guard.

It is, however, a fair presumption that the novels written by men, taking them as a class, portray the qualities of woman most admired by men, and with equal reason we may expect the novels of women will portray the qualities of men most admired by women.

In glancing through a large number of books by men, we find their favorite women characters peculiarly feminine, and, on the other hand, the favorite male characters in women's novels are forceful and masculine, often to an extravagant extent. The difficulty of man in fathoming the heart of woman is somewhat removed by the unconscious exposition of a woman's own heart, which her novel is. As is the excellence of the novel so is the truth of her own reflection. Women's novel heroes are often portrayed as ugly but not weak.

A study of women's novels will show a man that he has nothing to hope for in gaining a woman's love by throwing away his manhood and his manliness.

A woman studying men's novels will find little encouragement to the masculine type of women for securing the love of man.

A man seeking a wife, therefore, should never neglect to make an aggressive and persistent fight for the woman he loves. Some strategy, however, is not out of place. Long absences cool love and diminish interest, but short ones intensify the fire. Thus a lover, if he finds his suit not progressing favorably, may increase the girl's interest by a short absence, and increase by the same opportunity for reflection his own inventions and energy for conquest.

Many minor matters, looking to successful love-making, might be suggested, but the instinct of love is so domineering when it takes possession of one, that advice to the lover is like water to the back of a duck. Neither make any impression. What we must work for is to form the character beforehand, so that love will take the true course and attach the young man to the proper type of persons only. The reason may eventually be a better guide to marriage than is love. This can hardly be said to be the case now.

An inquiry well worthy of attention is the effect of the vocation of the parents upon their children. Dr. Down, in the *Medical Record*, has given a number of figures on this point. He says that the percentage of idiots and of persons afterward eminent in the whole population born to fathers in three of the professions is :

	Idiots.	*Eminent Men.*
Lawyers . . .	3 per cent.	11 per cent.
Doctors . . .	4 " "	9 " "
Clergymen . .	18 " "	4 " "

As far as these figures are reliable, they show either that the strongest minds tend to select the law or medicine as a profession, and the weakest, theology, or that the effect upon the parent of these vocations is very different.

A woman complete and sound on the reproductive question, both as to wish and capacity, comprises in this qualification all things necessary for a wife. For this she must be suitable to the man in type, of sound body and developed intellect, and withal well reared in manners and modesty. She must be a virgin, and possess a strong instinct of motherhood. She must be so possessed of virtue that her husband may feel complete security in the paternity of his children.

The writings of Francis Galton and of Henry Maudsley show the influence of heredity on the capacity of the individual. Read them, so that you will understand the importance of some investigation into the family record of a proposed mate. You cannot find the perfect in humanity; it would be but a waste of time to look for it. On the other hand, it is of great importance to you to avoid unions with families that are behind the average in either physique or brain capacity, or tending to sterility.

You cannot make a silk purse out of a sow's ear. Bad seed, poor crop. Bad mother, poor child. The choice of a wife is the one event of life more than any other which establishes our happiness or misery here, and, through our children, our destiny in ages to come.

Some appreciate its importance so much that the instinct of reproduction is overcome, and they never marry. This is like the sailor on the desert island with two lots of food, one poisoned, the other good. In this story the sailor, fearing the poison, ate neither, and died of starvation. By a little judicious tasting, the sailor could doubtless have discriminated between the two foods, but in any case it would have been the part of wisdom to have selected one of the foods and eaten. In that way he would have had one chance out of two for life, while a refusal to eat meant a painful and slow death by starvation. So in marrying, you may be successful or you may not, but choose a wife you must. The question is one of life or death. Children and immortality in promise, or death and extermination in sterility.

If the choice of a wife gives you the disaster of a sterile woman, you must divorce her and choose again. No children is the one thing that is beyond all pardon in a wife. Knowing the risks, use care in choosing; but, knowing also the certainty of extermination without children, do what you must bravely and in time. If you fail, you may still choose again. Choose then wisely if you can, but choose, and do it in your prime.

The orange blossom is the emblem of marriage. It is the flower of that fruit which produces more to the acre than any other known in the temperate zone. It is the emblem of fertility. So wisely chosen an emblem should point the married to the great object of married life—that is, to fruits.

CHAPTER V.

THE CHILD.

THE treatment of the child involves so much more than it is ordinarily considered to do, and the improvement of our immortality as represented by the child is of such paramount importance, that it seems reasonable to consider this subject from a very wide point of view.

Our lives are affected by events of to-day and still more by those accumulated influences from the past ages of the world's history. Those events already accomplished are beyond our control. The effects of our deeds will likewise be beyond the control of our descendants. While the past cannot be changed, it may still act as a guide to prevent the repetition of error. Thus is the utility of the study of the bygone made clear. The history of a family is interesting in its indications of the weaknesses to be anticipated and overcome, and of the strong points to be developed and brought out in the children of such families.

These ancient influences may well deserve our attention and repay some study, in that they show the importance of regulating our own lives to secure the best heritage of health and character for our children. We may transmit an inheritance physical, mental, and moral from our life of to-day to our lives of to-morrow. The inheritance may be one for salvation or one for damnation.

It rests largely with the individual as to which it shall be. As we are influenced and our lives colored by the acts of our fathers, mothers, grandfathers, grandmothers, and ancestors, so our children's lives will be largely stamped and controlled by what we do before their birth. A young man or woman who contracts preventable disease through ignorance, carelessness, or folly, and thereby injures the physique, or who by idleness or excess enters the camp of vice and thereby injures the moral nature as well as the physical, is injuring not only himself or herself, but is likewise inaugurating a line of suffering and misery that may, through children, curse his or her life through indefinite ages, or it may exterminate such person altogether.

The law of Moses expresses this penalty (we must say dreadful penalty) clearly enough : " I, the Lord thy God, am a jealous God, visiting the iniquities of the fathers upon the children unto the third and fourth generation of them that hate me." As we suffer in constitutional defects, or gain in force either physical or moral, or both, from the acts of our ancestors, so will our children suffer for our bad acts or benefit by our good ones for periods of indefinite time. Thus our own suffering for sin must go on in our children, and in them we ourselves have a direct personal suffering, for we are the child and the child is ourselves.

From these considerations, conduct leading to physical or moral deterioration will have less standing and less excuse as the results of such acts are understood ; while conduct leading to physical and moral health, and consequently to happiness, will be given increased incentive with the increased knowledge of the duration of the reward.

So in the treatment of children, the first point is the treatment of ourselves even long before the period of conception of the child, for we thus treat the child in futuro. These are matters to impress upon the young, for doubtless by such means increased value will be set on physical and intellectual work and upon morality.

While physical, intellectual, and moral activity is essential to those who would bear children equal to or better than themselves, it must also be remembered that excessive physical work, over-athletic training, and exhausting mental exercise are alike opposed to reproduction. The vitality of the individual is increased and maintained by a due amount of physical and mental work. No one can be healthy without this, and no one can be the parent of a sound child without reasonable bodily and mental exercise. But excessive or premature effort of body or mind exhausts the vitality, though the muscle or brain tissue, according to the line of activity, may be increased.

By such means the development of the whole man becomes uneven and one-sided. Thus our years may be shortened by too much athletics as well as by too sedentary a life ; the mind may become deranged by the overwork of a business or literary man as well as by the intellectual inactivity of the shepherd or of the prisoner in solitary confinement.

Excess of idleness or excess of work tends to extermination. The effect on the individual is of necessity reflected in his reproductive powers. In idleness, license and lust prostitute and injure the body, morals, and mind. Through the non-use of bodily and mental qualities, the vigor of these disappears, leaving a hyper-delicacy and refinement which dims, if it does not extinguish, sexual feeling and the reproductive instinct ; or it may abnormally develop this, with an equally exterminating effect. Such children as are born under either condition will tend to be inferior to the life, at its commencement, of the parent, and will tend to reflect the parent's condition at the time of fertilization and conception.

On the other hand, exhausting body or mind work will weaken the sexual and reproductive instincts as well as the vitality of the individual, so that a parent thus worked out will be unable to transmit superiorities of muscle or mind acquired, by the excessive strain practised. Men of the greatest muscle and athletic power and men of transcendent mind development, whom we call geniuses, have, as a rule, no children or children of inferior constitution and rarely transmit the superior endowments of the parent.

We must not suppose from this that superior power of body or mind is opposed and fatal to reproduction, or that improved qualities can not be transmitted.

Man has continually progressed through many ups and downs from a universal use of rough stone instruments to the civilization of to-day. The progress has been chiefly mental. Mental work, impossible to primitive man, is doubtless easy and commonplace to the higher types of to-day. We may affirm this from the fact that tribes of men in a condition similar, as to the use of tools, to what all primitive men at one time were in, have a mental capacity inferior to our own, and an average brain weight of males running six to twelve ounces less than the brain weights of native male Americans.

Thus the genius of these people might have a brain below our average. Mental work in such a savage genius, that would prevent reproduction, at least with improvement, would with our average man be perhaps insufficient to produce the best results in his children.

There is an amount of work excessive and opposed to the best results in reproduction, which varies according to the development and power of the individual. What we must look to in this matter is a conservation of vitality with which to reproduce acquired improvements. Work alone will give us this vitality, and work alone will give the improvement to transmit. Excessive work may give an improvement to the individual, but through an exhausted vitality such improvement cannot be transmitted. Idleness is fatal. While overwork may not be fatal, or may be recovered from, the effects of idleness prolonged to the second generation are rarely overcome.

Each individual must draw the line for him or herself. It should never be forgotten that the brain power giving intellect and a possibility of the highest morality of the superior races of the world is a precious inheritance, the result of indefinite ages of time in development through pain, sacrifice, and sorrow. To perpetuate this brain power is a duty, to improve it a grand achievement.

It is a great misfortune to the world to have one superior brain lost in sterility. The work of a Shakespeare will not compensate for the loss of a Shakespearian mind. A Shakespeare's mind transmitted with its full force may compose poems and plays at any time. Such a mind once lost, what ages will it take to develop another so great. Certainly Shakespeare's children did not show his mental power. Whether this was owing to a great inferiority of brain in his wife compared to his own, excessive brain work, or to something else, such as dissipation, etc., we cannot say. A race-horse bred to an ass may produce a very fine mule, but always a mule—ears, heels, and sterility,—and never a race-horse. Thus a Shakespeare, to perpetuate his mental qualities in any force, must breed to a woman with a brain of at least good development, and can expect but poor progeny from a woman whose brain is below the average of her sex in the class to which the man belongs.

It may be said that the intellect of husband or wife, whichever be the stronger, must be modified and diminished by the ever inferiority of the mind of one of the partners. It is true that this adulteration will pull down the higher, but, also, it will improve the lower, and with the child the improvement gains the possibility of permanence.

No written book or individual act can perpetuate life as does the child. Books and acts may be forgotten, or deemed right to-day may be found wrong to-morrow. Of the billions on billions of men who have lived, how few are remembered ; of the millions on millions of writings that have been made, how few are of use to-day.

The transmitted intellect, however, will live, and though its achievement be lessened to-day, by the necessity of reproduction, its possibilities of achievement in the future are unbounded.

The slowness of evolution and improvement must not discourage us. When we reflect upon the extraordinary development of man since the historical period commenced, and upon the fact that our own race is of recent emergence from barbarism, with no probable physical inheritance from Egyptian, Greek, or Roman, or any other highly civilized race, we may be surprised at the shortness of our development, reckoning by generations. Two hundred and fifty generations, calculating each one at twenty-five years, carries us beyond the accepted age of history, say seven thousand years. Fifty-six generations will more than cover the development of the Anglo-Saxon race from a condition of barbarism to its present high estate.

While appreciating the difficulties before us in the attempt to reach immortality through our children and to improve them to a point not now comprehensible, we must not exaggerate these difficulties.

For the purposes of this chapter, the treatment of a child may be said to commence at conception. But, while this limitation is set, it is only so set because the chapter would be otherwise, and properly, a history and catechism of life. The treatment of every child born and to be born has been going on from time immemorial, and every act done, or to be done, was or is to be a treatment of the child. Such a discussion of this subject would require a library in itself.

These reasons make it perhaps permissible to take up the treatment of the child when its individual life commences.

The first budding life of the child, still unrecognizable in its individuality, involves the existence of all the lives and influences which enter into it and of the universe itself. It will be apparent to any reasonable person that all human qualities, whether physical, intellectual, or moral, that will preserve or improve, should be guarded and developed, while such as tend in an opposite direction should be discouraged and if possible destroyed; all for the sake of one's self renewed or to be renewed in the child.

When the spermatozoön of the male meets and fertilizes the ovum in the female, a new life has commenced and the lives of the father and mother are renewed. Let us proceed to the treatment of the mother and child from this period.

Conception in the vast majority of cases takes place from sexual connection either a day or two before or a few days after the menstrual flow. Its most marked and general first sign is a cessation of the menstrual flow. The other signs may be learned in an obstetrical work. The duration of pregnancy is about 278 days. The extreme term is set down by Playfair at 295 days, by L. M. Maur at 334 days, and by Simpson at 336 days.

Dr. E. J. Abbott of St. Paul, Minnesota, reports a case in which the last menstrual period occurred on April 3 to 6, 1888; symptoms of pregnancy commenced about May 1st; quickening was clear and certain in October; delivery occurred April 20, 1889, a term of over a year: the child was taken by forceps and weighed ten and one half pounds.

Pregnancy is the condition of a woman after conception and until the child is born. The simplest method of calculating the probable time of delivery of a child in utero is, add seven to the date of commencement of the last menses and then count back three months: thus, if the last menses commenced on November 5th, we add seven which makes twelve, and count back three months and determine August 12th as the probable day of delivery.

From the moment of conception the mother should avoid nervous or physical shocks or undue strain upon the nervous system. On the other hand both mind and body should be occupied with some useful work. In this connection, it may be well to call attention to the fact that work to which the pregnant woman is accustomed is safest. Thus horseback riding is exceedingly dangerous for a pregnant woman, still I have known the case of a woman who being an habitual rider continued this exercise after conception and nearly to the day of the child's birth without ill effect. There are certain kinds of exercise, and horseback riding is one, that should, as a rule, be avoided.

Overhand movements are bad, as are any exercises in which jars, jerks, or falls are likely to occur. Miscarriage is somewhat more likely to happen about the times the menses would have appeared had not pregnancy supervened. The seven or eight days corresponding to these periods, therefore, should be specially watched to prevent misfortune.

Dr. Verdi's advice in his book *Maternity* is good. "Take daily exercise in the open air ; do not lace, do not run, do not jump ; do not drive unsafe horses ; give up dancing and horseback riding ; do not plunge into cold water. Many women, in your condition, will tell you they have done these things and no harm befell them ; still, do none of them." To this may be added : Do not drive over rough roads or engage in exercises where overhand or reaching movements are required, such as clothes-hanging, etc. It is also said by Holbrook, that treadle work, as on a sewing-machine or organ, is bad. When an accident does happen that is deemed liable to bring on a miscarriage, rest and your physician are the friends to invoke. Everything should be done to quiet the woman's apprehensions, for the fear of the loss may be so strong as to bring on the abortion which otherwise would not have occurred.

Miscarriage sometimes happens without any sufficient apparent cause ; in other cases nothing seems able to produce it. Perhaps no authenticated relation will do so much to tranquillize a woman, at this time, as that of the native in Bombay, who, when far advanced in her term, was knocked down in the street by an English physician's horse and run over by the wheel of his carriage. His interest and fears followed her case and to his wonder everything went on as though nothing had happened.

Exercise and work have other excellent reasons to be practised. Of a moderate kind, they are essential to the welfare of both mother and child. By such means the woman's constitution is kept up and through it the child's also. Malformation in the child or unusual presentation at birth becomes less likely. The muscles of the woman are kept in better tone and the birth will be shorter and easier, and the recovery of the woman prompter, than if useful outdoor exercise had not been had.

As a rule, pregnant women have an instinctive desire to seek seclusion. It is a useful safeguard within proper limits. This feeling protects women in this interesting condition from the risks and dangers which a general participation in the outside activities of life would incur. Thus, they avoid balls, crowds, travelling, etc. This is good. Amongst civilized women, however, the instinct often induces to a morbid avoidance of all outdoor life and of social recreation of any kind. A pregnant women should be encouraged to visit her friends, to take reasonable social recreation, and to maintain quiet outdoor life and interest up to the latest possible period. A woman mewed up alone in this condition tends to a dwelling upon dangers she imagines, to a nursing of customary symptoms into disease, to abnormal fancies and to magnifying minor troubles into a real suffering. Therefore, while appreciating the fundamental advantage of the instinct for seclusion, its abuse should be carefully warded off. If no other ill happens, such excess of seclusion will make the woman's life so much a burden by loneliness and deprivation of customary resources that she will dread pregnancy. Thus must grow a feeling antagonistic to the family and to its immortality. The benefit of the doubt should be given toward doing too much rather than doing too little.

The retiring disposition of women, when pregnant, is most prominent in cities. In city life such feeling must be accentuated both through the number of persons the woman meets when out, and also by the general attitude of antagonism to childbirth in our Sodoms and Gomorrahs. From these facts, it will be seen that a country life is an essential to the mother of a family, both as to her health and comfort and as to that of the children she bears. It must be said, however, that city women walk more, as a general rule, than do country ones. Shopping and gadding about the streets is doubtless a cause of a good deal of exercise to these women. The woman in the country is not from that fact alone living a healthy life. She must have a useful occupation. Exercise for health is so monotonous that it is rarely long continued. It may be helped by games, but utility or object is that alone upon which the parturient woman must rely to keep up a good muscular and mental condition of the system. City life is objectionable from another point of view, and that is, that it is in all probability exterminating to the race as it is now constituted. Children in the country have a great advantage over those in the city, physically, mentally, and morally. On account of the earlier sexual development of city-reared children, I was under the impression that there would also be a mental precocity among them. On an investigation of this subject I find that this is not the case. All the teachers I have questioned, with city and country experience, state to me that, at the same age, children in the country have a better and stronger brain development than those in the city. The risks of disease, such as puerperal fever in the mother and the diseases of childhood in the babes are much reduced in the country.

The diet of the mother should be nutritious and easy of digestion.[1] The common idea that she should eat for two is a mistake. Her appetite when eating slowly will be a safe guide in a great majority of cases for the quantity of food. Certain cravings frequently occur at this time. When there is nothing clearly harmful in them they should be gratified.

Inconveniences of various kinds often occur to women during gestation,—morning sickness, constipation, etc. Considerable fruit in the diet seems beneficial in both these cases. When such troubles become serious and affect the health of the mother, or endanger the carrying of the child, a physician must be called.

The situation of the house is important. It should be sunny, well drained, accessible to pure water, and the soil under it healthy. The drinking-water and drainage should be examined with special care. Drinking-water is a general means for the maintenance and diffusion of certain disease germs. Well water is always dangerous, and river water, in a settled country where the domestic drainage and refuse of the population is certain to more or less pollute it, is also to be avoided. All water for drinking should be boiled before-hand for the purpose of killing any germs or parasitic life it may contain. This rule should only be relaxed when the source of supply and its watershed are thoroughly known.

In a dry country, where the waters are heavily charged with alkalies, some provision of rain water or distilled water should be made, especially where the individual tendency is toward the forma-tion of calculi. The importance of care with drinking-water is shown by the study of epidemics. The typhoid-fever epidemic at Plymouth, Pa., was directly traced to one case on the bank of the stream supplying the town with water. Very many sufferers and a large number of deaths were the result of this epidemic.

Recently the chronic cholera prevailing at the Takashima Coal Mines, Japan, has been completely stopped by the substitution of distilled water for that brought from the mainland, while the islands

[1] See Chapter on Treatment of Wife.

about, using the old supply, still continue to be devastated by this fell disease.

The Chinese city of Canton is on a nearly level plain. It has no system of sewerage. The refuse water and filth flow off in shallow drains in the middle of the streets with slabs of stone over them. Part of the time even these are choked up. The dung and urine, however, are to a great extent taken away as fertilizers. The water supply of this great and filthy city is derived from wells four to fifteen feet in depth. The comparative healthiness of Canton must be attributed to the practice of drinking only boiled water, as in tea. Villages are not as desirable as the country, plain and simple.

Around the woman objects of beauty should be placed and also things that will lead to high thoughts of heroic deeds and great performances. The books read should also be of superior character. In the courts of Europe, amongst the ruling families, where the welfare of the children to be born, who will become nobles and kings, is much considered, the rooms of lying-in women are carefully arranged. Beautiful pictures, statues, and works of art adorn the chambers, and the mental condition of the wife is much looked after at this time. The story of Jacob and Laban shows that the surroundings of animals, as they conceive, were recognized as important in ancient times. Jacob and Laban made a bargain that for certain services Jacob was to receive the parti-colored animals of the flocks and herds. Jacob then placed before the stronger animals at the watering-places streaked stakes, so that these animals should conceive among them. The story goes that he waxed rich by this arrangement. The strong animals, owing to their environment, produced a large proportion of parti-colored young. We suppose, too, that the frequent resemblance that insects and animals bear to their surroundings is not only a survival of the fittest and a result of natural selection, but also a tendency of life in reproduction to be impressed by the conditions under which conception takes place. There is a general opinion that sudden frights, impressive events, and, in general, unusual circumstances or sights experienced or seen by pregnant women may influence the character or appearance of the child in utero. This opinion has sufficient support to warrant attention. The following is one of many cases that might be cited :

CIRCUMCISED BY A MATERNAL IMPRESSION.

Dr. John G. Harvey, of Blue Mound, Ill., relates the following: "On August 11, 1884, I performed the operation of circumcision on a boy, three years of age, for the relief of a nervous trouble. On March 31, 1885, just seven months and twenty days later, his mother gave birth to a boy who was as perfectly circumcised as the child upon whom I had operated ; even the scars from the sutures were reproduced in the exact numbers and location of those on the organ of the boy upon whom I had operated."—*Medical Record*, Nov. 3, 1888.

PRE-NATAL CIRCUMCISION.

To THE EDITOR OF THE *Medical Record.*

SIR—In the *Medical Record* of November 3, 1888, page 535, I reported a case of circumcision by maternal impression.

In the *Medical Record*, of December 15, 1888, Dr. M. G. Lowrey, of Boulder, Col., thinks the case of so much importance to the profession that it should be established beyond question. I therefore enclose the certificate of Dr. R. Tobey, who assisted me in the operation and afterward attended the mother in confinement.

I do not propose to account for the phenomenon on a scientific basis, but can furnish the doctor and the professor with indisputable evidence as to the facts.

J. G. HARVEY, A.M., M.D.

Blue Mound, Ill., February 10, 1889.

[COPY.]

I hereby certify that I assisted Dr. Harvey in circumcising the son of Mr. S——, as reported in the *Medical Record* of November 3, 1888, and that I attended his mother in confinement on March 31, 1885, just seven months and twenty days after the operation, at which time she was delivered of a male child, which was perfectly circumcised, and presented exactly the appearance of having been circumcised in the same manner as the boy previously operated upon, even showing the marks of each suture.

R. TOBEY, M.D.

Macon, Ill., February 10, 1889.

I have been unable to find any similar record of pre-natal circumcision amongst the Jews. The long-established custom of the Jews would doubtless tend to prevent the performance of circumcision from so much affecting a Jewish mother.

If the extraordinary has such influence in one event, it is but reasonable to suppose that the every-day and oft repeated events of a mother's life must influence the life of the child. Some physicians think that it is not so much some particular event that influences the child in utero, as it is the mother's dwelling on the event, or dreading its effect on the child, that is likely to influence it. A number of cases have been collected to sustain this point. There can be little doubt that maternal dread of an evil influence on a child in utero would tend to produce the effect dreaded, or by the nervousness induced lower the child's vitality. The mother, therefore, should be informed of these tendencies. Some physicians deem influence of events in the mother's life to be without effect on the child in utero. The weight of testimony and the general indications of nature in evolution and development indicate some effects as being produced by circumstances occurring during gestation.

As poor food for the body taken by the mother will weaken the constitution of the child, so poor food for the mother's mind will be likely to affect the capacities of her child, and so the probability extends to all things entering into the mother's life.

Dr. Wm. Hunter, of England, undertook a scientific examination into the effects upon the child in utero of circumstances or shocks occurring in the life of the mother. He questioned two thousand mothers immediately after delivery as to influences that they could think of as likely to affect the appearance of the child that occurred during gestation. He then examined the child, and in no case found any correspondence or connection in the condition of the child with the circumstances related. He found marks where nothing gave expectation of them, and found none where severe shocks and fright had been experienced.

While this physician's testimony will not entirely overthrow other contrary testimony, it must lend a color to the opinion that some of the authenticated cases of birth-marks corresponding with maternal impressions might be due to an accidental concatenation of circumstances rather than to a real impression upon the fœtus through the mother. At least, such extreme views as those of Mrs. Kirby and Mrs. Farnham are not sustained. Were their views correct as to the over-powering influence of the life and thought of the mother, while pregnant, upon the child, we should find it impossible to account for the frequent preponderance of the father's physique and character in the child except upon the hypothesis that the mother herself is continually impressed by the father. As the mother might be equally or more impressed by other men, and as children are not observed to resemble those about the mother in moral families, this hypothesis will not help us to avoid the difficulty.

Galton, in tracing out the parental influences upon eminent men, finds that the father's is more often noticed in all pursuits except that of the divine. In that occupation alone does the influence of the mother preponderate. Galton's figures are as follows: In 100 cases of judges, statesmen, commanders, men of literature or men of science, 70 are found to derive their talent mainly from the father and 30 mainly from the mother. In 100 poets, 94 will be found to derive their talents mainly from the father and 6 only from the mother. In 100 artists, 85 have their talents from the father and 15 from the mother. In 100 religious teachers these proportions are reversed, and the ratio is 73 to 27 in favor of the mother. In musicians the talent comes very rarely through the female line,—in the wonderful Bach family, for instance, not in a single instance. Galton's figures, however, are considered by him as more likely to err against the influence of the mother than for it on account of the difficulty of tracing the female line. He finds as the degrees of relationship are removed that the female influence rapidly weakens, perhaps largely due to the cause named. For instance, of kinships of eminent men in the second degree he finds 41 through the male line and 19 through the female; in the third degree he finds 19 kinships through the male and 1 only through the female. Galton also calls attention to the fact that male qualities not visibly possessed by the mother may still be transmitted through her.

Dr. H. R. Storer states that hereditary insanity flows more commonly from the father than from the mother. A child with an insane mother, therefore, is more apt to escape the taint than one with an insane father. He states the same thing as true in regard to hereditary alcoholism.

Fournier shows that there are numerous cases of women infected through the fœtus with syphilis; the father being in the non-contagious stages of the disease at the time of conception, and the mother never having had the initial lesions. So also children have been born with constitutional syphilis, though the mother had never suffered from it, the disease coming from the father. Two cases have recently been reported from Scotland by Dr. Felkin, of Edinburgh, where the fœtus suffered distinct intermittent malarial chills in utero and where the infants were born with enlarged spleens. In the first case the child had seven chills after birth, but recovered. In the second case the child had two chills, the first followed by fever, temp. 102°; it died in the cold stage of the second attack, twenty-four hours after the first. In neither case was the residence malarious. In neither case had the mother ever had malaria. In both cases the husbands were suffering at the time of conception with severe malaria contracted abroad.

On the other hand, according to Galton (natural inheritance), consumption is nearly always inherited from the mother; that is, a child with a consumptive father has a good chance to escape the malady, while the chance for a child with a consumptive mother to escape is poor. It may in this case be reasonably supposed that the almost inevitable intimacy of mother and child might infect the child with the mother's disease after the birth of the child.

We cannot reconcile these results with a preponderating influence of pre-natal surroundings or occurrences upon the mother. It is, however, certain that every circumstance in our lives previous to the creation of a child will, to some extent, influence that child, and we may well suppose that circumstances immediately previous to conception are more influential upon the child than remote occurrences of equal importance.

It would seem upon the whole that circumstances of life in the father and mother immediately previous to or at conception are those most likely to impress the type of the offspring. In evolution it is pretty well demonstrated that the parent has the power to impress its progeny with a tendency to vary towards a harmony with surrounding conditions. At any rate, we observe that the seed of wheat grown in the north for several seasons will mature earlier when planted in the south than seed from wheat grown in the locality. So, also, the northern seed will stand frost the best. Farmers avail themselves of these tendencies in seeds for their own benefit. So, also, with trees having a wide range of habitat, we observe that the seeds produced by individuals in the extremes of a tree's range will give seedlings in each case better adapted to the locality where produced, than the seed from the same kind of tree in the other extreme of its habitat. The same thing will help us to account for such comparatively rapid changes in man as that divergence of type found in the American descendant of the English Puritans.

Geoffroy Saint-Hilaire shows that monstrosities in the fœtus are recognizable very early in gestation. M. Dareste's investigations confirm this fact, which indicates that monstrosities are probably such from the very moment of fertilization. On the other hand, Flourens produced red coloring in the bones of the fœtus of a female mammal by feeding madder, and Coste's experiments with salmon trout showed that the eggs when placed in water where only the white trout lived became pale and the fish lost their red color. These facts indicate a great influence upon the still unborn by the surroundings of their gestation. We should, therefore, do all that is reasonably possible to have the circumstances surrounding conception and gestation of the most favorable kind. Healthy, beautiful, moral, and improving surroundings are of great importance to the parturient woman, for the conditions of life of the woman will, of necessity, impress the child indirectly if not directly. It is not demonstrated, as yet, that environment affects the fœtus, still there is sufficient ground for such an opinion to warrant the precautions suggested.

Work is of great value to the child when performed by the woman before its birth, therefore we may repeat the advice that a wife should always have some useful occupation or occupations in which she will be employed before conception, to gain the habit of work, and to make it safe after conception, during which time she will continue the work to secure an easy labor and prompt recovery. The main object of this course is for the benefit of the child's physical and moral strength. Work prevents feelings of loneliness, discontent, and the abnormal development of passion. It is a great safeguard to the woman, and cannot but be beneficial in its influence upon the character and constitution of the conceived but unborn child.

Birth is the time from which, by a convenient convention, we date the individual life of each human being. It is indeed an important moment. The mother at this time should be in a sunny and well-ventilated apartment and at home. No stationary drain pipe or wash basin should be in the room. If it seems impossible to avoid this, close any such breeding-place and highway of disease tightly, by means of corks. Stationary wash-stands are ugly and dangerous. The best plumbing I have seen will not make them thoroughly safe. Their dangers are out of sight and often odorless. Traps, which are relied on, with pipe ventilation, to prevent sewer gas from coming into the room, do not wholly shut it off; and, besides, it requires but a short length of pipe to produce gases, which, if not filled with disease germs, still 'so lower the general vitality of a person long exposed to them as to render the individual less able to resist a shock of nature or to overcome disease germs introduced in other ways. The long and close confinement of mother and child after labor causes the condition of the indoor air to be a matter of special importance.

A quiet and reliable midwife should be employed. Great care should be exercised in such a selection. In case the means of the family render such professional aid impossible, a relative or friend may be secured to help the mother. A good and experienced physician should be in attendance to render aid should nature seem incapable of completing the task.

Anæsthetics are used a great deal in labor. How far the weakness of civilized women may make this advisable it is difficult to say, but a common-sense view points strongly to the propriety of a much lessened use of this practice. Chloroform and its allies, from the information at my command and as usually given—that is, before the extreme pain of expulsion—lengthen labor, cause the pains to come more slowly, increase the danger of post-partum hemorrhage, and delay recovery. On the other hand, by their use the supreme pains of delivery at the close of the third stage are passed in unconsciousness or semi-consciousness. The administration of chloroform in a judicious manner is not accompanied by danger ; only one death is on reliable record of a woman in labor under the influence of chloroform. When, however, an excessive amount is given prematurely, and say to the point of muscular relaxation, it may well be doubted whether chloroform does not in a secondary way cause death to the mother or to the child in numerous cases, although the death of the mother does not take place under the influence of the anæsthetic.

Indirectly chloroform may advance the interests of the family by encouraging women, otherwise too fearful of the labor pains, to bear children. Anæsthetics in labor on many occasions are invaluable. The use of these agents is probably now abused. The bad effects of chloroform arise largely from its use prematurely in labor. It should in almost all cases be confined to the last and supreme pains which expel the child. These it mitigates. In the primipara the perineum is liable to laceration and especially so in the case of strong, athletic, high-type women.

Chloroform properly applied is deemed a preventive of this. Its action, if favorable, is probably accomplished by a general relaxation and by a diminution of the co-operation in expulsion of the voluntary muscles.

This subject is worthy of careful study. The weight of medical testimony is decidedly in favor of the use of chloroform at the proper time in childbirth when indicated. The most phenomenally successful obstetrician whose record I am acquainted with, Dr. Henry Worthington of Los Angeles, Cal., never uses an anæsthetic when he can avoid it. Chloroform should in no case be given by gaslight. It combines with gas and forms an irrespirable vapor, C.O.Cl². A number of fatal results in general hospital practice have been noted recently as due to this cause. It is well to have chloroform together with forceps, scissors, catheter, thread to tie the severed cord, etc., ready at hand to use if required.

The occasional benefit of chloroform and similar drugs in labor may have for its cause the simulation of death by certain of the nerve centres. We know that in trees, plants, and animals there is often noticed a desperate attempt at reproduction when by a wound or otherwise death threatens ; and this too in spite of the fact that the attempt to live on in a new generation hastens the death of the individual. This is the philosophy of pruning fruit trees, and is at the bottom of the extraordinary numbers of oranges and other fruits frequently seen on trees wounded to death by gophers or by other means.

Judging by analogy one would be justified in concluding that any such disarrangement of nature's work in healthy human individuals could not generally be productive of good. For the advantage of pruning is where the tree goes to wood, not to fruit, and the wound awakens the dormant reproductive powers, or redundant fruit is cut off to allow a greater perfection to what is left. Some procedure of this kind might be appropriate with the sterile man or woman, but it could be of no advantage to the woman fertilized and carrying one child.

Anæsthetics in general practice are dangerous in heart troubles, kidney complications, and to some nervous conditions. They occasionally produce effects opposite to those expected. Chloroform is the best agent to produce unconsciousness in labor and is most commonly used ; but ether is deemed the safest of the anæsthetics. While this drug is not often used in labor, something may be said about its effects now that anæsthetics are under discussion.

Dr. Robert F. Weir has recently shown from the records of the New York Hospital that there is one death under ether in two thousand cases. This is not considerable, but this agent, like its congeners, adds to the shock of an operation, and, it must be presumed, prevents recoveries that would have been secure without its use. It may be said here that the method of inducing etherization should be gentle and gradual ; ten minutes will complete the work.

The sudden or drenching method is not productive of the best results. Ether is much more dangerous in kidney troubles than chloroform. It is also inflammable, having been known to ignite fifteen feet from a flame.

The clover inhaler does away with many of the drawbacks of ether. Its advantages may be summarized by saying that it reduces the time required for producing anæsthesia to from one to two minutes ; when properly used does away with struggling and unconscious resistance of the patient, prevents the dangerous chill to the air passages unavoidable in the old methods, and consequently obviates the old bronchial irritations which were sometimes fatal. The advantages of this inhaler are so great that it is indeed strange that it has not come into general use.

The most recent formalization of the use of anæsthetics in surgery is the following :

Dr. Kocher has been led by his researches upon the comparative advantages of ether and chloroform to formulate the following conclusions : 1. Before proceeding to general anæsthesia, it is indispensable to examine the patient thoroughly and submit him to preliminary treatment. 2. It is useful, and even necessary in many patients, to stimulate the heart's activity by the administration of alcohol or other stimulant (tea) before proceeding to anæsthesia. 3. The patient should be put to sleep only when in the horizontal position. 4. When the subject has not been properly prepared beforehand, chloroform should never be employed. 5. When the subject is affected with heart disease, or with any functional cardiac affection with accompanying implication on the part of the respiratory organs, ether should be preferred to chloroform. 6. The opposite course is necessary when an affection of the respiratory tract is present with hyperæmia of the tracheo-bronchial mucous membrane. 7. When the anæsthetic sleep is to be prolonged for a relatively long period, chloroform should be used first and then ether administered in small quantities to keep up the anæsthesia. 8. Chloroform should never be given mixed with a large proportion of air; during the whole duration of anæsthesia fresh air should, however, be admitted freely to the respiratory passages of the subject. 9. For long operations, or for one reason or another, the use of ether seems to be contra-indicated, a preliminary injection of morphine or morphine and atropine should be made, so as to restrict as much as possible the quantity of chloroform necessary to secure anæsthesia of sufficiently long duration.—*Gazette Médicale de Paris*, October 17, 1891.

The after-effects of ether, the safest of the anæsthetics, are often one or more of the following: inflammation of the bronchial tubes, headache, suppression of urine, choreic symptoms, and temporary insanity. One case is on record of a patient who remained insane after etherization for four days. Sometimes nervous symptoms commencing immediately after taking ether persist through life. When we consider that recovery is retarded and that more or less discomfort generally, and actual danger frequently, is the result of the use of even the safest anæsthetics, it may not seem unreasonable to lay down the following rule for the application of these agents:

The security of the surgeon in completing an operation doubtful if the patient could move or resist; the security of the surgeon in doing the work thoroughly; the security of the patient against injury or failure through his own incapacity to control his muscles, especially the voluntary. These are the certain indications for anæsthetics physically, Policy will induce us to use them at times when they are not physically necessary. The most sensititve nerves are on the surface in man. The interior of the body is but slightly sensitive and it is probable that in actual suffering there is less saved by the use of anæsthetics than they cause.

It must of course be understood that in many surgical operations the involuntary contraction of the muscles would prevent success were the patient conscious; consequently in such cases the anæsthetic is absolutely essential.

Prof. T. G. Thomas says that labor is, as a rule, and in a great majority of cases, a normal physiological process and requires no treatment whatever by drugs. The most rapid increase of population by birth-rate alone has always been in country districts, and especially in pioneer communities such as those founded by the early settlers of North America of both English and French stock. In those early times little indeed was known of gynecology or obstetrics, and such knowledge as existed was unavailable for the great mass of mothers.

Such well authenticated cases of mothers passing through labor with safety to themselves and to their children without the new knowledge as our first settlements offer, and the failure of the medical men to make any radical improvement in the death-rate per birth outside of maternity hospitals, show that much of the present method may be superfluous if not positively harmful.

The *46th Registration Report of Massachusetts* (1887) shows the general death-rate of the population without special epidemics to have been 20.28 in 1,000. This is higher than it was in the previous twelve years, and higher than between 1850 and 1862. This indicates a sanitary retrogression instead of advance, and incidentally sustains the point on death-rate of women in delivery.

The population of Massachusetts, however, is now more crowded and lives under much changed conditions probably less favorable to health, and it must also be remarked that the birth-rate of the State has decreased with the increased death-rate. These facts also incidentally show that the avoidance of childbirth diminishes the prospect of life.

Certain drugs have at times and in particular cases been found advantageous in labor. From such cases the formalism and devotion to tradition that more or less creep into every trade and profession have propagated and made general the use of these drugs and procedures. There can be little doubt that amongst many physicians this mechanical and blind traditional treatment of labor is not unusual.

I have been present at but a small number of labors, but what I have seen strongly prejudices me against anæsthetics. In my limited experience with anæsthetics the labor appeared to be delayed, the child's life proportionately endangered, subsequent hemorrhage in mother made more probable, and the mother generally left after the labor in a condition of half sickness which I have known to last · for a considerable time. On the whole I am opposed to these agents and as far as labor is concerned advise avoiding them.

The agent of an anatomical manikin of considerable merit, Dr. Henry F. Frisius, who in the course of his business has visited a vast number of physicians, tells me that only about one in a hundred of these retain more than a smattering of anatomy and physiology. This gentleman is a good anatomist himself and a very intelligent man. We may reasonably surmise from this information that a great number of physicians are equally ignorant upon other vital matters. Consequently it is not at all out of the way to give some hints on medical subjects.

Such a drug as ergot does probably more harm than good in labor cases. Its exhibition to induce labor or expedite delivery is harmful. Under its action still-births increase in ratio, and tearing and injuring of the parts under the violent and irregular pains it causes are common. Its use in labor is to prevent or stop post-partum bleeding. In this case its spasmodic action probably expels blood clots from the uterus, and may induce beneficial contraction of that organ. Thomas, King, Lusk, and Playfair recommend its use after the birth of the placenta.

Besides the mistakes so common in the administration of drugs, those who rely on them must contend against their extraordinary variability in strength as at present sold. Not long ago a committee of the New York State Pharamaceutical Society examined the drugs in a great number of country drug-stores with the following results :

Spirit of nitre varied in strength from 134 to zero. 76 samples of dilute acetic acid showed 11 too strong, 19 fair, and 34 very weak. The strength should have been 6.12 per cent., but the samples varied from 0.8 to 29.8. Of 46 specimens of Hoffman's anodyne only 5 were good, etc., etc.

When labor is delayed a much better practice than the use of drugs is to encourage indolent nature by such simple and innocent means as changing the woman's position, manipulation, and occasionally by manual dilation of the os uteri, etc. Nothing, however, should be introduced into the generative tract without thorough antiseptic precautions, and only in clear necessity.

Dr. Geo. J. Engelmann in his *Labor among Primitive People*, shows that nearly every possible position is taken by women in labor amongst such people. Standing up, lying down, kneeling, squatting, tied up, pulling on a rope or stick, on the belly, on the back, half recumbent, pushing with the feet against a wall, being held around the thorax by an assistant, ditto with downward pressure on the uterus by the arms of the assistant, hanging of the woman upon the neck of an assistant, etc., etc. Engelmann's investigations show that there is no natural position for the woman in labor. This has also been demonstrated by several German physicians by placing primiparæ in labor alone in rooms, with freedom to do as they liked, and no information as to what to do. Several hundred such experiments gave negative results. We may, therefore, feel sure that a change of position can do no harm, while it is strongly probable that this work of nature is facilitated by movement.

In post-partum hemorrhage, water heated to the point of tolerance may be used to irrigate the uterus with benefit. Such water should be boiled before use so as to sterilize it.

The bowels and bladder should be emptied before the child is born. This is the first thing when labor commences.

Dr. M. L. Holbrook has published an interesting small book entitled *Parturition without Pain.* If it be correct, then anæsthetics may be banished from every birth. Its chief object is to show that an easy and practically painless delivery may be obtained by a certain course of diet. The main points in this diet are the eating of large amounts of fruit, especially of the acid kinds, and the avoidance of food containing considerable earthy salts. What he advises against are, table-salt, wheaten bread, and all preparations of wheat, pepper, cinnamon, nutmeg, cloves, ginger, coffee, cocoa, Turkey rhubarb, liquorice, lentils, cinchona or Peruvian bark, cascarilla, sarsaparilla, and gentian. The best forms of farinaceous food are sago, tapioca, and rice. For drinking, only rain water or distilled water should be used. The theory of all this is, that if the earthy salts be withheld from the mother's diet, the bones of the child will be less fully formed, consequently softer, and that, therefore, the birth will be easier on account of the compressibility of the child. His proof is in citing Indian and Hindoo women and a number of special cases. In some of these the child was born when the mother was asleep, or standing on the floor, thus indicating an absence of preparatory pain. Pain and trouble were at a minimum in all his instances. Were it a patent medicine which he recommended, I should say that the proof was too incomplete to merit attention. Cases of sudden and painless birth come frequently under the observation of every experienced obstetrician without any special dietary regimen having been followed.

However, this system is simple and deserves a trial where a previous labor has been difficult or painful.

The pains of women in childbirth have a very excellent reason for at least a moderate existence. The human child in civilized communities require a great deal of care at the time of its birth. To have a child born while walking far from home, in a carriage, in the streets, or without due notice, would be very inconvenient in all cases, and very dangerous in most. It is not every woman who can be delivered of a child through the water-closet of a moving train, stop the train, and pick the child up alive as a railroad conductor's wife is recently said to have done. The pains are not only a warning but a positive command of nature to make ready, to bring in assistance, and to be so located as to make the child's appearance safe. When we reflect upon the necessities of reproduction and upon the careless-ness and folly of mankind in this their greatest duty, we may per-ceive that the pains of labor are a great safeguard to the race. Without them, child-death and child-murder at full term would be much more prevalent than at present. The average duration of labor in civilized women is in primiparæ seventeen hours, and in multiparæ twelve hours; but exceptions are so numerous as to render a knowledge of this average of little importance.

The tendency of to-day appears to be too much interference with this supreme work of nature in reproduction. However, as develop-ment is complex so is the difficulty of reproduction increased, and as civilization increases so does the difficulty of childbirth seem to increase with it.

In civilization it is at least certain that marriages take place later in life than amongst barbarians, and the proportion of lateness doubtless bears a close relation to the degree of civilization. Labor and childbirth must consequently come later in the life of the women in more civilized countries than in less civilized ones. It is equally certain that childbirth becomes progressively more difficult in primiparæ every year after twenty.

After twenty-seven the increased difficulty of women with first births becomes very noticeable. As the parts, muscles, and bones become more rigid, the difficulty augments. Abnormal presenta-tions are more frequent; the proportion of still-births increases and the children born are more likely to be deformed in body or to be deficient in mind with every year the first birth is delayed, certainly after twenty-five years of age in women.

Laceration of the perineum occurs more frequently also. When-ever this accident happens the lacerated surfaces should be sewed well and firmly together at once. The physician should never wait until the parts swell. After the sewing-up the knees must be kept tied together for from eight to ten days. Some doctors practise the Goodell system of retarding the birth of the head to save the peri-neum. A general adoption of this practice by the young physicians in a New York hospital increased largely the proportion of still-births.

Under the management of a skilled and experienced physician this system probably does good, but unless you have a man in whom you absolutely know you have such a physician, it will be best to condemn this procedure.

A manual dilatation of the vulva and stretching of the perineum when carefully performed from the commencement of labor diminishes the chance of tearing of the perineum. Its effect is upon the same principle as that seen in the dilatation of the rectum for surgical work. By gradual and careful dilatation of the rectum it may be so stretched that the hand and arm of the surgeon may be introduced into it without injury. The same gradual dilatation of the urethra enables surgeons to introduce without injury large instruments into the bladder for crushing stones formed there.

Accidents also occasionally occur to the cervix or other parts of the generative organs in labor. Such cases should be treated at an early subsequent period. Much suffering is thus prevented, and a prolonged and sometimes permanent sterility is avoided. Many women injured in childbirth live for years as semi-invalids, incapable of full life action, when they could just as well as not have been happy and complete wives, full of health for themselves and joy for their husbands. In most cases of this kind a short surgical operation would have cured them and opened their lives to happiness. Thus it may be seen that the meddlesome obstetrician may be a necessity. A first-class physician, the best you can get, should always be employed to superintend labor and childbirth, to be at hand in case operative interference be required, and to examine the mother afterward. A physician, by timely knowledge, may save a mother and child that otherwise would die through loss of time. He may promptly sew up a tear that without action might occasion long suffering.

The modesty of the mother should be protected as much as possible, and no persons should be introduced into the apartment except those absolutely required.

People and lights vitiate the air of closed rooms and should in these supreme moments never be allowed in excess of what is absolutely necessary.

In the royal families of Europe a different policy is followed. The members of the family and the principal officers of state must attend the birth of every royal child. The object is to secure the certainty that the heir to the throne has actually arrived by the proper and legitimate channel. In France, to the second child of Marie Antoinette, this custom was extended to admit the general public to view the birth and to thus carry assurance to the masses, at least as to the maternity of the princess. The crowd that roughly rushed into the chambers of this Queen, and even climbed on to the furniture to view the delivery of her first child, very nearly caused her death. Subsequently the family and principal officers were deemed sufficient, and the rabble was excluded.

The Mormons in this country have some curious customs about the delivery of the child. Four elders are expected to be present, but neither they nor any one else may render assistance to the woman. The idea seems to be that if God wishes her to breed He will carry her through, and if not she must die and be exterminated. This custom changes from the curious to the cruel when complications arise. On the other hand, the inquiries made by me in Utah show a very low death-rate in delivery, and indicate that the dangers that may be overcome by timely interference are more than neutralized by the dangers created by unnecessary meddling. As to the system of delivery and the presence of the elders at births, it is, I confess, all upon untrustworthy evidence.

If the husband be a man of nerve he should be present and should have beforehand studied as much as possible in obstetrics so as to know what ought to be done and what ought to be left alone. He should observe great discretion in the use of such information ; the employment of a new doctor in case of bad management is its best application. Nature ought to do this work, and, if the woman's life has been healthy, in the vast majority of cases it will do it. If the woman's life has been artificial and without healthy occupation, or if she be weak and sickly, trouble is more likely to occur. The history of labors in a woman's family, and the history of her own labors, if she be a multipara, are always of value. They may enable you to guard against peculiarities that would not otherwise be thought of.

The greatest danger in labor is from infection and septic poisoning. To guard against this, neither nurse nor doctor should be employed who has had within a considerable period cases of puerperal fever. Both nurse and doctor should be required to wash their hands in antiseptic fluid before going into the labor or to the woman pending her recovery. A basin of antiseptic water, renewed frequently, should be kept for this purpose. A good preparation for this object is one part of bichloride of mercury to one thousand of water. This destroys the life of any bacteria after an exposure of 45 seconds. Superficial washing of hands or instruments is not sufficient. The instruments should be soaked in the antiseptic fluid.

Doctors are often touchy about advice in such matters, and it may be well to exhibit this rule to them in the family book rather than to tell it with explanations. A doctor that requires cleansing, it must be said, is a pretty poor customer to deal with, but no precaution of so simple a character should be avoided where so much is at stake. The life of a true wife, of a mother who has immortalized you and kindled anew the fires of your youth, commands your every solicitude and care.

Septic poisoning in new mothers arises from two causes : the first cause being contagion, the second being from imperfect contraction of the uterus and the consequent absorption through its unclosed sinuses of the decomposed contents of this organ, blood clots, etc. The defective contraction of the uterus is generally due to a prolonged *second* stage of labor. The first stage may be long without harm, but after the presenting part has passed the cervix, the child should be born within an hour and a half, and if it is not born within three hours of the second stage instrumental interference is strongly indicated. The skilful physician can ascertain by the heart-beats of the unborn child, and by other signs, the time when delay would no longer be safe for the mother or the child. For more exact information you should study a work on obstetrics.

Some figures recently published by Dr. Down indicate at once the importance and the danger of instrumental interference in delayed labors.

Dr. Down says that of idiots born, 9 per cent. are due to instrumental interference, and 20 per cent. to delays in birth. One of the best practices I have seen in unduly delayed labors is a manual dilatation of the cervix. This hastens the labor and the dangers of injury to mother and child are at a minimum.

Antiseptics or drugs fatal to germ life are numerous. Two or more of these should not be used together without a full test of their action after combination. Many drugs fatal to germs when alone, lose much of their force when combined with other drugs also fatal to germs without mixture. Even soap should not be used with antiseptics, as it prevents the complete action of several such drugs. All secretions of the sick should be disinfected at once and before they are thrown out.

No nurse with syphilis, consumption, cancer, or any contagious disease should be employed upon any terms. Such diseases are communicable and might be given to the mother or to the child. It is not certain whether cancer is communicable. Recent experiments in Germany show that it may be inoculated. Dr. Hahn of Berlin experimented with a woman admitted to the hospital for recurrent cancer of the left breast. He transplanted some of the cancerous skin to the right breast. A microscopical examination after death showed that a cancerous growth had taken place where the inoculation had been made. Alibert derided the theory of cancer contagion. He inoculated himself with the juice of a cancer and died shortly after of carcinoma. Hanan of Zurich has recently transferred carcinoma from one rat to two others. If cancer be not contagious a child's vitality would be lowered by contact with it.

Cleanliness is the shibboleth of the lying-in room. Every precaution should be taken on this head. Soiled linen, excrementory matter, and all slops should be promptly removed. There is a superstition, based upon the necessity of keeping the mother quiet for some time after childbirth, that the sheets should not be changed for a certain period after the event. The sheets can be removed without any injurious disturbance to the woman, and should be removed at once and changed frequently. It is dangerous to have soiled sheets under a woman at this time.

The mammary glands and nipples of the woman about to become a mother require careful attention. This is especially the case before the first confinement. Some time before confinement, the nipples should be manipulated gently and rubbed twice a day with brandy to which a little alum has been added. Where the nipples are sunken, nipple shields with openings should be worn. White rubber should never be used. Proper care at this time will make the nipples hard, prevent cracking, and allow the mother the full delights of suckling without pain.

Where from malformation in the mother, excessive size of the fœtus, or from any cause the birth is impossible through the natural channels, there are two methods used, embryotomy and the destruction of the child being one, and caesarian section being the other; this latter by making an incision into the uterus from the exterior, and thus extracting the child. By this means the child may be saved. The objection to this procedure has been the supposed increased danger to the mother. The recent improvements in surgery and antisepsis show that this is not now to be feared. The operation of destroying the child now has no better statistics for the mother than has caesarian section. Hertsch has performed caesarian section seven times without a death, and of Cameron's ten cases but one died. On the other hand, the European figures on embryotomy show a death-rate varying from 5½ per cent. to 45 per cent. I am decidedly in favor of the operation to save both lives. Another operation has recently come into fashion. This is called symphysiotomy. The operation consists in cutting through the symphysis and so enlarging the opening for delivery. It is a good operation in certain cases, and is more easily performed than caesarian section.

The eyes, mouth, and nose of the new-born child should be promptly sponged clean with lukewarm water. The importance of this may be realized when we learn that 27.50 per cent. of diseases of the eye are contagious, and of these 1.69 per cent. are due to conjunctiva neonatorum contracted at birth. The percentage is not large, but it may as well be guarded against at so small a cost.

After labor the bowels of the mother should be moved, if nature is indolent, after the third day. Laxatives in such case should be given, and, if necessary, be aided by injections. An enema should be taken early in labor if no natural evacuation has occurred.

The child should not be generally exhibited to friends or kissed by any one except the mother. Frequently a child when born does not breathe. Prompt action is required in such case. The nose and mouth should be rapidly sponged, a dash of cold water on the spine may help, the arms should be moved to expand the chest, a breath may be forced by the operator into the child's lungs, or the mucus sucked from its throat. One excellent method is to hold the child's head downward by one leg for a few moments. These, and a number of other, procedures bring on the breathing by reflex action. When these methods fail, the system of artificial respiration practised by Dr. W. E. Forrest should be immediately commenced. As long as the ear, not the hand, can detect heart action in the foetus there is hope, and the efforts to save should not be relaxed. Forrest's method, in his own words, is as follows:

" When it is evident that the asphyxia is so profound that reflex irritation will not remove it, and that artificial respiration is necessary, the child is first laid for a moment on its face, head a little lower than the pelvis, and pressure is made upon its back to expel any fluids that may have been drawn into the mouth and trachea. Then the child is placed in a sitting position in a common wooden pail, half full of hot water, so that the water comes up to or just above the child's heart. The operator's left hand grasps the child's wrists or hands, the child's palms being to the front, so that when its arms are raised they will be rotated outward. The operator's right hand supports the child's back across the shoulders, with the child's head fallen back and resting in the crotch between the thumb and finger of this hand.

" The infant being in position, the first movement is that for getting air into the lungs. The child's arms are carried steadily upward and a little backward by the operator's left hand, until the weight of the body comes upon the shoulders, the back steadied by the operator's right hand, the head supported between the thumb and forefinger. In this position the child's arms are drawn up and rotated outward, and the muscles extending from shoulders to ribs made tense. Thus the ribs are raised. As the child is in the sitting posture the abdominal muscles are relaxed, and thus do not tend to prevent the raising of the ribs, as is done in the Sylvester and Schultz methods. In the latter methods one force tends to counteract the other. This is avoided in the method here given.

" Having enlarged the thoracic diameters to the fullest extent by raising the ribs, or rather, made it possible for them to be enlarged, we next proceed to force air directly into the lungs. When the ribs are raised the child's head extends sharply backward. This throws the cervical vertebræ forward and draws the larynx backward. Thus the flaccid œsophagus becomes compressed between the bones of the vertebræ on one side and the firm cartilaginous larynx on the other ; as a consequence, the œsophagus is effectually closed and the air cannot be forced into the stomach, and must enter the lungs. This effectually disposes of the time-worn and false statement that mouth-to-mouth insufflation must force the air into the stomach instead of the lungs. This position of the head also draws the tongue and epiglottis forward far better than it can be done with the forceps, and there is no possible chance for the tongue to fall back and close the larynx. We have now an open passage-way through the mouth and larynx to the lungs, and there is no necessity of inserting the catheter.

"The next step is to force air into the lungs. The arms still held up, the operator bends forward, and taking in a breath as he does so, places his mouth over that of the child and blows the air directly into the lungs.

"The air must and does enter the lungs and distend the collapsed air-cells, as can be determined by the fact that it can be heard leaving the lungs at the next step in this method. No great force need be used in doing this, although there is but little danger of injuring the air-cells, however great the force. It will be noticed that a safety escape is provided in this method for excess of air. The nose should be, and is, pervious, and any excess pours out through that aperture, thus relieving the pressure on the lungs. This completes the movement for introducing air into the lungs.

"Expiration is brought about by doubling the child's body forward upon itself so as to crowd the abdominal organs against the diaphragm ; at the same time the arms are lowered to the side, and the operator's left hand, still retaining the hands of the child, is brought against the front of the child's thorax, and then gently and steadily presses the ribs and sternum downward and backward. Thus every requisite is provided for forcing the air out of the lungs : the diaphragm is pushed up, the abdominal muscles are relaxed, the shoulders are lowered, and the thorax is compressed between the operator's hands, one on the child's back, the other across the front of the thorax. After a dozen or fifteen complete movements, when a sufficient number of the collapsed air-cells have been distended, one can hear the air rush out of the lungs when the pressure is made upon the thorax by the operator's hands. This completes the movement for expiration. Again the hands are carried upward and backward, the child's body is just raised off the bottom of the pail, so that the weight of the body is on the arms alone, the head falls back, air is again blown into the lungs.

"Now as to the philosophy of the method. It will be noticed that during the whole of the process much of the child's body is in the warm bath. This I conceive to be of great importance, and it is something that has not been applied, so far as known, in any other method.

"The important thing in attempts at resuscitation in a bad case of asphyxia in the new-born babe is to keep the child's heart acting. It is easy enough to supply air artificially to the lungs for the oxygenation of the blood, but unless the heart sends the blood to the lungs, and then on through the tissues of the body, the oxygen put into the lungs is useless. Now, if the child's skin is allowed to get cold the blood in the capillaries ceases to move, and the effect is soon manifested on the feebly beating heart. If the blood leaves the capillaries cooled it enters the veins at a low temperature and thus chills the heart itself. Again, the heart lies near the surface of the body, and in a half-hour may be directly chilled through the loss of heat from the surface of the body.

"On the other hand, if the body is kept in a bath with a temperature of from 105° to 110° F., the capillaries are dilated, the blood can circulate freely, and heated blood may be carried to the heart. It is claimed by physiologists that when the circulation is active the whole mass of blood in the body passes through the capillaries of the skin in a few minutes. Now, if the body is in a warm bath the whole mass of blood has its temperature raised, and thus the muscles themselves soon become heated. Any one can demonstrate the fact on themselves by getting into a hot bath up to the neck. The thermometer in the mouth will soon show a rise of two to three degrees Fahrenheit. M. Morey's experiments proved conclusively that muscular tissue loses its contractility when its temperature is lowered, and regains it when the temperature of the muscles is raised up to a certain point. It has been ascertained that the maximum aptitude for contraction is exhibited by human muscles at about 40° C. = 104° F. This is about the temperature of the body of a healthy adult when immersed for some time in a bath at the temperature of 110° F.

"The heart is a muscular organ, obeying all the laws of muscular action, and it seems evident that in an asphyxiated infant it will act with more force if the infant's body temperature is raised and kept at 102° to 103° F., than if it is lowered to 96° to 94° F., as it will be if the skin is exposed to the air for a short time.

"Theory and practice both prove that the continued warm bath is a most important measure in the resuscitation of badly asphyxiated infants. The importance of having the child in a sitting posture during the respiratory movements has already been commented on.

"In comparing the method here given with the best three methods heretofore used, namely, Sylvester's, Schultz's, and the catheter in the larynx, it will be seen that this combines all the advantages of the three usual methods without any of their drawbacks. For instance, in the new method, we have direct insufflation of air from the operator's lungs, as when the catheter is employed. We have exactly the same method of raising the ribs and sternum as in the Sylvester method, with the additional advantage of having the abdominal muscles relaxed. We have in the new method the descent of the diaphragm that is claimed as an advantage in the Schultz method. We have in expiration the same doubling of the child's body forward and pushing up of the diaphragm as are found in the Schultz and Schroeder methods. We avoid shock and exposure that are so often fatal in the Schultz method, and, at the same time, keep up the vital or animal heat in the infant during, perhaps, a long operation.

"In recapitulation it may be said that the steps in the new method of artificial respiration in bad cases of asphyxia in the new-born are as follows:

"1. Lay the child on its face for an instant with the head and thorax lower than the pelvis, and make quick but not violent pressure on the child's back. This is done to expel any fluids that may have been drawn into the child's mouth while passing through the pelvic canal.

"2. Place the child in the sitting posture in a pail or tub containing six to eight inches of water as hot as can be borne comfortably by the operator's hand. The child is supported in this position by one of the operator's hands across the child's back, the child's head bent back and resting in the crotch between the thumb and forefinger of this hand. The child's hands with the palms to the front are held in the other hand of the operator.

12

"3. The child's hands are carried upward until the child is suspended by the arms, the buttocks just raised from the bottom of the pail. The child's head now falls back, and the operator leans forward, and, mouth to mouth, blows into the child's lungs.

"4. The child's arms are then lowered until the hand of the operator holding them rests across the front of the child's thorax. Then the body of the child is doubled forward, and, at the same time, its thorax is compressed between the operator's hands, one in front, the other behind. This expels the air from the lungs and completes the movements.

"CASE I.—In March, 1890, I was called by an Italian midwife to assist her in the delivery of a child. The mother I found to be a stout, healthy primipara, aged twenty-one. The waters had come away forty-eight hours before I was summoned and there had been labor pains ever since, but no progress had been made. On examination, I found the os only one fourth dilated, the lips thick and firm, the pelvic roof but little retracted, and the vaginal canal wholly unfitted for the passage of a fœtal head.

"I decided to wait a few hours ; the patient meantime to receive hot rectal douches. Six hours later I was called again. Little if any change, except that the soft parts were more relaxed. The position of the head was face anterior.

"Taking into consideration the conditions of the case, *i.e.*, the position of the head, the early discharge of the waters, the leathery condition of the soft parts, the large size of the child's head, and the fact that the mother was a fat, plethoric young woman, I felt sure that I had a tiresome task before me. Needless to say that I was not disappointed. The forceps were applied, and it took three hours of almost continuous traction of the strongest kind to deliver the child. The child's head did not rotate, and in spite of every care during delivery, the mother was badly lacerated, down to, but not into, the rectum. The child was apparently dead, no pulsation of the cord, and not the slightest pulsation of the heart could be felt by the hand. The midwife attended to the delivery of the placenta, while I gave all my attention to the attempt to resuscitate the child. There was no pulsation of the heart that could be felt by placing my hand over the child's præcordial region ; but on putting my ear to this region I could very distinctly hear the heart beating at the rate of about sixty beats per minute.

"Let me say here that in my opinion the practitioner should never trust to his hand to determine whether or not the new-born child's heart beats. It is really startling to put one's ear to a child's chest where the hand can feel no pulsation, and then hear with such distinctness the dull thud, thud, of the child's heart. Dependence should always be placed on the ear instead of the hand in determining whether or not an infant's heart has ceased to beat.

"In attempting to resuscitate this child I employed for a minute or two the usual slapping with the hand, rubbing with brandy, dipping into hot and then into cold water, but all to no purpose. The case was beyond the effect of reflex irritation.

"The method of artificial respiration mentioned above was then employed. That it caused air to enter and leave the lungs could be determined by the blue color leaving the child's lips. Still there was not a single voluntary or spasmodic effort at inspiration.

"I have said that at the beginning of my efforts the heart was beating at the rate of sixty beats per minute. This gave me a little confidence that I might revive the child.

"At the end of fifteen minutes I removed the child from the bath, put my ear to its chest, and counted the heart-beats by my watch. The pulsations were one hundred and twenty per minute, I slapped the child quite vigorously, and it drew up its legs with a slow, convulsive movement. But it made no gasping efforts to draw in the air, a movement that usually cheers the physician in these cases. Meantime the water in the pail had been renewed by fresh hot water, I set the child in it, and with my hand laved the water upon the child's breast and neck. Under the influence of these hot douches the capillaries could be seen to fill with blood, as shown by the skin turning red, thus showing that the heart was doing its part. Still no respiratory efforts. I commenced artificial respiration again, and continued for ten minutes more. At the end of that time, the midwife stated that she could not deliver the after-birth, and that the woman was flooding. I was compelled to leave the child for a short interval. Laid it on the table and told the midwife to rub it while I attended to the mother.

"I was detained five minutes and then returned to my little charge. I found on putting my ear to its chest that the heart was beating only thirty times per minute. I had little hopes of resuscitating it, but wished to see what the effect of artificial respiration might be, and so replaced the child in the hot water and renewed my efforts. At the end of three minutes I removed the child, and found the heart beating at the rate of ninety per minute. At the end of ten minutes more the heart was beating one hundred and ten times per minute.

"It was now a little more than three quarters of an hour since the child was born, and in spite of the fact that the heart was beating quite normally, and that there had been two reflex drawings up of the legs, there had not been the faintest effort at an attempt toward spontaneous respiration. It seemed to me that the nerve-centres governing the respiratory function or the nerve-connection between these centres and the lungs had been injured, and the lungs could not voluntarily act. Artificial respiration, as I practised it, seemed to answer to supply the blood with air, and thus favor the heart's natural action. I resumed my efforts and continued them for fifteen minutes, making an hour since the child's birth. Heart beating over a hundred per minute, and skin and lips a good color. I suspended operations for three minutes; heart ran down to thirty beats per minute. Resumed my efforts, and heart was soon beating at ninety per minute. I had given up any hopes of establishing natural respiration, but was simply carrying on an experiment. An hour and fifteen minutes after the birth of the child, I suspended work for five minutes, owing to my own fatigue. On resuming, the heart was beating very slow, less than twenty per minute, the child, however, made another spasmodic movement of its legs.

"My efforts soon ran the heart-beats up to sixty per minute, and there it remained as long as I continued artificial respiration. I had become very much fatigued by this time, and occasionally laid the child aside so as to rest myself. Every time I resumed artificial respiration, I could increase the rate of heart-pulsation.

"An hour and three quarters after the birth of the child the heart was beating very slowly, not more than eight or ten beats per minute. My efforts ran the rate up to forty beats per minute. I then definitely abandoned the experiment, owing to my own fatigue, not because my subject was exhausted. The child never made a respiratory effort during all this time. It seemed that the action of the heart might have been continued for many hours in this case had artificial respiration been continued steadily. I noticed that the more rapid the artificial respiratory movements were made the more quickly the pulse rose.

"Respiratory movements in a new-born child should be made forty or fifty times a minute instead of twenty times, as usually taught. An infant breathes naturally about forty times a minute, and this rate should be the rule in artificial respiratory movements.

"There are certain conclusions that may be drawn from this case :

"1. The method of artificial respiration advocated in this paper ventilates the lungs. This was shown by the fact that for an hour and three quarters the blood received a fair supply of oxygen, as shown in the capillaries of the skin, without the child making a single voluntary or spasmodic effort at inspiration.

"2. It was demonstrated that the action of the heart is stimulated and continued by supplying the lungs with air. The pulse-rate rose and fell in direct ratio with the attempts at artificial respiration.

"Flint's *Physiology* states that, in experiments on animals, 'if the heart be exposed in a living animal and artificial respiration kept up, although the pulsations are diminished in frequency and increased in force, after a time they become perfectly regular and so continue just as long as air is adequately supplied to the lungs.'

"3.—That in certain cases the respiratory function cannot be established, owing possibly to injuries to the medulla.

"CASE II.—Stout German woman. Multipara. I was called to the case, and reached the house, according to the mother's statement, a half-hour after the child was born. From the circumstances of the case, I do not think this statement an exaggeration. The mother stated that when the child was born it screamed loudly for a minute, but she had neither heard nor felt it since.

"The mother lay on a German feather-bed, resting on her elbow, in a semi-reclining posture, thus making at the hips, in the soft bed an artificial pond that contained about a pail of mixed blood and amniotic fluid, lying in which, face downward, was the infant, apparently dead—drowned. It could not have been in that position less than half an hour, as the child was born just as the messenger left the house to summon me. I removed it and quickly rubbed it off with hot water. No pulsation of the heart could be felt and the child was limp and cool. On putting my ear to its chest I could just distinguish a faint thud at the rate of about twenty beats per minute. I put the child into hot water and commenced artificial respiration after the method given in the preceding case. In five minutes I listened to the heart-beat and found it much stronger and at the rate of about ninety beats per minute. No respiratory efforts yet. I resumed my work, and in three minutes more (eight minutes from the beginning) the child made its first gasp. . In a short time thereafter respiration was well established. The child is now living and healthy.

"This was not a case of asphyxia neonatorum, strictly speaking, because the child cried immediately after birth and then was drowned.

"The case was introduced here because it illustrates two things : 1. The influence of artificial respiration on the heart ; the pulse-rate running up from twenty beats per minute to at least ninety beats before the child made any respiratory efforts. 2. The ease with which a child is resuscitated after it has once cried and thus distended its air-cells, as compared with the difficulty of resuscitating a child, no more badly asphyxiated, but whose air-cells have never been distended and are completely collapsed, as at birth.

"CASE III.—Italian woman, primipara. Large male child, face anterior. A very tedious labor. Child born at length after delay with the shoulders. Badly asyphiated. I commenced artificial respiration after the method described above. There were no reflex movements in this case. It was just three quarters of an hour before the child gave the first convulsive, spasmodic gasp; then ten minutes' unremitting effort before the second respiratory gasp was made. After this the respiratory efforts became gradually more frequent, but it was an hour and forty minutes before the function was established so that the child could breathe alone. Even then it breathed with difficulty, and it was more than twelve hours before the respirations were natural. The child made a good recovery.

"CASE IV.—Mother a young and fleshy primipara. An exceedingly tedious labor. Instrumental delivery after prolonged traction. The child was born with blue and swollen face, and apparently badly asphyxiated. Before the cord was tied, the child made a single convulsive effort at inspiration, and my hand could feel the heart pulsate. After tying the cord I asked the nurse to cut it. Unfortunately she cut it on the wrong side of the ligature, and, as a consequence, there was a quick escape of about three drachms of blood. The child immediately became blanched and relaxed, and made no further efforts at inspiration. I tried the usual methods of reflex irritation, expecting no difficulty in restoring respiration, but to no avail. I could now not feel the heart beat, and on listening at the chest could just hear that it was beating very faintly, and only about thirty times to the minute. It seemed to me then that the sudden abstraction of blood from the large umbilical vessels connecting so directly with the heart, had caused a shock that had nearly suspended cardiac action. It is an old and almost universally accepted theory that, in the words of Cazeau: 'When the child is born with a general injection of the capillaries of the head and trunk, it is evident that the first indication is to relieve the engorgement of the head and lungs, which is done by promptly cutting the umbilical cord and allowing a few spoonfuls of blood to escape.'

"It would seem that the theory on which such practice is based, however plausible it may seem, is unsound in fact. Even if there were any evidence to prove that there can be a dangerous congestion of the head and lungs during the labor, the active cause is over as soon as the child is born. Bleeding the child then is like locking the doors after the thief has left the premises. Such congestion, if present, would be best relieved by drawing the blood to the surface and by stimulating the heart, rather than by paralyzing it by abstracting blood from it. There are but eight ounces of blood in the new-born child and 'a few spoonfuls' may represent a respectable portion of the whole amount.

"Without dwelling further on this point, it may be said : 1. That it has not been shown that a dangerous passive congestion of the brain and lungs often arises from a prolonged labor. 2. That, even if such a congestion existed, abstraction of blood from the large vessels leading to the heart after the birth is completed is a useless and dangerous procedure.

"As a result of the umbilical bleeding in this case, what seemed a simple

case of asphyxia was converted into the most obstinate one I have ever en-
countered. After fifteen minutes of artificial respiration, with the child in the
hot bath, it gave a slight convulsive gasp. I removed it and listened to the
heart and found it beating faintly at the rate of about sixty beats per minute.
Even as I listened, the heart-rate grew less and the sound fainter, and a pallor
spread over its surface. I replaced the child in the bath and recommenced
treatment. The capillaries of the skin filled again, and after ten minutes there
was another attempt at inspiration. These respiratory gasps becoming more frequent and at more regular intervals, after a half hour I removed the child and
tried for a minute the Schultz 'swinging method' of artificial respiration. An
almost immediate collapse was the result ; no more efforts at inspiration, and
the lips became blue and the nose cold and white. Again artificial respiration
in the hot bath, for thirty minutes continuously (making one hour up to this
time), and the spasmodic gaspings were quite frequent, and it seemed as if
respiration were on the point of being established. I removed the child and
tried first the Sylvester method and then the catheter in the trachea. The
gaspings ceased, and very quickly the heart pulsations grew slower and fainter.
Throughout the whole time during which artificial respiration was kept up in
this case (a little more than two hours) the difficulty seemed to be in getting
the natural circulation established. In this case, unlike Case I., the respiratory
centres seemed ready to assume their function but were delayed by weakness in
the circulatory centres. It took two hours or more of almost continuous efforts
at artificial respiration before the function was established. Many times I
stopped my efforts for a minute or two, or tried other methods, when the heart-
rate invariably lessened rapidly, and the case went into a state of collapse.

"When respiration was at last established, it was slow and gasping for
several hours. The next day the child had several convulsions, but these were
overcome by the liberal use of bromide of potassium, and the child finally made
a good recovery. At this writing the child is eighteen months of age, and
mentally and physically bright and strong.

"During the more than ten years in which I have practised the method of
artificial respiration given above, there have been many remarkable cases of
recovery from asphyxia, but the above typical cases are sufficient to illustrate
the principles of this method.

"My conclusions are that in a bad case of asphyxia neonatorum : 1. Direct
insufflation of the lungs is imperative. 2. This should be combined with movements to increase the diameters of the thoracic cavity. 3. That throughout
the process the temperature of the child's body should be kept at or above 100°
F., in order that the action of the heart may not be impeded.

"These requisites can be met, so far as known to the writer, alone by the
method of artificial respiration given above."

Soon after the child is delivered and breathes, and even when it
does not breathe, within a reasonable time the umbilical cord attach-
ing it to the placenta and circulation of the mother should be twice
tied tightly by a narrow cord, preferably of linen bobbin. The first
ligature should be made one inch and a half from the child, and the
second three inches. It should be tied tightly. After the ligatures
are made the cord should be cut between them, and the placenta,

when born, be removed. The end of the cord between the point where cut and the point ligated should be treated as follows. A piece of soft linen, about three inches square when folded four times, with a hole burned through the centre large enough for the cord to pass, is pulled over the cut end to the point ligated, and then that portion folded carefully in and laid up, and to the right, and a bandage placed around the child's body to hold it in place. The linen should be well vaselined before it is used.

The general details of childbirth and of all complications should properly be left to experts when these can be had. Still the more important points should be understood by every one. It is sufficient to add here that a serious delay in the birth of the placenta is exceedingly likely to cause post-partum hemorrhage. It is through the placenta that the unborn child receives its blood from the mother. The placenta is attached to the child by the umbilical cord, and to the uterus of the mother in a general and complex manner. It should always be born within two hours after the child. If this is not the case your physician will help its expulsion by external manipulation, by changing the woman's position, or he should take it out by the hand introduced into the uterus. When no physician is present and no bleeding occurs the attendants may wait longer, but, when serious bleeding comes on, no delay is safe.

The Credé method is the best and safest way of expelling the delayed placenta. The operator in this method takes a napkin in his hand, and at the first pain seizes the uterus through the napkin, and then gently expels the placenta. This method, or something like it, is practised by a number of primitive peoples in delay of the afterbirth. (See Engelmann.)

In using the Credé method care should be taken not to compress the ovaries. If the patient complains of pain during the operation, a new hold should be taken with a view of freeing the ovaries from the grasp of the hand. The drawbacks to taking the placenta by inserting the hand are two. First, the danger of infection or injury to the parts, and second, the difficulty of taking out the placenta clean and clear, thus leaving after sources of trouble.

Almost all doctors of experience take the placenta, if it be unborn, as soon as their attention can be given to it. This is the best course. If nature has given out, the sooner the woman is relieved of everything, and started on the road to recovery, the better.

The child after birth should be carefully sponged. The water should be blood-warm, and may be used after the usual application of oil or lard. In babes born before term washing may be omitted, except as to the eyes, and the oil alone applied. The baby should generally be wrapped in loose, warm coverings, but not too warm, and may be dressed at the convenience of the nurse. The omission of the fatigue of dressing for two or three days seems especially advantageous in babes of doubtful viability. Babes after the seventh month are viable.

While the seventh month is generally considered the period of viability, there is now too much evidence in favor of the possibility of life at the sixth month to longer doubt upon this point. Tarnier, by his system of gavage, saved thirty per cent. of children born at the sixth month. Dr. Llewellyn Elliot even considers the child viable under some conditions at four months. When born before term, the greatest care must be exercised to save them. The practice in the largest New York hospital is to lay these little waifs in cotton in a box, and to maintain by artificial means a constant warm local temperature.

The child should be kept warm and put to the mother's breast very soon. The first secretions of the mammary glands of the mother are laxative, and clear the stomach and intestines of the child. When a natural movement does not take place within twenty-four hours, half a teaspoonful of syrup of rhubarb should be given. If this is not effective it should be supplemented by a lukewarm enema. The baby's bowels should move once or twice a day, but exceptions occur to this. The mother's milk is the natural and the best food for the child for the first eight or nine months. This is the fact to-day, but how long it will be so cannot be told. Children, particularly amongst the poorer classes, die in frightfully increased numbers when deprived of their natural nourishment.

If the passages are of good appearance and digested, a considerable variation from this rule may be allowed.

The mortality amongst children fed by wet-nurses is also much greater than that by the mother-nursed.

The importance of nursing, both to the mother and child, is great. Nursing prevents too quick new conception, it aids the return of the uterus to its normal condition, and prevents the origin of troubles that frequently become chronic without it. In nursing, menstruation rarely occurs before the eighth or ninth month, when the baby should be weaned. Dr. Winter's figures are: of 1,327 women only 125 menstruated while nursing. Of these 125, 40 were married and 85 were unmarried. Among the latter insufficient care must be considered as likely.

Nursing is advantageous often in post-partum hemorrhage. The excitement of the mammary gland causes reflex contraction in the uterus, tending to stop the bleeding. The mother who nurses her child must avoid frights, excitement, and especially anger. A number of curious cases are on record, showing the influence of nerve or mental conditions of the mother upon her milk, and through it upon her babe. There are several authenticated instances of even the death of a baby on being suckled after a violent fit of temper in the mother.

Consequently a quiet home-life is most advantageous at this time. The food of the mother will also affect her milk, and should be carefully watched. In cows the food influences the color, smell, taste, specific gravity, and chemical composition of the milk. It is equally certain that the human female is similarly affected by food in her secretions.

In nursing, both breasts should be given the baby, not necessarily at the same nursing, but so that, as far as possible, the child shall receive during the twenty-four hours the same amount from each. The breasts are kept healthier in this way, and the child also. Recent researches on this line in the hospital at Lyons show that the mortality of infants nursed on one breast exceed that of those nursed on both by twelve per cent.

The increased health and prospect in life in the child suckled by its mother is most notable. Wet-nursing I am opposed to. Prepared foods or cow's milk properly diluted can, in case of necessity, be given with due care and cleanliness, and the baby live, but nothing can overcome the drawbacks to wet-nurses. These are usually the victims of seduction. Their own babes must be dead or put out to be hand-fed. An examination by Dr. Joseph E. Winters of New York shows that the children of wet-nurses almost invariably die. This must affect the wet-nurse. Losing her child will cause her to grieve, which will through the milk react on the foster-child, or, if she do not grieve for her own child, then such a woman is of too hard a nature to entrust with a child of any one else. Wet-nurses, if married and deserting their own children, are unnatural and consequently unreliable.

If the child of the proposed wet-nurse is already dead, some weakness of constitution or liability to infection may be suspected. These women not infrequently suffer from venereal diseases which they are liable to impart to children that suckle them.

Fournier (*Syphilis and Marriage*, p. 181, *et seq.*) cites a number of cases showing the danger from infection of syphilis from this source.

First case, in Notes: "A nurse infected with syphilis comes into a young family, whose infant is confided to her. She infects the child. The nature of the morbid symptom remains unrecognized at first, as would almost necessarily be the case, so that no precautions are taken against the possible dangers of such a contamination. What happens? The infant on its part infects, first, its mother; second, its grandmother; third and fourth, two nursery maids of the family, girls of absolutely irreproachable character. And the young wife transmits the contagion to her husband some months later."

Second case, Notes from work of Amilcare Ricordi: "A syphilitic nurse going into a small village transmits syphilis to sixteen, eighteen, twenty-three persons, and becomes the origin of a small local epidemic."

Nurses of any kind introduced into a family ought always to be examined by the family physician to secure, in some measure, immunity from danger of infection, not only from the terrible malady of syphilis, but also from other diseases. Quite a number of wet-nurses become professionals. They have children only to gain the wages of wet-nursing, and regularly consign their own offspring to what the figures show to be practically certain death.

Dr. Winters gives some comparative statistics as to the rate of mortality of children nursed by mothers and those nursed by wet nurses.

EXAMPLE I.

400 children during period of five years:
Mortality of infants suckled by mothers, 16 in 100.
"   "   wet-nurses, 28 in 100.

EXAMPLE II.

Observations on 600 children from 1872 to 1879:
Mortality of mother-nursed, 10 in 100.
"   wet-   "   26 in 100.

EXAMPLE III.

Paris:
Mortality of mother-nursed, 10 in 100.
"   wet-   ".   29 in 100.

In Foundling Hospital:
Mortality of mother-nursed, 6 in 100.
"   wet-   "   36 in 100.

The sickness and weakness which each additional death means, make the contrast still more striking. The influence of the midwife and of the attending physician is shown by Dr. Winters to be very great in inducing mothers to suckle or not to suckle their own children. An inquiry on this subject showed that some physicians had but one in ten of their patients in the well-to-do classes suckle their babes, while others in the same city had nineteen in twenty of their patients perform this duty. Physicians or nurses with a bad influence in this respect should be avoided.

Suckling is of paramount importance to the health of the mother, but there are cases in which the welfare of the child demands that the function should be performed but a short time or not at all. Such cases occur when the mother has some constitutional disease, as consumption, syphilis, etc. Nursing under these circumstances may increase the tendency of the child at birth to the mother's disease. There are also at times abnormal conditions in the mother's milk, as excessive acidity, which prevents proper nourishment by washing out the phosphates and inducing rickets in the child. Under such conditions, which are exceptions, and with due care in marriage ought to be rare, hand-feeding must be resorted to.

Of prepared foods there are many kinds. Only standard ones freshly made should be used. Some of these will suit one child and not another, so in hand-feeding the idiosyncrasies of the child must be considered. Cow's milk is easily obtained and is cheap. It is a complete food, and properly treated agrees with most children. One method of using it is when sterilized. This is accomplished by boiling and by tight-sealing or corking of the bottle in which it is placed until used. Even a cotton plug is sufficient to prevent the entry of germs. It should be boiled but a few moments. The objection to this is the liability of boiled milk to induce constipation. While this method destroys all germs, still my own observation is against boiled milk in its effect on the child.

The most recent examinations of the effects of prepared foods are certainly unfavorable to them. The proportion of babies in a weak or rickety condition on these foods is very large. They are largely composed of starchy matter, neither a complete food in itself nor easy of digestion, such as it is. Some of them, fairly good if fresh, spoil easily, and must always be suspected of too long keeping. Consequently these foods should only be used as a last resort and with the greatest discrimination.

One good food, on condensed milk as a basis, is :

4 oz. water.

1 heaping teaspoonful Mellin's food.

2 teaspoonfuls condensed milk.

This is about right for a babe of ten months.

Dr. Arthur Meigs, Dr. Joseph Winters, and a number of other eminent men recommend the following food as the best substitute for mother's milk : milk 3 parts, cream 1 part, lime-water 1 part, boiled water 2 parts, sugar of milk 1 part. Solution of bicarbonate of soda, eight grains to the ounce, may be substituted for the lime-water in case the baby is constipated. In a healthy child, ordinary sugar may be substituted for the expensive sugar of milk. This formula is for a baby of six months. It may be modified in proportion to suit individual cases and different ages.

In all cases when cow's milk is used the greatest care should be resorted to in feeding the cow, in its housing, in washing the bag and udders upon milking, and in seeing that the milker has his hands thoroughly washed, finger nails clean, and the pail and filter scalded. The importance of these precautions may be judged when we learn that in a certain carefully conducted creamery the Lazell separator accumulated from one thousand quarts of milk enough cow dung to fill two hands.

The milk of a cow known by examination to be healthy diluted one half at least with boiled water is perhaps the best substitute for the mother's milk. Condensed milk is also good. In all cases where foods other than the mother's milk are used the greatest care must be exercised to keep out germs and to prevent fermentation. The bottles, pitchers, and vessels used should invariably be thoroughly scalded out before and immediately after use.

In hand-fed children rickets is exceedingly liable to occur. Dr. I. M. Snow says : " Rickets is largely confined to children reared upon artificial food. Thus, Trousseau found that among one hundred rachitic children, ninety-eight had either not been suckled at all or had been weaned very young." " The correct proportion of fat to the solids in human milk is 1 to 4, but many artificial farinaceous foods contain a mere trace of fat, from 1–20 to 1–200 of the total solids. Rickets is, according to Cheadle, a diet disease which may be caused at will by a rachitic diet and cured by an anti-rachitic diet." Artificial foods are also deficient in the earthy salts.

The most prominent symptoms of rickets are pallor owing to the poverty of the blood, sweating without sufficient cause, nervous derangement shown by irritability, convulsions, tetanus, etc.; muscular languor and weakness, abnormal condition of the mucous membrane shown by bronchitis, croup, and diarrhœa; weakness in the ligaments shown by yielding of the spine, relaxed knee and ankle joint ; and troubles in the osseous system shown by the bending or deformity of the longer bones, bending of the ribs, etc. These symptoms may be all or only partly present and may be much masked.

Another symptom is delayed dentition. The teeth should commence to appear by the ninth month. If they do not, the condition of the child and its diet should be carefully inquired into. When rickets is present or suspected the farinaceous food should be reduced to a minimum and cod-liver oil or other fats, chopped or scrapped raw meat, eggs, and all the milk they can take added to the diet. It is probable that in a given meal much meat should not be taken at the same time with much milk.

The importance of looking out for rickets in artificially fed children is clear when we reflect upon the large number of rickety children whose troubles are caused by their diet.

It may be further accentuated by the words of Sir. Wm. Jenner. This distinguished physician says that rickety children are exceedingly liable to pneumonia, bronchitis, and collapsed lung. He also speaks of the excessive mortality in such children when attacked with measles, whooping-cough, etc. According to Jenner more children die from rickets either primarily or secondarily than from any other cause.

When a baby is weaned it should be to the spoon and cup and not to the bottle ; this for safety on account of the difficulty of keeping the bottles sweet and clean and the danger in their almost inevitable retention of some residuum which ferments and so injures the child's digestion by polluting the food.

Teething is usually a troublesome and sometimes a critical time for children. If the irritation caused by the teeth in cutting through the gum is excessive a reflex derangement of the digestion is exceedingly likely to occur. Consequently great care in the diet must at this time be exercised. In case the teeth do not come through the gum readily, the difficulty may be decreased by lancing. Lancing the gums, however, if prematurely done, may have a contrary effect. The wound heals up before the tooth comes through and the cicatrized tissue is harder for the tooth to pierce than was the normal gum. Nurses to help in the care of children lighten the labors of the mother. The persons seeking this employment are usually irresponsible and unreliable. Sometimes they resort to very reprehensible and injurious means to quiet the child under their care. Anodynes and narcotics are common causes of injury to children from this source. Other and still worse things are done to quiet the child, such as tampering with the sexual organs, etc.

It is therefore necessary to watch all nurses closely and to use the greatest care in selecting them. The babe should always have a basket or a crib to itself.

It should never sleep in the same bed with the mother. The reason for this is the danger to the baby of being suffocated.

Every year in London a great number of babies lose their lives in this way, and the mother in her sleep unconsciously destroys the child so precious to her heart.

London is no exception to the general rule, for the average of infant deaths from this cause wherever it has been examined shows a similar condition to prevail. It is a real danger and should be carefully guarded against. Folding beds are dangerous. Fifty-six children were suffocated in New York by being accidentally shut up in these beds last year.

Medicines should be avoided with children. Hot applications, poultices, such as those made ot onions, flaxseed, etc., rubbings, etc., are good when necessary and can rarely do harm, but medicines in their effect are too uncertain, and, if improperly employed, too injurious to be used except in serious cases and with skilled advice.

In the sickness of children as in all sickness the nursing is what saves. A good nurse is more important than a good doctor. Every one should study somewhat of nursing. Care and cleanliness, clothing and diet, these are the vital questions. Over-attention and coddling will prevent a due development of the constitution and predispose to disease. This should be avoided. The importance of having the nursing done under the direction of a physician is very great. In all cases of a serious kind the best physician attainable should be employed at once. Never hesitate about sending for the best. He will be cheapest in the end.

In the sickness of children, the rule should be isolation of the sick one, not only from the healthy members of the family but from any other sick one as well; from the healthy ones on account of the danger of communicating the disease from the sick to the well. Even should no spread of the specific malady occur, there is a certainty of lowering the vitality of the well ones exposed, especially during sleep, to the air of the sick-room. From the sick ones the sick should be separated. This is on account of the danger of infection or contagion, if the diseases be different, and on account of the certainty of increasing the intensity of the disease, if the malady be the same, by every additional patient placed in a room or ward.

Experience has been general in showing that with equal care isolated patients always do best. This superior prospect of recovery holds good even where the care and conditions are very unfavorable to the isolated.

The mortality of children from cholera infantum and kindred diseases is usually greater in infant hospitals than it is anywhere else. The same thing is true of the hospital epidemics of infectious pneumonia, of erysipelas, of blood-poisoning in wounds and surgical operations, and of puerperal fever in lying-in hospitals.

In our late war it was shown that small-pox had an average increase of intensity and mortality in the individual corresponding with average increase of patients placed together. Owing to this fact, better results were obtained in every case where tents were used for hospitals than in even the best arranged buildings. In isolating sick members of a family, the attic or upper rooms should be preferred, for the top of a house may be shut off from communication with the rest of the house better than the lower floors. There also seems a greater facility of infection from below upward than from above downward. If the household arrangements do not permit of isolation in the house, a tent or tents should be bought or hired for the purpose. Such expense in the commencement will save in the length and intensity of the disease in the individual, and will prevent additional cases with their consequent increase of expense for doctor and nurse. In cold climates the use of tents is of course limited. Convalescence will be safer and quicker, and many lives will be saved that otherwise would be lost by the isolation of the sick. Thus the poor may calculate that a dollar spent in these precautions will not only diminish suffering and save life, but will save tens and perhaps hundreds of dollars in money.

The human system has a great power of resisting morbific influences. The blood corpuscles will encyst or destroy a considerable number of germs or active individuals of various kinds of minute life injurious or fatal in large numbers to the body. Some individuals and some conditions of the system have this power more than others : for instance, gouty persons have, according to some, a considerable resistance to all contagious diseases, and while great sufferers from their own malady rarely take anything else. So also, individuals capable of resisting contagion or infection at one time may be extremely susceptible at another.

The acid diathesis seems that most resistant to the specific attack of microscopic life.

The Italian system of treating malarial fevers seems, if this be correct, to rest on a secure basis. They give large amounts of lemon juice in these cases and have better results from this than from any other treatment.

It appears probable, therefore, that in cases of contagious or infectious disease, a large amount of lemon or orange juice would be beneficial. I have found this course of personal advantage in malarial fever. Large amounts of acid given for yellow fever at Panama proved better than the usual treatment.

In the body, in the ground, and in the air we are in continual contact with the minute life, capable of producing specific disease, and without which such specific diseases are probably impossible. Their dangerous activity in the system seems to be due to two causes :

first, the favorable condition of the system for their development, such as low vitality, wounds, etc. ; and second, the presence of such specific minute life in considerable quantity.

In some cases, diseases due to bacteria, etc., will arise more from the first of these causes ; in others, more from the second.

In the streets of a city, we must breathe many germs of certain diseases every day.   The air in the crowded portions of Paris has been shown to contain thousands of germs and germ life per square foot of air, to one such life in the square foot of air of country districts near by.

Consumptive persons spit in the streets, the sputa become dry, and the germ life of the bacillus tuberculosis must mingle with the dust of the city and be breathed by the inhabitants.   The micro-organism said to be the specific infection of pneumonia is found in the buccal secretions of healthy persons, so also are the pus organisms, staphylococcus pyogenes aureus, albus, and citreus.   The tetanus bacillus is widely distributed, and is especially numerous in rich loam, as that generally worked in by gardeners and farmers.

Still the frequent contact of these forms of life with the body is not necessarily infectious or fatal.   But when large numbers of them accumulate, as in hospital wards, cesspools, drains, tenement houses, etc., persons of lowered vitality are extremely likely to come under the influence of one or more kinds of them, and persons in good vigor may also become subject to these diseases.

A peculiarity of some of these micro-organisms such as those of small-pox, measles, scarlet fever, chicken-pox, whooping-cough, etc., is that once having run a course in the human body, they are as a rule incapable of another attack.   In practice we find that one attack by any of these organisms is a guaranty against a second one. Even when an exception occurs, the second attack is usually mild. This is the philosophy of vaccination to prevent or render innocuous the dreadful and disgusting disease of small-pox.

All children should be vaccinated in their first year and until the vaccination takes.   At the same time, the greatest possible care should be taken to have the vaccine secured direct from a reliable source, and to have the operator's hands and instruments clean. The reason of this is the frequent introduction into the body of dangerous germs with those of the vaccine, and the consequent disease or death of the patient.   A great number of diseases have been transmitted in this way.   Sometimes one source of infection, such as a diseased child, will cause an epidemic when virus taken from it is used to vaccinate others.

At about the sixth and fifteenth years children should be revaccinated. The importance of vaccination may be judged by the results of the vaccination and re-vaccination in the German army. During the Franco-Prussian war of 1870 the Germans lost during the whole campaign out of 913,967 effectives but 261 men from small-pox. At the same time in the less carefully tended French army there was a death-rate from small-pox of 67.60 in the 1000. Here is indeed a remarkable difference. A way will probably be found to prevent other contagious diseases such as scarlet fever in the same manner as is now practised for small-pox.

Other classes of micro-organisms seem on the contrary only the more likely to find a lodgment in the body after once running a course in it. Some such are those of diphtheria, all the malarial organisms, gonorrhœa, etc. Persons having had an attack of the first class of organisms are indicated as nurses or attendants for a disease produced by such a cause in others on account of the probable immunity from recontracting the trouble. In the second class it is exactly the reverse. The value of disinfecting sick-rooms, the clothing, the person, the excrements, etc., has been clearly demonstrated. Equally the value of cleanliness, care, and careful antisepsis in surgery is shown in the records of our hospitals and private practice. All this is known by the intelligent. It is also generally understood that various specific micro-organisms are widely diffused; that these accumulated in considerable numbers are dangerous if not deadly, and that therefore all means favorable to their reproduction, by which they become concentrated, as excrements, drains, piles of rubbish, swill, general uncleanliness, confined damp as in unventilated cellars, etc., should be habitually disinfected, removed, or destroyed.

In connection with infectious and contagious diseases it seems appropriate to call attention here to the frequency and intensity of so-called children's diseases in armies. The necessary crowding of soldiers and the customary if not necessary crowding of children in their sleeping-rooms may be the principal promoter of these diseases in both cases. From considerable inquiry, *only* children seem largely exempt from these diseases. Whether their exemption is due to no crowding or to other causes is not certain, but it seems reasonable to attribute some relation between crowding and the frequency of these diseases.

The health of the child is best maintained by fresh air, exercise, and good food.

The food should be administered at regular times, diminished in frequency as the child grows older, and until three meals a day is attained. This rule applies to suckled children as well as to those weaned or hand-fed. At about the sixth month healthy children should no longer be suckled or fed at night. By night is meant the time between the hours of 10 P.M. and 5 A.M., or 11 P.M. and 6 A.M. The interval may be gradually lengthened as the child grows older.

The times of exercise, sleep, and evacuations should all be carefully regulated, and the child be kept out-doors as much as possible. In the matter of sleep a child can not have too much. All young children should be given an opportunity to sleep in the middle of the day. When the baby's meals are at regular times, its hours of rest fixed, its excretions of waste matter encouraged at certain times, and its opportunities of free exercise and investigation made ample, the mother will find child-care easy and not excessive in its demands upon her time.

Even with a large family, the helpless ones will never be too numerous to make proper care by one woman impossible. At the fourth birth at least, the first baby will have become capable of partial self-care and of helping the mother as well. The order implanted in a child's life by assistance of the mother will remain with it through life, and the young child growing up will become, as it should, a help and not an increase to the mother's care.

One of the great things for a young mother to learn is, after doing the essentials for the child, to let it alone. The error of most mothers is interfering too much with the baby's investigations and in often rewarding it for crying.

The tendency of women of force and character, as well as of the foolish and ignorant, is often to do too much for the child. To think and act for the young child is necessary in many cases, but this should never go beyond what is necessary, for to the extent that it does so, the individuality and self-reliance of the child will be injured and its character lack development.

The rule should be to see to the evacuations of the baby at a regular time, to change it at regular times, to feed it at regular times, to give it rest at regular times, to wash it at regular times, to dress it according to climate so that it is properly warm, but not clumsily clothed nor decked in anything expensive, and then put the baby down on the floor or ground as soon as it can sit up and let it play and find out things for itself.

The fact may be borne in mind that our conduct to the new-born child is necessarily based on a reward for incapacity; but that in mature life the rewards of the world to the then grown child will on the contrary be based on capacity. Consequently the parent, while conforming to the first necessity, must prepare the child for the second.

The will-power and self-reliance of the child should be built up as fast as possible. A child should not be allowed to derive advantage by an appeal from the judgment of one parent to the other. The parents must sustain each other in public and before the child, and settle their policy in private.

A good night-dress for restless infants is one made like a loose bag to be fastened at the neck. It may have sleeves, but should not provide separately for the legs. This device prevents the child from ever being entirely exposed to the cold and chill winter nights. If the circumstances warrant the whole bed-clothing may be arranged on the same plan. In putting children to bed they should be accustomed to no adventitious proceedings. Stories should never be told at bedtime. A healthy child should never be rocked to sleep nor accustomed to anything unnecessary for its welfare. A well-trained child is as sleepy as an ill-trained one. All things likely to attract the child's attention must to some extent prevent or retard the approach of natural rest in sleep. When bedtime comes, a child should expect nothing but sleep. When it has been prepared for bed, to bed it should go. It should be saluted for the night, the light should be extinguished, and the child left to sleep. A considerable amount of wear and tear is saved by this system. No possible advantage is lost to the child, its temper is not tried by a resistance to excessive or inopportune demands for unessential rockings, songs, stories, or company, and the mother's energy is liberated for other things.

Very great care must be exercised by parents to avoid themselves and to prevent others from frightening the children by unreal creations of the fancy. Parents and nurses too often endeavor to maintain their authority by a weak method, that sooner or later will be found out in its falsity by the child. This method is to threaten the child with goblins, bears, devils, etc., and to people the dark with torturing terrors. A child seems to have no natural objection to the dark, and the frequent fear observable on this point in the young must be attributed to the faulty, nay, criminal influence of those around them. The reaction in the child, when the deception is discovered, is a fertile cause of silent alienation. This practice secures obedience less well than a plain, consistent, and straightforward course. It causes great and useless suffering in the child, and eventually confidence in the parent is undermined and the moral nature is shaken to its false foundation. A falsehood should under no circumstances be told a child. With children be silent or be truthful.

The child is imitative and is consequently much influenced by those who make up its entourage.

The language, the accent, the grammar, the mental bent, and the religious views of children are all largely influenced by the persons who surround them. Thus it must be seen that the delegation of the care of her children to servants, by the average mother of means, is fraught with danger to her progeny.

Accents and methods of speech of an inferior kind become fixed, and superstitious and other false and inferior views of religion are stamped into the nature of the child.

My nurses implanted in me, amongst other things, the idea that to see the new moon over the left shoulder was unlucky, and over the right, lucky. So strong was this conviction that during my youth I made a business of always seeing the new moon over my right shoulder, and when I saw it over the left, by any accident, it made me feel exceedingly uncomfortable. To this day my first view of a new moon brings up at once the idea that I ought to see it over my right shoulder, and I believe that I feel better, at least for a few moments, when I do. If a ridiculous and baseless superstition of this kind implanted in youth can take such a hold, must we not be compelled to admit that impressions in regard to the serious matters of life may be received by the child from the same sources and of the same untrue character.

The impressions of early childhood are hard to eradicate. Many of these remain throughout life in spite of everything that can be done to get rid of them. The impressions of children derived from nurses, servants, associates, and books cannot be too carefully looked after. Servants should be commanded to say nothing on religion to children. That should come from the parents. The child, of course, must not be enslaved and ruined in these cautions to prevent a possible ruin in the open world, but care can easily be taken to provide the proper surroundings, and, as the child grows older, to put the proper kind of reading matter in its way and throw it in association with the best class of children. A proper bringing-up will make a child despise and avoid the vulgar and low, both in books and friends. Cast-iron rules cannot do it. In extreme youth alone is the complete and absolute regulation of association service-able. It is then also that the child cannot be a free agent. Often when parents or mentors correct a child, they themselves do the very things against which they have cautioned it. I have frequently been caught in this way. When one's attention is called to such a matter, the error should be acknowledged and caution used to prevent a repetition. Example is too good a teacher to be given the oppor-tunity to inculcate error in a child.

Every freedom should be given a baby that is possible and consistent with safety from real danger. Little falls, bumps, etc., it must have in the course of its investigations, and the sooner it has them the sooner will it be able to care for itself. A child should be told " don't " and similar words as seldom as possible, but when you do say " don't," mean it, and make the baby stop what you object to. So with all things in a child's life, give them as much freedom as you can ; never nag them, but when you do give an order, mean it, and have it carried out.

Reiteration of advice and correction is, doubtless, to some extent necessary. Such action always weakens advice or correction in new matters, tries and irritates both parent and child, and should be avoided as far as possible.

The efficiency of natural penalties in early childhood to avoid physical harm is so clear that natural penalties for unwise conduct should, as far as possible, be availed of. This practice, with proper precaution, may be extended to moral matters. If a child be late in getting ready for meals, walks, etc., deprive the child of such meal or walk, as the case may be. One or two lessons will cure nearly any starting bad habit of this kind. Violent or personal chastisement is the last thing to resort to. It always drives the parent and child apart, and associates the rewards and penalties of conduct to the personal and often arbitrary opinion of the parent. A child may pick up a hot coal twice, but that is the extreme limit of ignorance as to its effect. Herbert Spencer, in *Education*, puts this matter very clearly. He says :

" Penalties which the necessary reaction of things round upon them—penalties which are inflicted by impersonal agency produce an irritation that is comparatively slight and transient ; whereas, penalties which are voluntarily inflicted by a parent, and are afterwards remembered as caused by him or her, produce an irritation both greater and more continued. Just consider how disastrous would be the result if this empirical method were pursued from the beginning. Suppose it were possible for parents to take upon themselves the physical sufferings entailed on their children by ignorance and awkwardness ; and that while bearing these evil consequences they visited on their children certain other evil consequences, with the view of teaching them the impropriety of their conduct.

" Suppose that when a child, who had been forbidden to meddle with the kettle, spilt some boiling water on its foot, the mother assumed the scald and gave a blow in place of it ; and similarly in all other cases. Would not the daily mishaps be sources of far more anger than now? Would there not be chronic ill-temper on both sides? Yet an exactly parallel policy is pursued in after years. A father who punishes his boy for carelessly or wilfully breaking a sister's toy, and then himself pays for a new toy, does substantially the same thing—inflicts an artificial penalty on himself; his own feelings and those of the transgressor being alike needlessly irritated. If he simply required restitution to be made, he would produce far less heart-burning."

Again Spencer says, p. 186 :

"It is a vice of the common system of artificial rewards and punishments, long since noticed by the clear-sighted, that by substituting for the natural results of misbehavior certain threatened tasks or castigations, it produces a radically wrong standard of moral guidance. Having throughout infancy and boyhood always regarded parental or tutorial displeasure as the result of forbidden action, the youth has gained an established association of ideas between such action and such displeasure, as cause and effect; and, consequently, when parents and tutors have abdicated, and their displeasure is not to be feared, the restraint on a forbidden action is, in great measure, removed; the true restraints, the natural reactions, having yet to be learned by sad experience. As writes one who has had personal knowledge of this short-sighted system : 'Young men let loose from school, particularly those whose parents have neglected to exercise their influence, plunge into every description of extravagance; they know no rule of action, they are ignorant of the reasons for moral conduct, they have no foundation to rest upon, and until they have been severely disciplined by the world, are extremely dangerous members of society.'"

The whole of Spencer's book is worthy of quotation, and I desire that it should be studied.

The dangerous dissipation into which many young men run when freed, or even partially freed, from restraint shows the error spoken of. Such young men are supposed to be well brought up, but they have to learn that a violation of nature's laws is always followed by a punishment, and that the laws of society, generally following the rules of nature, when violated, bring their punishment with nearly equal certainty. Many young people never escape from the muck they are thus ignorantly gotten into. The true formative and receptive moments in their lives having passed, they are no longer capable of a comprehension of the lessons of life, and, started on the wrong road, are unable either to come back or to be brought back. It must be evident to any one who will reflect that the true natural or social penalty of an offence is the one to invoke and to depend upon when possible. A child brought up as thus indicated has a sure and certain foundation for its acts. When the personal equation comes up in a child's government, as it probably must occasionally, be consistent and firm. It will require but a few struggles from time to time to convince the child that you mean business when you talk, and do but follow nature in your rules.

Thus, instead of the thorns so many plant in their own and in their children's paths, there will be roses full of beauty and pleasure. If you are continually nagging at a child, and saying "don't" to every effort it makes to answer nature's call for exercise and investigation, you will reduce a healthy child to desperation. It ought not to remain still, and it cannot without artificial restraint. You also weaken your control, and bring it into contempt. Your temper and that of the child will become irritated. Place the child where it can play and roll and get dirty and make a noise, and let it alone as much as is consistent with safety. It is a study well worthy of careful attention to learn to save yourself from unnecessary interference with the child, annoying to you and injurious to the little one.

A spoiled child is one unduly indulged, and is most often spoiled by too much interference without the interference having been complete. Thus a mother says "don't" and lets the child go on. It would be a thousand times better never to have said the obnoxious word. The child is annoyed and not controlled by such a course and soon becomes a nuisance.

Activity in a child is to be expected. When it is not found there is something wrong. The thing to do is to provide the youngster with a legitimate means of exercising it. Say "don't" to things that must not be done and do not allow them to be done. But be careful not to carry the word into unnecessary use, and make an earnest study to have nature give this command for you.

The cry is the child's first means of making known its wants. A certain amount of crying therefore is proper in a baby and probably does it good in the way of exercise and expanding the lungs, but unless guarded against, crying, as the child grows older, is likely to degenerate into a tyranny destructive to both the happiness of mother and child and in fact to the happiness of the household. The mother should therefore keep a judicious watch, not only on the child, but on herself to prevent the "cry" for food or attention proper in the infant from becoming a characteristic of the older child used to obtain its wishes when obstructed. The best means of preventing this result is by not giving the child what it cries for and not doing what the child cries to have done. In other words, *never* reward crying. This policy carried out in the household will put a prompt stop to crying as a tyranny. Children when hurt generally cry, and sympathy and care should not be withheld on this account.

All things unnecessary for a baby are more or less harmful and are often much more so in their ultimate effects than one might suppose. Babies and young children are often held in the arms when they are not feeding or at times are tossed or dandled. These practices are dangerous. A child much held is more subject to catch cold than if not so held, on account of the changes of temperature to which it is subjected. A child dandled or tossed is liable to serious injuries without any chance of compensating gain either in health of body or mind.

Several instances in the families of persons whom I know or know of, have strikingly illustrated the dangers of tossing. One baby's skull fractured, another thrown headfirst against the point of a gas chandelier, two children made cripples, three humpbacks, and two killed by tossing, is a serious list for a private experience. While the number of injuries is small to the total number of children amongst whom they occurred, it is still sufficient to lead us to avoid the practice, since the child can by no possibility derive an advantage from it.

A mother should avoid holding a child except when it is in the act of suckling. Sometimes a baby will cry continuously for no understandable reason, and the mother or nurse dandles or holds the child to quiet it. Such otherwise inexplicable uneasiness is occasionally caused by thirst and usually occurs after feeding. A little water that has been boiled and purified will correct such thirst and is not infrequently an aid to a baby's digestion and a great consequent benefit.

A most important thing with children is to keep them out-doors as much as possible. A plant taken into a house soon becomes sickly; it loses its bright green and tends ever more and more to an anæmic white. It requires twice as much care and can never remain healthy. Thus it is with the child; in-doors it will become pale, nervous, and anæmic, it will require more care and never be healthy. To the extent that a plant is deprived of air, to the same extent will it be injured. The same result is seen in cooped-up children. Probably they can stand such treatment less well, for to them oxygen is necessary and carbonic acid gas noxious, which is not the case with plants.

Health is the main thing to work for in the treatment of young children. Cleanliness, plain food in reasonable variety, plenty of exercise, and an out-door life are the essentials to health in children.

Taking up these points in the order named, we have, first,

CLEANLINESS.

Young children should be cleaned thoroughly once a day and babies twice a day. The climate of the residence and the constitution of the child will vary the methods appropriate for accomplishing this result. For instance, dry rubbing with a bath once or twice a week may be best for a thin-skinned, nervous child, while for a stouter one, with perhaps some skin trouble, an alkaline bath twice or even three times a day may be beneficial. In eczema bathing is generally injurious. No rule can be laid down then as to how the cleanliness is to be maintained.

A child requires less cleaning as it wears less clothes and more cleaning as it wears more clothes. The emanations from our own bodies are as a rule more hurtful, if not gotten rid of, than accumulations of outside dirt. The privates of children should be washed once a day and children as they grow older should be taught to wash themselves in these parts always once a day. Great stress should be laid on this point, for it is of much importance that this should be done in after life.

The boy at about the age of ten should be taught to pull back the prepuce or foreskin in washing. Sometimes there is a premature secretion of smegma, or at others an accumulation of urine, under the prepuce. Under these circumstances washing is always necessary. The boy should be warned against handling or exposing the privates at any other time except when absolutely essential for the calls of nature. See Acton on *The Reproductive Organs.*

A climate that is warm and moist requires more washing to maintain cleanliness than one that is dry and cold. The skin in a cold climate, especially when also moist, acts less and throws off less waste than in a warm one. As a climate is cold and dry, so is its capacity increased to encourage endosmose and exosmose of gases to keep up the balance of healthy air between closed rooms and the outside.

Thus the carbonic acid gas, etc., coming from the body of a man at a temperature of 98° in a closed room, with the outer air at 0°, will by these means be passed through wooden or stone walls without a visible aperture, and oxygen, etc., takes its place.

If the temperature be 20° or 30° lower outside the room than it is in it, and the air be dry, the replacement of bad gases or those deleterious to health by good ones, will be very rapid. The air in a closed room, under favorable conditions of temperature and dryness, often maintains its purity better than the air of the same room with a window open does, under unfavorable hygrometric and thermometric conditions. The tables showing the permeability of stone, wood, etc., to the gases of the atmosphere and the rapidity with which, under favorable circumstances, atmospheric balances can be established and maintained through solid walls of these materials is astonishing. On the other hand, the difficulty of proper air cleansing, when conditions are unfavorable, is clear.

It is consoling to know that when the necessity for the transmission of gases is greatest, it is easiest.

As it is with rooms, so it is with individuals. When the most attention is required to maintain cleanliness, that is, in moist, warm weather, then is bathing easiest, while in very cold weather, bathing need not be frequent, and if carried too far may even injure the constitution.

In arctic regions winter bathing is practically impossible.

Baths of children should rarely be in cold water : lukewarm water is best. Bathing may vary from a sponge off to an immersion. It is essential to use judgment against overdoing the use of water.

The nails should be kept clean. The dirt in them, especially in the nails of nurses and physicians, is a frequent vehicle for infection. This fact, pointed out to children, will doubtless add to their interest in this point.

The teeth should be carefully cleansed night and morning. A great deal of suffering from the teeth in after years will thus be avoided. But besides this, food and the secretions in the mouth, if allowed to accumulate in and about the teeth will decay, and with the decay of the teeth this induces, will produce ptomaines, inimical to digestion, and consequently lowering to the vitality.

I have recently seen some reports of recurring diphtheria, that is, where one or more attacks of diphtheria occurred in the same individual every year. These reports show that the diphtheritic attacks were prevented by a careful cleansing with antiseptic fluids of the mouth, throat, and nose. The checking of these results seems to have been carefully done. The residence was the same, and in several cases members of the family thus troubled, not taking the precautions mentioned, were attacked, while the more susceptible member or members taking the treatment were not.

These results indicate that the abnormal secretions or contents of the nose, mouth, and throat are a breeding-place for any germs that may be introduced into them, and that the resisting power of our healthy blood and tissue against injurious germ life has little or no influence in dead tissue or decaying matter. A child having catarrhal conditions, or defective teeth, or furred tongue should be encouraged to the greatest care in keeping the parts affected clean. Bedding should be carefully aired every day, and whenever practicable, that is when the sun shines, should be sunned in the open air an hour or two a day. The sun is a great disinfector. Its direct action is not only usually fatal to minute disease life, but is often so to the germs also.

Plain healthy food, with fair variety and occasional change, is of great importance to the child. A proper diet varies with the constitution, activity, and residence of the child. Constitutions differ in all respects and often in curious and exceptional ways.

Thus strawberries are generally a wholesome fruit, but with some they cause a rash to break out, accompanied by a great deal of irritation. Milk is usually a wholesome and advantageous diet at all ages, but quite frequently children shortly after weaning cannot digest it well. With some it will turn acid and cause diarrhœa, while with others nausea causes the milk to be thrown from the stomach; in other cases, it causes constipation. One of my own children, now two years old, is unable to eat eggs or anything prepared with them ; even a piece of cake with egg in it will cause an immediate attack of nausea and general malaise.

Tomatoes, generally friendly to the digestion, are not suited to some, and occasionally even salivate persons eating them. Apples eaten to any extent by some persons will bring on an increased flow of urine. It is, however, with stimulants, narcotics, and medicines that we notice oftenest the idiosyncrasies of constitution in man.

Some persons, instead of being narcotized by the usual doses of such drugs as chloroform, opium, etc., are greatly excited. Some can tolerate strong doses of mercury, arsenic, or other powerful medicines, while others on taking even small doses suffer such general injury as to counteract any good effects on a specific trouble these drugs may produce. Some are poisoned by a whiff of air from a poison oak plant, while others can roll in it without effect of visible harm. There are certain general rules as to diet that should be followed with children, but at the same time peculiarities of constitution should be watched for, and food that is unsuitable to a child in experience should not be given, though the general rule favor it.

What should compose a proper diet varies with the age of the child, its activities and manner of life, and on the climate in which it lives. These are matters for investigation and study which open an ample field for the scientific investigation of the parents, and especially of the mother. Too much importance cannot be attached to the diet of children. A mistake will cause suffering to the child and consequently to the parents, and may result in death. Food absolutely requisite in a cold climate may bring on indigestion, diarrhœa, and fever in a warm one.

The extraordinary mortality of infants during the excessive hot periods of summer in such cities as New York is now accounted for by the effects of the heat on the milk and food used for the babies as well as on the babies themselves. Here then is another matter for consideration. Milk exposed in warm weather is a food especially liable to spoil. It turns acid and the babies' powers of assimilation being already weakened by the heat, indigestion sets in to be followed often by cholera infantum and death. Various single methods may be used to diminish this danger, such as care in seeing that the milk is fresh and sweet when received and when given, boiling the milk, putting lime-water in when received, etc. The first should always be done. The cow or cows from which the milk is received should be examined occasionally. Cows are frequently subject to diseases common to man, especially to tuberculosis. As milk is a good vehicle for disease germs caution should be used on this point. For the same reason some track should be kept of the health of the family furnishing the milk. The best road out of this difficulty is to keep your own cows, but the means of the family may not justify this.

After we have taken all the pains and pleasures of creating a human being in our own likeness we cannot be too careful of its life. At the same time we must remember that the child's future success depends on its character. This can only be well and forcibly developed by throwing the child as much as possible on its own resources and building up its own self-reliance and self-respect. Coddling and care by others are inimical to these results. It will not be easy to draw the line between proper care of the child and care that will injure its future life. It is a matter that should be looked into, and the care appropriate for children will doubtless vary with different individuals and places.

Children may often derive advantage from a temporary change of climate and scene. But travelling with children in general is to be avoided. The risks of exposure, changes in diet, dangers of infection, etc., are very great.

Numbers of cases of the loss of children from diphtheria and zymotic diseases through exposure while being dragged about by parents in their pleasure or sight-seeing tours have come to my notice.

A child may grow up cautious or careless according to influences around them and these are largely the result of the activities of associates. It may not be amiss to point out to young people as an inducement to good manners in the home that they are never so well thought of if they treat their family or friends with disrespect. It is a disrespect to themselves. The reading of young people is an important matter. Every effort should be made to keep it on a high plane. While doing this it is essential to consider the development of the child's mind and to suit the matter to the machinery for its working up.

Exercise is an absolute essential to the welfare of children. This exercise should be in the open air as much as possible. While the dictum admits of no amendment it is important to have a clear idea of the object of exercise, so that the abuse of it or its usurpation of the energies of life may not take place. Exercise of the body is a means and not an end. The body without exercise, especially in the young, does not remain healthy. Without a healthy body the full possibilities of the mind cannot be realized ; consequently to use the mind, as humanity is now constituted, a good body is necessary. The true object of exercise is then to develop or maintain a body that will carry the mind and enable it to exhibit its work and improve its quality, and to reproduce this mind with its accompanying body.

Physical education to insure physical perfection is good, but it is not realized when the physique detracts from the mental or reproductive powers. These may all be considered physical powers, as they are, but they are here separated for convenience. From these reasons any physical education for superiority in acrobatic exercises, etc., is exceedingly liable to abuse. We do not want prize fighters or circus actors. The improvement of the race and of life is not on that line. It is in the mental line, and the mind will triumph over brute force. The mind only requires a vigor and vitality in the body to allow it to do its work. The best means for a proper physical education is the child's self-learning acquired in sports and games. The development of the body is in such sports more even, the exercise is outdoors, and excessive exertion, while quite possible, is not so likely to occur as in gymnastics or feats of strength. Interest, discipline, combination, etc., are also cultivated in games.

Hard work of body or mind should not be permitted in children. Excesses of this kind, like all excesses, are especially injurious to the child.

The vigor necessary for development is abstracted by premature overwork, and the child thus abused is either arrested at a stage of evolution lower than it would otherwise have reached, or fatally injured in its future reproductive powers ; perhaps not prevented altogether from reproduction, but so devitalized as to be unable to transmit superiority of body or mind.

A colt worked hard when young is ruined, or at least does not become so good a horse in all respects as would otherwise have been the case. An animal so treated does not develop so well, does not live so long, and a precocity—say of speed—is developed at the expense of the future matured horse. Human beings we have less positive data about. But it is a subject of general remark that the youthful prodigies and acrobats of the circus are of short life, and very rarely are athletes of any mark in manhood. So also the prodigies of precocity in the school are not usually those who take the prizes of life at maturity. Some exceptions, such as the celebrated

Pascal, must occur to the thoughful ; but even this remarkable child and remarkable man is not so much an exception after all. His powers commenced to wane before thirty, and before his death he was at least partly insane. He died prematurely old at thirty-nine, and left no progeny.

John Stuart Mill is more nearly a complete exception to my views. This eminent thinker was both a precocious child and a celebrated man. He was born in a city, in London, and lived to a good old age. He, however, failed to perpetuate his mental abilities in children. His father was a strong and celebrated man, and he came from the country in Scotland. According to my theories, had the son remained in the country, been discouraged in precocity, and reserved a sufficient energy to perpetuate his superiorities, the Mill family might to-day be achieving greater things than any they have done, and possess no end of future possibilities.

Many of the eminent men of the past showed a development of talent or genius at an age which we must indeed admit as precocious. Alexander the Great, for instance, commenced his experience in government at 16, and his career of conquest at 20. He died at 32, leaving a child born after his death. This infant was murdered when 12 years of age. William Pitt, the second son of the great Pitt, was Chancellor of the Exchequer at 24, and Prime Minister at 25. He died at 47 without children.

The rarity with which those showing great precocity of talent have left children, or children who became eminent, is to be noted. Precocity is consequently not to be encouraged, and never to be artificially produced.

The pressure of reading and study upon the eyes is now so great that many children suffer through life from the consequences of imprudence in the use of these windows of the soul. The rule should be never to allow reading or study at dawn, twilight, or by a bad light. No study should be allowed by lamplight, gas, etc., until twelve or fifteen years of age, and then only in moderation. Studies necessitating before twelve night work may from that fact be deemed excessive and should be reduced.

Reasonable body and mind exercise is usually what a child takes of its own volition when under the proper influences. In mental exercise it is well to keep the fact before us that the child first understands or grasps the homogeneous, and only afterward the heterogeneous ; consequently, generalizations should follow the acquirement of the facts upon which they are based. Plain as is the propriety of following this order, frequent violations of it are observable in ordinary education.

In considering the treatment of the child the general course of its evolution should govern. In the fœtus all the vitality goes to growth. In the baby nearly all the vitality has the same destiny. In the child this still remains true, and it is not until nature has completed the reproductive powers of the individual that she diverts vitality for a great superiority in any other line. Vitality thus diverted prematurely is taken at a heavy cost.

Children of the two sexes should be brought up together. The two sexes must meet and live together in after life, and I believe that they should never be separated as is so often done in schools. The separation of the sexes is invariably followed by awkwardness and uncomfortableness when a child so separated is brought in contact with the opposite sex. The reproductive instincts, swelling in the bud long before they bloom, drive girls and boys separated from each other, with the whips of a natural curiosity as, to each other, to think and do many improper things.

The natural curiosity when they are separated turns to a morbid form, both sexes become foolish about each other, and the results too often are self-abuse, escapades, and elopements. The girls are often misled and are ruined beyond repair, and the boys often slink into houses of prostitution to gratify a natural and healthy curiosity that, with more familiarity and daily contact with good girls, would never have taken so dangerous a form. Girls and boys brought up together in the common schools, as far as I have observed, seem to look at each other as a matter of course, and play and romp together with little if any unclean language, thought, or deed. On the other hand, boys separated from girls' society and girls in carefully kept boarding schools become possessed with a romantic folly about the opposite sex, and while so possessed are easily led away to error.

It is important to impress children with the danger of intimacies with strangers, kissing and caressing unknown persons or children, using clothes, sheets, towels, handkerchiefs, etc., used by other people. The reason of this is that many kinds of disease are transmitted by germs or by already developed minute organisms. These may be carried in the clothing or in articles used, and thus infect persons subsequently using them ; or the transfer of the disease may take place by actual touch. In this class of diseases are small-pox, scarlet-fever, diphtheria, measles, chicken-pox, whooping-cough, cholera, gonorrhœa, and various skin troubles, and, most of all, consumption and syphilis. Consumption, fortunately, is not so easily transferred as the others. Syphilis is a deadly and terrible malady. One can never know when its march is done. Even death to the individual will not stop it, for it will march on in the children, directy or indirectly, if happily the children be born alive, for a large proportion of conceptions by or in syphilitics are not born alive.

In these matters a consistent caution should be followed. The care taken should be systematic, reasonable, not excessive, yet great.

A schoolmate of mine lost his eye from a gonorrhœal attack caused by a soiled towel with which he wiped his face. Thus venereal disease may endanger the eyes though no venereal license be practised. I personally know of one case where syphilis was given by a kiss. There are undoubtedly transmissions of syphilis without sexual intercourse, and the kiss is of these secondary means the most frequent spreader of this fell malady. The importance in care as to syphilis may be understood by the number of its victims in the community.

One writer estimates 25 per cent. of the population to be more or less tainted with it. A friend of mine, who is a physician in large practice, estimates the proportion injured by it in one way or another to be from 35 per cent. to 40 per cent. Both estimates seem to me excessive, and may arise from the proportion of this disease or its sequelæ to all others treated. An estimate founded on correct data as indicated, need bear no true relation to the condition of the whole population.

The value of care and education on this subject is shown by the frequency of venereal diseases in the armies of Europe as compared to the care taken to guard against them.

The treatment of venereal diseases is annually :

1 in 19 in the Prussian army.
1 " 10 " " French "
1 " 3 " " English "

The care and education on this subject are greatest in the Prussian army and almost nil in the English.

Unclean water-closets are also a source of infection, especially in venereal diseases. In cases of epidemics of typhoid, typhus, or cholera public water-closets should be avoided. Care in looking into the health of playmates and nurses should be taught children, and the parents must not sleep in the matter.

One thing in the treatment of children and young persons is of great importance to their health, and especially to their moral well-being ; it is to give each one a separate bed to sleep in and, if possible, a separate room or compartment.

(See Acton on *The Reproductive Organs*, p. 54, sixth edition.)

The sleeping apartments and arrangements bear a direct relation to the development of modesty.

One thing is always to be remembered in the treatment of children. You must gain their confidence. While holding up to them a high standard for all attainments you should make it clear to children that you understand their humanity and their liability at times to fall below the standard set. Our standard should always be progressive—that is, higher than our own lives have attained. Such a standard can only be come at with struggle and effort.

These inevitable struggles toward perfection can not, in the nature of humanity, be each time completely successful, otherwise humanity would be very different from what it is. With a high standard it is consequently more than ever necessary to commend it with a sympathy to the child and I believe also with a confession of the difficulties you yourself have experienced only to overcome with effort. If this be not done, then any proper standard for our eventual efforts being too high for immediate realization by the human child, the child will feel a shame and disgrace at its inevitable lapses and will keep them secret. What the child needs in such failures is the sympathy and help of its mentor.

Our efforts should ever be towards a condition superior to anything hitherto attained, but the road to it is the human one over at best a cobble-stone of imperfection.

This must be recognized and admitted, otherwise we do but prepare ourselves for an inevitable reaction such as has thus far invariably accompanied the high aims of man. These remarks apply especially to morality. The attitude of the parent to the child should be in the following line.

I teach you, my child, what is good and what is error. I have not been perfect and I know much of what I teach by bitter experience and the observation of the still more bitter experience of others. I hope to help you to avoid my own mistakes. In this undertaking it is your welfare I consider, and my effort is to make you, my new self, better than I, your old self. You cannot be perfect. It is toward perfection that you should work. Fear not then when you fail to come to me for counsel. Be not ashamed when you do wrong to come to me for help. You, my child, are my own life renewed. You are the best part of me. Then believe always that you are my hope. Your secrets I will never betray. Your interests, your growth, your achievements are mine. Let now your inexperience profit as far as possible from my age. My heart beats in your heart and my hopes grow new with yours. Consider me what I am, a reserve force to cover your retreats where these may unfortunately be necessary, and to push home your victories when these you achieve.

14

Exaggerate nothing. Exaggeration is sure to bring reaction. Nowhere will it be more felt than in the young trusting child. The idea should not be given that the parent knows everything, for this brings the child to the parent instead of to nature. The inquiring child should always, when possible, be taken direct to nature. You will yourself always find something to learn, and you should admit it to the child to encourage its inquiries.

In the treatment of the child, as has been said, it should be clearly formulated as well as indefinitely felt that the new-born babe must receive services and attention in no way connected with its own services—for of these it is incapable.

Conversely, the interest of society and ultimately of the individual also demands that the rewards to the grown person should correspond with their merits and with their services rendered. In the first stages of life the conduct of the parent toward the child must be according to affection and generosity; on the other hand, the conduct of society toward the mature individual must be according to justice and to render to him by the measure he renders to it.

The parents, while recognizing the first necessity, should so govern themselves and their children that these, when going out into the world, will be prepared to meet the contest of life upon the lines of justice.

Society cannot live much less progress in treating the individual in a general way upon the lines of generosity which are an absolute essential to the treatment of the babe by the parent. Therefore a grown person leaving the family for the fight of life with the expectation of being treated in the generous policy appropriate to the child is handicapped. If he or she succeeds, it must be by learning and avoiding the error. It is to be supposed that the failure of many persons is due to the impression of youth, unmodified in the family experience, that subsistence, kindness, and reward in the world are matters of generosity and not of justice.

When children come to the age of puberty and commence the change that is to make them men and women, they have arrived at a crisis in their lives. At this age the body grows rapidly both in size and weight, and the vital forces in great activity go to the perfecting of the reproductive organs. It is not expedient to press mental efforts during this period. On the contrary, young people should be kept out-of-doors in light occupation or sports to a greater extent than usual while they are passing from the age of children through the development of the reproductive power to the age of manhood and womanhood. Examinations and extra pressures are often allowed to push young people at this time. It is always at the expense of their future health and vitality.

As reproducing an improved being should be our aim, it being the grandest achievement of which we are capable, so a course interfering with this is a fundamental error.

In the treatment of children nothing is more important than to carefully look after their welfare at the age of puberty. Girls having a sure sign of this in the appearance of the menses their age of puberty can be accurately established. It is true that the descent of the egg in some women is accompanied by no sign, this fact being known by the pregnancy of women without a menstrual flow, but such cases are like five-fingered men, albinos, etc., too rare to require attention.

The boy's age of puberty is, however, not so easily known, and must be watched for more carefully. Usually the hair commences to grow on the lip and chin, the voice to change, and a self-consciousness appears that requires judicious treatment. If the course of the chapter on education has been followed, and the boy and girl understand something of the functions that are taking such a hold on them, and comprehend the dangers of abuse of these, and, above all, realize their grandeur and importance, less trouble will be experienced in inducing the young to a wise life at this time.

After the age of puberty childhood is over. The reproductive instinct then dominates life. It is for us to say whether this domination shall be for evil in lust, dissipation, prostitution, and self-abuse, or for good in marriage and children with the healthy and renewed life these bring.

With the robust this is the choice, but it must be said that in our in-door and sedentary civilization there are numbers who without strong health are also without an aggressive reproductive instinct. These are our weaklings. Extermination threatens their ill-balanced constitutions and they on their part court extermination by repressing or perverting these our grandest powers. The repression or perversion only hastens the end. Such people rarely enjoy good health ; insanity and death ever dog their heels.

For the wise man there is but one choice—the wife, the child, the happy home. Renewed and immortal there, such a man may smile at old age and threatening death. The time that furrows and whitens him is but developing and bringing on his new self in his children.

CHAPTER VI.

HINTS TO THE HUSBAND.

M ARRIAGE is the official sanction of the union of two lives in one by means of the child. By marriage alone is the man or woman complete.

The proper treatment of a wife in the almost entire absence of any education as to the duties, greatness, importance, and joys of matrimony is a conduct now come at by intuition alone. That intuitions alone are not sufficient in a large number of cases we now see.

Religious forms and dogmas which have supplied the lack of a rational education in this, the most important matter of our lives and of our future, have lost much of their hold on our actions. Thus troubles in matrimony are more prevalent than they were formerly in America, and are becoming still more so. It is indeed true that experience is our only real teacher, but may we not learn how to obtain that experience and have our attention drawn to what will occur, so that we may see the facts when they come in their true light.

Every one who is married can appreciate the difficulty of making clear the difference that takes place in one's life through matrimony. In this relation in its perfection the individual is at once halved and doubled—halved in that the individual is but a part of a new life made by the union, and doubled in that two lives thereafter make the united pair.

In the new and grand relation formed by the union of marriage the first thing of importance is to become acquainted with one's better half. Before marriage this is impossible, because you have no other half. The intimacy of marriage will introduce the husband to the wife; nothing else can. Therefore the great voluntary step of our lives, marriage, should at first be so regulated as to prevent any interference with or drawback to the intimacy and communing of the united ones, lest the union should be less complete or be slow in its growth.

No man or woman can be complete until they create. Marriage

which provides for creation in its joys and mysteries is in a sense a birth. It is the birth from the single man and maid of the united couple, husband and wife. As the first influences on the child are the most lasting, and do most toward moulding its character, so also the first influences on the bride, as on the husband, are the most important in marriage, for it is these that do most to fix the destiny of the union.

In the newly married there is an opening of the heart, a tenderness and exchange of confidence that should be given every encouragement. It cannot have full sway under the eye of friends and relatives, for they will criticise and appear at inopportune occasions.

Near relatives especially seem at these times exacting and unreasonable in regard to the new member of the family, and often enough suggest doubts that become the seeds of much unhappiness ; or, while the beings are adjusting themselves to the great change of marriage, interfere with the heart and reason of the interested ones in moments of the almost inevitable friction that occur, and with very good intentions do incalculable harm.

The custom of a bridal trip after marriage, however it originated, is clearly a good one. Understanding the why, you will be able to make this trip one full of good results. The voyage in most cases should be to a quiet place or places with no excessive fatigues. In all cases it should be without relatives and where relatives and friends will not be seen. The husband at this time should not forget the embarrassments of the new relation his wife has undertaken, remembering that she in receiving the ring, the emblem of eternity, has given him her life. Her honor and happiness are in the husband's hands. The separation from her old associations and the fulfilment of the wife's duties cause a great strain upon the delicate sensibilities of an inexperienced wife so recently a maiden. The husband should be tender and should not abuse his privileges.

It is too delicate a matter, according to our present popular opinion, to enter into any useful detail as to the more intimate relations of marriage. In fact the rules and laws of Solon, Moses, The Mishna, Mahomet etc., as to these matters have not done much good. Recent researches on this point, such as those of Acton, are equally unsatisfactory as a positive guide. They are all, however, useful and suggestive.

To lay down rules for the marriage embrace of a camel-driver, as distinguished from a sailor, to exact heavy duties from the vigorous idle man and relieve altogether the sage and scholar, as all these authorities more or less do, would be to perpetuate the idle and worthless, and to exterminate the wise.

It is sufficient to say that excess in marital privileges is bad, and that the true and grand exercise of the reproductive function is for reproduction. Anything beyond this, any use without hope of fertility, is to be scanned with suspicion. The presumption is against it. It may be said here that the marital privilege of the husband should not be exercised for six weeks after the birth of the child nor during the menstrual flow.

There is no need to make a bridal trip costly. Servants should never be taken on a wedding journey ; they are as dangerous as relatives—nay, probably more so.

The husband should take his wife after the bridal trip to a home. A boarding-house, a hotel, or the house of the parents on either side should be excluded. A home, if it is only a tent or a shanty, is an essential to a marriage. A married couple can live as cheaply and in as much comfort, as to worldly matters, in a home of their own as in a hotel or boarding-house. The comfort and happiness possible in a home is altogether and completely impossible anywhere else. In a home only can the husband and wife really taste the full joys and greatness of marriage. A home will make both greater, nobler, more useful, and more successful than any half life in detestable boarding-houses or hotels.

In the formative years and until the first children are born, there are few good reasons for the permanent introduction into the house of a relative—none for the introduction of a stranger.

The development of the children and their improvement upon the original stock depend on the development and the use of your faculties and your wife's. These can be most fully developed under the full stimulus of a sound home life.

Outsiders, whether friends or relatives, cannot be introduced at the commencement into the home for a length of time without endangering it. The direct mischief possible is great, especially when the person, whether male or female, brought in is attractive. But this danger is not the only one ; it is the indirect effects which are to be most feared. The presence of outsiders has two tendencies : the first is to lessen the full home life by lessening the confidences and the freedom of man and wife,—it is a constraint ; and secondly, to make misunderstandings between the married ones tend to quarrels, and quarrels that become difficult to make up.

Pride in holding up one's self-esteem before an outsider has caused many an unhealed breach in married life.

As no one is perfect, not even a new wife or a new husband, so perfection cannot be presumed ; consequently occasional criticism in personal or household matters should be expected in the adjustments of the newly married and probably later on in their united lives.

These criticisms, all advice, misunderstandings, and embraces should never be before witnesses. The sting is out of a senseless squabble if no one knows about it ; while on the other hand the joys and caresses of the married excite the comment and ridicule of the world when improperly thrust into public view. Therefore, keep your family life strictly private.

A husband, conscious of his headship in the family and of his power, should not cavil over small things. When a domestic squall breaks, as it occasionally may, it is usually good policy to follow the practice of shipmasters in open roadsteads when storms come up— that is to put quietly to sea under storm sail, and cruise in deep water far from the rocks and breakers till all is quiet again.

The first years at least should be spent by husband and wife together, and free from the dangers of friends or relatives in the household. Later, when children have made marriage a real union, more freedom in these matters may be allowed. It is, however, never a wise plan to introduce to the intimacy of your home life young men.

By intimacy is meant the entry into the home at all times, and social intercourse with the wife without check. Women at certain times have moments when they are scarcely themselves. At such times designing men may ruin a really good woman. It is not only the actual ruin of the wife which may take place through such imprudence, but the confidence of the husband in the wife may be undermined and his peace of mind destroyed, even though the wife be really innocent of any impropriety. The happiness of the home may thus be more or less cut down, and perhaps altogether destroyed.

A home destroyed is the wreck of the wife, and in many cases of the husband also. Such an event is a blot in life that will not out. Such extraordinary penalties demand a withdrawal from risks. As the pleasures to be gained bear no sort of relation to the risks incurred, it is clearly a bad business proposition to be careless in these matters. Nothing said in this connection should be taken as advising a mewing up of the wife, nor should a course of conduct be pursued likely to destroy her own self-respect and self-reliance, for on these your honor rests. Do not place your wife in temptation, but lead her by just reason from the first to avoid these risks herself and thus keep her reputation free from the treacherous stabs of scandal.

In case a man becomes persistent in attentions, it is advisable to have a plain talk with him, not necessarily of a quarrelsome nature ; say, if you like, what you have at stake, and be plain and firm in refusing to allow the attentions to continue. In such an open approach to any one, you will find yourself thrice armed. You are right and he is wrong. You have on your side your own force, the opinion of the best, and the necessity society is under to maintain the purity of the home for the reproduction and the life of the race. He will stand alone, weakened by his own sense of being an intending thief. You need, therefore, never fear to be open in the matter, being careful never to throw doubt on your wife, but to confine yourselves to the motives of the man. It is to be hoped that such a necessity may never come to you; but spying, crossness, etc., arising from a proper jealousy, are bad. Unconsciously you show your skeleton to the world, while taking no sound remedy to get rid of it. Thus the reputation of your wife, and consequently of yourself, suffers, her strength for future occasion is weakened, and you knife your happiness.

There is another way of dealing with intruding men—by a sound thrashing or death. Extremity is the only excuse for such a course. Observation will show that women, whose husbands take this action, become more disposed to flirtation than before. They lure men on careless of consequence, or perhaps secretly pleased in the power of making men run risks for them, or of the notoriety which a conflict gives society of their attractions.

If a man be married to a woman, unable or unwilling to guard and insure the paternity of the children in all her conduct, the best remedy in our society is divorce. Still it must be admitted that a husband whose character and courage mean death to intruders, will probably have more respect shown toward his preserves than one of an indifferent and careless disposition.

As the husband demands and must have chastity in his wife, he should be most careful to set her no bad example in his own manners in this respect. There is an old saying that the first person who will know of a man's sexual infidelity is his wife. Certainly such a discovery by a wife, as women are now educated, would cause her to feel a just resentment. Such conduct on the part of the man would, therefore, be likely to cause unhappiness in the home and weaken the family tie. For this reason, and on account of the liability to introduce venereal disease in the family, the husband should maintain strict chastity to all beside his wife.

Infidelity on the part of the husband weakens his love of his wife as well as his wife's love of him. It almost invariably leads to sexual excess, and consequently tends to sterility.

A wife who loves can not be expected to be indifferent to sexual license in her husband. It is exceedingly likely to cause trouble.

Rachel and Leah, the wives of Jacob, in their desire to increase his family, sent each one her maid-servant to him and gloried in their conceptions. Such generous rivalry can hardly now be counted on. The husband may well remember that the heart is a realm and kingdom of which one may be sole monarch. He should aim at such dominion and prize and maintain it when secured. As he aims to be absolute pontiff and king in the heart of his wife, so he should make the wife, as a means to his own end, the absolute queen of his own heart.

The home which you establish should by all means be in the country. The rapid transportation we now have enables a man whose business is in the city to live in the country. It is frequently the case that places in the country fifteen or twenty miles from a city office are reached more quickly and easily thanplaces within the city itself. This hint is given because the rewards of the world are now so largely found in cities, that it cannot be anticipated but that many of my descendants, if I am so fortunate as to have many, will be lured into the towns. In fact, in many occupations, such as the law or medicine, a man can find opportunity for the highest use of his faculties in cities only, and ought consequently to have his headquarters in one of them. Would that it were otherwise. Cities are destroyers. From the country pour the thousands of recruits into the city. Its great men and its leaders are aliens strong from the fresh, pure air of nature. The recruit comes strong, but is weakened and in his children still more weakened, which goes on progressively with the end, death to the family, as certain as death is to the individual body. The city convert thus condemns himself to extermination, while had he remained upon his native fields he might through his children and descendants have reached the perfect race and lived on forever.

In a paper read before the Section on Theory and Practice of the New York Academy of Medicine, March 19, 1889, by Henry Ling Taylor, M.D., appear the following thoughts:

"There is little doubt that the specialization of occupations and pursuits which is such a marked feature of modern civilized life, notably in our cities, has been in some respects a detriment to our physical development. If the hard worker is now less frequently starved outright, he is perhaps more often deprived of sufficient light and wholesome air, and his physical and mental activities restricted to a narrow range. In the commercial and head-working classes excessive competition stimulates, and often necessitates a war of wits, which is usually associated with sedentary habits, and frequently results in starvation of the tissues, in a spindling or flabby physical type, diminished fertility, and stunted asymmetrical offspring. When we come to analyze it, we find that modern city life among all classes, in spite of much superficial variety, is characterized by nothing so much as narrowness if not monotony, and this is as true of the leisure classes as of any. What can possibly exceed in inadequacy of neuro-muscular experience the routine activities of a man or woman of fashion? Probably nothing; but many of our professional and business men, working in narrow grooves, under continuous strain, and innocent of the rudiments of a common-sense hygiene, many of our overworked women and high-pressure children, certainly run a good second."

Thus it is probable that, contrary to the generally accepted opinion, city life is really more narrow and belittling than that of the country.

Samuel Hough Terry has written a small book called *Controlling Sex in Generation*. In it he maintains, amongst other things, that a danger signal to families is the reversal of the rule and the production of more daughters than sons. His statements go to show that accompanying this is a diminished virility of the males born and also a diminished vitality. It is not until about the age of puberty that this is reversed. At that time the female deaths become for a time slightly higher.

Well-to-do families in cities continually tend to the production of female children. The male children which they bring to maturity seem to amount to little in life and to be effeminate. In the chapter on " Marriage " some further examination of this matter is had. Terry's statements require close scrutiny.

In another place, cities as places of residence are again discussed. The paramount importance of judging rightly as to the situation of the home, makes it advisable to neglect no point of view when considering so vital a question. The weight of testimony appears to me to be against cities, but the intense nervous strain of these great centres, one of the things to which I object, may be the means, nay, the only road by which humanity is to make further progress. At the risk of repetition, city life deserves some further consideration.

The ranks of the great are filled from the country. It is seldom in our age that a man of prominence in any country is of city birth and rearing. Whether this is owing to a diminished virility and vitality in city children, to the artificial life and artificial landscape and surroundings, or to some other cause, the fact remains that a country life, during the formative period, is almost a necessity to greatness. Taking up average life, we must conclude that, other things being equal, a boy reared in the country will achieve more than a boy reared in the city.

Premature sexual development is also a certain danger in city-reared children. This probably is nature's first notice of approaching sterility. Sexual precocity is a sign of weakness. It is the sick tree that bears the first fruit—a fruit poor in color, size, and flavor. So, frequently persons with constitutional disease and incapable of procreating healthy offspring hasten their own death by sexual excesses.

There seem, however, to be exceptions to the exterminating influences of cities. The Jews certainly for a long period of time have resided almost exclusively in towns and cities. Whether their city population has been recruited from country towns, I am unable to say, but it is evident that a sound family life with domestic tastes amongst women have a counteracting effect upon the generally unfavorable conditions of cities. The Jews certainly maintain themselves very well, although they are *par excellence* a city population. With this race male births exceed the female to a greater extent than is normal in civilized countries.

While unlike the Egyptians, Greeks, Romans, etc., this people has escaped extermination ; it has not progressed as it should have done beyond the races that have come up around it. The last Federal census shows the reproductive condition of the high-class Jews in America to be weakening. The failure of this race to dominate the world indicates that their superior families or breeds must have been exterminated like those of the lost civilized peoples.

The traveller, W. W. Rockhill, tells us that the Chinese of the populous province of Ssu-ch'-uan live altogether in towns of about 10,000 inhabitants, going out to their farm work. As this condition has prevailed from time immemorial we may perceive that at least a non-progressive population may survive in full reproductive vigor, a city centralization with country work. The experience of Europe in the forced concentration of the agricultural population into towns during the feudal age, which still largely persists in most of the continental districts, shows the same thing. The more purely agricultural and country life of the English and early American yeomanry deserves our study and investigation. While not producing a population that has averaged in individual genius anywhere near that of Greece, or of the Italian republics (largely city populations), it has given the world a strong and materialistic progressive race never before equalled. Out of sixty odd millions we do not produce as much known mental genius in a given time as came from the sixty odd thousands of the city of Florence, and nothing at all compared to the two hundred odd thousands of free Greeks.

If Terry's suggestions be true, that life in a city by parents will diminish the strength in all ways of the children, we have strong reasons indeed for refusing to live in one. I believe that city life has not only a dwarfing effect on the intellect and physical force of the children born in cities, but also upon those who come into them to reside, who were born in the country. In the country we may take the hand of Nature, in the city everything is artificial. In the one case, Truth predominates, for Nature is Truth; in the other, all is artifice, and for the most part far from the truth indeed.

The death-rate in cities is much higher than in the country. This is especially the case with young children. In some cities, as New York for instance, this death-rate is so high that, were the city population dependent upon its own reproductive powers, it would soon disappear. The laws of health are becoming better understood and sanitary measures are being everywhere undertaken on a large or small scale, so that some of these disadvantages are being overcome.

At the present time and upon our present incomplete information, we may affirm that an American family living in a city is doomed to extermination within four generations. One individual only of the fifth generation of London birth was found in that city by an eminent and careful observer. Bowdin could discover no pure-blooded Parisians beyond the third generation.

Marriage being to get children for the continuation of the life of the individual through them, it becomes an idle thing to marry and then live where the children are either certain to die early or else are certain to kill the breed and family in a short time through their weakened reproductive powers.

The future of the family in the children is the most important consideration in counselling against cities as places of residence. Added to the above reason is this, that the home is never so completely a home in the city as in the country. The attractions and diversions of a great city, the crowd even, that ceaselessly tramps along the hard stones, have their fascinations.

The welfare and amusement of the husband or the wife seem less dependent on each other under these conditions. The happiest marriages and the most complete unions are therefore in the country.

Besides all this, city life in its attractions and ambitions, and in the continual presence of a strange crowd, is not favorable to maternity. The modesty of the pregnant woman, and the exercise necessary for her health, are at war. Thus city families have fewer children than country ones, and there are more marriages quite sterile in cities also.

It must be said, however, that some of the small towns in New England are an exception to this rule. Small families and sterility are more noticeable in some of these than in many of our large cities. This is owing to a false education that teaches nothing as to the value and necessity of child-bearing, and at the same time implants in the girls ambitions inconsistent with maternity.

You cannot hope to lead a complete married life without children, nor to have the complete happiness a wife can give in their absence. As the city is so inimical to the grand object of matrimony, it should be avoided, at least for the home. The sickness and weakness city life usually produces in children, it is to be expected, will diminish the happiness of your wife, the mother, and consequently yours also.

The vice and wickedness of cities presented to you every day, as it must be should you reside in a city, will assuredly injure your character. Can you touch pitch and not be defiled?

Recent statistics in England show that, at the same age, the country resident weighs more than the city man. The figures are:

	Height.	Weight.	Breathing.	Pull.	Squeeze.
Cambridge (country)	68.9 in.	153.6 lbs.	254	83	87.5
Kensington (city)	67.9 "	143 "	219	74	85

It will thus be seen that physically there is a marked advantage to the adult in the country. The difference is the more noticeable as the district of Kensington selected to represent cities is an exceptional and superior one. The common observation of an inquirer, merely looking at any gathering of country and then at one of city children, will be convinced that the inferiority of city adults compared to country people is shared by the children also. The intellectual grasp of the country children, being shown in another place to be greater than those of the city, the disadvantages of city life become clear.

When we consider that the highest rewards for effort have generally been found in the cities of the world, and that consequently the strongest and most ambitious have been for centuries drifting to the cities, we may well note with attention the fact that our leaders and thinkers, speaking generally, are, as they have been, born in the country. The continued recruiting of the city population from the cream of the country has not in all time enabled it to produce its own leaders.

The city then is a place where we can hardly hope to maintain for our children a grand superiority, much less make an advance. If the cities, after ages of immigration of the best and strongest of mankind, are unable, from a thus selected population, to produce the leaders of mankind within their own precincts, there must be something fatally deteriorating in their influences. It may be that a race will eventually develop with superior mental endowments, able to overcome the drawbacks of cities, while reaping their material rewards. This possibility should be carefully watched for.

Quatrefages in his *Human Species*, page 224 *et seq.*, cites a number of facts which go to suggest this possibility. He shows in these that animals and men emigrating into new climates often suffer an increased death-rate and diminished birth-rate. Sometimes this goes so far as to indicate extermination. A death-rate higher than the birth-rate must eventually end in this way. But he shows that a condition of this kind is frequently overcome.

The goose, when introduced at Bogota, seemed doomed through diminished fertility and vitality to extermination. It is now, however, passed the crisis, and seems as vigorous in its new home as in its old one. The introduction of chickens at Cuzco was beset by the same difficulty. Infertile or addled eggs showed a lack of fertility in both the male and the female. The eggs laid were few, and the mortality of the chicks hatched was excessive. Now, however, the chickens at Cuzco have become established by the survival of the fittest, and they seem as thrifty as elsewhere.

The negro slaves introduced into the Southern States, to Brazil, Jamaica, Cuba, and the French Antilles, showed for a long time a death-rate greater than the birth-rate, and the fact was often cited to show that without the slave-trade the plantations could not long be manned. We see, however, the black race now established in all these places.

So, also, with the whites in Martinique, Isle of Bourbon, Algiers, Louisiana, and in many places, the death-rate was at first excessive and above the birth-rate, but we find these conditions now overcome and the whites maintaining themselves in all these places. The acclimatization, however, cannot be accomplished when the conditions are very unfavorable without a great loss of individuals and without a heavy risk of failure.

During the Civil War of the sixties in America, the figures of the medical department and the observation of many field officers indicate that the regiments from the cities were less subject to sickness, that their members wounded recovered more quickly, that they marched better and generally had more endurance than the soldiers from the country, and suffered less from night work and loss of sleep. These statements, in the main, rest on sufficiently good authority to demand attention.

In imagining an explanation to fit our other information, it must be remembered that an explanation of unfavorable facts is usually more or less faulty. With this condition the following points are offered to reconcile the divergence :

1st. That the campaigning life to the city resident was a medicine and healthier perhaps, even with all its hardships, than the one from which he came, and that consequently his constitution and condition improved.

2d. That the composition of regiments could only be approximately known, and that many of the city soldiers were born, if not reared, in the country.

3d. That the exposures of city life had weeded out largely those subject to disease, such as measles, small-pox, scarlet fever, etc., while the country man, brought suddenly into crowded camps without this full weeding process, became peculiarly liable to epidemics of such diseases.

4th. The figures apply as far as they go to the Northern armies alone. The Southern armies were almost exclusively composed of country-born and country-bred men. In endurance of poor clothing, poor food, and hard marching, they surpassed the Northern soldiers. Whether they would have done so had the case been reversed and the Northern homesteads and sovereignty been at stake, is a question. The Northern army was comparatively a city army ; the Southern, a country one. In this aspect, man for man, the country army must be considered the best as to endurance.

The army officers with whom I have conversed on this point nearly all noted the superior facility of making good soldiers quickly out of city men as compared to country ones. Contagious disease and homesickness seem the most troublesome things to country men newly enlisted. After the acclimatization, however, the country man seems, generally considered, to have been the best man.

One Western officer, Col. Miller, expressed the opinion that the pioneer or frontiersman made, by far, the best soldier. One of the principal recruiting officers in the army says that he would take a countryman as a recruit every time in preference to a city man.

Gen. Irwin McDowell and Gen. Crittenden are my principal authorities on the deficiencies of the country man on first enlistment in the army. Col. C. Mason Kinne thinks that the city soldiers stood the hardships of the war better throughout. His explanation is that those who could not stand the irregularities and strain of cities died young, and that only those of superior vitality were left to enlist. These, if they had been reared in the country, would have been stronger and hardier than they were, in his opinion.

Col. Volkman, on the other hand, thinks the country men always the best. His extensive experience as First Aid to Gen. Sheridan, as recruiting officer for many years, and in other positions of vantage in this question, make his testimony valuable. The proportion of recruits rejected for physical defects is very materially greater in cities than in the country; if to this cause were added moral defects, the disadvantage, in this officer's opinion, would be still greater.

As a rule in history pastoral tribes or hunters, such as the Huns, Goths, Vandals, Arabs, Mongols, Turks, etc., have been superior in fighting qualities to the educated and civilized people with whom they have contended. Such tribes were all country men, while to a large extent their victims, the civilized, were citizens of cities.

Even in late years with all the superiority of civilized weapons in war, we find naked bands of Zulus near Natal, of Bedouins in Nubia, with swords or spears destroying the splendidly drilled and armed troops of England.

The wild Indians often worry the American army, as witness the destruction of Custer by the Sioux, while even in peaceful Samoa, a band of German marines, we hear, are defeated and driven off by the naked natives.

The medical history of the war in America, while worthy of careful study, does not seem sufficient to shake our general facts as to the effects of cities, so far, upon mankind.

A theory has been advanced to account for the superior qualities noted in the city regiments, based upon a supposed storage of energy in the city man through good feeding. It is true that the food of the city man is generally better and better prepared than that of the country man. Some force is given to this theory by such facts as the superior endurance of cold in the Russian campaign of Napoleon by the soldiers of Southern France and Italy. This has been much remarked on, for with less protection they stood the cold and privations better even than the Russians themselves. It was the Germans of the central provinces who had the least vigor in this respect, and their losses in this terrible campaign practically swept whole corps of their soldiers out of existence.

It has been said that the temperate climate, with but few extremes, of Provence and Italy allows the energies of the food eaten by man to accumulate in some unknown way and thus to furnish a storehouse to draw upon in emergency; consequently men from such climates may be expected to support the rigors of a more northern winter for at least a year or two better than those born under the bear. People from Southern California seem to resist the cold of their first eastern winter better than the eastern residents themselves. This explanation is not satisfactory.

Another important consideration in this connection is that the moral health is as much benefited by the country as the physical. Immoral acts are more difficult in the country than in the city, for they are more difficult to conceal.

The mode and system of life make all crime comparatively easy in cities. The excitement, the crowding, the luxury, the strain on the nerves, and the decoys to lead one on are all in the city. In the country a man and his habits are known for miles around. In the city one may never even have seen his next-door neighbor, and in a few blocks any one can get into a locality where no person knows or cares for him. Thus in the country fathers, mothers, and later the children are removed from the grosser temptations to crime. With the nurses and servants it is the same. They must lead better lives in the country than in the city.

The city offers the only exception to the rule laid down that we must work either productively or unproductively, either in virtue for the good or in vice for the bad. The exception is, it is true, but a partial one. A city does give more capacity for idleness, and consequently for death and extermination of the family, than the country. The amusements, theatres, gardens, and even the crowds moving in the streets visible from a window seat, give an occupation to the mind that is no occupation. The outside movements of the city permit an individual idleness that would be intolerable in the country; consequently, this possibility for nonentity, for the decay through non-use of the faculties, should be avoided. Many city persons now cannot endure the country; when in it they are the victims of ennui. Such persons with few exceptions are non-producers and belong to the useless or dangerous class.

The city amusements, such as theatres, etc., stir up the emotions without creating any action. We sympathize with the hero, weep with the afflicted, condemn the villain,—and do nothing. Thus theatrical representations in excess form in us the habit of being stirred to our nature's depths without action. This is their worst feature. Never select a home in the city.

Every wife should have an occupation in the home. The larger part of her time should be taken up in regular duties of some useful kind. This is necessary for your happiness, for her happiness, for her health, and for the development through use of her faculties, so that these may add force to her children by inheritance. No one can be healthy who has for any length of time nothing to do. The health not only of the body but of the morals and of the mind is involved.

15

You should have something to do, so should your wife, and so should your children. Idleness is the true devil. It leads to the hardest and most painful kinds of work, paid in distressing wages. The work of vice is born of idleness.

Therefore give your wife an occupation, see to it that she has some useful duty to interest her. Vice is but too likely to capture idle hands. The alternative is inanity.

If idleness did not endanger morality and chastity it would be still most reprehensible. In idleness the faculties fail ; without use our bodies and brains get into a rust. A man who does not use his body soon loses the power to do so. He either becomes obese or else emaciated with dyspepsia, muscular force decreases, the physique retrogresses. So the sedentary lose the health of the body. The health of the mind depends equally upon reasonable use. It is the shepherd, who, of all employed men, has least use for his brain, as it is the shepherd also that furnishes of all occupations the largest proportion of insane. All results of a true or of an improper life are transmissible ; therefore, for the children's sake, for the future, the wife should be usefully employed in both body and mind. Her first employments should be in household works. These will be found sufficient in the majority of cases. In fact, domestic life, being the key to the future, is the most important in the state. In *Tasks by Twilight* the chapter on the " Education of the Girl," shows that chemistry, engineering, medicine, etc., may be brought into the every-day home life of the wife. Thus the highest attainments are useful in the home, and a strictly home life is perfectly compatible with an interest in the most important· knowledge acquired by mankind.

The charms of home life depend on the useful, but the ornamental is important also. So the wife has a place for surplus energy in music and painting. The most important of the home duties is, of course, the rearing of children. The wife in this work forms the next generation, which is the most influential work of life.

The only point to be considered in providing for the employment of the wife is that it should never place her in dubious positions. The security of the paternity of his children is of the first importance to the man, and all things throwing the least doubt on this in the past, present, or future are dangerous. So, also, all ambitions should be directed to childbirth, or things immediate to it.

True development of the physique, brain, and faculties must improve the children born. No development is too great for the mother, provided her child-bearing capacity and will for it be not interfered with.

In home matters the wife should have charge and be responsible. Thus by responsibility will her character be strengthened. Feeling her responsibility, she will take an interest in the household welfare and economy that could not otherwise be expected. Put her in charge of these matters. Express household wishes to your wife and let all orders proceed through her. If this practice be adopted, many sources of friction will be avoided. Under this scheme servants have one head to look to, cannot receive contradictory orders from different chiefs, and can never give the excuse for non-performance of orders that some one else told them to do something else. The wife's self-reliance and standing in the household will be increased, and her interest in domestic affairs must be improved if slight, or maintained if strong.

A woman is much more emotional than a man. It is therefore necessary for the man to make an extra effort in keeping up the little attentions and marks of affection so much prized by a wife. Husbands often become lax in these matters and lose much happiness by doing so. A husband should be as polite in speech and conduct to his wife as he would be to any strange lady in similar circumstances, nay more so, for the stranger he may never see again, while the wife is his companion for life. So often one sees this rule violated, so often one is shocked and made uncomfortable by the rudeness of married people to each other, and their neglect of the common courtesies of society·when outsiders are present to see, that we must believe that these practices are usual in private married life. What an amount of unnecessary friction, mortification, and loss of life's sunshine this mistaken conduct means, it would be difficult to tell. Avoid this rock.

Never nag. Never be less considerate in your dress or address when alone with your wife than when with strangers. Carelessness in these matters is both common and foolish. A little verse taught to children has a power of wisdom in it :

> " Little drops of water, little grains of sand,
> Make the mighty ocean and·the beauteous land ;
> Little deeds of kindness, little words of love,
> Make the world an Eden like the Heaven above."

Life is made up of little things. An accumulation of little irritations will bring discontent if not a passionate outburst after they have reached a climax. It was the straw that broke the camel's back. On the other hand, little attentions and care in the detail of life make happiness when many larger considerations would counter-indicate it.

If you can afford it take two morning newspapers, one for your wife, one for yourself. A thousand and one little directions of this kind can be given but cannot be remembered. Consequently the general principle of treating the wife with a consideration greater than that given to friends, must be the standard set up to govern the minor happenings of life.

Good manners are the result of rules followed in conduct, that by long experience have been found most conducive to happy and smooth intercourse amongst mankind in the social state. Least of all should these rules be neglected in the home. The last shred of politeness a man possesses should be wrapped around the hearts he loves.

The home is the holy of holies of society. From it springs the future. It is the inspiration to greatness, the sanctuary of the heart. Nothing is too good for it, no diplomacy too high, no manners too fine, no science too grand. On the contrary all these and all inventions are servants to the home and secondary to it. The home or family is the foundation of society upon which all else rests, to which all else is servant. Let the wife then know the importance of her position, that as mother and as influencer and former of her children, as manager of the home, it is she who holds the key to the future of the race, and in reality holds the most important position in society. The occupations of men and their strength when properly directed are all for the support and defence of the home, which is the citadel of society held by the wife.

Often married people who have an affection for each other get into the unfortunate habit of nagging, speaking crossly, and generally treating each other as they never would think of treating a stranger under the same circumstances. The rules of social intercourse are for the avoidance by mankind of grating and unpleasant occurrences, and to promote ease and happiness in our general relations. If we find these rules useful for our welfare in dealing with society, the members of which we may meet once a day, once a week, once a year, or perhaps never again, how much more essential are they in the family whose members we are with so much ; especially are they important for the wife and husband who are together more or less both at night and in the day.

In Deuteronomy, Chap. xxiv., the following rule is made : "When a man hath taken a new wife, he shall not go out to war, neither shall he be charged with any business, but he shall be free at home one year, and shall cheer up his wife, which he hath taken."

The first year of married life, as Moses indicates, is the formative one. It is important to pay more than ordinary attention to the wife at that time.

The general strategy of successful sexual companionship is worthy of some consideration. For with the proper points before one many minor errors leading to discord and unhappiness may be avoided.

A woman may give herself to a man in spirit—that is, she may be willing to give herself corporeally, and thus give herself in wish, though not in act. This is capable of producing great devotion on the part of the woman.

When the willingness to give is followed by the woman's surrender of her person to the man, there is in this act and at that time an intense instinctive worship of the man.

She gives, he takes. She demands to be dominated. She surrenders and abdicates every command and power. She leans upon him, lies in his arms at his orders and in his power. As her body has merged in his, so she desires to merge into him and be part of him in all things. There is nothing too much for her to do for him, no self-effacement too great, no act to indicate devotion or worship too menial or too much a confession of conquest for her to make.

Here is the point of strategy for the husband and wife to consider. She must give. He must take.

This is the key that commands marriage.

If this essential to all marriage be properly started and properly maintained, the marriage must succeed. No matter what other conditions may fail, the due acceptance and holding by the man of the woman's surrender will make all else secondary. He may beat her, she will forgive it. He may squander her property, she will give him more. He may be untrue and she will welcome him again. If, on the other hand, this strategic situation does not stand, no wealth, position, or anything can cure its absence.

Indeed, in the first case, a divorce or marriage-breaking may occur. But such division, as far as the woman is concerned, is adventitious, formal, nominal, not real, and no matter what injuries her husband may heap on her, she will still bear a fuller and better rounded life,—happier, in fact, than if separated from him and freed from his abuse.

So, on the other hand, no ease, idleness, comfort, wealth, position, nor power can fill any wife's heart or life if this marriage-give-and-take, this strategy of situation, be not there.

Do not confuse a continued corporeal application of this principle with spiritual strategy, so difficult to describe and which is here intended.

No one in his or her senses expects a happy marriage where the husband beats his wife like some primitive savage, or uses his masculine ascendancy to get hold of her property to waste it. None of these things mean happiness, but a woman is more capable of devotion to a man who beats her, than to one she beats.

It is the husband's business to understand the importance of care to his wife during pregnancy and childbirth. Some points are given on this subject in the "Treatment of the Child," but the subject is only touched on. A husband should make a study of what is proper at these times and should certainly read up on obstetrics, and if possible take a course in this study. This is not for the purpose of making him a midwife, but so that by accurate information he can see that the proper attention is given by those practically qualified.

Childbirth is the true realization of marriage. The mystery and grandeur of creation are then possessed by the happy pair. It is the grand crisis as it is the grand moment when hope is made captive and your life is renewed. Neglect no precaution at this time, deprive yourself of no assistance, for your fortunes, your studies, and your efforts when truly directed are all for the wonderful achievement of your own new birth in the child.

CHAPTER VII.

A WORD TO THE WIFE.

THE primary reason for marriage is to secure the paternity of children. Therefore, when a woman becomes a wife, the principal duty of her life is to bear children, and to so guard her virtue that not even a doubt of it can find lodgment in her husband. She should not permit intimacies to grow up between any man other than her husband and herself. What is called flirtation in a married woman is simply damnable. The more sound a man the husband is, the more certain it is that such destruction of the sanctity of the home will alienate him from the wife.

No true wife will be untrue in fact or in semblance. It is exceedingly bad policy on the part of a wife to be flirtatious with other men. She sees them to-day, but may never see them again. Their interest at best is but a passing one, intense perhaps for the moment of to-day, but gone in the hours of the to-morrow.

The attentions of men to the wives of others is at base nearly always due to improper motives. Once gratified in their wishes, it is not long before these butterfly seducers fly to new flowers, and abandon to a life of reproach and misery those whom they betray and ruin.

Upon the husband the wife depends for her position in society, and on him also for her happiness. If he throws her off for cause, society frowns upon her, for society depends on the family for its existence, and as it is healthy, so will it resent unwifely conduct leading to the injury of the family.

If, however, the wife has not gone into the gulf, only played on the edge, and lives on with her husband, his confidence will be shaken in her, and a shadow will be on the hearth. The complete happiness of home life will be impossible. The risk being so great, the wife should not only maintain her virtue in fact, but should avoid as well the slightest cause for scandal. Scandal is much decried, but it is a great protector of society and of the family. Beware of it, for it sees when you least suspect.

The web in which the wife has caught her husband she should

ever work to transform into a safe and close cage for his heart. A husband caught is not yet fully secured. The ceremony of marriage is but the conventionality to be followed by other things. It is after the vows are passed that the wife enters into the business of really securing her husband to herself. If she leave him in the web of fancy in which he was caught, doing no more for him or to fasten him, but, on the contrary, devote herself to weaving other webs for piratical bachelors and society men, she will find marriage a lottery indeed, and herself no prize-winner.

Where the substance goes the shadow must follow. The child is the substance of marriage. To the extent that marriages are childless, to the extent that husbands and wives seek to avoid procreation, so do they take the substance out of marriage. Its shadow, the form, convention, and habit of society, cannot remain when the substance is gone. So we find with decreasing birth-rate increasing divorce. Let wives remember this.

In certain times, places, and societies, cosmetics for the face are or have been used, and doubtless will remain in use, or come into fashion again. Whatever may be said for this practice before marriage, every indication is against it afterward. Cosmetics on the face are not a bait for kisses. Their effect is, besides, to injure the skin, and consequently to diminish its natural attractiveness.

Good cookery, good housekeeping, good dressing, these are the means to an end—The Happy Home. Sometimes one or more of these is allowed to so dominate a wife's life that the means destroys rather than makes the end.

She is a housewife instead of her husband's wife. So other hobbies, industrial, social, or intellectual, good as means to develop the faculties, to make life successful, and to transmit superiorities to children, are sometimes so exaggerated as to destroy home happiness and to destroy the true end of every life—perpetuation in the child. Remember, then, the end while using the means.

The general policy of a wife in regard to her husband's business should be helpful, interested, and sympathetic. At the same time she should be careful to avoid criticism or censure in public, even when just.

In the matter of gossip or tale-bearing involving her husband or children, she should defend him or them before others, reserving advice, protest, or correction to a private meeting. As a rule, a wife should refuse to listen to gossip or scandal regarding her husband. The wife should bear her husband children, the more the better. Every true man wishes for children of his own, and is delighted when they come, even though he deny it, or propose sterility to his wife. This is certain, a childless wife, as her charms pass away, loses her hold on her husband. The more vigorous the man, the more sure is the result. The wife should remember that artificially produced sterility brings wrinkles, loss of beauty, loss of health, and premature old age.

The bearing of children is the surest means of preserving the health, vigor, and youth of the wife, as well as the respect and love of her husband when her charms have faded. This being the natural function of woman, it must be utilized, otherwise, like a non-use of the muscles, the senses, or the intellect, a decay commences in the part so neglected, only to spread through the whole organism.

The youngest-looking women for their age and the most vigorous are those who bear children. The woman of the greatest vigor in advanced age I ever knew was a mother of fourteen living children. She is now eighty-four years of age. The most vigorous woman past the menopause I have known is a woman of fifty-three, the mother of twenty-three children.

Any reputable physician will inform the inquirer as to the almost universal invalidism prevalent amongst American single women after the age of twenty-eight. Two physicians in Los Angeles, who are enjoying a large, if not the largest, practice in that city and county, tell me that the proportion of single women amongst native Americans, who have trouble after twenty-five with their reproductive organs, is fully nine tenths, or ninety out of every hundred. (A specialist is liable to overestimate all figures in his specialty ; we must then put a grain of salt into these estimates.)

Amongst married women who prevent childbirth by abortion or other means, disease, physical or moral, and a life of bodily or mental suffering is the sure consequence.

The first effect of uterine diseases is upon the vigor and happiness of the woman, and the second, through incapacity on her part to fulfil the duties of wife, to disgust, and consequently to alienate, the husband, and to tempt him to infidelity.

No woman who is unwilling to bear children should ever marry. Nature has nothing but punishment for those who violate her laws. The wife should make it a rule not to throw the care of a baby or of children upon the husband, especially at night. His work is outside ; for this his temperament is suited. If he performs this part of the contract, an additional performance of the wife's duties is likely to injure his health. If he does not perform his proper duties, there is nothing so likely to keep up the weakness as a continued diversion of his energies to the wife's field of action.

The wife should be careful of her mental and bodily health. She can best do this by useful occupation.

The home should be made and kept attractive, so that the husband will find no place pleasanter and no welcome warmer than at his own home. A man a-courting is one thing, and a man a husband is quite another. In the first case the man is pre-eminently the one who seeks to please; in the second case this is the pre-eminent business of the wife.

A bride should expect to find shortly after marriage a great difference between her lover as a husband and her lover as a beau. He enters with marriage the serious business of life, and must give time and attention to his work. Too often, indeed, husbands devote their whole energy to the outside fight to the neglect of the home, but a husband can be a true lover without continuing the customs of courting. In fact, such a continuation in its full vigor would practically push all other activities to one side. Moses contemplated this when he commanded the newly married man to leave all business and to devote himself entirely to the bride for one year.

A wife may have great power over her husband; when such is the case, she should never show it in public, nor thrust the fact upon the husband. In other words, don't rule your husband, and if you do rule him, don't let any one know it, not even the husband.

Every undertaking, partnership, or combination that has to submit to competition must have an executive head to be successful. A number of young women in our day reflect the tendency of the times toward individualism at the expense of family unity, by a revolt against the headship of the husband in marriage. The protest of women against even the word *obedience*, still contained in the marriage service of the churches, is very often heard. By such persons marriage is made a dissolvable compact without a head. The family, like any other combination, to be successful, must have a head. There can be no head unless there is final jurisdiction in some one. What would be thought of the prospects of an army whose captains maintained independence against their colonels, their colonels against their generals, and their generals against their commander-in-chief? The army is a plain illustration, but may be considered to be inapplicable to civil life. Let us then look at civil life. What would we think of a business firm's prospects where the clerks declared independence against the junior partners, and the junior partners against the head of the house? So in the family, if the children do not recognize the mother as an adviser to be heeded and obeyed, and the wife does not recognize the husband as chief, there can be no unity or cohesion in the family. Such a family can have no executive capacity as a family, no force and no influence. What would be said of clerks, partners, or officers who refused to recognize a chief on the ground that such a recognition was a disgraceful confession of a non-existing inferiority ?

The presence of a chief is necessary in every undertaking. Without such there cannot be unity in direction of force. A wife who will not agree to a head and chief of the family sets up a doctrine of revolutionary anarchy that must permeate and weaken the family throughout. Her control over her children and servants is overthrown by her own doctrine ; if she will not have a chief, why, indeed, should they ? The acceptance of the husband by the wife in marriage should be like the acceptance of a commission in the army. It should involve obedience to the chief. As a bad general is better than no general in an army, so a bad or inferior chief is better than no chief in a family. The exceptions that may be thought of as applying to one apply equally to the other. In either case " no chief " is a condition of radical defect and weakness. In the army it is injurious to its members and its cause. In the family it is injurious to its members and to its future.

Never tell your husband that he does not love you, or that he no longer loves you, etc. Such talk tends to tiresome repetition, and may suggest doubts in the husband's mind on the point you desire assured. The maxim may be laid down that it is unwise to suggest an idea which you do not wish carried out.

Avoid having animals, birds, etc., as house pets. Numbers of persons are frightened or bitten or injured by such pets every year. The most prominent recent case of this kind is that of the Princess de Sagan, who was bitten by her monkey diseased with hydrophobia. Animals carry and disseminate disease. Some diseases come to man from them, such as hydrophobia, anthrax, tetanus, etc. Animals are short-lived and a favorite must soon give pain by its useless age or early death.

Such pets usually annoy friends, often exasperate the husband, and must always divert duty from him and distract the attention from the true household pet, the child, and prevent its production or its due care, if happily born. Animal pets are the resource of the childless, and sometimes may cause persons to be satisfied with sterility who otherwise would have married, or if married, have had children. They have no proper life in a true home.

Never nag or scold your husband ; it is a risky business, and eventually makes the life of the wife nearly as unpleasant as that of the husband. The efforts devoted to recrimination are not remunerative. If the husband behaves badly, use your efforts and ingenuity to bring him to a right course. Scolding at one extreme and maudling caresses at the other are not good strategy.

In such unfortunate cases, love and patience judiciously handled are the best remedies. Well cooked food, an economically and well ordered household, a neat and becomingly dressed wife, true to her vow, together with children, make the home a place that has no equal for any normally constituted man. There is no fear that the club will draw any man except a fool from such a home.

By neat and becoming dress, it is not meant that a wife should wear a ball dress in the kitchen; on the contrary, the dress should be suited to the occupation, but no sensible wife will ever appear before her husband in unclean clothes, in curl papers, or go slipshod and slovenly in the house. It would be better for a wife to thus destroy her womanly attractions in public streets amongst strangers than in the home and before her husband.

The love which induces a man to marry a woman is born of and based upon the reproductive instinct, which is expressed in sexual desire. A wife should never lose sight of this fact, and should always keep herself neat in dress and in person. Nothing in the home is more attractive than a clean, simple dress upon a pretty woman engaged in household work.

The woman at the ball with silks and laces, corsets and cosmetics, decked in jewels is often a work of art beautiful to look at, indeed at times even magnificent. Amongst all the women I have seen thus splendidly arrayed in the court balls of Europe and the parties of America, I can say that those most simply dressed pleased me the best. But none of them ever had for me the same peculiar warm attraction that the maid at or fresh from household duties in her appropriate garb has had. My taste in these matters is probably more the rule than the exception. At least judging others by myself, I can advise the wife that household duties and a neat and natty garb are attractions to the husband irrespective of the addition such duties well performed make to the comfort and happiness of the home.

A woman who has accomplishments should by no means neglect these after marriage. Music, painting, etc., are both a pastime and an occupation for a wife. Besides these considerations, accomplishments tend to enlarge the mental horizon of the woman and benefit the children, not only as they grow up, but while still in utero before birth.

A wife should be advised against giving up any accomplishments she may have because after marriage, say by the third year, she will find that the happiness of the family depends upon them to a very slight extent.

The attraction of the wife to the husband is, it is true, after marriage very little affected by accomplishments directly. Indirectly, however, they have a considerable influence. While accomplishments should not be neglected, they should never be allowed to interfere with the home duties of first importance, or that care of the health and person essential to happy married life.

The care of the children in the family is an important element in the relations of husband and wife. Upon the mother through the decrees of nature the principal part of this duty devolves. Well mannered and useful children, healthy in body and mind, form an essential feature in every happy family. With such children the continued life of the father and mother has a bright future. They can with good reason hope to perform better deeds in their children than they themselves could do alone. A future of promise is a happiness actual though in anticipation.

A wife should therefore give much attention to the forming and rearing of her children. Their proper care does not involve coddling them or so fencing them about as to prevent a due development of character and individuality. The proper course is to lead them to perceive for themselves the dangerous path to be avoided and the good path to be followed.

With children it is as much a science and about as important to know how and when to let them alone, as it is to know what to do and when to do it.

The wife should always suckle her children, because this function aborted means always a slow return of the reproductive organs to the normal condition and generally a tedious recovery from childbirth, together with danger that disease may supervene especially of the mammary glands. The suppression of the activity of the mammary glands also induces a premature return of the menses with probable conception before the constitution of the woman is in the best condition for it. Nature should therefore be followed.

Jealousy is an instinct in the males of the higher vertebrates. Birds mate, and the male drives away other male birds. The cock protects his favorite hens and attacks intruders. The tomcat will not endure a rival in reproductive matters. The bull will fight a bull intruding amongst his wives; his own son will be gored as promptly as any other bull. The stallion and the stag possess the same instinct to secure the paternity of their offspring, and to protect their females from being basely impregnated by inferior animals. The females amongst these animals seem to have no development of the instinct of jealousy. Its development among women is an exception to the rule prevalent in the animal kingdom in this respect.

Marriage with mankind is a formal recognition of the necessity of the instinct of jealousy in reproduction. The proper carrying out of the wedding vow does away with the usefulness of the animal manifestations of a demand for purity on the part of the mother by the father.

The laws of marriage are intended to do away with the necessity of personal violence to protect the purity of the breed and to secure the paternity of children. In this regard, law written and unwritten and the machinery of society play the same beneficent part that laws for the protection of property have done in securing a peaceful enjoyment to each person of the results of their labor, thus doing away with the primitive necessity of violence for this purpose. It is true that both the law of property and of marriage are imperfect and full of error. Their objects, however, are just. Nature demands and the law recognizes that a man should not live with or breed to an unfaithful wife. A wife should therefore excuse even abnormal jealousy in the husband as a too large development of a useful and widespread instinct that serves to supplement the still imperfect law.

The security of the paternity of children necessitates a faithful wife, but does not necessitate a faithful husband. Infidelity of the wife is fatal to the family. Infidelity of the husband is not necessarily so. Therefore a wife is not wise in leaving a husband whom she discovers to be sexually untrue. A revolt against the continuance of such acts is sometimes good, but the best policy is for the wife to look to the improvement of the home, to add comfort to it, and, above all, to improve her own manners and to be attentive to her personal appearance. She must make her home and herself attractive. The normal man, with a healthy wife and a well-regulated home is but little tempted to leave it for stolen sexual indulgence.

Jealousy in man is of greatly more importance to the welfare of the race than in woman, but it has good cause in women also. Amongst animals the females have little or no manifestations of this instinct. But the conditions are different in the essentials of reproduction with mankind. .

Our children are helpless for a long period, and therefore require a protector and supporter during this time, which office is naturally the part of the man, both on account of his strength and on account of the absorption of the mother's energy and time in the care of the helpless young.

Venereal diseases are the exclusive property of humanity. The effects of these diseases, especially of syphilis, are terrible, and endure from one generation to another ; consequently, promiscuous intercourse on the part of the man renders him liable to infection, which it must be expected will equally disease and ruin his wife. But, worse than this, the child of such a parent must carry the curse, and the father and mother thus suffer in the child, and, through the debilitated constitution of the progeny, extermination stares them in the face.

Thus jealousy in woman is shown to have a foundation in these two reasons, if in no others. A wife, however, should bear in mind the radical difference to the family of the husband or wife's infidelity. In the first case it is a venial offence, unless disease be contracted or the support of the family endangered.

No uncertainty as to the children of the wife is possible, and no stamp or life from an outside source is introduced as a burden to the family. With the wife infidelity is ruin to the family. The husband no longer feels certain that the children born are his, and the wife becomes either sterile or may bear into the family a child of some dissolute man, not the husband, and carry through life the stamp of such inferior man to plague the fool-husband in children subsequently born to him.

A faithless woman is also liable to neglect her children, if she have any, and to bring venereal disease into the family. Therefore, a dissolute man is bad, but a dissolute woman is intolerable.

A wife should never have a secret from her husband. Dickens wrote a story, called *The Cricket on the Hearth*, that incidentally shows how dangerous even a good scheme may become to a family by making a secret of it. Husband and wife are too near for one to have a secret from the other. Where secrets exist, acts will be misunderstood, letters and words misconstrued, love wear the livery of jealousy, and happiness be kicked out of the home.

The wise wife will show an interest in her husband's occupations and ambitions, for by such a course she will secure his confidences and live his life, thus securing a powerful hold upon him, second only to that given by a fine child.

As a wife should not be down at the heel in her personal appearance, nor in her housekeeping, neither should she allow herself to be down at the heel intellectually. She should read, think, and keep herself informed in the world's movements. This is advisable for two reasons : first, on account of her children ; and second, to make herself companionable mentally to her husband. Without some activity of mind on the part of the mother, the mind from disuse will inevitably grow weaker, and consequently the children born will inherit the diminished mind power of the mother. The mother's influence to improve the children will also be impaired.

As the children are the mainhold the wife has on her husband, it should be ever her object not only to have children, but to have better and more forceful children than her own parents had in her, and thus to make her husband glory in the renewed life she has given him and herself in the fruits of the marriage.

While a wife should on no account allow society to interfere with her home duties she should not altogether neglect it. A healthy society has a code of unwritten laws that does much to benefit humanity. Intercourse of a social kind with one's fellows broadens the view and causes us to keep our dress, manners, and wits in tidy and presentable form.

Balls and dances are some of the means used in society to bring people together. These forms are the least suited to the wife. It should be remembered that society balls are most useful as matrimonial bazaars, where young people of opposite sexes may meet and become acquainted.

The low-necked dress of the young lady enables the young man ready for a wife to judge somewhat as to her physical qualifications and suitability, and is in the same useful line as the bathing costumes worn in the water by women at seaside resorts. A wife, however, has no reason to display her charms even well within conventional usage to the world. In this connection a French saying is apropos :

" La femme est comme une armée : elle est perdue si elle n'a pas de reserve."

This saying is commended to the wife who would guard the respect of society and the confidence of her husband.

Society balls are for the unmarried of both sexes, and the place of the married in these is merely a service of pilotage, or as lookers on. A married woman who flirts at all is a fool ; one who flirts at such balls is a thief as well, for she steals the chances of her single sisters.

The first duty of the wife is to preserve her faith to her husband and secure him in the paternity of her children born to the marriage, and the second to strengthen and build up her own and her husband's better qualities so that these may be more prominent in the children. As the wife is the better part of the husband, so also the husband is the better part of the wife. That wife is truest to herself who is truest to her husband. Her treatment of her husband is a treatment to herself.

The wife, like the husband, has every reason to devote her best efforts of all kinds to the home. The home contains for her the only true happiness, the only true greatness, and within its mystic circle lies hidden in the child—her future.

CHAPTER VIII.

RELIGION.

IT is impossible to conceive God. It is equally difficult to imagine the universe without a First Cause. The mass of mankind have found the lesser difficulty to be the doctrine of a Supreme Omnipotent Being. Man calls this Being God. Those who think, must think of God with awe. Man cannot conceive with his weak senses what God is, nor why the laws of nature, which are His, are what they are. The thinker merely feels able to recognize some of these laws. They cannot be broken without paying the penalty. Therefore man, if he lives, if he lives in perpetuity through repro-duction, must observe them.

It has been inconceivable to man in general that the continued development of the world from chaos to the appearance of organic life and the development of this through ages of progress to the pos-session by matter, in man, of intelligent thought, reason, and action, is for nought. It cannot be believed that all this is to end in death. The progress must go on. Every presumption from the history of the globe, of life, of man, points to further development. If we believe in evolution, the reality of the progress from the first prim-itive life to reasoning man is not more wonderful than the belief that life by man will reach immortality, the power of self-continuance without individual death.

How this is to be reached, no one knows. The most probable way seems to be along the same lines that the progress of life has already followed. If this be correct, we have but one means of reaching immortality—by our children and by their children to the perfect race. Thus will our spark of life burn on. The father dies, but does not die. His likeness, his life, is still marching on in his child to the grand future of perfection ; and so also of the mother.

Every form of religion framed by man has had for its object the good of mankind. The general plan has been to secure material results in this world by the promise of penalties or rewards in an-other. Owing to the ignorance of the masses of the people in the past, still existing to this day, but which all thinkers hope to see cured, doctrines for the good of man were not receivable on reason alone. Information and proof were generally lacking to support doctrines demanding self-denial, and where proof existed it was not communicable to the people ; therefore, the early leaders of mankind invoked supernatural authority for their creeds, forms, and laws. The credulity of ignorance, the tendency of primitive man to attribute the phenomena of nature to anthropomorphic forces, and the early belief in spirits arising probably from dreams, etc., made the claim of supernatural authority for wise laws one easily imposed on the masses. Doubtless mankind has benefited by religious forms. But as man has advanced in brain power it has become more difficult to control him in this way.

First he loses faith in the communion with God of men in his own generation, gradually working to complete negation of such direct advice and counsel by God to men about him.

He comes, secondly, to lose faith in such things ever having occurred.

It is to this second stage that civilized man has again arrived as he has so often before. Our laws in this country are at present all mundane and supposed to be based on reason and use. The canons of the Church do not affect us materially and seem to me to be losing their hold daily. Our code of morality and unwritten law, being based originally on this sinking foundation, is now sinking with it. I do not mean that what is known as crime is more rife than formerly, but that character and morality are less vigorous to-day than they were a few decades ago ; as there is less belief, so there is less earnestness in life. This idea may be a mistake, but it seems to me that the young people lack purpose and high aims and shirk work and responsibility more than formerly, and are more guided in their social relations by the written law than by their honor.

If it be true that the religious forms of our day are losing their capacity to hold the faith of the people in their supernatural authority, then the whole structure of the moral code they have raised is undermined and may fall. The breaking down in the past of religious forms through incredulity in their divine origin, as in Greece and Rome, was followed by corruption and crime. It may be that similar dark ages will overtake us. It is very doubtful whether the world is ready for a religion founded on the reason alone ; at any rate all attempts at founding such a religion have hitherto failed. Men are not governed by reason. The masses never have been. What governs and has governed humanity is more or less a combination of the following :

Force of leaders who impose their interests on the masses, self-interest, passion, prejudice, sentiment, superstition, anything but reason. Who ever heard of a race receiving wisdom by reason alone. It may be, but it has not been. It is not wise, therefore, to attack the prevailing forms of religion nor the authority on which they are based.

The present religions of America are of two kinds : those that are receptive and capable of change, and those that are not. The value of these religions is great, especially those of the first class. Through religion capable of change without ruin we may, indeed, hope to see adaptations maintaining the religious feeling in man in harmony with his advancing science.

The origin of the religious idea in man has been clearly and cleverly traced by a number of scientific men, best perhaps by Tylor and Spencer.

Amongst the most primitive men there is practically no more religion than we find amongst the higher animals. With the evolution of man socially we find also an evolution of religion. Step by step this evolution has been traced to our present position.

The strange and, to the ignorant man, inexplicable metamorphoses in nature, such as the formation and disappearance of clouds, the wonderful changes in the life of insects, at one time crawling worms, at another beautiful flying creatures,—these and other phenomena of nature, storms, whirlwinds, earthquakes, tides, floods, etc., are by savages looked upon as a confirmation of the dual life of things. The shadow of the cloud, of the animal, and of the man, the echo that answers, and the dream that transports one to distant places or brings us face to face with the dead, doubtless originates this belief in a spiritual life separate from the corporeal.

The starved like the glutted savage tends in sleep to dreams. The psychologic knowledge of the savage is incapable of explaining a dream upon true grounds. To him the only rational view is that there is another self which may leave his body and go to distant places with the rapidity of lightning while the body does not move. The apparitions of those dead must be to him the spirits or shadows. of such and give the basis of belief in a future life. From nothing, we can study in such a book as Spencer's *Sociology* man gradually progressing to the most abstract religious conceptions.

The first dawn of religion is in an indefinite dread of the dead on account of the supposed possibility of their return. The first church where a sacrifice or service is held is the burial-place. The origin of the sacrifice is clearly the desire of the living to give, on the one hand, to the spirit of the dead the weapons and food necessary for the journey of life it is supposed to take ; and, on the other hand, to propitiate the shade that might otherwise be malignant. Amongst tribes that have migrated the general belief is that the dead will in spirit return to the old home which by lapse of time has also been spiritualized.

If the migration was down a river, or across a river or a sea, so the spirit journey will be supposed to take a return course requiring boats, ferrymen, etc. One dark river to cross is a common belief, continuing from the savage who buries or burns his dead in a canoe, or burns a mock one for his dead kinsman's spirit to use, to the Ferryman Charon and our own Christian doctrine. If the migration has been by land, and crossing water has not been a prominent feature, then we find the sacrifice of the horse or beast of burden to facilitate the return journey of the spirit. These beliefs in a future life, at first indefinite and ill-defined, then limited to immediate ancestors, at last include all ancestors. Great chiefs, warriors, or benefactors are longer remembered, more dreamed of, more invoked, and tend to an attributed ascendancy in the spirit world similar or greater than they had in this world.

The dreamer or enthusiast may at first esteem that he has had real interviews with such leading spirits, but the utility of spirit sanction in controlling men will soon lead to claims of supernatural authorship of various laws and rules deemed useful by living leaders. Deification of one dead leader will lead to the deification of others; so may arise the conception of many gods, and at last, with the organization of society under a powerful ruler with subordinate chiefs, will inevitably come the idea of a similar constitution of the spirit world. We in our religions of to-day conceive a ruling God with subordinate spirits, saints, angels, or demons. Only in the most advanced thinkers can the abstract idea of a single Supreme Being arise. Even in Christianity in its least involved form we have a belief in a mysterious Trinity. Amongst the Catholics many angels and saints are credited with supernatural influence in mundane affairs. To such, shrines are erected, pilgrimages are undertaken, and gifts and offerings are made. According to the opinion of this large congregation, the Mother of God has an extraordinary influence in averting storms or disaster and in giving fortune and advantage to mankind.

A few small sects without vitality, as the Unitarians, believe like the Mahometans in one God. It must be said that this nominal belief in one God by the Mahometans is often accompanied by a belief in the supernatural influence of various saints, spirits, and demons, and of Mahomet himself.

The idea of sacred animals may arise from the habit of certain animals, as bats, owls, serpents, etc., of frequenting tombs, houses, or other places where spirits are naturally supposed to be. A spirit whether friendly or inimical is likely to seek the object of its attention ; so a serpent, which has always an attraction to the warm houses or bedding of man, can easily have a spiritual life attributed to it in countries where the climate favors constructions accessible to them.

The association of ghosts with the animal life found in or about tombs, which were originally so often caves, is still shown in the story of vampires and in the common description of ghosts as squeaking or gibbering as bats do. All our religious forms, or at least the popular beliefs accompanying them, bear clear traces of an origin in ancestor worship.

The family domicile became the church after or with the tomb. The Lares and Penates of the Romans perpetuated the early belief from which their more generalized religion had grown. The Chinese have never progressed much beyond ancestor worship pure and simple. The one idea of a Chinaman is to marry, to have a son. Everything must bend to having a son, because without a son the proper sacrifices cannot be made on a man's tomb at death, and the spirit wanders aimlessly in endless torture. This belief has doubtless been the cause of the perpetuation of the Chinese race and stamp through every mutation of time. To be happy in the indefinitely living spirit, reproduction is absolutely essential. So the most earnest Chinese have reproduced, and the clearly recognizable race is still here. The defect in their system is that the individual independence going with intellectual progress must eventually overthrow the foundation of their system. Investigation and reflection must with progress destroy the unprovable belief that the spirit of an ancestor depends in an individual separate existence upon the sacrifices of a descendant. This overthrown, the whole system must fall with it. This Chinese doctrine is far indeed from my idea of an actual immortality had by the parent in the child, but there is a suggestion of similarity.

So the receivers of my view may gain confidence in observing the wonderful persistency of the Chinese race against decay and extermination, although so long in a stationary or reactionary condition.

Other animal worship may have arisen through the worship of dead chiefs named, as is so common with savages, after animals, and the imperfection of all savage languages in expressing the difference between an animal and a man named after an animal. It is, however, immaterial how the religious idea arose, for the general view remains the same.

We cannot escape the conclusion that all primitive religions, from inchoate dread of ghosts to definite ancestor worship, and so on to a ruling God and a pantheon of subordinate spirits, are of purely human origin.

The most extreme devotee of form in religion must equally admit that all modern developed religions, but one excepted (his own, of course), have a similar origin.

It is not conceivable to a reflective person with any brain power, and with the information as to physical and psychological facts now available, that a Supreme Creator would directly transmit or permit to be transmitted to man, His creature, religious information fatal to the everlasting welfare of his soul. It is equally impossible to suppose a Divine Creator of the universe capable of leaving the vast majority of humanity in every generation for the long ages of human existence ignorant of doctrines essential to their everlasting salvation. We are from the limitations of our reasons driven perforce to attribute a mundane origin to all religions, excepting, perhaps, our own, and, if still clinging to special forms taught us in childhood, to at least admit so wide a tolerance for those who differ with us as to leave the belief in our own doctrines unessential either as to damnation or salvation.

Tolerance is no twin brother to faith. Intense faith must be accompanied by an equal force of intolerance. When a person or people believe that a particular course or doctrine will lead to eternal salvation, or its disregard to eternal damnation, any mundane matter becomes of infinitesimal importance, except as leading to the everlasting future. So suffering in this world to reach heaven is a splendid investment, while joy here and hell hereafter is a bad one. Equally, any suffering imposed on others to everlastingly save them, or to prevent the spread of damning doctrines, is, with faith, thoroughly justifiable. Therefore faith, in proportion to its intensity and political power, will persecute dissent.

The universal tolerance of our age is consequently a demonstration of the weakness of the old religious forms and the necessity of something different to pervade the lives of our children with a religious ardor. The Christian religion more than any other spiritualizes the unity of mankind, and inculcates a sympathy that is limited only by the limits of life, and takes in the whole human race.

Its doctrines are distinctly those forming the ideal toward which the highest humanity tends. Its chief weakness in an incredulous and inquiring age lies in its claim of supernatural authority and authorship. Without at all denying the correctness of this claim, we cannot but perceive that the prevailing demand for demonstration in all things is extremely exacting for it.

It is indeed strange to learn through well authenticated history that this beautiful religion, in which love and sympathy, suffering and resignation, are foundation pillars, has by its disciples been guilty of the most cruel persecutions often upon technical and trivial points, has sanctioned and preached war for no just reason, has praised and encouraged unsocial and unsympathetic seclusion in the name of religion contrary to the spirit of Christ, and has often, on the other hand, sustained in good standing not only its lay members but even its preachers and leaders while living and practising notorious crime and immorality.

A perusal of the Gospels and then of the theological dogmas that have been declared by the saints as essential to salvation must surprise a thoughtful person. How the one could have come out of the other is most curious. The confusion of contradiction amongst Christians in their catechisms and the practices of the pious as professing Christians are certainly inexplicable as originating from divine inspiration. The leaders of our Christian sects, as a rule, no longer have a full conviction in the truth of their technicalities. When they had this, the humanity consigned to everlasting hell by these pious persons would cast into the shadow the doings of a demon. In fact, no other religion has painted so uncertain, black, and hopeless a picture of the future as the Christian. Some sect always had a door open direct to hell for the trembling votary. If the rules of one Church were followed, the very fact condemned the individual to everlasting damnation by the rules of another. To go forward, to go backward, or to stand still was alike damnable according to some saint. Thus we can observe the difficulties and uncertainties of every religion or rule of conduct derived from an interference of God Almighty through man.

Some of the prevalent doctrines of Christianity are worthy of examination to indicate that their votaries may mistake a true interpretation of the Gospels. Let us see what they say. Salvation can only come by faith, not by deeds. Man is incapable of self-salvation, and can only hope for it through the vicarious sacrifice of Christ. Any amount of sin may be obliterated and the soul snowed into whiteness by the superabundant virtues of another. These votaries set up as the ideals of life resignation, mercy, and to do unto others as you would have them do unto you; resignation and submission in peace to outrage, wrong, oppression, to anything, even unto death; if smitten on one cheek, turn the other. These votaries are probably wrong in taking the text upon which these views are based too literally. These doctrines have not and cannot be lived up to in any society that has existed since the Crucifixion.

As to salvation coming only by faith, how shall faith be demonstrated except by deeds? If this be accepted, salvation coming by faith comes by deeds. In the matter of obliterating sin, the Old Testament tells us what we know in our daily experience to be true —that the sins of the fathers shall be visited on the children to the third and fourth generation of them that hate Me. They are not washed away by a profession of faith. The vicarious sacrifice, as understood by many, would make the perfect life one of dreams, enthusiasm, and inaction. It did so in the Dark Ages. Resignation and meekness carried to extremes lead to nothing. We cannot be resigned to wrong without reaping ruin as a harvest. The brotherhood of man is another idea completely misunderstood. As it is often comprehended, we might with equal truth speak of the brotherhood of the primates, the brotherhood of mammals, the brotherhood of life, the brotherhood of matter; all true, but not leading to the conclusions adduced by the saints from the first. We might also allege the brotherhood of dogs as a reason for receiving the cur and the collie on an equal footing; we might assert the brotherhood of equines as a reason for placing the ass in the stable of the thoroughbred.

In doing unto others as you would have them do unto you, who, we may ask, would ever be imprisoned, hung, or in any way punished? The rule is good in a sensible interpretation, but it is nothing when run into extremity.

So the professors of Christianity through mistaken zeal have rushed or been pushed into no thoroughfares, into impossible impasses where conduct conformable to conscience was ruin, and where denial was damnation.

Christianity is a religion of love. Its Gospels are full of parables and allegories, and should be interpreted as to what they are and in harmony with common sense. It is a sufferer from the deformities that have been imposed on it. Its superserviceable devotees by the impossible positions in which they place themselves live in contradiction to their professions. They set up a standard that brings before us a set of rank hypocrites. Good men and true live oppressed in their souls from the recognition of the incompatibility of creed and of human duty.

In the French Revolution the beautiful and useful doctrines of Liberty, Equality, and Fraternity were preached, received, and acted on by a whole nation. But men ran to a wild extremity. Their excesses turned truth into a lie. Liberty became license. Equality pulled down the superior only to make rulers of the incompetent or cruel. Fraternity presided over the guillotine, the Noyades, and the massacre of the best lives of France, including even founders of the Republic, and still worse of even women, children, and babes at the breast. Thus great and progressive doctrines in incompetent hands became the cause of the worst reign of terror civilized man has known.

Man cannot live by terror, and so the reaction came with a Napoleon, as it must have come with some one. Thus we may perceive from the injustice and cruelty of crime committed in the name of the brotherhood of man the danger of extreme and technical interpretation of a great and true doctrine.

Every great leader of early man has claimed a divine or demoniac origin for his rules and regulations. In the weakness of human reason this was doubtless necessary and may be still. Its inconvenience lies in its contradictions. Moses and Mahomet, Buddha and Brahma, Confucius and Christ, cannot be reconciled. How can the evidence of like miraculous kind be deemed more authentic in one than in another? If we deny the revelation of the Mormon prophet, Smith; if we deny the passage of Mahomet through the rock at the call of God, a rock with its manhole still visible to the curious, how shall we admit the inspiration of Moses or of any one?

The most curious circumstance in the consideration of this matter is that not a single, solitary sect known to me lives to-day up to the exact letter of the revelation from God upon which its rules are founded. We may dismiss a dangerous discussion with the admission that all religions, or all but one, each person excepting his own, were founded by man, who, to secure conformity to his plans by the ignorant mass, invoked the general floating belief originating from dreams and unexplained phenomena of nature in a spiritual world, and set up moral and material laws said to emanate from the Ruler of the Universe. Such laws were in reality the creation of a great human mind bent on improving his race, the world, or of advancing a personal ambition. We can thus understand how codes suited to the savage, the barbarian, or the civilized man were invented as the race required them, and further understand how every code has been modified often beyond recognition to suit the growth of man or the change of his circumstances or condition.

Thus what is good and advantageous in a savage state of society may be injurious in a civilized condition, and consequently as a savage race advances its moral code must change.

The great leader like Moses or Mahomet invokes God or Devil to sanction the innovation necessary for advance, and in this way secures a conformity that at least amongst primitive men could be secured in no other manner. The philosopher should consider the general use of the invocation of supernatural authority to secure morality. The fact that mankind has never continued sound without a religion in form founded on Divine reward or demoniac punishment, and that decay in religion has been accompanied heretofore first by a hectic flush and rush of intellectual advance, followed in every case by social disease, decay, and death, should make us slow in attacking any religious forms.

The emergence into history of every race has shown it to be devoted to religious observance. So in extremes, or when immorality has almost extirpated the people, it may also be observed that the grossest superstition and the most devoted duty to the ritual is the rule of the survivors. The escape from the formality of faith to freedom and reason finds man in the middle career. He comes to this point at or near the highest of his achievement and holds to it at least for a time on the thus far inevitable reaction.

In each of such of these numerous epochs of advance and retrogression we find man going a little higher in his glory and achievement, and falling a little less low in the reaction. On the whole then man must be advancing, and also we may say that the advance in each case is becoming more widely diffused and affects a larger class.

So the general doctrines of the faith have lived, while those not appropriate to the advance or change of society have been overthrown or left as dead letters.

In matters of revealed religion a facility for fraud is unfortunately found. A communion with God may be claimed by any one, for such communion is not susceptible of scientific proof even in the admitted saint. We cannot secure a conformity of belief in any religious dogma similar to that which we may secure for the law of gravitation.

The first is a declaration incapable of demonstration, while the other may be proved without regard to time or place, and cannot escape reception wherever intelligence has reached even an ordinary advance above the most primitive types.

The old dictionary definition of religion becomes inadequate to convey any enlarged idea of religion. "Religion is a belief which induces morality." This definition carries with it the idea that the morality induced requires neither political law nor the opinion of society for its practice.

The belief that religion is necessary for man, together with the doubt as to the permanent acceptance of any religion dependent on faith and not capable of demonstration, is the cause of setting forth these views.

What we need is a religion or belief capable of demonstration. Such a belief is the one I offer to my children. It is the body immortality secured by reproduction.

One should not consider the immortality of the body through reproduction to be in any conflict with the immortality of the soul.

The one is a belief based on demonstrable fact ; the other is a faith founded on revelation. A belief in the first will conduce to conduct that will insure the soul salvation of the second.

In any case, what better work could one of holy life do than to procreate a line of souls to be saved? Given a holy life, the presumption is that such a life will impress the progeny, and that, other things being equal, such children will be more likely to be saved through goodness than the children of bad parents, like, let us say, the children of the celebrated criminal family of Juke in New York. It would appear then that the holy ought not to be satisfied with their own sterility and extermination, leaving the world to the domination of the damned. Such a course would certainly diminish the proportion of souls saved and increase the proportion of souls lost through all time.

Good conduct without faith is not sufficient for soul salvation according to most religious creeds, but faith and good works is according to all a good combination. Good works then are to be encouraged, and those who, doing good works, have children in turn inclined by inherited qualities to do good works, should be encouraged in reproduction.

A belief in a possible human improvement through improvement of one's self, perpetuated and intensified in one's children, each generation seeking improvement for the sake of improvement in the children to succeed them, and so on toward perfection, may help faith-religions, and certainly has no element to hinder them. The Roman Catholics carry out my ideas in this respect as to their laity. Their confessional and rules for the married oppose all practices leading to sterility and encourage child-bearing. The care with which the priesthood seek to control the religious training of the young leaves us no doubt as to the objects of their rules for the wife. Every child is another soul to be saved, and another glory to the Saviour.

A reward or punishment for good or evil is as a rule felt by the individual, immediately as well as remotely, in some form or other. Our deeds and thoughts recorded in our minds and bodies for good or evil and going to modify our individuality are reflected from us and appear in our undefinable expressions.

Thus persons of evil life but beautiful in form and feature repel us and become ugly from the thoughts and deeds recorded in their expressions ; on the other hand, plain persons may become attractive, nay beautiful, from the goodness shining out of them. Everyone's deeds and life are to be found in their expressions. As the face is deformed by evil or beautified by good deeds, so also is the mind. In the end we may presume that a perfect beauty of face and form will only be found with a perfect beauty of thought and action. Evil diminishes the power for greatness. It weakens. Truth gives strength. Our mental as well as bodily health depends on our being in harmony with truth. To achieve the most that is in us we must be moral. This motive and the good or bad opinion of society are not enough to make an earnest belief leading to good deeds and away from bad ones.

The effect of our actions on our children may do so when we perceive the results of our morality on them and appreciate the renewed existence achieved in progeny.

Every bad thought or act must leave its trace on the mind or body, and lower one's renewed life in any subsequent child. Thus is established a future punishment. This punishment can be proved as certainly as can the doctrine of gravitation. Every good and noble thought and action will leave its trace and improve one's immortality in the subsequent child. Thus is established future reward—a reward perfectly provable.

The child is the parents united and renewed. There is no doubt of this. Here then is a sequence of demonstrable beliefs that are no more attackable than is the revolution of the earth around the sun. These beliefs cannot be held by any one without leading to a desire for immortality in the child and to a desire by a moral life to improve oneself as renewed in the child. The child is the new life of its parents. It is their immortality. This new life is the parents fused. According to their forces the parents' life-renewal will be good or bad, weak or strong. The parents have the power to govern this their future in a great measure. If their bodies are kept in health, the presumption is for bodily health in the child. If their bodies are diseased, disease must be expected in the child. So also in matters of the mind: we may have health and strength or disease and weakness in the intellect according to the condition of the parents. Everything tells. As it is our future life, our immortality that is at stake, so must the value of every act and even thought become appreciated. An earnest and intense life devoted to improvement is more productive and profitable with this belief than with any other. To secure immortality in the child a large family is necessary to guard against accident and inevitable dangers. A large family is one of the best means of inducing and guarding morality that we have. From every point of view it would appear that a belief in the spirit or soul, as well as in the physical likeness of the child to the parents, giving the idea of a material and immediate immortality, the condition, hopes, and future of which depend on the parents' acts, would lead to a religious life with high aims and a pure morality.

Life's object is not cultivation, not content, not wealth, not individual greatness. It is the development of power for progress to the future of perfection. We can only gain this through the child from our own loins. To secure this improvement of self in the child our highest capacities must be used. We have this reason, then, aside from any other, for good and great action. Most religions preach content either here or in a heaven. The most perfect conception of content is the Nirvana of the East, and the nearest approach we make to it in life is in sleep. As we do nothing in sleep, so we do nothing by content. Discontent is the spur of progress. Content leads to nothing. It cannot exist with ambition nor even with any desire for improvement for such desire must grow from discontent. This frequent idea in religion must be denounced. Teach every one to look for and glory in discontent, and still to use its power with due discretion. Declamatory discontent in small household or personal matters is an error so complete as to come close to crime ; while discontent in large things is the spur to improvement.

All living religions have a great deal that is good and useful in them to the peoples and conditions where they are received. Consequently missionary work to replace one with another where the people's conditions are not the same is of doubtful value. The rule should be to let people's religions alone.

The form of any religion may be followed that does not interfere with or discourage reproduction. Any doctrine of this latter kind should be condemned out of hand in your own family. One may, however, preach with perfect propriety a religion to those who have none. A large proportion of Americans have no religion. Thus it is seen that in our country there is an ample field for missionary work.

The missionary work most essential in America for its material welfare is something in the line of this work. We certainly could spread with advantage some doctrine that would diminish divorce, that would make marriage happier, and that would secure our patriotism in the expectation that the generations succeeding us will be Americans not only in name but by descent from our own loins.

Immortality in the child is a fact. Its thorough conception upon the highest plane cannot but lead to good.

Never be a monk, a fakir, or a fool; but have children and assure your continued life and continued youth and participation in future glory. It cannot be that the death we see striking right and left and which we know will one day strike us, will kill completely. No, if we follow the road God has marked out we will gain immortality and we will not die. We may catch a glimpse of that road that our poor senses can comprehend and realize and believe. It is our children. I hope for other immortality, but this I understand and can harmonize with what I know of what has taken place and what is taking place.

Every one should have a religion. Religion is necessary to every one. Intellect makes religion possible, and with each increase of brain in man true religion may become truer and stronger. Its forms are many and are suited to the intellectual grasp of those who hold them, though not always best suited to their changing conditions and to their progress. Religious forms, like all the institutions of man and more than any of the others, tend to fixity and oppose change.

Whatever form religion takes, it is but an expression of the universal craving of man for something better, purer, and grander than he at present knows. When the forms have been perverted and used by the designing for their own profit and aggrandizement, we must overlook these passing defects, and study the reason and core of the religion which is afflicted by them. Religion has been and will be an important aid to the progress of mankind. True religion is devoted to truth, and is capable of any sacrifice to find it and secure it. Too often, alas, truth has been opposed by corrupt and antiquated forms whose followers arrogated to themselves to be the only religion. Every real scientific man is a light of religion and has a heart full of it though he may follow no creed or form.

While some are capable of thus standing alone, and by so standing gain in breadth and power, in mental grasp and feeling, the great mass of mankind is still doubtless dependent on form. In Egypt the instructed priests had a religion for themselves involving a belief in one God, and for the people another with many allegorical forms and many gods. The conditions justifying this, if they ever existed, still exist, for even where the nominal forms are the same, as in the Catholic Church, the different grades of people adhering to that faith have created a practically different religion within the fold each for itself. Thus we have the extremes of the Neapolitan devotee of St. Januarius demanding the liquefaction of the dead saint's blood on pain of stoning his statue, on the one hand, and, on the other, St. George Mivart, the scientific writer, holding for a freedom of research that would have called for excommunication in the Middle Ages.

So forms must exist for a long time yet, and they are still neces-,sary. Reverence these then for that of which they are the emblem.

In the Hindoo religion there is held a doctrine of progression. The sinner at death according to his sin goes back in the chain of evolution and recommences life in some animal, to return to man again only after ages of probation.

In my doctrine there is but one sin that so condemns man. This is the absence of progeny. A sterile man or woman at death is the unpardonable sinner. Ages of progress have combined the atoms in him or her in a wonderful complexity, and given them an identity which we may call soul, together with a capacity for reproduction and improvement. The sterile in exterminating themselves shatter this, the work of ages, and sin beyond redemption.

Like the Hindoo, the religions of the past and of to-day have much to admire and to imitate.

While I counsel reverence to religious form, I equally counsel you to avoid it as a faith. The danger of all religious forms is that man so often comes to regard the form as the religion. When this happens man's spirit dwindles, progress stops, and religion is lost. Let form, as a faith, alone in religion, for it is but the skin of it. Make truth the guiding star of your lives, and never fear to follow where it leads. Immortality by the child is the core for your religion.

A great deal of the religious thought of man has been devoted to things he knew nothing about. As might be supposed, dogmas about unknowable subjects were incapable of securing the unity of faith we have, as has been said, in the law of gravitation. The bitterest contest, the bloodiest wars, and the most cruel tortures have been caused by religious disputes about subjects which neither side had any capacity of comprehending.

We can neither think of God nor picture to ourselves what such a being could be, nor can we think of the universe without a cause and without a commencement, and here again we are confronted with the unthinkable character of a first cause without a beginning and without a cause. So we find ourselves in a vicious circle, in which the complacent ass may trudge blindfolded by dogmatic statement, but from which the wise man will flee.

The defect, to my mind, in most modern religions is that they deal too much with another world of which we know nothing, and

neglect a study of present conditions, which are capable of comprehension. Some of these, to me idle doctrines, may have done good.
For instance, the dogma, so frequently found, of a hell or place of
everlasting torture in which worldly sin will be punished, may have
prevented the ignorant from sins that otherwise would have been
committed. A great deal of ingenuity has been devoted to picturing
the kinds of punishment that would take place in this unending hell,
of which we are all perfectly and completely ignorant. Milton knew
nothing of it, nor did Dante, nor does any one. The things we know
of sin and its punishment would better occupy us than such idle
speculations.

If we sin against nature we are *always* punished : first, directly
in this world ; and secondly, again in all children conceived subsequent to the sin, we are still punished and still in this world. Each
act of ours and, doubtless too, our thoughts are at every moment
moulding us and giving a stamp which will pass to our children.
A drunkard's child must suffer for its father's sin ; thus the drunkard
again suffers in his child what he at first suffered in himself.

It seems to me that this doctrine, so easily proven, would be more
conducive to morality than some fantastic picture of a sulphurous
pit without bottom, and which, after all, may be avoided by acts of
repentance. With innumerable short cuts from the broad path full
of pleasure to the narrow, thorny way, there is little wonder that the
business man takes all the broad path and forbidden pleasure consistent with taking the last possible short cut to the straight and disa-
greeable path. His position in heaven is rather improved than
otherwise by such a course. The truth is, nature never forgives.

For what you do you must take the consequences. There is no
repentance that can avoid the results of deeds already done. The
best that we can do is, by wise deeds to counteract the results of foolish ones, and, as we live and learn, to suppress the foolish deeds and do
only wise ones. A man knowing that his act of sin is a permanent
injury to him and stamps and lowers his character will avoid such sin
much more than if he believed that some subsequent act could
entirely wipe away its results.

There is other sin than sin against nature. This is sin against
society, and it may be against a written or an unwritten regulation
of man made for the general good. The punishment of a sin against
the laws and customs of man, but which is not a sin against nature,
is to a considerable extent dependent on whether it is found out, but
not altogether. We are generally educated and impressed from
youth up with the necessity of observing the regulations of the

society in which we live, and we consequently suffer more in conscience from a violation of man's rules than we do from a violation
of nature's Thus we may suffer much from a sin against society
though it be not found out. It is also to be noted that many, in fact
most, sins against society are, if not injurious to oneself directly, at
least so to oneself renewed in the child. An injury to society, the
medium upon the conservation of which our social activity depends,
must eventually injure us in our descendants. There is a good deal
of dovetailing between these two classes of sins, but attention is called
to the difference now because the unforgivable and most fatal sins—
that is, those against nature—are often considered venial, while the
less important and not necessarily injurious sins—that is, those
against the rules of man—are considered as serious or deadly.

Thus a man or woman who spreads syphilis is left free to curse
generations that follow them. Constitutional and preventible diseases
are spread broadcast every day, and those committing this sin against
nature are termed in society, if any attention is paid to the circumstance, unfortunate. On the other hand, a hungry person taking a
loaf of bread is jailed, and a man walking into a field that some one
has enclosed and calls his by a convention of society is arrested for
trespass. Religion should deal with those sins, and they the most
fatal, with which man has been unable to cope by law.

The present system of ethics has many points susceptible of improvement. Such a rule, for instance, as the one that a wife who
has an "incompatibility of temper" is a sinner and may be divorced,
while a wife who refuses to bear children, or is incapable of having
them, is all right, and against her fatal sin—her sin that exterminates
both herself and her husband—the husband has no remedy, is the
ruling of the monumental ass.

Children are a religion for any one. To improve your own life as
renewed in the child is, when understood, a motive that will draw
from evil and lead to the true and good. As soon as a human being
thoroughly realizes that every excess and every crime must be ex-
piated by the child, and perhaps by the child's child of his or her
own loins, for many generations, such aberrations will become rare.
And equally, when knowing the character stamp of good acts and
noble thoughts, and the physical, intellectual, and moral improvement in the child's nature by such improvements in one's self, a
human being must attach an importance to a sound and true life that
nothing else will give.

Every true man has a religion. Every such person has a standard
of right, which is followed irrespective of direct enforcement. In

fact, practically all humanity has such a standard, though it be narrow, or perhaps bad for the general public. We have honor even amongst thieves. A man without religion is a man without sympathy. He is like an oak with the heart rotted out. He may be fair externally, but he is a sepulchre within. He can only stand in fine weather ; when the storm comes he will be beaten down.

For success we must have earnestness. For earnestness we must have a belief. Therefore, to use our capacities to their best, we need a religion. It may be in heaven, in hell, in liberty, in honor, as in the days of chivalry, or what not. But some overmastering motive from belief in something we must have for the full realization of our possibilities.

This Religion of Children offers such a motive. A religious man in this view is one with a high standard of right, which he follows, without the compulsion of written or unwritten law, for the sake of himself in his child. The basis of this true religion is life, its continuance, and, above all, its improvement. This true religion followed is to so live that the noble thoughts and good acts of our lives will be ingrained in our children by inheritance, and place them upon a plane from which improved lives will flow. So by reproduction we multiply and may improve our life and fasten fortune for the future. It is in our children, ourselves renewed and immortalized, that we have tangible means of enjoying true religion.

A person without children exterminates himself, and, as far as he is concerned, has no chance to perpetuate or to improve the life-flame confided to his care. This is the unpardonable sin. It is the blackest in the category. For sterility there is neither repentance nor forgiveness. The spirit of the father or mother passes on in the child to do the work of perfecting humanity, and to carry the father and mother on for countless ages to pick the fruit from the lives whose seeds planted in the unfathomed past have been so long struggling toward perfection. The spirit of the sterile is thrust by death into outer darkness.

Religion demands the child. Children are a religion. The home is the holy of holies. It is the true church. The parent is the priest. Immortality is in the child, and paradise is the perfection to which by procreation we progress without plan or perception.

Has not the time come when a plan is possible ? Let us believe it. We can with such a belief take the world and its details into a broad conception, and instead of being sunk into ruts of routine or confused in complex circumstance, we may treat the incidents of life as the means through the child to reach to gladness and to glory.

When the human egg is fertilized the Phœnix is rampant. In reproduction we deride the dark demon of death. Hope and youth and life are born again in the child. With each new flame of life, with each new descendant, we renew ourselves in reproduction. With each new child we create a new sun and system in the heavens of our immortality, and by so much are we fixed faster in this firmament of fortune.

www.ingramcontent.com/pod-product-compliance
Lightning Source LLC
Chambersburg PA
CBHW020346030726
47496CB00007B/2028